AFTER DUNKIRK

LEE JACKSON

SEVERN RIVER
PUBLISHING

AFTER DUNKIRK

Copyright © 2020 by Lee Jackson.

Severn River Publishing
www.SevernRiverBooks.com

ISBN: 978-1-64875-477-7 (Paperback)

ALSO BY LEE JACKSON

The After Dunkirk Series

After Dunkirk

Eagles Over Britain

Turning the Storm

The Giant Awakens

Riding the Tempest

Driving the Tide

The Reluctant Assassin Series

The Reluctant Assassin

Rasputin's Legacy

Vortex: Berlin

Fahrenheit Kuwait

Target: New York

Never miss a new release! Sign up to receive exclusive updates from author Lee Jackson.

severnriverbooks.com/authors/lee-jackson

Robert Gordon Hall
You were one hell of a pilot.
Your family and friends are proud of you
and miss you.
RIP

"We really ought to be waterskiing!"

PROLOGUE

June 9, 1940
Sark Island, Guernsey Bailiwick, English Channel Islands

The Dame of the tiny island of Sark in the English Channel hurried from her home onto *Rue de la Seigneurie* for a better view of the northeastern horizon. Far out over the water, black smoke rose to the sky in huge billowing clouds. She knew fully what caused them: the good citizens of Normandy had blown up their oil storage tanks, an early act of resistance to the armies of Adolf Hitler, *Führer* of Germany.

Five days ago, the British Royal Navy, in a herculean effort, had evacuated the British Expeditionary Force, commonly called the BEF, and large units of the French army in a ten-day evacuation of over three hundred thousand troops at Dunkirk. They had faced overwhelming pressure from Nazi forces that had flanked the Maginot Line and descended into the north of France in a blistering *blitzkrieg*. The German divisions pushed south along the Atlantic coast in a wide swath to overrun and control the northern and western regions of France, and threatened Paris.

Hitler would no doubt set a priority on occupying Sark and the other islands belonging to Great Britain in the Channel simply for the propaganda value of taking British territory. And Normandy was only twenty-five miles across the waters.

1

One day earlier
Dunkirk, France

Jeremy Littlefield held his breath, a near-impossible feat after crawling in whatever shallow ground he could find in the low hills and dunes above Dunkirk's flat beaches. He scrunched under a small outcropping of sand held in place by protruding roots of scraggly vegetation, willing his body to meld into the space he had hurriedly carved at its base.

Just as he pulled in his legs, his back to the crumbly wall of sand whose grains already worked their way between his sweat-soaked blouse and skin, he heard men above him speaking in German. He could not make out how many there were—at least two, maybe three—but they did not seem to be searching for him. On the contrary, these soldiers he had barely avoided seemed to be casually looking out to sea.

Jeremy had used every bit of cover and concealment in his headlong flight to the beach for one purpose: survival, ahead of the German behemoth that pursued the escaping British and French armies. Out of ammunition, the bolt of his rifle broken, he had lost the weapon as he lunged from one hiding place to the next through a wretched night of crackling small arms fire, blasts from tanks obliterating another of their opposite number, brilliant flashes from artillery breaking the darkness, and then the whistle of projectiles followed by ear-splitting concussions until he emerged at dawn among the dunes and furrows leading down to the shore.

Spread before him, the carnage of war assaulted his senses with sights of dismembered bodies, separated arms and legs, animals caught in unworldly repose, crumbling rooftops, cratered roads, and every sort of vehicle cast at odd angles amid the stench of torn and scorched flesh, all under an overcast sky.

Jeremy's hope, one he expected to be futile, was the same as that of thousands of soldiers who had protected the evacuation and fled to the beach for want of any other alternative to avoid capture: *maybe there's one last boat to take me home to England.*

Now, despite the voices overhead, curiosity overcame him to see what remained of the British and French armies that had been trapped there. Far in the distance along the shore, lines of abandoned cars, trucks, tanks, and field artillery vehicles were set in well-ordered ranks stretching into the gently lapping wavelets, with some buried halfway up their wheels in the sand. Rifles leaned against cars and trucks. Boxloads of ammunition had been stacked in neat rows, the machine guns they accompanied still looking menacing.

As the murmur of voices above Jeremy continued, he looked across the vast expanse of sand marked with the patterns of huge formations of soldiers who had waited anxiously to be rescued over nine hair-raising days while being shelled by Hitler's armies or strafed or bombed by Hermann Göring's air force.

For indiscernible reasons, Hitler had stopped his ground forces short of finishing off the escaping British and French troops of Operation Dynamo, and he had held back as the flotilla of small boats, yachts, and warships loaded desperate soldiers onto their decks and sailed away ahead of the Nazi onslaught. High in the skies, British Hurricane and German Stuka fighters left vapor trails as they dueled, some spiraling downward amid black smoke to crash in the ocean.

The ragged British and French armies had completed an evacuation out to sea four days ago, and then the *Wehrmacht* had hurled its might at their rearguard north and east of Dunkirk, mercilessly slaughtering any who continued to oppose them, and taking prisoner or executing those who surrendered. As far as Jeremy knew, he was the last of his unit still alive and free. Driven ahead of the *blitzkrieg* wrought against him and his comrades, he had crawled in the shallow runoff gullies between the dunes on the sides of the low hills and berms down to the beach.

Now, Jeremy slowly, cautiously let out his breath and took in another as he fought panic. To his left, not fifty meters away, a British soldier, mouth gaping, eyes staring, lay sprawled on a low embankment while seagulls wheeled and screeched overhead and then plunged to feast on carrion.

A gut-wrenching cry broke above the breeze beyond a dune to Jeremy's left. The soldiers above him uttered startled, muffled exclamations and took off at a run, almost stepping on Jeremy's face and causing more sand to cascade in on him.

He dared not move, and he held his breath. From a distance he heard further shouting and sharp commands. He inched one hand up to wipe the sand from his eyes and peered out in time to see another British soldier being clubbed with rifle butts, hauled to his feet, and led away a broken, wretched man.

All day, Jeremy lay where he was, exhausted, daring to move only his eyes as he searched the horizon for any hope of rescue while resigning himself to the notion that none would come. He was alone. And then, as the sun dipped in the western sky, and despite himself, he slept.

When Jeremy opened his eyes, dawn had broken. Far up the beach, hordes of German soldiers systematically moved among the long lines of abandoned war machines and equipment, searching for and hauling off anything that might be useful. They worked their way down the shore steadily, relentlessly, toward him.

Too tired to be afraid, Jeremy dropped his head into the crook of his elbow, feeling the stubble of five days' growth of beard pressing against his bare arm. He snickered involuntarily. *What would the ol' man think if he saw me now?* Then he remembered the last time he had seen his commanding officer; the man had been face-down in a pool of blood and muddy water.

Jeremy pushed his body against the wall of his hiding place and wedged his face around to scan the beach in the opposite direction. It was empty of men and equipment but provided no cover. Along the edge of the break that marked the joining of sand to the low rise of land, dark seaweed and detritus gathered, thrown up by breaking waves, and Jeremy studied the shallow gullies where rainwater ran down to the sea, the same ones that had covered his escape to the beach. They snaked toward higher ground and at the top, more cover and concealment.

Famished and thirsty, Jeremy glanced toward the enemy soldiers continuing their search of military equipment. *I can't stay here.* He took another look at his only possible direction of escape, and began a long, slow crawl to the northeast.

Amélie Boulier scanned the beach below her house. For days she had watched in disbelief as the huge army of British and French soldiers gathered by the hundreds of thousands in endless formations stretching along the shore toward Dunkirk, their vehicles and large war machines parked in long rows. Then, two weeks ago, boats of every description had appeared along the coast, some ferrying back and forth between warships and other larger crafts, while overhead, aircraft from Göring's squadrons strafed and bombed the soldiers huddled below.

After nine days of steadily emptying the beach, the flotilla disappeared, leaving mounds of waste, the lingering smell of armies struggling to the death, and the moan of wind whipping through the ghostly lines of abandoned equipment.

On the second day after the boats had disappeared from the coast, Amélie had ventured onto the road above it with her younger sister, Chantal. Until then, they had remained sequestered in their home. Situated at the northern extremity of the beach, the cottage was beyond the periphery of furious combat yet close enough to see, hear, and feel its fearsome power. Despite its proximity to battle, the house remained the safest place for the family to shelter, relegating its members to the windows to watch the epic events revealed just beyond their garden gate.

On this first outing, they were aghast at the enormous size of the area trampled by the escaping armies, smoke still rising from the vast number of war machines. Here and there, seagulls and other scavengers fought over clumps that must be the remains of unfortunate men cut down by machine gun fire from the sky in their last desperate scramble over the remaining yards to be rescued.

As Amélie and Chantal walked along the row of burned-out shops along the beachfront at the base of destroyed apartment and office buildings, they ran into friends and acquaintances, each with expressions of disbelief at what they saw in the tragic panorama before them. They greeted each other gravely, mixing the joy of encountering friends safe and well with sorrow for the death and devastation that had come to pass and dread for what must surely lie ahead. Then, the sound of guns and small arms fire had sent everyone hurrying back to their shelters to bide through the further annihilation of the city by the advancing German army.

Guns pounded, and soldiers scurried and bled and died. From their home, the Bouliers had no view of the destruction south and east of them where lay ancient cathedrals, parks, municipal buildings, schools, markets, and the neighborhoods of friends and loved ones. They could sense but did not know the extent to which Dunkirk had been leveled. Finally, an unnerving quiet returned, and with it, the sight of Germans in dark uniforms, moving to the coast and then descending to the sand to inspect the hoard of arms and machines left behind.

Today, Amélie watched intently as the soldiers moved like marauding ants from vehicle to vehicle, throwing open doors or breaking windows, leaning or crawling inside, and sometimes emerging with objects that they placed in a pile or hurried up the beach. She drew back from the window, her eyes arrested when they came to the innumerable flocks of scavengers squawking over scattered dead bodies. *Mon Dieu!*

Now, as her view trailed toward the stretch of beach far down in front of her house, she caught sight of a long, dark object pressed against the brown line of detritus where wavelets rose to the land at high tide. Seen from hundreds of meters away, the object looked like it could be another body not yet discovered by scavengers.

Amélie sighed. *Le pauvre.*

She shifted her attention to the activity among the vehicles again, seeing that the Germans worked efficiently, methodically, and thoroughly as they moved northward toward her end of the shore.

Dark clouds intensified in the overcast sky, and rain descended in driving sheets. The soldiers on the beach first pulled out their rain slickers and continued to work, but then as the downpour became torrential, they retreated up the slope to gain shelter.

Amélie's eyes swept across the sand to the place where she had seen the presumed dead body, and her forehead wrinkled in puzzlement. It was not there, and the tide was not yet high enough to sweep it out to sea. She searched back and forth, and then thought she spotted it several yards north. She peered more intently through the rain and gasped as the body flopped over on its back. Then as she watched, it appeared to lift its head skyward.

Jeremy cast his eyes to the heavens in thanks as heavy raindrops fell. Within moments, he was drenched, but the sheets of rain provided limited concealment. He drank in the rejuvenating water and then struggled onto his stomach and began crawling faster. Daring at one point to look back across the beach, he saw the Germans first cover themselves against the downpour and then climb the slope to seek shelter.

As he watched, fresh energy surged. After a few moments, he dared to rise to his knees and examine the ground nearby. To his front, he saw a gully deeper than the others. It would allow him to ascend from the shore in a low crouch for some distance before again having to revert to crawling on his belly. Glancing at the dark, looming clouds, he crept into the gully and began his climb.

"Chantal," Amélie cried, her voice unmistakably urgent. "Chantal, come quickly!"

Moments later, Chantal appeared at her shoulder, staring out the window. "What is it?"

"Shh," Amélie cautioned with one finger over her mouth. "We don't want Papa to hear."

"What are you talking about?"

Amélie pointed. "There. In the gully, the deeper one. I saw a soldier go in there. He must be British and trying to escape the Germans. He'll come this way."

Chantal fixed her eyes on the gully. "Are you sure? In this rain, how could you see anything?"

"I noticed him before the rain started. I thought it was another dead body, but then I saw him move, and he crawled into that gully." She glanced over her shoulder as if checking to see that they were still alone. "We must help him."

Chantal's eyes widened with alarm. "Are you a fool? If the Nazis catch us..." She made a slicing motion across her throat.

Amélie shrugged impatiently. "They don't need an excuse. That man is here because he fought for us, for our country. He needs our help."

"What are you two whispering about?" Ferrand Boulier, the girls' father, appeared behind them. Thin, wizened, and bent, he regarded them with dubious eyes and then stared out the window. "What is it? What did you see out there?"

The sisters exchanged glances. "It's nothing, Papa," said Chantal. "We were just watching the German soldiers running up the beach to get out of the rain."

Ferrand eyed them. He pointed a finger by his head skyward and wagged it, an eternal French gesture. "Don't be watching them too much. They are not our friends, and I'm going to have enough trouble keeping them from you."

Amélie swayed back and forth on her feet, anxious to end the conversation and get back to the window. "We know, and we don't like them either. Seeing them run for cover was fun, that's all."

Ferrand's eyes narrowed as he examined his daughters' faces. "You could never lie to me," he told Amélie. "Every time you tried as a little girl, you twisted back and forth on your feet just like you're doing now. What else is going on?"

"She saw a British soldier in that gully," Chantal blurted. "She wants to help him."

Ferrand whirled on Amélie, whose cheeks flushed as she glared at her sister. "That's not true. I thought I saw another dead body on the beach where the gully ends. But it's gone. I must have been mistaken."

Her father stepped closer to the window and stared down at the beach where Amélie had indicated. "My eyes are not what they were," he said quietly after a moment. "I can barely make out the beach." He turned and craned his neck toward Amélie, his expression muted. "Tell me exactly what you saw, and don't lie to me. Twisting on your feet is not the only way you gave yourself away."

Amélie sighed and told her father everything she had seen. "We have to help. If we leave him out there, *les Boches* will either capture or kill him."

Ferrand listened carefully, then remained in thought for several minutes.

"You are to do exactly as I say," he said at last, "which is nothing. If you saw such a soldier, he is not your concern. I won't risk your lives."

Amélie looked furious. "How can you say that? He risked his life for us. That's why he's down there in the mud. We can't leave him. Our duty—"

"I know our duty," Ferrand stormed. "I know *my* duty. I fought in the last war, and my obligation now is to protect my daughters. If your mother were alive, God rest her soul, she would tell you the same thing. I'll have a hard-enough time keeping you from being raped by these pillagers without you going out and inviting it." He pointed a finger at them. "You are not to leave this house until I say so. Is that understood?"

"But Papa—" Amélie interjected.

"Is that understood?" Ferrand repeated.

"Yes," Chantal replied.

Amélie only nodded, her face pinched in anger.

Ferrand exhaled. "Now, I have to go to my brother's house for bread. We have none, and the baker was closed today. He's already short of supplies, but luckily, his shop still stands. When I get back, I expect to see you both here, dry, and no strange man in my house. Do I have to say that again?"

Both girls shook their heads. Ferrand nodded brusquely. Moments later, they heard him rummaging about in the kitchen for his raincoat, and then the back door slammed.

The heavy rain collected in the gullies and poured mud and water down their beds to the ocean. It produced a new challenge to Jeremy as he struggled to reach higher ground, his boots either sinking in the ooze or slipping without traction. Progress was slow, but better than when he was low crawling on the beach.

Ahead, the gully narrowed, and above it he saw flat ground that appeared to be a road crossing in front of him. *Finally.* From his desperate flight to the beach, he recalled stands of trees where he could hide while gaining his bearings. He had dodged between houses then, and now thought he might find a place between or behind them where he could shelter. *Maybe a garage or a garden shed.*

As he approached the gully's tapered upper end, he saw another channel running at a right angle to his left. When he reached it, he heard a hiss, and a small, thin man stepped into his path.

"I am Ferrand," the man said in heavily accented English. He motioned to indicate the direction of Dunkirk. "Nazis!" He turned in the opposite direction and gestured for Jeremy to follow.

Jeremy hesitated.

Ferrand turned to him, his face expressing urgency. "*Vien,*" he called. "We help." He beckoned again and started back in the direction he had come.

"Why did you have to tell Papa?" Amélie demanded of Chantal. "We could have saved that soldier." They huddled on the floor together, staring out the window.

"He would have found out anyway. You were never good at lying."

"Now we're stuck inside when we could be doing something."

Chantal sighed. "You're always more adventuresome than me. I'm not brave. I just want this war to end so we can get back to normal."

"This is no adventure. We can't let the Germans overrun our country and do nothing."

Chantal buried her face in her hands. "But they kill, and they take everything. If we resist, they will make us pay."

Amélie embraced her sister, caressing the back of her head. "We'll get through this, little one, but I think we'll both have to be braver than we ever thought possible."

Chantal whimpered and rubbed her eyes as she straightened to look once more out the window. "Look!" She pointed at two German soldiers making their way up the road from Dunkirk. They would pass right above the head of the gully where Amélie had seen the British soldier.

"They might see him," Amélie gasped. "We must do something."

She flew into the kitchen, emerging moments later with her raincoat. Before Chantal could protest, she headed out the front door while still wrapping and clasping herself in the garment.

The rain came in torrents as she stepped out. She halted to regain sight of the two German soldiers and pull the hood over her head. They had moved past the house and stood over the gully, staring into its recesses.

Amélie hurried through the garden gate, leaving it open behind her. "*Allô*," she called after the soldiers. They did not hear her, so she ran to close the distance and called again, "*Allô*." Without waiting for a response, she darted to the soldiers and tugged on the sleeve of the nearest one.

Startled, he whirled on her, and seeing his sudden movement, his companion did the same.

"We need food," Amélie yelled in French above the roar and splash of the falling rain. With her hand she mimicked eating.

The soldiers eyed her at first with anger and impatience, then amusement. One smirked, a salacious gleam in his eye. He said something to his comrade and then reached to the top of Amélie's raincoat as if to pull it open.

Amélie drew back, her eyes betraying her horror. "*Essen*," she screamed, using the German word for food, one of the few she knew. "*Essen*," she repeated, standing her ground.

The second soldier grasped his companion's shoulder and shook his head while locking his eyes on Amélie's face. "*Abendglocke*," he said slowly, his tone stern. Then, more deliberately, he said in French with a heavy Germanic accent, "*Couvre-feu*." Curfew.

The soldier who had tried to open Amélie's jacket reached out again, shoved her, and waved her off. "*Raus*," he commanded. Then the two moved away from the gully and recommenced their patrol.

Breathing with relief, Amélie stood on the drenched pavement in the rain, watching them go. For good measure, she bleated out again, "*Essen*," but the soldiers paid her no heed and continued on their path.

In the gully, Jeremy watched Ferrand go, and hesitated. Then, above them, he heard voices. Pressing against the side of the gulch and hardly daring to breathe, he craned to see through the rain to the street surface. Ferrand also froze in place and lifted his eyes toward the road.

Two German soldiers stood there peering into the channel. Jeremy pressed himself harder against the mud wall.

A woman's voice joined those of the soldiers. Her utterances were few, and she stooped against the wind and rain. One of the soldiers reached for her twice, but the other restrained him, and they motioned for her to leave. Then they proceeded on their patrol, away from Dunkirk.

Jeremy glanced at Ferrand. Even in this light, he saw that the thin old man's grim face had taken on an extra layer of anxiety.

"We go," Ferrand called, motioning for Jeremy to follow. His urgency was palpable.

With a quick glance at the road, Jeremy followed. The water ran ankle-deep with a rapid current, and the walls, slick with mud, offered no place to grasp for balance. Soon, this second gully curved upward, where a culvert emptied below the roadbed.

Ferrand crawled into it with no difficulty, but being much larger, Jeremy struggled through, squirming against the flowing water and fighting down a claustrophobic panic. When he emerged on the other end, Ferrand stood waiting and helped Jeremy out.

"This way," Ferrand said, moving swiftly to a stand of trees and then to the shadows of an alley behind a row of houses. They came to a garden gate. Immediately inside stood a toolshed. He opened the door and motioned for Jeremy to enter. The shelter was dry and long enough that Jeremy could lie down. "You wait here," he said.

Ferrand stepped inside behind him and leaned into the shadows. When he straightened, he handed over a blanket and a small pouch he had packed before leaving the house. "Food," he said. "You eat. I come back, yes?"

Exhausted and grateful, Jeremy only nodded. He collapsed on the floor and pulled the blanket over him while clutching the small bag of food. Even before Ferrand had shut the door, he closed his eyes in sleep.

2

Ferrand's eyes blazed when he entered his house through the back door. He pulled off his raincoat and threw it across a kitchen chair before striding into the front room, tracking thick mud behind him. His daughters sat on the floor, still staring out the window; however, at the front door, he spotted a puddle of water that trailed into the living room.

"Don't play innocent with me," he fumed. "One of you went outside the house, against my orders, and into the rain. Stand up."

Crestfallen, the girls climbed to their feet. There was no hiding Amélie's wet shoes. "Just as I thought," Ferrand said. "You disobeyed me." He directed his attention to her. "Are you trying to get yourself killed along with our family? Why did you speak with those soldiers?"

Amélie looked up sharply. "What soldiers?"

His anger rising further, Ferrand snapped, "Don't play with me. I heard you begging those soldiers for food. How did you know that word in German?"

Ignoring his question, Amélie stared at him. "I confess. I went out to talk to them. I couldn't let them catch the British soldier."

"You were foolish," Ferrand retorted. "There is no British soldier, and even if there were, he's not worth your life, or your assault. That Nazi had his mind on doing bad things to you."

Amélie's eyes dropped to take in the muck caked around Ferrand's boots and the trail of mud leading from the kitchen. She glanced at her father's face. "You were there. How else could you know what happened?"

At a loss for words and still angry, Ferrand could only stare with wide, yellowed eyes. A smile broke across Amélie's face. "You went to help him."

She crossed the room and wrapped the old man's head in her arms. "You talk so tough, but we all know what a soft heart you have." She pulled back suddenly. "Did you see him? Where is he?" Leaping away from Ferrand, she ran toward the kitchen. Seeing it empty, she turned back into the living room. "What have you done with him?"

"I didn't see him," Ferrand grunted, shifting his eyes.

Amélie's laugh had the excited, musical tone Ferrand had known and loved since she was a child. "You're no better at lying than I am," she said. "Tell me. You know I'll find out."

"Is he really here?" Chantal broke in with mixed excitement and fear. "Can we see him?"

"He's in the shed, isn't he?" Amélie watched Ferrand's face closely, then turned and started toward the kitchen.

"No," Ferrand bellowed. "He cannot come in here. It's too risky, and he's filthy and wet. At least if the Germans find him in the shed, we can say we didn't know he was there. But if he's in the house..." He shrugged, leaving unstated his fear of impending doom.

"We can't leave him out there," Amélie said. She embraced her father again. "You already risked your life for him—"

"You did too," Ferrand interrupted. "We've done our part. We can't do more."

"He's cold and wet." Amélie laid her head on his shoulder. "He could die from exposure."

She stood and once more moved toward the back of the house. "Chantal," she called, "I'll need your help."

Her sister clambered hesitantly to her feet, her eyes on Ferrand, torn between Amélie's command and her father's wishes.

He breathed deeply and nodded, his reluctance showing on his face. "I'll help."

As though through a fog, Jeremy heard piano music. The melody was familiar, one he had often heard his sister, Claire, play while growing up. It was a classical piece, thunderous, moving, and requiring great skill as the concentration on bass notes moved to light trilling at the higher end of the scales.

Jeremy thought he dreamed the tune, bringing as it did images of his sister at the piano in his home in the English Channel Islands, and slowly he realized he was awake. He had no idea how long he had slept. He vaguely recalled horrific sights and sounds of war, thrashing among images of dark-uniformed soldiers tromping him into the sand and of a skinny little man leading him into a dark, tight tunnel. He squirmed against the panic of being unable to move. In the recesses of his mind he heard the voice of a woman, maybe two, and remembered the sensation of being half-dragged and half-carried through rain and wind into a warmer place.

He awakened by degrees, first sensing dim light, then the warmth of blankets and a soft bed, and then the enchanting music.

When he finally opened his eyes, his first view was a blurred image of a figure standing next to his bed. As his eyes cleared, he perceived a young girl smiling at him. She spoke, but he was too groggy to make out her words.

He shook his head to clear it and looked again. The girl was still there, and she held his hand. She let it drop. Then he felt her hand again, wiping his brow with a moist cloth.

She had moved closer, and he saw that she was perhaps in her early teens. Her hair was dark with a reddish hue, her skin white and soft, her stature smallish, but he could not make out the color of her eyes.

He tried to sit up.

"Shh," Chantal said. "You rest." She spoke in broken English.

He sank back into the sheets. "England," he croaked. "I must get back." He dropped his head onto the pillow and reached behind his head, noticing that his hair was soft and clean.

"Wait. I get my sister." Chantal rushed out of the room.

Moments later, the music stopped, and almost immediately, Chantal reappeared leading Amélie, a version of herself only a few years older.

"He's awake," Chantal said, "and he says he wants to leave."

"Not now," Amélie said firmly, her French accent strong. She carried an air of authority. "You rest. I get food."

As she left, their father entered the room. Jeremy studied Ferrand's face, his memory flashing to the small man who had helped him escape the gully and the Germans on a dark, wet night. He raised up on his right elbow and reached forward.

"You saved me," he rasped. "Thank you."

Ferrand nodded and clasped Jeremy's hand. Chantal stepped forward.

"My father not speak English," she stammered. "My sister—"

Jeremy fluttered his right palm to interrupt her. "I speak your language," he said in French.

"Ah, *bon*," Chantal replied, delighted, and reverting to French. "My sister speaks a little English." She laughed and held her thumb and forefinger close together to demonstrate her meaning. "I do too. We studied it in school. My father speaks only a few English words, but he understands a lot, and yes, he saved you. My sister, too." She twisted from side to side and laughed again. "Not me. I'm too afraid."

Jeremy smiled and shifted his eyes to Ferrand. "Thank you again." He squeezed the old man's hand.

"I did nothing," Ferrand said.

"My sister saw you on the beach," Chantal broke in. "She ran out in the rain to distract the soldiers." She detailed what Amélie had done. "My father was very angry with her."

Jeremy closed his eyes. "Thank you so much." He put his hand behind his head and again felt his clean hair. "Who—"

Anticipating his question, Chantal's eyes flashed with amusement. "We cleaned you, Amélie and I. You were cold and shivering. My father watched us. He wouldn't let us see or touch..." She indicated Jeremy's middle parts. "You have to do that yourself."

In spite of his fatigue, Jeremy chuckled. Then his face became grave. "I must leave. I'm a danger to you."

"You'll go when you're strong enough," Ferrand said. "You need rest.

We'll watch the Nazis. If they come, we'll move you. You stay here." His tone was one of finality.

Amélie reentered with a tray bearing warm soup, bread, and coffee. "You eat," she said in English, setting it on a nightstand. She sat on the chair next to him again. "I watch."

"He speaks French," Chantal chimed in.

Overcome with emotion, Jeremy studied Amélie. Maintaining his composure, he said, "Your father and sister say you saved my life. How can I ever thank you?"

Amélie waved away the comment. "I did nothing. My father saved you. I just talked to the Germans. I made them think we are weak." Her face took on an impish expression. "We are not weak."

3

"Was that you playing the piano when I woke up?" Jeremy asked the next day.

Amélie smiled shyly and nodded.

"My sister plays that piece," Jeremy said. "It's the 'Revolutionary Étude' by Frederick Chopin, if I recall correctly, and takes a great deal of skill and practice to do it as well as you do. How long have you been playing?"

"Since I was a little girl. My mother taught me. She was a great pianist before she died."

Jeremy sensed an onrush of melancholy. "I'm sorry—"

"That was four years ago." Amélie dismissed the subject with a toss of her head. "You have a strange accent when you talk in French. Sometimes you sound British, sometimes American."

Jeremy chuckled. "That's because I'm both. My father was born an American, but he became a British citizen, and my mother is British."

"Then do you have family in the United States?"

"Many uncles, aunts, and cousins."

Two nights and almost two days had passed since he had entered the Boulier home. He had remained in Ferrand's back bedroom while he recovered. With food and drink, he already felt strong and had become comfortable with the family, but uncomfortable in the threat he posed to them.

"I can't stay here," he told Amélie. "It's too dangerous."

She remained obstinate. "You're not leaving yet. That's more threatening." She cast him a curious look. "Where do you live?"

"You're changing the subject. I must go."

"You don't know where to go," Amélie insisted. "The Nazis are putting checkpoints in place. When the time is right, we'll help you." She grinned in her impish fashion and asked again, "Where do you live?"

Jeremy sighed. "If you must know, my home is on Sark Island. I was born there. It's off the coast of Normandy near Guernsey. It's one of the English Channel Islands."

"Ah, I know of them. We call them *Îles de la Manche* or *Îles Anglo-Normandes*. Do you speak *Sercquiais*?"

"Those are the right islands, and yes, I speak *Sercquiais*. Even though it's a French dialect, no one who didn't grow up there understands it. Children are taught both French and English. We learn our *patois* on our own. Sark is a backward place."

Amélie wrinkled her forehead. "What do you mean, 'backward?' The education sounds like it must be good."

"The culture is dated. We don't even allow cars."

Amélie nodded with a bemused expression. "Maybe it's good that your island is backward." She indicated their surroundings beyond the confines of the room. "Look what we have now in Dunkirk."

Jeremy first nodded, and then shook his head grimly. "You have a point."

"So, you fight because you're British. Do you think the Americans will fight?"

Feeling a downward pull in mood, Jeremy's shoulders slumped. "I don't know. This war has already gone on nearly nine months. Americans want to stay neutral."

"Then they will fight. Hitler won't let them stay neutral. He's already taken Austria, Czechoslovakia, Poland—"

Suddenly, the door burst open and Chantal rushed in with a look of horror. Tears ran down her face. "The Germans have entered Paris," she cried. "I heard it just now on the street. The Nazis are celebrating." She wrung her hands together in despair. "What will happen to us?"

Amélie gasped. Then they heard the front door of the house open and close, and Ferrand hurried into the room.

He spoke rapidly to Jeremy. "The Germans are searching all the houses in the neighborhood. I'll hide you. Come with me. Now." As he headed out the door, he told his daughters, "Stay in the house. Look normal."

Jeremy bolted after him while pulling on his dirty uniform. Then he stopped and turned to Amélie. "I will never forget you. After the war..." His voice trailed off.

With tears brimming, Amélie nodded. "*Oui.*" Her voice caught and she wiped her eyes. "After the war. Go!"

Amélie and Chantal sat in the front room staring out to sea. Occasionally, Chantal searched Amélie's face for a clue to her thoughts, but Amélie remained impassive. Finally, unable to restrain herself, Chantal asked, "Do you think you'll ever see him again?"

Amélie shrugged. "I don't know. Right now, we can think only about how we get through tonight. When the Germans come here, don't be so inquisitive. Be quiet, answer their questions, volunteer nothing, and look scared."

"I am scared."

"Good. Stay that way."

"You don't have to be so cross with me."

Amélie smiled gently. "I'm sorry. You've been wonderful."

Chantal remained quiet a moment, but curiosity overcame her judgment. "Do you love him?"

"Don't be silly. I just met him two days ago, and he was unconscious."

"But you cried when he left."

"Of course," Amélie deflected. "Those Germans on the road could have killed us."

Chantal darted to the window. "Look, they're coming. The soldiers are leaving the neighbor's house and coming this way."

"And where's father?" Amélie cried. She rushed to the kitchen, doused cold water on her eyes, and returned to the living room to sit and wait.

Chantal sat across the room in a chair, her legs kicking, her eyes wide. She bit her fingernails.

They heard the garden gate creak open, the stomp of boots on the sidewalk, and then an abrupt knock on the front door. Amélie went to open it.

The officer who met her was dressed immaculately in his uniform. He exhibited flawless manners and a friendly attitude, whether sincere or not.

"Good afternoon, *mademoiselle*," he greeted in French with a perfect accent. "I am *Hauptman* Bergmann. But I see that you've been crying. Is anything the matter?"

Bergmann personified Aryan good looks with a square jaw, blond hair, and blue eyes, and he carried himself with a confidence just shy of arrogance that repulsed Amélie. She sniffed and wiped an eye. "Of course I'm crying. I just heard that your army marched into Paris. Dunkirk is destroyed, and everything in our country is turned upside down. I don't even know if I'm allowed to leave the house, or when."

"I understand. Please accept my assurance that we are here with the greatest of intentions." Bergmann's condescension grated on Amélie. He continued, "When this mess is finished, we'll all be friends in one big country. Right now, we ask for patience while we settle in." He turned to an orderly standing just behind him.

Amélie recognized the soldier as the one who had jostled her when she had gone out in the rain. Involuntarily, she froze.

"Who lives in this house, Kallsen?" Bergmann asked.

"The Boulier family," Kallsen replied, after checking a list on a clipboard. "Ferrand Boulier lives here with his daughters, Amélie and Chantal. His wife is deceased."

Bergmann turned back to Amélie. "My condolences regarding your mother. May I assume that you are Amélie Boulier?" She nodded. "Is your father home?"

"My father went out right after we heard the news about Paris. I think he went to find out more detail."

Bergmann feigned hesitance. "May I come in? I want my soldiers to check out your house. Nothing invasive. We've had reports of British soldiers still loose and hiding, and we want to apprehend them before they cause damage to local residents."

Mindful of the irony of a German officer concerning himself about destruction amid the ruins of Dunkirk, Amélie stepped out of the way and motioned for Bergmann to enter. He turned to Kallsen and indicated that he should join them.

Two more soldiers followed. They immediately went to other parts of the house to carry out their search. Kallsen remained inside the front door, prepared to take notes.

Looking around the living room, Bergmann said, "Very nice. I'm happy to see that the fighting did you no harm."

"We were fortunate. It stopped a few houses closer to town."

Noticing consternation on Chantal's face, Bergmann crossed the room to rub her cheek.

Chantal blanched. Her eyes widened further.

"You have nothing to fear from me, young lady. We're here to make you safe. How old are you?"

"Fourteen." Chantal trembled, but dared not move her face from the officer's hand. Meanwhile, Bergmann had glanced around the room, his eyes resting on a set of photos atop a piano. He moved over and picked up a family portrait.

"Such a lovely family." He pointed at one of the girls in the picture. "Is that you?"

Before Chantal could respond, she heard the back door open and close. Then, Ferrand appeared in the passageway leading from the kitchen. "I brought a fresh loaf of bread," he called out, and then he saw Bergmann.

"Forgive the intrusion," the captain said, and crossed the room to introduce himself.

Ferrand shook his hand perfunctorily. "I was not expecting guests," he said, "or I would have brought more bread."

"Don't trouble yourself. My soldiers will be finished momentarily, and then we'll be on our way. As I explained to your very charming daughters, we've had reports of stray British soldiers annoying local residents, so we are alerting everyone to help round them up. We just want you to let us know if you see them."

Bergmann's men returned to the front room, having completed their search. They made eye contact with him and shook their heads.

"Is there anything out back?" Bergmann asked.

"Just a shed in the garden. You can have your men check it if you like."

A flick of Bergmann's wrist sent the soldiers out the back door. They returned shortly and shook their heads.

"Good, then," Bergmann said. "We'll be on our way. If you need anything, do not hesitate to contact me. I am at your service." With a click of his heels and a sharp nod, he departed with his entourage.

Jeremy breathed a sigh. The German soldiers who searched the shed had just closed the door, and he listened to their boots clomping up the concrete garden path and entering the house through the back door.

He waited several minutes, and then pushed against the false wall that Ferrand had hurriedly built overnight in anticipation of such an occasion. The shed was barely long enough for a man to lie in, and only a few feet wide. Its steepled roof allowed standing to full height, and the low door was built into the wall nearest the garden path and faced the house.

Ferrand had taken old pieces of wood stacked in the back of the shed and constructed the moveable false wall that looked more like a floor-to-ceiling tool rack. He had done it in the early morning hours, tapping the nails lightly and repeatedly with a cloth-covered hammer to minimize noise. The construction was not held together well, but when placed upright behind the door, it provided sufficient space for Jeremy to stand against the front wall and hold it in place. Ferrand had hung rakes, shovels, and other garden implements on it, and he had thrown a pile of rags in the opposite corner. With Jeremy concealed behind the wall, Ferrand had leaned a wheelbarrow against it.

When the soldiers had swung the door open, one waited outside while the other probed the interior.

Jeremy's hiding place stood in the door's shadow. He held his breath, wishing he could calm his thumping heart.

Flashlight switched on, the soldier had crossed to the pile of rags and kicked them aside while keeping his rifle ready with his free hand. Finding nothing, he swept the light around the shed, searching the nooks and crannies. Then he moved to the door and swung his weapon toward the space behind it.

Jeremy had pressed into the dark recess behind the false wall, but he had no more room. Between him and the muzzle of the rifle pointed at his chest were only the boards and garden tools. But the soldier took only a perfunctory look, switched off his light, exited the shed, and returned to the house.

Several minutes later, Jeremy pushed the wall forward at an angle sufficient for him to slide through. Then he opened the garden door a crack to peer at the house.

Images of Amélie flooded his mind—her standing stooped in the rain facing the German soldiers, the strands of music that stopped as he caught his first blurry glimpse of her following Chantal into the room and then sitting next to him and tending to him. Her impish smile and melodic laugh burned into his psyche so that he smiled slightly as he thought of her. And once again, he heard her play Chopin on the piano.

He pictured her large, honey-colored eyes. He imagined her turned-up nose and full lips. She was petite, but under her loose clothing, he could not see her figure...

I don't care. She's the most beautiful woman I've ever seen. She risked her life for me. He thought she must be around twenty, roughly two years younger than he. Then he brought his thoughts under control. *Her* family *risked for me.*

He thought of Chantal, a younger version of her sister, also bubbly, exuberant, and fearful; an adolescent facing challenges no one should have to endure. Yet, there she was with the Nazis in her living room. *She must be terrified.*

Then Ferrand. The old veteran who had fought in and survived the trenches of the Great War had gone out into the storm to save a stranger. This father's love and protection of his daughters manifested in his anger at the exposure to danger Amélie had initiated, yet he had put his own life on the line for the same purpose. *He might be old and bent, but he's noble and crafty, a true hero.*

Jeremy sat in the dark, his thoughts and emotions jumbled. Dulled by days of fighting and evading capture, his ability to analyze and choose a course of action seemed impaired. But one driving thought prevailed. *I put them in danger. I can't stay.*

With a lump in his throat, he opened the door only enough to slide through. Closing it softly behind him, he ducked and shuffled behind a hedge growing along the low garden fence. He sat there for a time, listening, and when he heard no sounds indicating anything amiss, he parted the branches so he could take one last look at the Boulier family home. Then, crouching, he stepped over the fence and made his way along the alley, staying close to its edge until he found another garden with an unlocked shed where he could wait for darkness.

He looked down at his uniform. *If I'm caught, I won't be shot as a spy.*

As soon as Bergmann and his men had left, Amélie turned to Ferrand. "That soldier standing next to Bergmann, the one he called Kallsen. He was the one who reached for me on the road yesterday."

Anger flaring, Ferrand asked, "Did he recognize you?"

"I don't know. He didn't seem to. The rain was falling hard, the sky was dark, and I was in my raincoat with a hood."

"Let's hope he didn't. He could throw us under suspicion."

Amélie nodded. "Where did you hide Jeremy?" Uncharacteristic urgency tinged her tone.

"In the shed," Ferrand replied.

Amélie started for the back door.

"Listen to me," Ferrand commanded. His tone arrested her. "You can't go running out there. Everything we do must appear natural. Hurrying to the shed without being dressed for gardening right after *Hauptman* Bergmann was here could seem suspicious to neighbors who might see and report you."

Amélie faced him, fury in her eyes. "You don't believe that anyone living around here would report us." Her expression softened as she saw the added stoop of his shoulders and the strain on his face.

"I don't know," Ferrand said. "Two years ago, the Austrians had their

Anschluss and welcomed this madman Hitler into their country. Why would they do that?"

"Austrians are German," Amélie replied, "and Hitler came from there. He just joined two countries that should already have been together."

"That's the popular view," Ferrand replied. "Austria took a lot of land from their neighbors before the last war. There was a reason why the Allies wouldn't let the two countries unite after the armistice." He paused, gathering his thoughts. "Several months after the *Anschluss*, the Nazi Brown Shirts destroyed hundreds of Jewish synagogues across Germany. They ransacked over seven thousand of their businesses and huge numbers of homes, hospitals, and schools. The rioters left so much broken glass in the streets from looted stores that they call it *Kristallnacht*."

"I remember vaguely, but I was still a teenager."

Ferrand chuckled. "You are still very young, my daughter, but unfortunately"—he looked at Chantal sitting alone across the room, glued to their conversation— "your generation will have to mature fast." He sighed. "A lot of people who attacked the Jews had been their friends. Many of our countrymen sympathize with Hitler's aims." His tired eyes studied Chantal's face and then Amélie's. "We don't know who to trust. The danger is constant. We'll survive by acting normal all the time."

"You mean give in?"

The lines on Ferrand's face creased in a barely perceptible smile. "If the last day hasn't proven otherwise, I cannot convince you that I will never give in to *les Boches*."

A look of chagrin crossed Amélie's face. With outstretched arms, she moved to her father and hugged him. "I'm sorry. That was stupid of me to say." She sniffed and pulled away while patting his chest. "I'll put on some gardening clothes and go make sure Jeremy is all right. Don't worry, I'll putter around before coming back in."

Ferrand exhaled grimly. "You won't find him there."

"What?" Amélie's voice caught. She whirled around. "Where is he?"

"Gone. He knows he can't stay here. I drew him a map."

Startled, Amélie could only utter, "To where?"

"Best that you don't know. If we are going to keep each other safe during this war, the less we know about what others are doing, the better. Learn that. Jeremy is a capable man, and he needs to get to safe ground, home in England."

Amélie sat with her eyes closed, not moving for a time. Then, fighting back tears, she leaned her head into her father's chest. "How will he get there?"

"He'll have help. I can't say more."

For several minutes, Amélie snuggled against Ferrand, who put his arm around her shoulders and held her. "He'll be all right. I'm sure of it."

"Oh, Papa, I'm so afraid for him. I close my eyes and I see him, the way he was on the beach, and then when we brought him into the house, and after we cleaned him up. He was strong. When he woke up, he was gentle and nice." Her chest convulsed with an involuntary sob as tears flowed down her cheeks. "I can't bear to think that I'll never see him again."

"There, there, *ma cherie*. You feel like you're in love. This has been an emotional time for all of us, more so for you because you found and saved him."

"*You* saved him," Amélie choked. She shook her head and straightened up, wiping her eyes. "I don't know what I feel. I only know I—*we*—cared for him. He fought for us, and we risked our lives to save him. There's goodness about him." Her tears continued to fall. "I don't want him to die."

4

Two days earlier, June 8
The northeast outskirts of Dunkirk

Lance Littlefield stared in turn at each of his comrades circled inside a thicket at the edge of a dense forest. His stomach gnawed with hunger; his parched throat was thirsty for even a capful of water. How much longer he or any of the small group of soldiers of the 51st (Highland) Infantry Division could hold out was something he dared not think about. The guns had fallen silent a few days back; how many he no longer had the ability to count. The previous day's storms had blurred his sense of time. He inhaled, fighting despair.

Images of his family plagued him. His parents had been against his enlisting in the army amidst the inevitability of war, but he had been determined to do his bit for king and country, and so here he was in this desolate place.

The situation had not been this way when he arrived, nor had he intended this place as his destination. The notion of fighting the Hun had appealed to him in a romantic way. As an adventurer, he sought challenge, undeterred by danger, and he had expected to be in the thick of combat. He had not expected to provide rearguard protection for an escaping army while pitted against overwhelming force, or then to have been abandoned along with his brothers-in-arms whom he fought for most, those to his left and right during battle.

The young, gaunt faces around him were new to Lance. Like him, they had been separated from their units and scattered when the German juggernaut strafed, bombed, machine-gunned, mortared, and engaged with small arms and fixed bayonets as it rumbled through the last strands of British and French defenses on its way to the beaches at Dunkirk.

Each of the lads had witnessed the capture and slaughter of thousands of their fellow soldiers, and they observed from barely concealed hideaways as prisoners were stripped of their arms and led away. Their faces, seeming old despite their youth, showed the shock of the brutality they had witnessed. No one smiled, and they clung close to each other for mutual support. Without asking them, Lance knew their thoughts, because they were his own. *Will I ever see home again? Will I see tomorrow?*

Three of his companions were in almost catatonic states. One of them had been among roughly a hundred captured members of the 2nd Battalion of the Royal Norfolk Regiment who had been marched to a farm in *Le Paradis*. There, the SS Totenkopf Division machine-gunned their captives. At the first sound of gunfire, he had fallen to the ground and lay there with heaving breath and gushing tears while around him, his comrades screamed and groaned in agony as bullets ripped through their bodies. They fell over him, covering his face and uniform in thick splashes of blood. For hours, he lay there until the Germans departed and darkness allowed him to crawl out and escape into the underbrush.

The second soldier in severe shock had witnessed a similar atrocity in which members of the 2nd Battalion of the Royal Warwickshire Regiment, captured near Wormhout, were forced into a barn. There, the Germans lobbed hand grenades into the outbuilding until no sound of life emanated. Finding himself physically unharmed but covered in blood, he lay still while the captors moved among the corpses, firing into those still showing signs of life. He continued to lay among his dead mates for hours after the Germans left, waiting for darkness and silence.

The third was a medic who had been in the passenger seat of an ambulance and narrowly escaped into the woods when a squad of German soldiers fired on them, despite the Red Cross markings. The engine block had spewed smoke thick enough to conceal him as he jumped from his seat and plunged into the shrubbery, unseen. From there, and to his horror, he watched as the enemy secured the back door so that it could not be opened from the inside and set the vehicle on fire. Within seconds, screams filled the air as the wounded were incinerated.

Not daring to move, the soldier could only cover his ears while tears streamed down his face. Then, the stench of burning flesh had assaulted his nostrils.

All the men in this small group with Lance had seen huge numbers of their compatriots rounded up at gunpoint and marched to heaven-knows-where. Each had likely avoided detection because the Germans had their hands full managing the thousands of prisoners they had already taken.

Some soldiers evaded capture by squirming behind shrubs, berms, hedges, and whatever concealment they could find, including massive numbers of dead bodies and the hulks of burned-out war machines. They headed away from columns of prisoners marching east under armed guard. In the dim light of dusk or dawn, from hearing the crack of branches or catching a glimpse of movement, they had found each other, recognized by their filthy olive-green British uniforms. For days, they had scavenged, only daring to approach garbage bins of the most isolated homes in the darkness of night and scurrying away at the sounds of barking dogs. In the mornings, they licked dew from leaves and sought water from wherever they could find it, including puddles in the road. Now grimy, unshaved, starved, thirsty, disoriented, and with no plan, they offered each other the only solace they could, company during shared misery.

Numb, Lance realized after a time that, as a mid-level sergeant, he was the ranking member of his group. The weight of responsibility for these lives descended on his shoulders like a dark, heavy cloak. As he looked dully from face to face, he saw that some with sufficient presence of mind stared back, expectant, questioning, despairing, looking to him for glimmers of hope that they would live and find a way home.

Home. The thought now seemed a surreal notion, a distant place remembered but real only in the sense that a dream was real, mercurial and wispy. Lance pictured his stepfather, tall, thin, a jocular personality who had nevertheless frowned on Lance's choices in life. His mother was a prim and proper woman, always ready to help anyone who needed it, but seemingly incapable of deep emotional attachment, or at least the expression of it.

Then there were his brothers, Paul and Jeremy, and his sister, Claire. Always-dutiful Paul, the eldest of the four siblings, had taken his mother's personality. He had been the first of the brothers to enter the British Army, accepting a commission and leaving for London to serve. At last word, he was rising rapidly on the staff in the War Office, but his job seemed to be very hush-hush.

Next came Claire. Fair-skinned and fair-haired, she had refused to let her status as the single female sibling interfere with her participation in whatever escapade her brothers dreamed up. Adventurous in her own right, she was the artistically inclined member of the family, loving the piano and gifted on any instrument she picked up. She had been accepted into the Royal Academy of Music in London two years earlier and had lived there ever since.

Lance was the third in line and had joined the army for reasons completely different from Paul's. He had always sought adventure, shirking studies while in school, and as a result, his prospects for advancing scholastically were dim. That bothered him not in the least but inflamed his mother. *Not that she would ever show it.*

He had enlisted as war clouds gathered, only informing his parents the night before shipping out. He had relished the training, earned quick promotion into the non-commissioned officer ranks for his natural leadership abilities, and looked forward to engaging the Hun in combat.

Then there was sweet Jeremy, the baby of the family, a perfect blend of his older siblings. Jeremy was fun-loving but always respectful. He was studious and a gifted athlete, and while he enjoyed joining in Lance's adventures, he never initiated them or pushed the limit. Having always been good with numbers, his choice of an engineering degree surprised no one. The shock had come when he had volunteered for service in the army to build infrastructure in France in anticipation of war with Germany.

Lance closed his eyes and let his chin drop to his chest. *I hope Jeremy got out.*

Picturing his siblings was not difficult: they were images of each other with only those slight differences that family and friends used to distinguish between them. They were above medium height and build with variations of musculature dependent on their physical activity, meaning that Paul was thinner and softer than his brothers, athletically capable, but more inclined to study. Lance was rock-hard. Jeremy was, well, Jeremy, as physically talented as Lance but giving more time to his numbers than to following the physical regimen of his more rambunctious middle brother. As for Claire, despite the hours she spent practicing music, she spent almost an equal amount of time roughhousing with her brothers.

Despite the differences between the siblings while growing up, they wrestled and boxed with their stepfather and each other, spent hours climbing among the cliffs on the shoreline, or played with a ball of some sort on the flat ground of their island home. They were each other's best friends, and they idolized their stepfather.

Paul and Claire had brown eyes, their brothers both had green. All four had straight noses, dirty-blond hair, and firm jaws.

Their mother had her own peculiar warmth. It seldom expressed itself in long hugs or high blandishments, but she was always there, standing aside with a smile more detectable in her eyes than on her lips. She was at once apart from them and yet with them, and always doing small things that made life good—baking favorite desserts, bringing home a new board game, or just being there and helping when they worked through problems.

Thinking about his mother now, an overpowering ache welled within Lance's chest and he felt tears spilling down his cheeks, a recently frequent occurrence. Glancing up, he saw that some of the men noticed. He coughed and wiped his eyes.

Without quite knowing why, he climbed to his feet. His impulse had been to rise abruptly, but he found the effort slowed by exhausted muscles and painful joints. On finally standing upright, his legs wobbled beneath him, and he found himself at a loss for words. He reminded himself that he was the senior man present and opened his mouth to speak.

The sound that emerged was almost unrecognizable, a weak, unintelligible croak. He coughed to clear his throat and tried again, hearing his voice barely above a whisper. Looking about, he saw that he had gained the detached attention of the soldiers, their weary eyes, sagging skin, and drooping shoulders a testament to the deprivations they endured.

Lance sucked on his tongue to pull whatever moisture he could muster into his mouth to wet his throat. Then, he tried for a third time to address the small group.

"Chaps, we're in a pickle." He tried to grin but saw that his attempt at humor had bombed. "No help is coming."

Several of the men closed their eyes, and their heads dropped further. Some turned away. Lance saw that he had only plunged them into deeper desolation.

He straightened his back as best he could and tried to put force in his voice. "We are British soldiers," he said. "We have a mission. Our job now is to evade capture and get home."

Several of the men raised their eyes to meet his, some with a stray ray of hope, some with deep skepticism.

"Just how are we going to do that, Sergeant?" one asked, his tone thick with sarcasm.

"I don't know," Lance admitted, "but we bloody hell won't do it by sitting in a circle with our jaws in the dirt." Feeling a slight rush of energy from unknown reserves, he continued. "We are soldiers of His Majesty's Army, and as the senior member present, I will ask you to please speak to me and your fellow soldiers with respect."

By their startled faces, Lance knew he had at least dented their senses. "The first thing we are going to do is get to know each other," he continued. "Right now, all of you, get on your feet. That's an order."

No one moved. Some turned away.

Lance scanned the weary faces. Then he walked over to the soldier who had seen his comrades machine-gunned at *Le Paradis*. Despite his own shaky legs, he squatted in front of the man, really still a boy. "Where are you from?" he asked gently.

The lad raised his eyes as if unsure that he was the person being addressed. "Aysgarth, sir. I mean, Sergeant."

Gratified that the soldier could still comprehend and respond, Lance pressed him. "Where is that?"

"It's..." The soldier started to reply and then had to stop to think. "It's in the middle of the country, in North Yorkshire. It's a tiny place."

"Is it beautiful?"

A slow smile crossed the soldier's face. He nodded. "It is. Just a stop in the road, really, but I grew up there."

Lance clasped his shoulder. "What's your name?"

"Private Tobias Stewart."

"What does your mother call you?"

"Toby."

"Toby it is, then. Do you want to go home, Toby?"

The young soldier nodded, and Lance saw a spark in his eyes and slight color appearing in his slack jaw.

"I'm going home, Toby," Lance said. "If you'd like to come with me, would you please stand and wait for me over there?" Lance pointed to where he had begun speaking.

With excruciating effort, Toby climbed to his feet and ambled to the place Lance had indicated. He stood on unsteady feet, but Lance saw that he had set his jaw.

Lance sought the soldier who had witnessed the massacre with the hand grenades. Before Lance had even kneeled in front of him, the man struggled to his feet.

"I'm Private Ian Chapman, Sergeant, and I'm from Hoylake on The Wirral, on the west coast. I'm going with you." He made his way across to stand with Toby.

Lance turned to a third soldier who, without prompting, used his rifle to help himself to his feet. "Corporal Derek Horton. I'm ready." Using the weapon as a crutch, he limped over to Toby and Ian.

Watching him, Lance called after him, "Corporal Horton, what's wrong with your leg?"

Horton turned and, looking sheepish, he replied, "It's nothing, Sergeant. I sprained it jumping into a ditch." He grinned through mud-streaked lips. "That was better than munching on incoming artillery."

Lance managed a slight smile and turned to face those still seated. His attention fell on the medic sitting alone and apart, his eyes almost vacant. Lance moved over and sat down beside him.

For a moment he said nothing. The medic did not look up.

"We're going home," Lance said gently. "Would you like to come with us?"

The medic did not stir.

"What does your mother call you?"

No response.

Feeling his own despair rising, Lance looked around. Horton, Chapman, and Toby stood together awkwardly, Horton still leaning on his rifle.

Forcing his aching muscles, Lance stood up and looked about. The battle had long since moved past them and they were no longer within earshot of enemy soldiers. He glanced at those remaining seated and then back at the trio waiting for him.

Suddenly, he summoned all the energy he could muster and yelled as loud as his weakened condition allowed, "Medic! Medic!"

Startled, the soldier at his feet looked up, eyes wide, and whirled around, searching.

Lance reached down and grabbed his collar. "Over there," he called, pointing at Horton. "That man has a wounded leg. He needs you. Now!"

He yanked on the medic's collar again. "What's your name?"

The man looked confused.

"There's a soldier over there who needs first aid. Do your job. Help him."

The medic looked slowly over toward Horton and started rising to his feet. Lance reached down and helped him. "What's your name?" he asked again.

"T-Tickner," the medic stammered. "Private Kenneth Tickner."

"Well, Private Tickner, take care of Corporal Horton, and get ready to go with us."

Now standing on shaky legs, Tickner looked into Lance's face. Then he turned to Horton and stumbled toward him.

Lance shifted his attention to the remainder of the group. They regarded him with expressions ranging from gaping to startled. Some started the painful climb to their feet. Then, without another word, the entire group got up and clustered around Lance, awaiting his direction.

"Good," he said. "From here until we get home, we are each other's closest friends." He made his next statement to the medic. "Private Tickner, you've got a big job ahead of you. We have a long way to go, and you have to keep everyone healthy." He then addressed the full group. "Get acquainted. Learn each other's names and backgrounds. First order of business — we're going to find food and clean water." He looked around at the haggard faces staring back at him with traces of hope. "And then we're going home."

5

"Do any of you speak French?" Lance asked.

Horton raised his hand. "Enough to get along."

"Good. I'm fluent. Between the two of us, we should have it in hand. Now listen carefully. There are"—he did a quick head count—"nine of us, and we might pick up more. The French are not our enemies. They probably feel worse than we do. This is their country that's been savaged. We need to make contact with locals who would give us shelter and food. We'll have to take every precaution, so we don't walk ourselves into capture, but we need to take fast action while we still have a smidgeon of strength left."

"What's your plan?" Horton asked, looking around at the anxious faces.

Lance told them.

At dusk, the loosely formed squad of men crept into position around a solitary farmhouse. Dogs barked, but the soldiers paid them no heed.

A man walked out onto the porch and looked about, but seeing nothing, he called to his dogs to be quiet and re-entered the house.

The soldiers had watched from a distance all day. A few laborers had shown up for work and then left in late afternoon. A woman hung clothes in the backyard, but aside from them, they saw no one else.

The guns of the previous days had fallen quiet, the Germans had marched their prisoners of war away, and the area where Lance's group sought refuge had seen only light fighting. It was dormant. Lance was sure that more German soldiers would pour into the area, but at present the army was preoccupied with gaining control of Dunkirk, cleaning up the battlefield, removing their own dead and wounded, and moving the POWs. Those activities provided time for him to act.

They had moved in the dark to surveil this farmhouse, choosing it after much discussion regarding what each soldier had seen while fleeing from the battlefield. This particular farm was isolated, well away from the gunfire. It showed little damage from a passing army, the fields were lush green, and water was nearby. As they had moved into position, they came across a narrow irrigation canal, drank their fill, and washed off their filthy bodies and uniforms.

Just after dark, they moved in closer to the farm and set up a perimeter on the east side of the house. The dogs barked again, a maddening howl that immediately warned their owner that they were serious. Fortunately, they were tied up.

The farmer lumbered out onto the small covered porch, rifle in hand, silhouetted against the light above his head and that of an interior lamp spilling out behind him. Lance and Horton crouched below in shadows on either side of the entry.

"Psst," Horton called. "Here," he said in French, just above a whisper. "I'm English."

On the other side of the porch, Lance watched, ready to spring if the farmer raised the rifle toward Horton. At first, the man seemed confused, or at least startled, perhaps torn in deciding what he should do.

"I'm English," Horton called again. "I'm hungry. I need food."

Lance held his breath, but then the farmer edged over to Horton's side of the porch and looked into the darkness. Horton stood, his arms spread at shoulder height, his hands empty. "I need food," he said again, and then, sweeping his arm toward the dark fields, he added, "We need food."

The farmer stood silently. He was big and wore brown rough-cut trousers with suspenders over a soiled white shirt. He stared at Horton without speaking for a full minute. Then he lowered the barrel of his weapon and beckoned.

"Come, come," he said. "We have to get you out of sight. How many are you?"

"Nine."

The man stopped in his tracks and turned to Horton. "Nine?"

Horton nodded.

The farmer looked again into the darkness. Then he pointed to a barn barely visible against the night sky. "Take your men there. I will meet you." One of the dogs barked. "I'll get them to be quiet."

Fifteen minutes later, the farmer, Alain Coste, watched as nine hungry men devoured all the bread, cheese, and cold cuts he could muster on short notice. "My wife is making stew," he told Horton," but that will take a while longer." He also brought out fruit juice and water.

"You must remain quiet," he said, his large eyes worried over a bulbous nose and bushy mustache.

"We understand," Horton told him. "We won't stay long. Maybe a day to rest up and get some strength back. We're headed for Switzerland or Spain, to get home."

"And then you come back to fight *les Boches*?" Coste queried dubiously.

Horton chuckled. "Of course. If we don't, we'll be fighting them in London."

"Ah, *bien sur*," Coste remarked. "You rest. My friends will help, but please, don't do anything to endanger my family."

Lance had remained in the background, content to let Horton take the lead with the kindly farmer. Now he stepped forward and said in French, "You have my word, and thank you for your help." He extended his hand. Coste alternated his eyes between Lance and Horton. Then he took Lance's hand in both of his own and shook it.

———

At first light, the farmer entered the barn and beckoned to Lance and Horton.

"You can't stay here," he said, his eyes wide. "The Germans are coming this way, and they are searching every house and barn." He pulled a large cloth bag from over his shoulder. "There's bread, fruit, cheese, and meat in here." Looking around at the gaunt men gathering around him, he added, "It's not much for so many, but maybe it will hold you up a while." Handing the bag to Horton, he reached across and grabbed Lance with both hands. "Listen to me. There is a port south of Dunkirk where the British are still picking up soldiers. If you can get there, you might have a chance, but you must hurry."

Lance stared at him, not quite comprehending. "More evacuations? Are you sure?"

Coste heaved a sigh. "Nothing is certain anymore, but I spoke on the telephone with a friend in Veules-les-Roses." He reached into his pocket and pulled out a folded piece of paper, then handed it to Lance. "My truck is broken down, or I would try to take you myself, but I've sketched a map." He indicated the paper. "Go back to that irrigation ditch. Follow it south, where it joins a spring that feeds it. Follow it upstream to a wooded area. On the other side is another farm. The owner is a close friend. He'll take you, but you must do exactly as he says. He's prepared his truck with a false floor on the bed. It'll be tight, but you all should fit, and he'll cover it with hay and a load of vegetables. The Germans are setting up checkpoints, but he knows how to avoid them. He should have you there in a few hours."

For the first time in days, real hope flooded Lance's senses. Overcome with emotion, he leaned over and hugged Coste. "Thank you," he choked. "We can never repay you enough."

Nodding, Coste grasped Lance's upper arms. "You came to fight for France. That is enough. Now go. Hurry."

Lance told his men what Coste had said. As they prepared to leave, one by one, they expressed their gratitude. The farmer shook off the compliments, but then took Lance aside one more time.

"Don't trust all Frenchmen," he said gravely. "Some sympathize with the Nazis."

Startled, Lance could only stare. "How will we know—"

"Trust only the people our friends introduce to you. Avoid the rest. I wish I could instruct you better, but there's no time. You must leave, now."

6

Two days later, June 10
London, England

Lieutenant Paul Littlefield hurried up the front steps of the requisitioned Metropole Hotel situated between Northumberland Avenue and Whitehall Place near the center of town. The trappings of the once gracious old building made no impression on him, most of its fine ballrooms and halls having been divided and subdivided long ago into sterile bureaucratic cubicles, its rooms and suites converted to offices, and most of its gilded and marble detail covered over with plywood and plaster.

As he strode down the hall, he ignored the incessant ringing of telephones and the cacophonic clatter of typewriters mixed with the rhythmic staccato of telegraph machines and the low hum of many people engaged in discussion. Because he had been assigned to the Secret Intelligence Service, commonly known as SIS or simply MI-6, he had the clearances despite his junior rank to push his way past need-to-know checkpoints.

He marched directly to Room 424 housing MI-9, a new organization under the War Office's military intelligence section. This latest element had formed in anticipation of fighter and bomber pilots being downed during air raids, soldiers being separated from their units in battle, or a mix of both types of combatants being captured or simply needing to escape and evade the enemy after being stranded behind enemy lines.

It was organized and led by Major Norman Crockatt, a veteran of the Royal Scots Regiment who had fought during the Great War and left the army in 1927. With war again on the horizon, he had returned to service.

Paul burst through the door and headed straight for the major's desk. Crockatt, a tall, fit man with dark hair, a high forehead, and piercing eyes over a well-groomed mustache, saw him coming and cast a slightly deprecating glance his way.

"You again, Lieutenant? I suppose you have the same questions?"

"I do, Major."

"And my answer is the same as I gave you this morning, and twice yesterday and the day before. Have you checked the Red Cross again?"

"I have, and still no news."

Despite the lieutenant's neutral expression, Crockatt detected the worry behind it. "I sympathize with you, but our office is not set up to gather the information you seek. Nor do we use what we collect in the way you seem to think. We've only been in existence for nine months or so, and we've barely started operations. We still have no one in the field, and even if we did, their jobs would not be to locate particular POWs."

Paul nodded. "I know, and I appreciate your indulgence. I just thought that maybe information might flow through here that would identify where my brothers are."

"Are you sure they were both at Dunkirk?"

Paul shook his head. "All I know is that my youngest brother, Jeremy, was sent to France to build military infrastructure. His unit ended up getting thrown into the rearguard at Dunkirk. I only know about that from reports coming through MI-6."

Crockatt grimaced. "I like you, Lieutenant, and I feel I should give you some friendly advice." He furrowed his brow. "Don't misuse the information you're privy to. Doing so could cost you."

Paul heaved a sigh. "I know, sir, and thank you. I'm sure that Jeremy was there. I keep hoping he made it to the beach and got onto one of the boats."

"I've heard that some in the rearguard did manage that," the major remarked encouragingly, "but there was such confusion and such a mishmash of boats in the flotilla that units are still trying to sort out who made it home and who didn't. Don't give up hope. What about your other brother?"

"Lance. Not a clue where he is. I think he was with a company that was supposed to cross France from the south, but when our army was pushed back from the Maginot Line, other units rushed in. I think his was among them, but I'm not sure."

"With two sons there, your parents must be terribly worried. Didn't you tell me they live on Sark Island?"

"Yes, and communications between here and the island are very difficult."

"I imagine they are. I wish I had better news and advice for you. Unfortunately, I don't, except to say that the odds of ever having relevant news from this office is slim to none. That's not our mission, and I still have only a skeleton crew. We don't have the resources. Your best bet is the Red Cross."

"If the Red Cross gets word, it'll probably be months. I was hoping to learn something I could get to our parents to ease their minds."

The two stood in silence, and then Paul turned to leave. As he reached the door, Crockatt called to him. "Lieutenant, would you wait a moment? I'd like to speak with you on another matter."

Surprised, Paul retraced his steps to Crockatt's desk. "What can I do for you?"

"MI-9 is the new kid on the block, so to speak, and MI-6 is at the top of the heap, the old venerable intelligence organization that helped win the last war."

Paul allowed a smile. "You sound like you've been around Americans. I believe those are across-the-pond expressions."

"Right you are, and as I recall, your father is American, so they are not wasted on you."

"Almost correct, sir. My father is a naturalized British citizen."

"I see." Crockatt clasped his hands together and held them over pursed lips. "Mind you, I'm mulling out loud, and what I'm thinking would require difficult-to-get approvals..." He let his voice trail off while his mind was clearly still at work. "You know there will be tension between our two sections."

"How do you mean?"

"MI-6 is tasked with running foreign agents overseas, and MI-5 handles domestic counter-espionage. MI-9 is chartered to train our forces for survival, escape, and evasion, and to develop networks to assist them in the combat zones. I can see instances where we might use the same people and methods. In fact, I can see that MI-9-developed assets might independently gather intelligence that we would then deliver to MI-5 or MI-6; and by the way, part of our mission is to invent devices to help POWs escape and get that equipment to our men inside the prison camps."

Paul gaped. "That's a tall mission, sir. Why would there be tension?"

Crockatt chuckled. "There should be none. We're all in the same war. But let's face facts: war is led by generals and managed by bureaucrats. Anywhere you find generals and bureaucrats, you find turf wars. We'll have both types of people with MI-5 and MI-6. Of that I have no doubt."

"There could be another player in the mix soon," Paul said.

Crockatt's head jerked backward in surprise. "How so?"

Having second thoughts about divulging what he knew, Paul chose his words carefully. "Mind you, this is only rumor at this point. I've seen nothing official yet."

Eyes taking on a steely expression, Crockatt scrutinized Paul. "You've piqued my interest," he said, a note of command entering his voice. "Go on."

"Yes, sir. Rumor is that Churchill is contemplating a new element to train and assist partisans in the occupied countries in carrying out acts of sabotage directly. It's to be titled the Special Operations Executive."

"I'd heard," Crockatt replied brusquely. As he spoke, he rose from behind the desk, ambled to its front, and leaned against it with his legs spread out and arms folded across his chest.

Alarmed by his demeanor, Paul was at a loss for words, finally managing after an interlude of heavy silence to say, "I've heard rumors, but nothing definite." Another uneasy moment passed, and then Paul asked, "Did I cross a line, sir?"

Crockatt heaved a sigh and shook his head. "Maybe. Maybe not. I'm disturbed that the information about the SOE has reached you. At this point, it was to be known only at senior levels."

Paul felt blood rise in his cheeks. "Sir, I'm an intelligence officer. I work in the section that runs foreign agents. My job is to keep my eyes and ears open, my mouth shut, and to add two and two. I apologize if I've said too much."

Crockatt eyed him momentarily and then broke into a half-smile. "Of course, and you are a good intelligence officer." He circled back to the other side of his desk and sat down, then leaned back with his hands clasped behind his neck and inhaled deeply. "What have you heard about the German resistance?"

Keeping in mind Crockatt's earlier manner, Paul hesitated.

The major spoke to set him at ease. "I suppose you've heard of attempts by senior members inside the German military and regime to contact British officials in hopes of negotiating an armistice. Such a move would require toppling Hitler in a coup."

"I'd heard," Paul said cautiously, "but nothing beyond what you just said."

Crockatt remained quiet, scrutinizing him. "We're still building this organization," he said at last. "I'd like to transfer you here." He searched Paul's face for a reaction.

Paul remained impassive.

"You might get advance news of your brothers' whereabouts," Crockatt continued, "or, who knows? You might help one or both of them escape back to England."

7

Late at night, June 13
Dunkirk, France

Jeremy had left the Boulier house with a great sense of loss. Following the sketch map Ferrand had penciled, he first hid in the shed a few houses down the alley until darkness descended. Then he moved through ruined backstreets and rubble, clinging to shadows, headed to a particular address Ferrand had indicated.

Progress was slow, with only enough light from a sliver of moon and an occasional working streetlight that silhouetted the landmarks he was to follow: the shells of bombed-out homes, churches, and schools.

Alert to crossing paths with German patrols, he stumbled over wreckage and debris, counting streets and alleys and feeling for the waypoints Ferrand had specified, while the stench of damp, scorched ruins spoiled the air.

After two hours, he entered an undamaged barn and found a hay-covered entrance to an underground room indicated on the map. Then he descended into its darkness, closed the trapdoor, and waited on the cold floor. Unable to sleep, his mind wandered to the events that had brought him to Dunkirk, and Amélie.

Despite the gloom, he imagined her honey-colored eyes, her soft skin, her full lips, the auburn highlights of her dark hair, and her slight figure. He heard the music of her laughter and recalled the directness of her conversation and the courage of her actions.

Don't get carried away, he warned himself. *We're still at war.*

Deliberately, he recalled having left home, saying goodbye to his mother and father, his trip to northern England for training, and then the short hop to France. There, he had enjoyed his time in the British Army as an engineer, building roads and airfields in anticipation of the expected war, until the Germans had attacked rapidly and fiercely, driving the BEF and the French 10th Army south to Dunkirk. He had been among thousands of non-combatants thrown into the fray to provide rearguard protection for the evacuating troops, with only cursory training, under the command of the 51st (Highland) Infantry Division.

For ten days, he had heard reports of boats coming and going from the Dunkirk beaches, and wondered, with his comrades, when their turn would come. Then, an unexplainable lull in the battle had persisted for four days. Two nights later, field artillery shells whistled through the air, and then shocked the senses amid concussive explosions that threw dirt skyward with body parts and war machines fragmented into distorted pieces.

As he sat in the dark cellar below the barn, images he had witnessed entered his mind unbidden, and then trailed to his rescue by the bent little man and his daughter.

Then the cycle of recollections started again as he forced himself to cease thinking of Amélie by redirecting his thoughts to home, and when he had left, and how he had come to France, and then Dunkirk and when he was rescued by Ferrand and his beautiful daughter. He found the cycle uncontrollable and relentless.

Am I in love? He immediately derided himself. *I've known Amélie barely two days. What do I know of her?* He answered his own question. *Only that she's strong, brave, daring, beautiful, and I can't get her out of my mind.*

Undeniably, he had an overpowering emotional attachment to her, as he did to her father and younger sister. *As I should, from gratitude.* In the dark, he dropped his head. *I'll probably never see them again.* He put Amélie out of his mind once more and started the cycle of remembrance yet again.

Before dawn, sleepless, he heard soft tapping on the ceiling, and then the trapdoor lifted. The shadow of a bowed figure resembling Ferrand Boulier appeared and beckoned to him. Apprehensively, Jeremy climbed the stairs and looked into a face very similar to Ferrand's.

"I'm Claude," the man said in French, "Ferrand's brother. He says you speak our language." He handed Jeremy a paper sack. "Food."

Then he opened another sketch map. "We're here." He indicated a point on the map representing the barn. "You're going here." He moved his finger to another place on the paper. "I'm sorry to be so abrupt, but time is short."

Jeremy nodded without replying.

Claude nudged his arm and pulled another, larger bag from behind him. "Here are clothes for you."

Jeremy pulled back. "If the Germans catch me in those, they'll shoot me as a spy." With both hands, he mimicked the act of shooting a pistol.

Claude grasped Jeremy's shoulder and looked him in the eye. "They don't need a reason," he said slowly. "They'll shoot if they see this." He grabbed Jeremy's uniform sleeve to make his point and stuffed the bag of clothes in Jeremy's hands. "Your chances are better if you wear these, but you must be alert."

Jeremy took the clothes with lingering doubts.

"My son will be here in an hour," Claude said. "He has papers. You'll play a fool. You won't talk."

"A fool?" Jeremy echoed while examining the map.

Claude circled his finger around his temple, the universal gesture for "crazy."

"I'm crazy." Jeremy chuckled. "You're not the brightest man I've ever met either." Despite his good nature, his pique showed.

Claude shook his head patiently. "Nicolas will explain. He's my son."

Understanding dawned on Jeremy. "I see. I'll act crazy." He laughed. "I can do that."

Claude looked relieved. "Eat and get dressed. We'll burn your uniform. When Nicolas gets here, he'll take you to the next destination."

"The next?"

"He'll explain."

Jeremy nodded and gathered the items Claude had brought. Before descending back into the room below, he reached over and grasped Claude's hand. "*Merci.*"

An hour later, Jeremy heard another soft tap on the trapdoor. When it opened, a younger, bigger version of Claude appeared. As Jeremy ascended, the man reached a hand down to help him up the final stairs.

"I am Nicolas," he said. "We must hurry." He grinned. "You're the fool?"

"That's me," Jeremy confirmed.

"Let's go." Nicolas led him rapidly across the barn to a flatbed truck laden with hay. "You sit in the passenger seat. When we see Germans, don't speak. I'm your brother. You're sick in the head. Foam at the mouth. I'll carry your papers and show them if needed. I'll do all the talking. If someone talks to you, you grin, like this."

He plastered his face with a crazed grin and let his head flop around, seemingly out of control. "You understand?"

With that, they boarded the truck and drove out of the barn, down a driveway, and onto the street. When they had gone a short distance, Jeremy asked again, "Where are we going?"

"To my cousin's farm, southeast of Dunkirk. Tomorrow, you'll go to Paris."

Jeremy's reaction was immediate. "Paris? The Germans just took that city. They'll have soldiers everywhere."

"Not everywhere, my friend. Think. Here they have many soldiers controlling fewer people. There they have millions of people but not so many soldiers by comparison, and we French hate them. You'll go to some friends. They'll help get you through France and Spain, to Gibraltar. Then you'll get on a boat to England."

Jeremy regarded him in astonishment. "You'll help me that much? Why?"

"We're at war together," Nicolas replied. "Tell them in England how we helped."

They approached a German checkpoint. Without hesitation, Nicolas pulled to a stop in the line of vehicles waiting to have documents inspected. Taking on the attitude of a bored driver, Nicolas put a reed of straw between his teeth and leaned against the corner of the truck's cab.

"Remember, you're a fool," he said. "I'll show your papers. When the guards talk to you, smile big, let your head go like this." He wobbled his own again.

"I get it," Jeremy said. He let his jaw go slack, his eyes vacant, and his head loll about loosely. Despite his demeanor, his heart beat wildly as their truck approached the checkpoint. The vehicle ahead of them slid into place next to the German sentries who inspected thoroughly, taking time to read through identification documents, scrutinize passengers, and go through the trunk.

Then it was Nicolas and Jeremy's turn. Nicolas straightened in his seat while retaining his bored attitude. When he pulled up by the soldiers, Jeremy let his head roll in the direction of the guard on his side of the vehicle. He opened his mouth in an absurd grin and let loose an unearthly guffaw.

On the other side of the cab, Nicolas yelled something unintelligible, then reached across and slapped Jeremy's face while apologizing to the soldier. Then he reached into his shirt pocket, pulled out papers for himself and Jeremy, and handed them to the respective sentries. Meanwhile, Jeremy closed his mouth, letting saliva form in bubbles on his lips and drip down his shirt. He lolled his head and grinned again.

Disgusted, the sentry on his side of the truck backed away. Moments later, the other one waved them through.

"We did it." Nicolas laughed as they drove away. "Now we'll go on back-roads that I know, and they don't."

Jeremy sank back in his seat, and for the first time in many days, he relaxed completely. "Where did my papers come from?"

Wide grain fields rolled by, green and swaying in a gentle breeze. The sun had risen against a blue sky, and now that Jeremy felt safe to observe, he watched birds flitting between trees and cows grazing in their pastures with the occasional horse. For the first time in his recent past, his immediate world seemed at peace, the war far away.

"My Uncle Ferrand is an artist. He made your papers."

Jeremy's head jerked around. Momentarily, he stared at Nicolas in amazement. "He forged my documents?"

"Yes." Nicolas tapped his head. "He's very smart. He knows how to do things. But..." He shrugged. "The papers were not hard. They were my brother's. He altered them." As he spoke, his face became sad. "My brother was the same age as you. He suffered a brain injury in an automobile accident. He died two years later."

Horrified, Jeremy said, "I am so sorry."

Nicolas clapped Jeremy's shoulder. "Eh, not your fault. That's life. Today, you're my brother, and tomorrow. Forever." He laughed.

As they rumbled on in silence, Jeremy's mind again returned to home, and then the battle and the killing fields, and then came around inevitably to Amélie.

"Your cousins also helped me. I can never repay the kindness of your family."

"You owe us nothing," Nicolas replied. "But you can help. You tell the people in England what we did. Not just my family. Many people are helping to get you home. You spread the word that we are free French. We'll fight. We'll resist." His voice had taken on a grim note, and he glanced at Jeremy. "You tell them."

A short silence ensued, and then Nicolas grinned. "You like my cousin, Amélie?"

Startled, his cheeks flushing crimson, Jeremy turned to Nicolas. "Of course," he stuttered, "she saved my life. Chantal too, and your Uncle Ferrand."

Nicolas beamed wider and shook a crooked finger at Jeremy. "Yes, but you *like* Amélie. Why not? She's good-looking." Glancing at the road, he made a corrective maneuver. "You think she's pretty?" Then he leaned toward Jeremy and whispered conspiratorially, "I can tell you; she likes you."

Jeremy's heart skipped a beat, his throat caught, and he felt suddenly, involuntarily exultant, not missing the irony under the present conditions.

"You *like* her," Nicolas went on. "I see it. Your face is red like a tomato." He laughed uproariously.

In spite of himself, Jeremy laughed along. "Did she say that?"

"She didn't say anything. But I'm her closest cousin. We're the same age. I know her. She changed when she met you. She grew up."

"We're in a war," Jeremy said soberly. "She saw awful things. She had not met or even seen me up close when she risked her life, and that was not even three days ago."

"You're right. She'll help anyone. But"—Nicolas wagged a finger in the air— "she worries about you. I saw her last night. She's *very* worried about you. I could see it."

Feeling overwhelmed with unfamiliar emotion, Jeremy locked his eyes on the road and remained silent. "I'll probably never see her again," he muttered.

"Why?" Nicolas bellowed with genuine concern. "We'll win this war. You know where we live. You'll be back." He clapped Jeremy's shoulder again. "We're brothers. When you come again, you'll see that you and Amélie like each other." He set his jaw firmly. "I see it." Then he looked across at Jeremy. "Write her a note. I'll give it to her."

Jeremy exhaled. "I wouldn't know what to say."

Nicolas let loose a peal of laughter. "Don't worry. I'll write it for you. I'll be your Cyrano de Bergerac."

8

Two days later, June 15
A road northwest of Paris

Jeremy trundled along in the small farm truck on the outskirts of Paris with Nicolas at the wheel, trying to blend in while pressing ahead of a mass of humanity that clogged the roads, some in horse-drawn wagons, cars, and trucks of every description, and many on bicycles, all fleeing the German juggernaut. The two men had escaped Dunkirk by heading southeast for roughly forty miles to Hazebrouck, then turning south on tiny backroads through Béthune and Arras. At Roissy-en-France, a town north of Paris, Nicolas changed course again, and instead of going into Paris, they headed west to skirt the city.

They had expected to encounter refugees streaming to sanctuary, but the vastness of the fleeing throng boggled their minds. Now, the truck labored under a load of people that had climbed on unbidden, displacing the bales of hay as more and more men, women, and children clambered aboard to continue their desperate journeys.

Nicolas had shed his jovial countenance, and he glanced worriedly at the fuel and temperature gauges and then through his rearview mirror at the traumatized passengers on the truck bed. They left behind a torn countryside. Some villages had been flattened to rubble while others were untouched but abandoned except for the roiling, unending throngs of a terrified populace in search of safer ground.

Fathers pushed makeshift carts with elderly parents clutching precious mementos, mothers struggled with baby carriages laden with necessary articles heaped over crying youngsters, and older siblings struggled to keep up. Already, as whole families and communities pushed south, discarded items no longer deemed crucial to survival lined the roads along with abandoned vehicles that had encountered mechanical difficulties or simply run out of gas. Among the waste were bodies of unfortunates too old, weak, or young to continue who had slumped where they last stood or had been trampled.

The smell of the dead mixed with that of unwashed bodies and their waste, filling the air, as did the cries of anguished mothers and toddlers separated from each other by the press of the struggling crowds. As Jeremy and Nicolas slowly progressed, they passed farms with animals standing in barnyards, some waiting to be fed or milked, not perceiving that their owners had abandoned them. Some poor beasts sprawled on the ground with bloated bellies, their carcasses growing ripe under the spring sun, and already, packs of dogs ran loose, devouring food where they could find it, including corpses of any type that they encountered.

Although at first the two companions were stoic, the depraved scenes bore down on them. Nicolas fought to maintain his composure, but Jeremy saw that often his mouth quivered, and he wiped tears from the corners of his eyes. He viewed the horrors numbly, willing his mind to see past the most horrendous scenes, unable to fathom the depths of depravity that could lead to such conditions.

"Six million," Nicolas muttered. "I talked to my cousin last night. He told me that six million people fled Paris ahead of the German invasion, with everyone going this same direction." The truck barely moved, inching along within the exhausted masses tramping alongside them.

Edging through the ruined countryside northwest of Paris, they saw a dark cloud hanging over the "City of Lights." Nicolas nudged Jeremy and pointed at clumps of dead birds alongside the roads. "My cousin said that when the Germans entered the city, the smoke and dust were so thick that it suffocated the birds. The people of Paris burned garbage and fuel to create dark clouds so that German bombers could not see and destroy our national treasures." He stopped and glanced in the direction of the city center. "If not for the smoke, we'd be able to see the Eiffel Tower from here." He surveyed the teeming thousands snaking over the landscape. "We're fortunate. Most of the people have already gone before us. The air has thinned out."

Jeremy reached over and grasped his shoulder. "Go home," he said. "You have your own family to see to. I'll make my way to Marseille. In this crowd, I'll pass for just another refugee. The Nazis will need weeks to put up all the checkpoints for population control, France still has an army in the south, and your navy is intact."

"The French army," Nicolas grunted with disgust. "It was useless. Totally useless. The government escaped to Tours without resisting at all. And why hasn't our navy been active against the Germans? It's been sitting in port somewhere in North Africa." He stepped on the brake lightly, bringing the truck to a halt as an old man bumped into it with vacant eyes, oblivious to what he had just done.

As Nicolas waited for a few inches of road to clear ahead of him, he turned to Jeremy. "If we dare hope to get our country back, the French people will have to do it." His voice took on an urgency edged with hopelessness. "My cousin and I talked late into the night. We agreed that my job now is to get you home with the message that the French people will not give up our country without a fight."

"Is that why you're taking me farther south instead of into Paris? I thought that someone else would take me to the next contact, and so on until I got to Marseille, and then to Gibraltar to get on a boat."

Nicolas gestured toward the crowds with his chin. "We need help, and soon. The message you carry is more urgent. Our people are organizing to sabotage, get intelligence, and help soldiers like you escape France so they can rejoin the fight, but we need contact in England." He sighed and leaned his head against the back wall of the truck's cab.

Jeremy blew out the air in his cheeks. "What's the plan now, for me?"

Nicolas closed his eyes momentarily. "We're going to put you in greater danger, my brother." He opened his eyes and turned to look directly at

Jeremy. "You can say no, and I'll take you on to Marseille. Otherwise"—he inhaled sharply—"we have to get in front of this crowd and head west before the Germans get much farther south along the coast. There are ports to the west where boats are still able to leave. Not many are trying because the German U-boats patrol there, but if you can make it across the Channel, that will be the quickest way of getting you home to England."

Jeremy sat quietly, contemplating the implicit request. Having grown up on a tiny island in the often stormy and ferocious waters separating France and England, he knew intimately how furious Mother Nature could be there. With the added danger of German U-boats and fighter planes on the prowl, he understood in an instant the alternatives being offered, the equivalent of choosing to play between the paws of a hungry lion or slapping its mouth and hoping either way to emerge alive.

The sun had sunk to their right, casting its rays inside the cab. Nicolas raised his palm to block them so he could study Jeremy's face.

"You can't be pinning your hopes on me," Jeremy said after several moments.

"I'm a hopeless romantic, not a fool," Nicolas said. He shook his head sadly. "Amélie will hate me forever if she learns of the choice I offered you, but no, you are not the only one. Tens of thousands of your soldiers were captured after Dunkirk and are being force-marched to Germany. But a lot got away. Local groups are trying to find and help them. We hope one or two of you might make it to England soon."

Just then, the old truck sputtered and shook. Nicolas looked down again at the gas gauge. Seeing that it registered past empty, he let the vehicle coast its remaining few inches to a halt. "This is as far as we ride," he said with a wry grin. "Whichever way we go, we're on foot, unless we get lucky."

He reached down and grasped a cloth bag containing bread and cheese. Slinging it over his shoulder, he climbed down from the driver's seat onto the street. Without a backward glance, he started walking.

As Jeremy clambered from the truck, he noticed that the gaunt men and women still clinging to its bed barely took note for having known so many starts and stops. Now, if they noticed Jeremy and Nicolas' departure at all, they did so with blank stares.

With Nicolas leading the way, they continued their trek, two more exhausted men trudging through the ruined countryside. After many hours, they came to a major road intersection outside of Le Mans. Nicolas halted.

Turning to Jeremy, he pointed in the direction of a road headed south. "That way leads to Marseille," he said. "It's about a six-day walk, but we could probably get rides, and we have friends who will help us." Then he indicated the road leading west. "That goes to the coast, to Saint-Nazaire. It's about two days away on foot, and from this point on, I wouldn't trust anybody." He grasped both of Jeremy's shoulders and looked directly into his eyes.

Jeremy read the unspoken question. The ground below his feet seemed to buckle as if from a turbulent wave. Strength had momentarily deserted his legs. Blood drained from his face. For an instant, the cycle of memory took unbidden possession once again. Home. Family. War. Explosions. Small arms fire. Flight. Suffocation. Gritty sand. Burned-out war machines. Death.

Then, rejuvenating rain. A bent figure. A warm place. Soft hands. Blurry faces. The smile of an angel. Amélie.

Without a word, Jeremy shrugged off Nicolas' grasp and trudged toward the setting sun.

9

One day earlier, June 14
Dunkirk, France

Amélie glared out the window at four German soldiers patrolling past the Bouliers' garden gate. Since the first day of their appearance throngs of them had gathered on the beach with the task of searching and removing war materiel abandoned by the British and French armies. She glanced around for Chantal, and then remembered that her sister had gone to see if the bakery was open and selling bread.

"Everything will resume as normal," *Hauptman* Bergmann had announced at a public gathering the day before. "The schools, markets, churches, and all other public functions will reopen, and life will continue as it was before our arrival."

The irony of giving such a statement amid the city's bombed-out relics seemed not to bother him. With a sweeping hand, he had indicated his soldiers. "My men are here to protect you. Respect us and we will respect you." As he made his last statement, his ingratiating smile disappeared, and he cast a glassy eye at his audience. His implied meaning was clear and sent a shiver through the crowd listening with grim-faced stoicism.

Amélie had attended the gathering with her father and Chantal. They did not stop to speak to anyone on their way home.

As they hurried along, Ferrand growled to his daughters, "Nothing will open soon. There are no schools, shops, or churches to open." He kept them moving at a fast pace. "Pay attention to this advice I give you. Avoid eye contact with German soldiers. Try to stay away from them, but if you cannot and you meet them in the street, greet them civilly. Never stop to talk. If they call to you, move on as if you didn't hear them. Never trust them. They think of themselves as belonging to a superior race, but they are nothing more than conquering soldiers far from home, wives, and girl-friends, and some have more evil intent than others. Do you understand?"

Amélie had glanced at Chantal to see if her young sister grasped the import of what her father had said. Chantal's wide eyes and wrinkled brow gave the sense that she fully understood.

Now, seeing the time on her wristwatch, Amélie moved to the kitchen to prepare lunch. Chantal should be home soon. Then, standing in front of the window overlooking the garden, she noticed that the door on the shed was slightly ajar, unusual because her father was fastidious about keeping his tools put away and the door closed against the coastal weather. "The salt in the air will eat them up," he reminded them frequently.

Ferrand would be at his shop now or visiting friends. He was not home.

As Amélie took note of the door, she thought she saw the shed shake slightly. Thinking she might have imagined it, she stared at the small wooden building.

It shook again.

Amélie stepped out onto the back porch, shielding her eyes against the noontime sun. The shed shook again, and then she heard grunting and a fearful wail. *Chantal!*

Amélie flew off the small stoop, ran to the shed, and threw the door open. She was greeted by the sight of the prone, bare buttocks of a German soldier with his uniform trousers pulled down below his knees. Under him, he had one hand clasped over Chantal's mouth while he maneuvered his body on top of hers.

Chantal's terrified eyes beseeched her sister.

With sunlight suddenly illuminating the interior, the man turned his head, and Amélie recognized Kallsen, Bergmann's orderly. He squinted over a churlish grin.

On reflex, Amélie grabbed the shovel still hanging on the false wall and swung the flat of it down on Kallsen's face. He groaned in pain.

Stepping back to allow a greater swing, Amélie brought the shovel down again, this time hitting the edge across Kallsen's throat at his Adam's apple. He coughed, let go of Chantal, and tried to twist and sit up.

The flat of the shovel struck again, this time high on his forehead. He fell back, writhing on top of Chantal, his yelps of pain loud as he fell onto his back.

"Shut up," Amélie shouted in French, and she stomped on his mouth several times before stepping back and bringing the flat of the shovel down hard against Kallsen's nose.

He lay still, but Amélie kept hitting until his body convulsed. She stepped back, watching Kallsen shake out his last moments of life. Then, the full import of what she had done intruded on her conscious mind.

Chantal, still pinned under Kallsen's legs, managed to push off his upper body. Her wails had turned into sobs as she continued to push against the corpse.

Amélie dropped the shovel and helped her struggle from under the body to a sitting position. Sobbing, Chantal pulled her underwear up from around her knees and covered her legs with her skirt. Then she flung her arms around her sister.

Amélie let her cry.

After a few minutes, Amélie said with desperate urgency, "Listen. They'll be looking for him."

Chantal stared at Amélie without comprehension.

Amélie shook her. "Listen to me. We are going into the house. We must act normal at all times."

Chantal shook her head in protest, fresh tears running down her face.

"Chantal, you have to be strong. There's no time for self-pity, or we will be executed: you, me, father, our entire family."

By degrees, Chantal's face hardened, and she nodded.

"We are going into the house now," Amélie said. "You will clean up, eat—"

Chantal wiped her eyes. "I'm not hungry."

"But you must wash yourself. And when you leave the house, you can no longer go the back way through the alley. From now on you'll go out the front and take the long way. If you see your friends, you'll act as if nothing happened. If you see soldiers, you'll act just as Papa told us. Do you understand?"

Chantal turned to look hard at Kallsen's battered face. Then she wiped her cheeks and hugged Amélie. "I'll be all right."

Later that afternoon, Ferrand listened grimly as Amélie recounted the details of what had happened inside the garden shed. "Did Chantal say how he got her in there?"

"She said that she came home from the bakery and saw some of her friends. She spoke with them a while, and then turned off to come down the alley like she always does, and the others kept going to their houses. She had seen soldiers including Kallsen a little before the alley, and she behaved just as you instructed. She doesn't know how Kallsen got to be behind her. She had already moved a ways into the alley when he called to her. She pretended not to hear and kept walking, but he kept calling and getting closer. She ran to the garden, but he caught up with her at the gate and forced her into the shed."

Anger and despair tinged Ferrand's countenance. "They will come here, to our house," he said. "The soldiers with him will remember that he turned down our alley and that Chantal was ahead of him. Did you clean up the shed?"

Amélie nodded. "The body is still in there, but I shoveled dirt in to soak up the blood and tilled it into the flower garden. Then I spread some dry surface dust on the floor. We'll have to move the body and do some final cleanup, but it will look like a normal garden shed."

"At dusk," Ferrand said. "They will miss him by this evening, and the days are long. We can expect a knock on the door tonight."

10

The knock came just past midnight. When Amélie peered through the window, Bergmann stood at the door, a new orderly at his side and two men behind them.

"I'm sorry to bother you at this hour," he said when Amélie let him inside. "We are searching for a missing soldier. You might remember him. He was my orderly when I came by the other day."

"Yes, I saw him, in the alley this afternoon."

Chantal appeared in the hall by the kitchen, rubbing her eyes sleepily. "What's all the noise?" she murmured. Then she saw the soldiers and Bergmann and drew back.

"Chantal," Amélie said, "these men are looking for *Hauptman* Bergmann's orderly. Did he say where he was going when we saw him today?"

Chantal shook her head and yawned. She hoped her pretense looked real. Her heart beat unmercifully. "I had just arrived home from the bakery. You were gardening. He chatted with us a moment and went on down the alley. He didn't really say anything besides hello, telling us what a nice garden we have, and goodbye."

Ferrand appeared in the hall dripping wet and pulling a towel around his waist. Bergmann looked askance at him, slightly amused. "Isn't this a little late for a bath?"

"I'm having a hard time sleeping," Ferrand replied stonily. "It's been that way since your forces advanced on Dunkirk. How would you react if an invading army destroyed your town and took your country?"

Bergmann regarded him silently. He turned slowly to study the details of the room, taking in the family pictures on the piano. Then he reverted his attention to Amélie and Chantal. "You saw Kallsen here?"

The sisters nodded in unison. "He called to us just as I opened the gate," Chantal said. "We returned his greeting, and then he continued down the alley. We didn't see where he was going."

Bergmann crossed his arms and cupped his hand over his chin, his brow furrowing in thought. "All right," he said after a few moments. "That is consistent with other reports we've had. Did any of your neighbors mention seeing him?"

The Bouliers glanced among themselves. "We didn't think to ask," Amélie said, shrugging.

Bergmann took a breath and exhaled rapidly. "No matter. We'll continue down the street with our inquiries. My soldiers will need to check inside your shed."

"But of course," Ferrand said. He gestured with a sweeping palm toward the kitchen. "Be my guest."

The new orderly flicked his hand, and the two accompanying soldiers bolted for the back door. They returned momentarily and shook their heads.

"I'm very sorry to have disturbed you," Bergmann said, inclining his head toward each of the Bouliers in succession. "Please let me know if you hear of anything." With that, he departed with his entourage.

"It's not over," Ferrand told his daughters after Bergmann had left. "They will determine that you were the last ones to see Kallsen, and they will keep after us until someone confesses." He walked over to the piano, scanned the family photos absently, and dropped his forehead onto his curled fists. "I'll be taken in for interrogation soon."

Chantal ran to him, alarmed. "But you didn't do anything," she blurted.

Ferrand wrapped an arm around her and drew her to his chest. "You mean aside from disposing of the body? It wouldn't matter. They'll come for me." He drew back and alternated his look between them. "It was good you had the bath ready. I was filthy. You did good work on cleaning up the sand and dirt through the hall and kitchen."

"Where did you put him?" Amélie asked.

Ferrand sighed. "When they find him along the beach in several days, he'll look like the sea pounded him on some rocks. That might buy us enough time for what we have to do." He regarded his daughters with doleful eyes.

Seeing his expression, Chantal gasped. "We have to leave, don't we?" she cried. "And it's my fault." She leaned into her father with tears running down her cheeks. "I am so sorry."

"There, there, little one," he consoled her. "You did nothing wrong. Unfortunately, evil lives among us. We'll have to fight it every way we can." He stroked the side of her face. "And in the end, we will win."

"Oh, Papa," Chantal said, burying her head in his chest. "You and Amélie are brave." She wiped her eyes. "I'm not."

"*Ma cherie*," Amélie said, embracing them both. "You'll be the bravest among us. You'll see."

Ferrand gazed at his daughters as if from far away. After a moment, he said, "Let's go. Get dressed. Take only the clothes on your back and something to stay warm. We leave in five minutes."

The girls stared at him, and Chantal looked anguished as tears welled in her eyes. "Now?" She glanced around the warm room, at its furnishings and family photos, the fireplace with smoldering coals. "This is our home."

"It's a house that is no longer safe, no longer a home," Ferrand muttered. He leaned over to comfort Chantal. "It's dangerous for us now. We must go."

Amélie regarded her father as if seeing someone she had never known. His eyes pierced, and he set his jaw. His back even seemed straighter, his shoulders squared. When he spoke, his voice was laced with command, mixed with his usual kindness.

"We have to go," he said firmly. "Get ready."

Amélie stood and tugged her sister to her feet. "Let's go," she said, leading her by the hand into the back of the house. "Papa knows what he is doing."

11

An hour later, Bergmann turned on his heel and retraced his steps in front of the row of houses that included the Boulier home. Despite the time of year, the air was cool, almost frigid, owing to the overcast skies, heavy rain, and winds blowing in from the sea. With his orderly and the other two soldiers, he had reached the last house along the row, awakened its residents, and completed his initial inquiry.

Among the residents past the Boulier house, none admitted to seeing Kallsen. *I must speak with Ferrand and his daughters again.* He glanced at his watch in irritation and then smirked as he thought of Amélie. *I like that one. She's the perfect age.*

The houses on the street were dark, so he was surprised when he neared the Bouliers' dwelling and a dim light still shone. Remembering his amusement at Ferrand's wet body wrapped only in a towel, he thought maybe the old man might still be trying to relax himself. *He needs to keep his hostility to our army in check.* Then Bergmann sighed. *He'll learn. They'll all learn.*

For half a second, he thought of delaying his second round with Ferrand for the following day, but then thought better of it. *Since he's up, I might as well do it now.*

He recalled with relish the French *mademoiselle* he had courted into his rooms in the sumptuous house he had commandeered on entry into Dunkirk. *This way, I'll have more time with her.*

He opened the garden gate, strode to the front door, and knocked loudly. When he heard no answer, he tried the knob and found it locked. He stepped in front of the window and peered inside. The peaceful scene gave no hint of anything amiss, yet a sense of foreboding formed in the pit of Bergmann's stomach.

He moved aside and ordered the soldiers to break in the entry. One of them stepped forward and slammed his boot against the door. It shook but did not give. The soldier repeated his action until the door creaked and light filtered through a crack. Then, both soldiers put their shoulders to it and crashed it open.

Needing no instruction, they proceeded into the recesses of the house while Bergmann stood in the middle of the living room and looked around. Coals in the fireplace still gave off a bit of warmth. Light emanated from a fixture in the hallway. His new orderly headed toward the kitchen. "I'll check out the garden shed," he said.

Minutes later, all three soldiers had returned to the living room. "Their clothes are here, but the beds have not been slept in," one reported.

"Nothing in the shed," the orderly interjected. "We should look again in daylight."

Bergmann walked over to the piano and studied it. "There was a family photo here," he mused to no one. "I noticed it the other day when we stopped by." He cocked his head in thought. "It was there earlier this evening."

He stood abruptly and issued swift, terse orders. "Get a platoon out here and secure this neighborhood. No one leaves. Detain anyone coming in. Get all these fine French citizens up." His voice dripped sarcasm. "I want them on the street in their bedclothes in fifteen minutes."

Stone-faced, Bergmann paced along the line of frightened French residents standing in their pajamas, braced against the wind and damp night air. He stopped in front of a middle-aged man whose wife cowered against her

husband while trying to constrain her weeping. This neighbor lived in the
home preceding the Boulier house.

"You must know something about Ferrand Boulier," he barked in
French. "You lived next to him for decades."

The neighbor shook his head rapidly, his eyes revealing his terror.
"After his wife died, he kept to himself. He wasn't the same. We all thought
he would soon follow her."

"But he didn't, and now he's disappeared with both daughters, and I'm
left with a missing soldier." He pushed his face close to the man's. "Tell me
again what you saw."

"I only saw the soldier who was with you the day that you stopped by
our house."

"*Unteroffiziere* Kallsen?"

"If you say so. I didn't hear his name. I saw him hurrying down the alley
around noon. He wasn't really running, but he walked very fast, almost at a
trot."

"And you didn't see anyone else?"

"No. I had just come into our kitchen. Your soldier's motion caught my
eye, but he was then in the alley at the corner of our garden shed and
continued behind it. I barely had time to recognize him."

"You weren't curious about why he was in such a hurry?"

"I know better than to take interest in the movements of your soldiers."

"If *Monsieur* Ferrand wanted to hide with his daughters, where would
he go?"

The man shrugged nervously. "The city is barely recognizable. I don't
know what still stands. I have no idea at this moment how to find any
particular place in Dunkirk."

Bergmann stared at him. "Does he have family in the area?"

The man closed his eyes as if reluctant to speak.

"I asked if he has family here." Bergmann enunciated each word.

The woman looked into her husband's face, her own a mask of fear.
"Tell him," she cried. "Tell him."

Bergmann grabbed her by the shoulder and jerked her forward. "Tell
me what?"

"Leave her alone," the husband cried hoarsely, and tried to step between his wife and the captain.

A soldier standing next to Bergmann rammed the man in the stomach with the barrel of his rifle. The hapless man doubled over, and the soldier brought the butt of the weapon down hard on his back. He lay in the dirt, moaning and gasping for air.

"Ferrand has a brother," the wife sobbed. "He lives across town on a dairy farm."

"What is his name?"

"Claude Boulier." Her voice broke, and she tried to stoop to comfort her husband. Bergmann shoved her away with his boot. She too fell into the dirt.

He turned to a sergeant standing close by. "Radio headquarters. Tell them to find that farm and send out a platoon-sized security detail immediately." He gestured at the terrified couple lying in the road. "Bring them along, as well as every man here. The women may return to their houses, but keep security around this neighborhood. No one leaves. Detain anyone coming in."

"And you, sir?" the sergeant asked.

"Bring the neighbors from the other side of Ferrand's house. I want to interrogate them again. Here." He glared at the couple still lying on the ground. "Then these two will guide me to the dairy farm. I'll meet the security detail there."

12

Chantal stumbled along in the dark, following her father and sister, barely aware of her surroundings. She clutched a single picture frame to her chest, one that she had grabbed from the living room before staggering through the kitchen and out the back door. The frame contained the black-and-white photo that Bergmann had viewed. It had been the last family one taken of the Bouliers that included her mother. Now, she held onto the memory.

That had been four years ago when Chantal was ten, only weeks before *Madame* Boulier had contracted pneumonia and wasted away. Amélie had become Chantal's surrogate mother, watching out for her schooling, monitoring which friends she chose, making sure she was fed and clothed.

His wife's death had crushed Ferrand. For months, he had gone through the motions of doing his work, but without enthusiasm. He had spent hours on a chair in the living room staring out to sea, and often, he had to be coaxed to eat.

Amélie had shouldered the care for both her father and sister while still attending school. Now, with one hand, she led Chantal through the rubble of Dunkirk's streets and alleys while keeping a firm grip on her father's arm with the other. After what seemed like hours, they approached the back of a brick building that was mainly intact despite the destruction to its immediate neighbors.

"What is this place?" she whispered as they entered through a rear door.

"It was a restaurant," Ferrand replied. He smacked his lips in dismay. "No more. The front and the kitchen were destroyed. But it has an underground wine cellar."

He felt along the back wall until he reached a corner. Then, stooping, he knocked with a distinct rhythm against a wooden section in the floor.

Moments later, the panel lifted, a dim light shined out, and a dark figure appeared. Without a word, he motioned for the trio to follow, and then held the trapdoor up while they descended ahead of him. Then, he lowered it in place and followed.

At the bottom of the stairs, the two girls huddled together, Chantal still in shock, Amélie observing her surroundings. She could not see the full extent of the cellar, its walls leading into darkness, but she sensed that it was large and people moved quietly about. The wine shelves had been pushed against the walls for more room, the bottles still resting in them. Overhead lights remained dim, whether for security reasons or because that was the way they had always been, she could not tell.

One element immediately surprised her: the people gathered in this place deferred to her father. He called to a woman and asked her to take the girls to another room where they could rest. Before they left him, a man approached and spoke to Ferrand in hushed tones. Other men and women came to inform or ask for guidance. As Amélie tugged Chantal to their resting place, she could only stare back at her father with wonder.

Two hours later, Amélie awoke with a start as a hand pulled at her shoulder and called her name. She recognized her father's voice.

"Time to go," he said gently. "Wake up Chantal. You cannot stay here. I've arranged travel to the south of France, but we must hurry."

Looking into his face through bleary eyes, Amélie perceived his usual kindness, but also an ethereal strength. "Where are we going?"

"I'll explain all of that, but hurry. Get your sister up. I'll wait at the front."

He disappeared into the shadows.

When Amélie and Chantal reached the entrance, they saw Ferrand conversing with their Uncle Claude. Both men fell silent as the girls arrived. A third man stood on the stairs ready to lift the panel.

"Listen to me." Ferrand's urgency was intense. "Claude will take you to our cousin's farm. You won't stay there long, and then he'll take you farther southeast. We're trying to keep you out of the way of the German advance and the crowds of refugees."

As he spoke, Amélie stared at him. "And you, you're coming with us."

Ferrand shook his head and shoved a set of papers their way. "These are your new identity documents. We prepared them while you slept. Study them carefully. You must become Monique Perrier, and your sister is Blanche."

"And you?" Amélie asked stonily.

Ferrand inhaled deeply. "I won't be coming, my dear daughters." Tears filled his eyes. "We are in a war, and my place to fight is here."

Next to them, Chantal let out an anguished cry. "No, Papa. You cannot stay." She lunged toward him and threw her arms around his neck, her body trembling. "I won't go. If you don't come, I won't go."

Ferrand held her and guided her toward the stairs. "You must. I have a job to do, and I'll do it better if I know you're safe."

Amélie, who had moved with them, fixed her gaze on him. "What job?" Then she stopped and looked around the cavernous cellar. Tables from the restaurant had been brought down with chairs and set around the room as worktables, and furtive figures hovered over them, deep in conversation. "What are those people doing?"

"Today was traumatic for both of you," Ferrand said without replying. "Chantal was nearly raped and—" He looked deep into Amélie's eyes. "You protected your sister, and a man is dead, a German soldier."

"And now we lose our father," Amélie cried, wiping away tears.

Ferrand closed his eyes, breathed in deeply, and exhaled. "You'll never lose me, but you can't stay here. The Germans will come looking for you. I need for you and your sister to take care of each other in a safe place. I can work better then."

Amélie looked around again, gestured at the people moving about, and locked her eyes back on her father's face. "You're building an organization. To fight back."

For a moment, Ferrand only returned her gaze. Then he nodded grimly. "No one is coming to save us. We have to save ourselves. You have to go."

13

Two days later, June 17

Hauptman Bergmann strode into the morgue, his eyes fixed in anger. A nervous French policeman hurried to keep up. German soldiers stood guard inside and outside each entrance while a stooped, white-haired man wearing thick spectacles waited at a set of swinging doors. Bergmann swept past him without so much as a greeting and walked directly to a single gurney in the room. On it, a covered corpse lay flat.

Bergmann pulled back the sheet and stared. Then, he dropped the cover and addressed the white-haired man who now hovered over the body on the opposite side of the gurney.

"Are you the medical examiner?"

The man nodded.

"How long has he been dead?"

"At least two days. Maybe three. He was in the water for most if not all of that time, so it's hard to be sure."

Bergmann turned to the policeman. "Where was he found?"

"On the north end of the beach."

"Were there any rocks there?" As Bergmann asked the question, he spun around to a German sergeant. "Send out a patrol to search the area." Then he focused his attention again on the French policeman. "Well?"

"There are no rocks to speak of, sir. Not in that area."

Bergmann stared down at the dead man's mangled head. "Then how," he asked without looking up, "did he get this flat bruise on his forehead and this long one on his neck?" He threw a withering glance at the medical examiner. "What was the cause of death?"

Before the man could reply, Bergmann added, "I will have your work checked by our own medical examiner when he arrives. Meanwhile, I want this body kept well preserved. Is that understood?"

"Yes, sir. I'll see to it," came the nervous response. "The cause of death appears to be blunt-force trauma, but I have yet to perform an autopsy."

"Not drowning?"

"I believe not. No water drained from his lungs. I'll know for certain when I open him up."

"On second thought, just store him," Bergmann snapped. "I need competence. Our own pathologist will perform the autopsy." He wheeled about and walked briskly out of the room.

"Take me to the jail on *Rue* Henri Terquem," he ordered his driver as he climbed into his vehicle. "They call it the *maison d'arrêt*." Meanwhile, he radioed his headquarters. "Arrest everyone from that row of houses where Kallsen was last seen. Bring them to the jail at Terquem." He listened a moment. "I said everyone," he barked. "Men, women, children. We can't have people thinking they can kill a German soldier without consequences."

He fumed as the vehicle rolled through the streets. His commander had pressed him for details pertaining to Kallsen's disappearance, and he had been unable to provide any. The situation had been complicated by the Boulier family having vanished.

When he had arrived at Claude Boulier's dairy farm on the night Kallsen went missing, it had been recently and hurriedly abandoned, with unwashed dinner plates still in the sink, beds stripped of blankets, and empty hangers lying on the mattresses. In the hay barn, his men found a root cellar, its trapdoor left wide open. In another barn, the milk cows stirred restlessly, their udders full. Bergmann ordered that they be confiscated for German army use.

Over the next two days, investigations conducted by the *feldgendarmerie*, the German equivalent of the US Army's military police, revealed that Ferrand Boulier's extended family had uprooted hurriedly, and even some of their close friends had vacated their homes. Bergmann ensured that he was informed of developments in the investigation as they occurred. Meanwhile, news trickled up from the south of acts of resistance by the populace. At Normandy, partisans had reportedly blown up fuel-oil tanks to keep them out of German army hands. *And here, our soldier is murdered by the French. That cannot be allowed to pass unpunished in my area of operation.*

The Bouliers' next door neighbor who had been arrested on the night Kallsen went missing had been useless. The man had been afraid of his shadow, but even threats against his wife yielded no information. The two had observed no unusual activity, seen no unknown visitors, or witnessed anything to indicate that the Bouliers had been involved in Kallsen's disappearance. And yet the Bouliers and their extended family and some close friends had deserted their homes, apparently within an hour of Bergmann's visit on that street less than two days ago.

An hour after leaving the morgue, Bergmann walked down the wide, second-tier corridor of the jail. Keys jangled and metal doors clanged as he entered the cell where Ferrand's neighbor was held. On seeing the German captain, the prisoner cowered in a corner, holding an arm over his battered face.

Bergmann mocked him. "Your time with us is coming to an end. I have your confession."

The man peered at him through bruised eyes. "But I didn't confess to anything. I don't know anything."

"Ah, but you did. I have three witnesses who will swear that you admitted to seeing Ferrand Boulier attack and beat Kallsen to death with some sort of instrument, and you aided his escape by failing to report immediately and then by delaying your confession. Come along. Your friends and family are waiting to see you."

Two guards grabbed the hapless prisoner under his armpits and manhandled him along the walkway behind Bergmann, down a flight of stairs, and into a courtyard. Assembled in a fearful group at the other end were his neighbors and wife. She burst into tears on seeing him and tried to run to him, but she was restrained by the guards.

Halfway between the trembling cluster of neighbors at one end of the courtyard and the cringing prisoner at the other end, a squad of soldiers had spread out in a line. They held their rifles at their sides.

The two guards who had dragged out the prisoner stood him against the wall and tied his hands behind him. His body shook and he sobbed uncontrollably, looking alternately between his wife and the captain.

Bergmann strode to a position in front of the huddled neighbors. "I told you that you must respect my soldiers. This man confessed to witnessing your neighbor, Ferrand Boulier, deliberately beat and kill the one who went missing in your neighborhood two nights ago. We cannot and will not tolerate such violent criminal acts."

With a quick nod of Bergmann's head, a sergeant took charge. The two guards holding up the prisoner retreated behind the firing squad, leaving him weeping and wobbling.

After three quick commands, the courtyard erupted in gunfire that echoed from the walls. Children screamed and covered their ears. Women shrieked, turned their eyes, and buried them in kerchiefs. Their husbands stood, their faces devoid of expression, emasculated.

A thin cloud of smoke lifted into the air, spreading the smell of gunpowder. The prisoner lay in a heap on the ground. Behind him, a thick spray of blood ran in rivulets from the wall to the ground.

Bergmann spoke again. "Go back to your homes. Take care of your children. We want only peace between us. And remember, we will keep order, one way or the other."

When Bergmann returned to headquarters, the orderly at the security desk told him that his commander wished to see him immediately. Surprised at the apparent urgency, he navigated the corridors of the office building that had housed the local school administration building. That function had been moved to an empty warehouse, the superintendent and staff told to make do.

On arrival at the office of *Oberstleutnant* Meier, the battalion commander, a corporal announced Bergmann and showed him in. Meier looked less than pleased. He was a tall man, slender, with thinning hair, a narrow face that dropped into a strong jaw, and piercing eyes.

He left the captain standing at attention. "I've been informed of your initiative," he said. "You executed a man without clearing or even informing me of what you intended to do."

"Sir—"

"I'm not done. I'll tell you when you may speak."

"Yes, sir."

"Your action will inflame the population to take more extreme measures against us. Our job here is to secure this objective, and we don't do that by generating more enemies where they did not exist."

"They were in place already, sir."

"You interrupted me." Meier shot the captain a stern look. "We have the *feldgendarmerie* to carry out investigations. They've been doing their jobs. You know, and I know, that we had trouble with Kallsen. He's assaulted women before. You might be interested to know that his comrades were questioned, and that around noon on the day he disappeared, he followed a young girl home from a bakery. He had leered at her when she walked by, and he told his patrol members that he intended to get her."

Bergmann looked momentarily nonplussed. Then he regained his composure. "Sir, may I speak."

Obviously still angry, the commander nodded.

"I was not aware of the information you just told me."

"Did you miss that report? I'm told by the commander that you've taken a keen interest in the investigation."

"That is correct, sir, but apparently I missed that detail for pursuing my normal duties. I am sure that the young girl was Chantal Boulier. She and her entire family and their extended family are gone. Meanwhile, as you know, we're hearing rumors of resistance groups forming and of bombings farther south in France."

"You missed that detail? Seriously?" Meier's tone was slightly mocking.

"Your zeal for action seems to outweigh your duty to be thorough. As for events farther south, you're wading into matters far above your rank, *Herr Hauptman*." Exasperated, Meier waved a hand in the air. "What did you expect? This country fought ours in a bloody war that lasted four years and ended only twenty-two years ago. Many of those people resisting us probably fought in that war. They remember. Did you think they would now welcome us with open arms? Your recklessness will get our soldiers killed."

The captain remained at attention, silent, his cheeks flaming.

Meier paced for a few moments and then circled his desk. "At ease," he said.

The captain complied, noticing that, curiously, the commander suddenly looked deflated, even defeated.

Meier picked up an envelope from the desk. He opened it, pulled out a document, and scanned it. Then he circled the desk again and stood in front of Bergmann as if he were reluctant to speak.

"I am directed to inform you," he said at last, "that the background investigation for your application to the SS has been completed, and that you are accepted. You will transfer with your current rank, effective immediately. For the moment you are to remain on my staff until you receive further orders. Your command will be turned over to your executive officer until I select your replacement." He folded the document, returned it to its envelope, and handed it to Bergmann. "Congratulations."

A slow smile had begun to spread across Bergmann's face. "So, my bloodline is pure back five generations," he breathed. "No Jewish blood." He became effusive, breaking unbidden from his "at ease" stance and reaching to shake Meier's hand.

"Thank you, sir. This is the best news."

"I'm sure it is," Meier said, retaining his reserve but taking Bergmann's hand.

As the two men stood facing each other, both perceived a shift in relative authority. Bergmann straightened his back, his face becoming stern. "Thank you again, sir." He locked eyes with the commander. "I shall call SS higher headquarters immediately to discuss where I might best serve."

"Do you have something in mind?"

"I do, sir. I intend to root out these partisans who think they can stand in the way of our *führer's* plans. I will start with the group hiding the Bouliers."

Meier returned to the other side of his desk with an air of being forced to accept an unpleasant inevitability. "Keep our conversation in mind. We can have no more capricious executions. My advice to you is that you do not let this investigation become an obsession."

"I assure you, *Herr* Meier," Bergmann replied with a glint in his eyes and a frozen smile, "I will not forget our discussion." Without waiting to be dismissed, he clicked his heels, inclined his head forward sharply, and crossed to the door. On opening it, he spun about and extended his arm in a full-length salute. "*Heil* Hitler!"

14

Two days earlier, June 15
Saint-Nazaire, France

A scene like none they could have imagined greeted Jeremy and Nicolas as they entered Saint-Nazaire, situated on the north bank of the Loire River estuary where it ran into the Bay of Biscay on France's Atlantic coast. Despite the ancient town teeming with British and French soldiers, as well as other allied soldiers from Poland, Belgium, Czechoslovakia, and Canada, the war seemed a peripheral concern. It spawned a raucous carnival atmosphere with dark undertones driven by *the* overriding concern: personal survival, and a hoped-for rescue by the British Royal Navy.

The soldiers' moods ran a spectrum from abject despair to accepting inevitable capture, with hordes celebrating whatever hours of freedom they had left. Others, calculating the odds of rescue of so many by sea while the Germans closed in and routinely strafed from the sky, decided their overland chances looked better. They headed out on foot to Switzerland, southern France, or Spain.

Some soldiers were still fully outfitted for combat including rifles slung across their backs, while others had shed their kits and overcoats and stripped down to trousers and undershirts. Small groups clung to a semblance of military decorum, but the majority had reverted to boisterous first-name basis regardless of rank and wore wild-eyed expressions that dared anyone to try to impose authority.

Jeremy and Nicolas entered this maelstrom with the second overriding concern on everyone's mind: food, and where to get it. To that end, the two newcomers observed British soldiers standing guard outside of a gentlemen's club, presumably for pay. Another escorted young girls with nuns bound for a Catholic school. Others served or washed dishes in restaurants. Jeremy and Nicolas watched as one Brit asked a senior non-com where he could find something to eat. The non-com told him to hold his cap out, and yet another soldier hand-filled it with raisins.

Dressed in the civilian clothes Claude had provided, Jeremy and Nicolas went unnoticed as they made their way through the crowds. Unshaven for days and with unkempt hair, both men passed for refugees seeking sanctuary. Nicolas had brought money, and soon he purchased bread and meat sufficient to assuage their gnawing hunger.

Jeremy noted that Nicolas had a passing familiarity with Saint-Nazaire. After short conversations with fellow citizens, Nicolas determined how to reach a destination he had not divulged, and he led through narrow cobblestone streets.

They reached a stone dwelling overlooking the estuary near the port. Fortunately, it was on a backstreet without commerce, warehouses, or activity that would attract the soldiers, and so it appeared empty when they approached it. Nevertheless, Nicolas instructed Jeremy to wait in the shadows cast by a tree growing close to a wall while he crossed the road, mounted some stairs, and knocked on a heavy wooden door.

A few minutes went by, and then Nicolas reappeared and beckoned to Jeremy. With a sense of relief, Jeremy left his hiding place and sauntered across the road. Inside the apartment, Nicolas introduced him to Jacques, a serious-faced young man a few years older than himself. He had a stocky build, a deep tan, and dark hair. His eyes sank under bushy eyebrows over a straight nose, and he wore a heavy mustache.

"Another cousin?" Jeremy inquired, half-smiling.

"The less we know about each other, the better," Jacques cut in. "Within days, the Germans will be here, inside Saint-Nazaire. I can't afford to know anything about you or for you to know anything about me."

Taken aback, Jeremy only stared. Suddenly feeling overwhelming fatigue, he nodded.

"I don't mean to be unfriendly," Jacques added. "It is enough for me to know that Nicolas brought you here. I had to stop him from telling me more about you." He smiled tiredly as he rubbed the back of his neck. "I know you carry a message for us to England. It's an important one." He gestured through a door. "You must be starved. Come into the kitchen. I still have plenty of food. Then you must rest."

Jeremy slept long and hard, occasionally brought to semi-consciousness by far-off explosions or the rat-tat-tat of overhead machine gun fire as German fighters strafed the town. When he finally woke up fully, the sun was high in the sky, and he learned that he had slept through a full day and night.

Nicolas and Jacques were sitting at the kitchen table when he entered. Strong fresh coffee spread its welcoming aroma. Nevertheless, both men looked grim.

"We've been catching up," Nicolas said, while Jacques crossed the kitchen for coffee. He also brought buttered bread with marmalade back to the table.

"None of the news is good," Nicolas continued. He cupped his hands over his face and blew out through his fingers. "I've been in touch with my family. I don't have much detail, but my Uncle Ferrand and the girls have fled their house."

Looking up and reading Jeremy's concern, he added quickly, "Everyone is safe, but my mother and father had to vacate our dairy, and my cousins left the farm where we spent the first night. The Germans are overrunning the north and setting up checkpoints everywhere. You and I got out just in time."

A sense of profound dismay caused Jeremy to reel. "I'm so sorry," he said, dropping his head. "This was my fault."

"No, no!" Nicolas jumped to his feet and grasped Jeremy's shoulders.

"Uncle Ferrand began organizing to resist as soon as the Germans crossed the Maginot Line. My father joined him immediately, and so did I. He intended to send the girls to exactly the place where they are going now. The schedule was moved up for reasons I don't know, but you are not the cause of all this chaos and sadness. You are our hope of generating an early response and making sure that your countrymen know that we are ready, willing, and able to carry the fight on our home ground. With their help, we will beat this Nazi monstrosity."

Seeing that he felt no better, Jacques, who had watched and listened silently to the exchange, thrust a steaming mug into Jeremy's hand. "Drink this," he said, "you'll feel better." He shoved the bread with marmalade across the table. "You must eat too. You'll need your strength."

Jeremy raised the coffee to his lips and took a swallow. The aroma brought with it the feel of warm places and friendly faces, a stark contrast to the current reality. He set it down and nibbled at the bread but could not yet bring himself to take a full bite.

"What's the plan?" he asked. "How do I get across the Channel."

Jacques sighed. "I can't tell you much. As you've seen, a lot of soldiers hope to cross, and boats have come and taken them away by the thousands. That's been going on at Brest, Le Havre, La Pallice, Cherbourg, and other ports along the Atlantic coast, but unfortunately, tens of thousands are still here. They're angry, anxious, they feel abandoned, and they are losing their sense of good order and civility.

"They are particularly incensed that they did their duties, fought in the rearguard so that the British and French armies could escape, only to be left on their own while the German army closes in on them. Meanwhile, they're attacked from the air with only their small arms for defense since they were ordered to destroy and abandon millions of pounds worth of heavy guns and other equipment. Those strafing runs kill hundreds of civilians too."

Jeremy closed his eyes and shook his head. "So again, I ask. What's the plan? What will put me on the front of any of those boats? And *why* should I be at the front of the line? Some of these soldiers have braved the elements and attacks for days. For that matter, why can't any of them carry your message?"

Jacques and Nicolas looked at each other, startled, as if not having considered the thought. For a few minutes, no one spoke, each silent with his own thoughts.

Nicolas broke the quiet. "You make a good point, Jeremy, but let's be realistic about what you've done. You evaded capture against all odds, you broke out on your own so as not to endanger your helpers, you bluffed through German checkpoints, and you walked many kilometers with French refugees to get here. I think a better question is: who deserves to be at the front of the line more than you?"

When Jeremy started to protest, Nicolas held up a hand. "Our message sounds simple, but who should carry it? You might be unique in that you made it to the beach at Dunkirk, lived with the people building up the resistance, and are emotionally involved." Momentarily, his eyes twinkled. "And that's without even considering Amélie."

Jeremy smiled involuntarily and then shrugged off the comment.

"Seriously," Nicolas persisted. "You must tell them that our government seems to have given up the fight, but our people have not. As I told you before, you're not the only one carrying our plea for help. We're hoping one of you will get through and convince your Mr. Churchill not to give up on us. I don't know the others or anything about them or where they are. I know you. My mission, directed by our fledgling French resistance, is to get you on a boat to England. Please don't let me fail."

Jeremy took another swallow of coffee while staring straight ahead. "All right," he said after a time, "how do we proceed?"

Late in the afternoon, the three men assembled again. Jeremy and Nicolas had ventured into Saint-Nazaire and returned appalled again at the rowdiness and lack of discipline displayed by many of the troops awaiting rescue. Palpable resentment permeated their moods.

While waiting for the next wave of evacuations, gangs of soldiers of various nationalities roamed the streets seeking mischief. Some had found several train cars loaded with liquor and soon ran about in drunken stupors. The quick wits of an unknown soldier had put a stop to that plundering by the simple expedient of setting fire to the hay used as packing material within the cargo boxes. The flames quickly spread and soon consumed the entire train, including a boxcar containing large quantities of ammunition. As they heated up, the resulting explosion and flying bullets drove the crowd back.

"I made contact with British intelligence," Jacques said when the three of them had regrouped in his kitchen. "I have my own shortwave radio. An operator in London picked up my signal a few weeks ago and put me in touch. The intelligence officers put me through some paces, but apparently, I passed the test. We don't communicate often, but they take my calls. We keep them short. I could probably do better if we had a code established between us. As it is, we speak in euphemisms. When the Germans arrive, I'll have to shut it down." He paused in thought. "Jeremy, tell them in London that we could use some trained radio operators who know Morse code and can encrypt."

"I'll do it. Now, what did you learn today?"

Jacques took a breath and closed his eyes. "There will be a large evacuation here tomorrow involving many boats. We're to seek out the largest ship, a troop carrier." He opened his eyes and locked them on Jeremy. "You'll be on it."

"Why that one?"

Jacques shrugged. "It's the easiest to identify. I'm sure you'll get more instruction once you're aboard."

"Or maybe," Nicolas added, "because they could assure that you could get on that ship. If it's so large and full, one more passenger won't matter."

German Junkers struck during the night, their thunderous bombs shaking the apartment and rattling windows. After what seemed an endless time, the roar of engines, the rattle of guns, and the thunder of explosions ended, replaced by cries of the wounded and grief-stricken and the wail of ambulance sirens.

The three men left the apartment to help collect the dead and care for the wounded. When they returned many hours later, Jacques thrust a finger in Jeremy's face. "You tell them in London that we must win this war," he said, seething with anger. "We have no choice, and we French will fight with or without England."

Later that evening, while Jacques was out of the room, Nicolas told Jeremy quietly, "One thing I can tell you about Jacques is that he means what he says. He is a very brave man." He glanced around to be sure they were still alone. "He's Jewish, and as we've already seen, the Nazis don't like Jews."

15

Three days earlier, June 12
Veules-les-Roses, France

"We're too late," Lance muttered. From his hidden position on the cliffs south of the picturesque town, he observed an empty bay with five groynes stretching out into the water. He turned to the small Frenchman at his elbow whom he knew simply as François. "Are you sure this is the place?"

"Of course," François said. "I saw the boats here myself two days ago when I helped other soldiers escape. Small ones ran thousands of men out to larger boats and warships. The Germans bombed them from the cliffs north of the village, and Stukas came down to shoot at them."

As he leaned back against the rocks, the sinking feeling that had started in Lance's chest grew as it descended into his stomach. He gazed into the clear blue sky and then closed his eyes against the disappointment he would face when he informed his squad.

After leaving the Coste farm, he had led the beleaguered men back to the irrigation ditch, followed it to the stream that fed it, and then into the woods from which it emerged. On the other side, they had found the other farmer, as Coste had said they would. He had appeared to Lance as both eager to help and anxious about doing so. He had already constructed a false floor on his truck with planks and heavy plywood.

As the men climbed onto the truck bed, he instructed them to lie down on their backs, close together. He then fitted the false floor above them and piled a full load of hay and vegetables onto it. When the side slats were slid into place, the cargo looked normal, and the plywood protected against the possibility of probing pitchforks. The meals that Coste had provided revived the men's strength, and despite the new discomfort, they remained in good humor with the thought of moving toward rescue.

Unavoidably, the driver encountered German checkpoints. The first one stretched the British soldiers' nerves. Although they could not see the guards probing the load of hay, they felt the enemy presence and heard them speak. When the Germans prodded the bales with pitchforks, the Brits' nerves seemed to scream inside their heads. They relaxed a bit as the truck was allowed passage, and by the time they had endured two more checkpoints, although remaining alert, they were inured to the fear that had attended the first.

Six hours later, the truck stopped, and they sensed being inside a building. Soon, they heard the hay and vegetables being removed from above them, and then the farmer raised the false floor. With a finger over pursed lips, he cautioned them to silence and pointed to the back of what they now saw was a huge barn. Another man stood near a door and beckoned to them. He was old and thin and wore a straw hat and friendly smile, but he also did not speak. Lance, Horton, Toby, Kenny, and the rest of the men filed past him quietly. Both Frenchmen followed.

"We'll bring food," the farmer told Lance. "Then you'll sleep. Tonight, you'll walk many miles."

"Are you coming with us?"

"No. A friend will take you. His name is François."

"Where are we going?"

"Veules-les-Roses," the man replied. "It is on the coast two hundred kilometers southwest of Dunkirk, and the British Navy has been taking soldiers on its ships there. We are only thirty kilometers away now, but there is much fighting in between. The Germans have the roads blocked, so going by truck is too dangerous. François knows how to get there on foot, and he will take you in."

Sitting on the floor with his legs stretched out, Lance leaned back on one arm and massaged his forehead. "That must be dangerous for him."

"*Oui, monsieur*," the farmer replied, "but this is our fight. You sleep now. When you wake up, François will be here, and you will go."

François had been as good as the farmer had predicted. His skin was very white, and he wore a black beret over perpetually wide eyes, and although very young, his age seemed indeterminate. Lance guessed he was in his early twenties, and although on the chunky side, he moved rapidly and tirelessly. He seemed to be someone who could be easily underestimated.

Through the dead of night over unseen trails, François had led them on a twelve-hour hike through back alleys, over fields, and through forests. The men held onto each other's shoulders in the dark so as not to be separated. During the day, they skirted villages, staying as deep in forests as possible. François scouted ahead to ensure safe passage until they emerged on the cliffs above the Atlantic coast and maneuvered to where they had sight of their objective.

As they neared the town, François suddenly ducked to the ground and signaled for the others to do the same. His eyes widening further, he brought his finger over his lips and moved carefully back the way they had come. Lance and his men followed.

Having reached a safe distance, François whispered, "*Les Boches* are on the cliffs on both sides of the port. When I was here before, they were only on the north side."

With a sinking heart, Lance had asked if there was a place where he could observe more closely. His youthful zeal undiminished, François nodded, and while the squad waited, he took Lance to a place where they could see the waterfront with its groynes stretching into the sea.

"Never give up hope," François said on seeing Lance's downcast expression. "We'll go to Le Havre. They are taking soldiers out to sea there too."

For several minutes, the weight of leading eight men to safety in a fierce war immobilized Lance. Finally, he muttered, "What about Dieppe? Isn't it much closer?"

François shook his head. "It *is* closer, but there is nothing there now. It's dead. Le Havre is the closest point for evacuation. I will take you there." He forced a grin. "It's only seventy kilometers."

On the second night of the trek, while moving through the forest with no visibility and guided only by a compass, they heard others moving in the same direction, toward the coast. Only a few feet away, men called to each other in the crisp, modulated tones of the German language. In the darkness they were invisible.

Lance's men froze in place. When the immediate danger had passed, they turned their direction southward.

In the early morning hours, one of the men spotted a lone French tank. Approaching it, they found it deserted yet in full working order, complete with fuel and ammunition. Wasting no time, they mounted it, and with five men sitting out on its hull, proceeded toward Le Havre.

Several miles along their route, a French officer stepped into their path. "What are you doing with a French tank?" he demanded.

Lance hopped down from the turret and related how they had come across it. Although expressing surprise, the officer accepted his account. "I could use your help," he said, and explained that he intended to establish a rearguard action on the south bank of the Seine.

Lance agreed, and after crossing a bridge, his ragged squad helped blow it with tank rounds and then set up firing positions. No sooner had they completed their preparations than German infantry appeared on the opposite bank in trucks.

Lance's thrown-together unit targeted the lorries as they appeared, and then fired on groups of German soldiers descending to the riverbank. The melee lasted an hour, with more enemy troops pouring down the opposite side, bringing up armor, and launching pontoon boats filled with infantry.

The rearguard began to give way, with French soldiers streaming past Lance's position. "Time to go?" Horton called above the din.

Grim-faced, Lance took stock of his men's position and the approaching enemy and nodded. With a sweep of his hand, Horton signaled for their comrades to regroup on the tank, and once again they headed for the coast. They drove until they ran out of fuel, and then set out again on foot.

At dawn on the third day, having walked the forests and across fields to avoid more German troops and the mass of refugees that clogged the roads, Lance's small group rested in a wooded glade while François went to learn about the current situation from locals.

"That French officer was a bloody good fighter," Horton observed. "He gave it all he had."

"He was outgunned," Lance agreed.

When François returned, his face was grim.

"Le Havre has fallen," he reported. "The last evacuation took place a few days ago. Cherbourg too, which is the next port. The British landed troops there that had evacuated from Le Havre. They were supposed to join fresh Canadian units headed into battle, but the Canadians retreated the same day. The Nazis already occupy Cherbourg." He grunted. "I saw a military policeman directing traffic. Unfortunately, he was German."

Lance looked around at his men's gaunt faces. They appeared tired but not defeated, in healthier states of mind than when they first gathered on the outskirts of Dunkirk. The generosity of their French hosts had filled their bellies, and despite their arduous journey, they were in hardened physical condition.

"Where to now and how far?" he asked François.

"We could try for Brest. The Royal Navy has been picking up soldiers there. But that's four days away on foot. We'd have to travel west, and the Germans are moving down along the coast very rapidly. I think if we go south to Saint-Nazaire, we'll have a better chance. It's only three days away on foot."

Lance snorted. "Why wouldn't the Germans go there first?"

François shrugged. "I'm taking a guess. They're working their way along the coast to secure the ports. If they continue that way, they'll take Brest first. Saint-Nazaire is farther south. I suggest that we go straight there and bypass Brest." As he spoke, his wide, youthful eyes locked on Lance. "I could be wrong."

Once again noting that François was someone who could be misjudged, Lance smiled wearily. "You've kept us safe so far," he said. "Lead on."

They hiked, avoiding main roads and the ever-growing mass of refugees heading south. The first part of the journey was more arduous as they climbed grades to as high as fifteen hundred meters before the land gently sloped downward again. François invariably sought routes that contoured the steepest rises. When they ran out of food, he left them to rest in wooded areas, and returned with sufficient loaves and meat to take them through the next leg of their journey, courtesy of the local population. As they proceeded, Lance noticed that François too had trimmed down and taken on a more weathered countenance, but his youthful enthusiasm remained undimmed.

"Are you planning on going all the way with us?" he asked François at one point during a rest stop.

"It is my duty," François replied while chomping on a sandwich of French bread and cheese. "You came to help us. I can do no less."

"What about your parents, your family? Won't they be worried? You've spent a lot of time with us."

For the first time, a fleeting look of desolation crossed François' face. "I have no parents," he said. "My father was killed in the last war when I was an infant. My mother died before I knew her. I was raised by relatives. I do this for them. We cannot allow the Germans to take over our country." Defiant eagerness returned to his eyes. "My cousins know I can take care of myself."

Eventually, they approached the small town of Sautron, northwest of Nantes. It lay on the rail line to Saint-Nazaire. When François suggested they take the train for the rest of the trip, Lance reacted skeptically.

"Are we trying to get ourselves caught?" he demanded with more passion than intended.

"It will be all right," François responded, heedless of Lance's vehemence, crediting it to fatigue. "Thousands of British soldiers are riding the train." He grasped Lance's arm. "The sooner you get to Saint-Nazaire, the better chance you have of getting on a boat."

They approached the train station cautiously, with François walking along the platform first, followed by Lance, and then Horton and the rest of the squad. British and French troops crowded the station. The other seven men in Lance's group sidled along the platform, keeping a healthy distance from each other and feeling exposed in their worn and dirty British uniforms.

When the train rolled in, Lance and his men could not believe their eyes. It moved slowly enough that with minimal effort, anyone could sprint to get on it at any time. British and French soldiers filled the cars, sat on the roofs, and occupied every square inch of available space. Only disembarking French civilians made room enough for Lance's squad to clamber on.

"Try to keep together," he called as they struggled for free space, but his words were lost in the screech of steel on steel, the rumble of train cars, and the toot of the whistle as the engine struggled under its mammoth load.

When he had secured a foothold on the bottom step of one of the cars, Lance glanced around. Horton perched above him on the top stair and shot him a grin. Toby had made it farther inside the same car, but Lance could see none of his other comrades.

He heard his name called from the platform, and while still holding onto his place, he turned to see François running alongside.

"It seems I will leave you now," François called. "No room." He panted as he ran to keep up. "Remember, Saint-Nazaire. Go to Saint-Nazaire. I hope to see you again in happier days."

"Where will you go?" Lance yelled back.

"Marseille," François replied. "The resistance is forming there. *Vive la France! Vive la Résistance!*"

He fell back as the train puffed out of the station. Lance waved, a sense of loss overcoming him. "*Vive la France,*" he called back. "*Vive* François."

Then, as François fell back, a new sound filled the air: the low growl of German Stukas on the prowl. They had found a favorite target, an almost stationary train in a station filled with enemy troops.

The fighters descended, machine guns cut loose, and François' chest exploded. He went down in a bloody heap. Soldiers jumped from the train and ran for cover while the rat-tat-tat of machine gun fire raked them, followed by deafening explosions.

Almost frozen in horror, Lance reacted to screams around him and dove to the ground, nearly sprawling on his face. He felt a hand grasp his collar and jerk him upright, and he turned to find Horton beside him, dragging him to cover.

Minutes later, the attack was over, with bloody corpses strewn about. The train had not stopped, and now with much of its load discarded, it had picked up speed. The chaos of moments before reversed, with soldiers running to jump back on.

"Let's go," Horton yelled in Lance's face, but only a strange buzzing sounded in his ears. He gazed about, dizzy, and sensed another set of arms supporting him on his other side. The medic, Kenny Tickner, had wrapped an arm about Lance's back. Together, he and Horton dragged Lance toward the train, while a fourth man, Toby Stewart, the soldier who had survived the machine-gunning of his comrades at *Le Paradis*, cleared the way.

"Did our chaps make it back on the train?" Lance moaned. He had curled up against the corner of the last car, and his mind had begun to clear.

"I saw only four. Us," Horton replied while gesturing toward Tickner and Toby. "The others might be in the forward cars ahead. I don't know." He lowered his face close to Lance's. "You got your bell rung from that first bomb blast, so you rest easy and let me do the thinking for a while." Then he turned and called out to everyone in close proximity, "Hey, can you give us some room? This bloke's hurt. He needs air."

Lance grasped his arm. "It's all right. There *is* no room." He closed his eyes, and an image of François' last seconds framed in his mind. "François didn't—" He could not finish the sentence.

"I know," Horton said. "I saw." He remained squatting next to Lance. "I suggest we stay on the train and get as close to Saint-Nazaire as possible. We might want to jump off short of there to avoid being targets again."

Toby hovered on Lance's other side. "You have to lie flat," he cajoled, "get those feet elevated, and stay awake." While Toby and Tickner shoved against other soldiers to carve out space, Horton took his own helmet and placed it under Lance's ankles. Tickner put a field jacket under Lance's head as the train chugged toward Saint-Nazaire.

16

June 16, 1940
Saint-Nazaire, France

Lance and his remaining three comrades rambled into the tumultuous conditions in the port city. Despite the grueling challenges faced on their flight from Dunkirk, they viewed the seemingly complete breakdown of military discipline with mouths agape.

The train had stopped well outside of Saint-Nazaire. On the walk in, the group had passed field after field of British military gear, most now destroyed by its users for lack of space aboard ships to transport it and to prevent its use by the enemy. Among the equipment were brand-new battle tanks, trucks, field artillery guns, and every sort of supply an army would need to fight. They lay, battered, disabled, and rendered useless, by order of higher command.

They passed a field artillery officer protesting his orders to demolish his guns. His face red, his eyes bulging, he thundered at a superior officer delivering the order, "I did not drag those Bofors over four hundred miles just to demolish them."

"I can direct you in writing, if you'd like," came the patient response.

With a disgusted glare, the officer set about to comply.

Lance, still weakened but recovering, regained his position as leader of the group, to which Horton readily submitted. "Stay together and let's get to the waterfront," Lance said. They continued on, sometimes being passed by soldiers who ignored orders to abandon motorcycles and rode them into town. All around combatants broke into stores and dumped their respirators and other combat necessities to make room for pilfered cigarettes, beer, and other items.

While passing a supply depot next to a railway, a horde of unruly soldiers looted train cars filled with cases of liquor. Within minutes, men ran wild-eyed through the streets, pouring bottles of spirits down their gullets.

Looking closer, Lance saw that many of the liquor cases had been lined with straw as packing material. "Let's go," he ordered. "Set fire to those cars. It's either that, or this crowd will turn into a drunken brawl. They'll be incapable of being evacuated."

"Blimey," Horton exclaimed, whirling on Lance. "Do what?" But then a mischievous twinkle crossed his eyes, and he grinned. "I'm morally opposed to burning perfectly good booze," he intoned, "but that fire should be blinding."

Minutes later, flames leaped high in the sky and spread to the other cars. As bottles heated up, they burst, their alcoholic content further fueling the fire. Then the last car caught fire. Unexpectedly, exploding ammunition sent shockwaves through the air, and people ran for their lives. Driven back, the crowd could only watch in dismay.

Lance observed, emotionless. "Avoid the drunks and the listless. We're going home, and we won't wait around to be captured."

They pushed through the crowds to the port, noticing groups of civilians mingling with troops, hoping to be included among the evacuees. As dusk settled to darkness, they arrived at the waterfront. The atmosphere was less raucous but still filled with stress. The four men pressed on toward the queues of soldiers already lined up for passage to the hoped-for waiting ships.

Then a coaler out on the water steered toward the dock. The captain called over a loudspeaker, "I'm coming in. I won't tie up. Anyone wanting a ride can jump aboard as I pass. Then I'm headed to Plymouth."

Anxious men pressed against the edge of the pier. The drop to where the boat would pass was a good distance. As the coaler closed in parallel to the dock, men jumped to its deck and rolled before climbing to their feet. Others fell into the buffering arms of comrades. It continued past and quickly filled with more men leaping to their hoped-for escape.

Lance caught Horton's eye. "You go," he said. "Take the others with you."

"Why not you?"

"Too many privates need a lift. Go on."

Horton looked askance. "Can't," he replied. "My ankle's barely healed. It won't take the fall."

Briefly recalling the strenuous hike of days they had just completed, Lance shot him a skeptical glance and turned swiftly to Toby and Tickner. "Go. Now. Jump. You might not get another chance."

Wide-eyed, the two soldiers returned his gaze.

"Go," he ordered. "You don't have time to think it through. I'll see you in Piccadilly."

With that, Toby and Tickner leaped. Lance and Horton watched. They were horrified to see that many soldiers missed the deck and plunged into the water. Some on board managed to rescue several, but a few soldiers still wearing full kits sank below the surface and did not rise again. Amid the writhing figures, the tossing boat, and swirling waters, Lance lost sight of Toby and Tickner and could not see if they had completed the jump safely.

"We can't take any more," the captain bellowed over his loudspeaker. "We'll sink." He turned the boat toward the open seas.

While Lance continued to search the dark waters, Horton stepped away, threw his head back, and breathed in deeply. "Let's go," he said, grabbing Lance's shoulder. "It's just you and me now. We've got to get in those queues."

The bombing that night was horrific. The Junker bombers, flying in fast and furious amid roars of engines and ear-shattering explosions, delivered their payloads indiscriminately, centered on the port. Soldiers scrambled. Many cast aside concern for others in desperate attempts to save themselves. They collided with each other and the hopeful civilians among them.

Watching the bedlam with nowhere to seek shelter, Lance and Horton held their ground. Seeing a soldier push a woman aside to take her place in a questionable shelter, Horton shook his head and went to cover the woman with his own body.

When the planes had departed and the smoke had cleared, the cries of the wounded and the stench of spent explosives and burning flesh filled the air. Lance and Horton helped carry wounded people for triage and corpses for burial. Then they once again headed for the queues.

17

Sometime during the night, a fleet of vessels arrived and anchored roughly ten miles off the coast. Included among them were large troop ships that had been requisitioned by the Royal Navy and converted from cruise liners, as well as destroyers and a flotilla of yachts and small, seaworthy boats. The destroyers and smaller boats were to be used to ferry evacuating soldiers to the ships, and when all were full, they would take on their own load of evacuees, and the entire fleet would convoy back to England.

Lance and Horton hunched together to weather the rest of the night. At dawn, the ferries began their rounds, and then the Stuka fighters descended amidst their deathly staccatos. They, in turn, received the full anger of every available weapon, to include Ack-ack guns, Brens, and thousands of Lee-Enfield rifles.

Discipline strained against the onslaught. Despite the regalia of proud units including the Royal Engineers, the Pioneer Corps, and the Royal Army Ordnance Corp, an ominous sense pervaded that a tiny spark could generate a mentality of "every man for himself," brought on during the night by the Junkers bombing.

As the day wore on, and irrespective of the rain of fire from the sky, the lines of men moved forward into the ferries and onto the waiting ships.

Finally, early in the afternoon, Lance and Horton joined a group of men transported across the expanse of ocean to board the HMT Lancastria.

From the apartment window, Jeremy, Nicolas, and Jacques watched the huge numbers of soldiers ferried across the water. Early in the afternoon, Jacques stood.

"Time to leave," he announced. "The ships will be sailing soon."

"How am I getting aboard? Surely, we can't just walk out and be at the front of the line?"

"You're expected. That's all I can say. We'll help as many soldiers as we can get to the ship. Don't forget that we all face the Stukas."

Jeremy nodded as he turned to Nicolas. "What will you do now?"

Nicolas stood from the kitchen table with a dismal look. "I'll miss my friend, my brother—"

Jeremy chuckled. "Your brother, the fool."

Nicolas laughed. "You were a natural for the part." His expression turned serious. "The Germans will be here within days. I've agreed with Jacques to go inland. It should be safe to travel for a while, and we'll go south to Marseille. It's a city like no other, and the Germans will think twice before trying to subdue it. A healthy resistance will grow there, I'm sure of it, and since Jacques is already in touch with British intelligence, renewing contact from there should not be difficult." He grinned. "You didn't think you'd be rid of me so easily. If you do your part in London, we'll be in touch. Remember, I have Amélie's interest to protect."

"Ha! You never give up, do you?"

"I never do, and neither should you. I know you are right for each other."

Jeremy felt his eyes grow moist and his throat constrict, and for the space of moments, the three were silent. Then Nicolas exclaimed, "You must go." He grasped Jeremy's shoulders. "Be safe, my brother. We'll see you when this war is won."

"Thank you," Jeremy said hoarsely. "For everything." He pressed a slip of paper into Nicolas' hand. "For Amélie."

Nicolas chuckled. "Ah, so I am to be your Cyrano after all, at least in making the delivery."

With no other words exchanged, Jacques crossed rapidly to the door and held it open as Jeremy strode through. The two hurried down the stairs and then to the back of the building. Another set of stairs took them down to a boathouse on the waterfront.

Inside, Jacques boarded a small powered vessel. Before embarking, he tied three strands of material to the flag mast, one green, one yellow, and one red. Then he tied three identical ones to Jeremy.

"Show them to the receiving officer when you board the ship." Minutes later, he steered his boat along the shore to the lines of soldiers waiting to be ferried out.

Jeremy watched as a group scrambled aboard with mixed expressions of relief, anxiety, and wariness, all glancing at the sky for Stukas. Jacques turned his vessel out to sea, throttled up the engine, and steered toward the largest ship, the HMT Lancastria.

18

MI-9 Headquarters
London, England

Lieutenant Paul Littlefield once again paid a visit to Major Norman Crockatt in Room 424 of the old Metropole Hotel. The major noticed that the young officer, although always respectful, carried personal anxiety like a calling card.

"Nothing yet?" he asked as Paul stood in front of his desk.

Paul shook his head while fingering his service cap. "Nothing, sir. I was hoping you had something."

Crockatt scrutinized him as he stretched back in his chair. "You don't give up easily, I'll say that for you."

"They're my brothers, sir, and we've had no word of them in over a week."

"Nothing from the troops evacuated at Dunkirk?"

"Not so far. The units are still trying to sort out who arrived home and who was left behind."

"It's not even been two weeks. Give it some time."

"Give it some time?" The intensity of Paul's sharp retort surprised them both. He glanced down at his cap. "Sorry, sir." Then he looked up with an expression just short of defiance. "Within the last two weeks, Dunkirk fell, the Germans paraded into Paris, the French government fled and appointed a new head of state, and three hundred thousand of our troops arrived to a hero's welcome after an astounding defeat."

Crockatt sat forward. "I'd be careful what you say, Lieutenant." His tone was stern, but his face revealed compassion. "You apparently missed Mr. Churchill's speech. He claimed no victory. You can't blame people for being happy about the return of so many of our fighters. Why did you come to see me?"

Paul took his time to respond. "I hoped your group had heard something."

"Is that all? You haven't accepted my offer to transfer over here."

Paul hesitated. "Sorry, sir. I'm not understanding all the machinations going on at the national level. I rather hoped that you could shed some light."

Crockatt leaned back again in his chair and lit a cigarette. He offered one to Paul, who declined. "So, you needed someone to talk to." He gestured for the lieutenant to take a seat. "Why not your own boss?"

"It's not that easy. In MI-6, I'm one among thousands."

Crockatt chuckled. "And here we have a flatter, shallower organization. You can get to the top man more easily. Is that it?"

Paul nodded sheepishly. "I'm trying to understand, sir, why we gave up the fight so easily. Why did we evacuate so readily? More importantly, why did we leave so many behind without a shred of support and call the whole operation a victory." His eyes flashed. "We've deserted soldiers in port after port along the French Atlantic coast. Do we even know how many are still over there, scared for their lives, feeling abandoned, trying to survive? I don't feel victorious."

Crockatt blew smoke out and lowered his voice. "Having your two brothers missing doesn't help." He puffed on his cigarette and cast a side-long glance at Paul. "You seem to know a lot of things you're not supposed to."

"I dig for information, sir. I can't just let my brothers disappear."

The two sat in silence. Then, Paul blurted, "Why did Churchill abandon all those soldiers in France? I did hear his grand speech you mentioned about the spirit of Dunkirk and what a success that operation was. The evacuated soldiers were feted as heroes, but we left tens of thousands behind, maybe hundreds of thousands. The press isn't telling that part of the story. I'm not alone in worrying about family members left over there."

He looked to Crockatt as though he had more to say, so the major remained quiet.

"We've had more boats arrive from other beaches since the flotilla returned from Dunkirk. The later returning soldiers aren't being treated like heroes. Some of them had not eaten in a week. Some were still in shock from all they'd seen and experienced. They fought to allow our main force to leave. We abandoned them, and when they made their way home, we treated them like pesky vermin."

"How do you know all of this?"

"Because whenever I hear of another boat coming in, I go to the docks. I stand with mothers, sons, daughters, fathers. Just like them, I peer into every face, hoping against hope that I'll see Jeremy or Lance. And just like those family members, I hold out pictures of my brothers, praying that someone had seen them. Then, when the procession of half-alive men passes by after being mistreated by port officials checking their papers and questioning their right to be in England, I see the shoulders of those waiting family members droop, and they leave in anguish with tears running down their faces, just like I do."

"Silence.

Crockatt extinguished the stub of his cigarette in an ashtray. "I can't offer much comfort," he said quietly, "but let me ask you a question." He waited until Paul's eyes met his own. "What do you think the prime minister should have done differently?"

Paul took in a deep breath. "I know, I know. He didn't put the troops in France, and he warned the country and that cowardly parliament for years about the danger Germany presented. They laughed at him. But Dunkirk happened on his watch."

"Agreed. No argument. But how would he have defended our homeland if almost our entire army was imprisoned in Germany? He had to get a fighting force home, and in the process, he handed the British people something we've needed for a long time, something to celebrate, the spirit of Dunkirk."

"I understand that, sir." Paul sounded haunted. "But why not support those who remained behind? Why mistreat those who got home later?"

Crockatt arched his brows. "I don't have a good answer for your second question. I suppose the worry is that spies could infiltrate with escaping troops.

"With regard to your first question, we give the soldiers still in France whatever support we have available; but unlike Hitler and against Churchill's advice, we did not build up our bomber forces between wars. We send over warships and flotillas of boats manned by civilian volunteers, and our fighters provide cover as much as possible. Many of the pilots in those planes pay with their lives. For that matter, so do a lot of the crews on those ships and boats. I'd call that support."

Crockatt took a minute to study Paul's face with curiosity. "What caused you to come in here, now, to have this conversation?"

"Sir?"

"Why did you come here today? Why not yesterday, or the day you first went to the docks, or tomorrow?"

Paul was at a loss for words. He sat silently. Neither man knew where the conversation would lead.

"You're a good intelligence officer, Lieutenant. You put things together and you keep them to yourself, for the most part." He added the latter comment with a touch of irony and the ghost of a smile. "I have the honor of being your excepted audience. I gather you've heard about the operation at Saint-Nazaire today?"

Paul hesitated, and then nodded.

"You're hoping your brothers are there."

Paul drew back, closing his eyes and sighing. "I don't know." Looking up again, he continued hurriedly, "I don't want to be wishy-washy, but I've followed the success of each evacuation operation. We brought home a lot of our comrades, but we lost huge numbers of them too. The results at Veules-les-Roses were mixed at best. Cherbourg was a disaster, but at Brest, there was little German resistance. The difference appears to be how much support the air forces provided."

Crockatt pursed his lips and nodded. "I see what you mean, but I don't know what can be done about it. We're still building up our air capability." He gave Paul another studious glance. "Why should that concern you today in particular?"

Paul drew a deep breath. "Because a convoy of transport ships, destroyers, and another flotilla of small private boats are at Saint-Nazaire now, being loaded with tens of thousands of soldiers. I believe it's called Operation Aerial. The *Luftwaffe* rules the sky there. Without support from the air, our ships are sitting ducks, and so are the soldiers we're trying to bring home." He stared directly into Crockatt's eyes.

"I see," the major said. "I don't know what can be done on that score from this office. You know, I'm familiar with the support that *is* there now, and it's formidable. I can't discuss it with you, but Britannia still rules the waves, and that's all I'll say on the matter." He let the moment ride, and then changed the subject. "Have you given any more thought to transferring over here? The offer is still open."

"I have, sir, but I've made no decision."

"Please do give it consideration. You've developed a keen concern about our soldiers caught behind enemy lines, and our mission is to help precisely those men."

Paul sensed that the conversation was ending and stood to leave. "Thank you. You've been most courteous." He headed toward the door, then paused and turned back. "If you have any influence at all, perhaps you could call one of the higher powers to direct air cover for those ships."

Taken aback a bit, Crockatt arched his eyebrows and smiled. "I'm afraid you've overestimated my power, but I'll try."

Paul nodded his appreciation and departed.

As soon as Paul had left the office, Crockatt summoned his secretary. "Get Air Chief Marshal Sir Hugh Dowding on the secure line for me, would you, please?" He stood, rocking on his feet, deep in thought.

"Will that be all, sir?" the secretary asked.

"No," he said, pulling himself back to the present. "Do an inquiry for

me. Call down to the unit of Second Lieutenant Jeremy Littlefield. I believe
he is from Sark in the Channel Isles. I think he deployed to France with one
of those engineer units building infrastructure during the Phoney War, and
that he went missing in action at Dunkirk. I want to know which unit he
was with, and if he shows up, I want him here at first opportunity. If I need
to speak to his commanding officer, I'll be happy to do so."

"Anything else?"

"Do the same for Corporal Lance Littlefield, and please stay on it."

"Right, and I'll put that call through straightaway."

When Crockatt answered the phone an hour later, he recognized
Dowding's thin, high-pitched voice and clipped manner of speaking.

"You must want something, Norman. We haven't spoken in some time."
Dowding's notorious irascibility marked his stern tone. "What can I do for
you?"

"Yes. Well there has been a war on, as I'm sure you've heard."

"And neither of us has time to joust, even in jest. What's on your mind?"

Crockatt related his conversation with Paul regarding the ships at Saint-
Nazaire and their lack of air support.

When he finished, Dowding sighed tiredly. "That lieutenant deduces
too much, but he's exactly right. The truth is the fighters are spread thin on
higher priority targets."

"With all due respect, sir, what priority could be higher than covering
the escape of tens of thousands of men who've already given far beyond
what could be expected?"

A short silence ensued. "We've been friends a long time, Norman, but
what you imply with that question toes close to the line. Besides the three
hundred and thirty thousand men we brought out of Dunkirk, we have
since rescued at least another one hundred and twenty thousand more.
We've not been negligent."

"So, these men at Saint-Nazaire represent a small fraction of the whole
and should thus be considered expendable?"

Dowding's response was terse, bordering on exasperation. "Nothing
disastrous has happened to any of those boats. One was fired on from the
air this morning, but no major damage was done. At least we've received no
reports in that regard. You're browbeating me about a calamity that hasn't

occurred. We just don't have any fighters to spare, as I'm sure you already know." He paused a moment and softened his tone. "I wish I could do more, but I just don't have the assets. Even if I could divert some, it's too late in the day. They wouldn't arrive at Saint-Nazaire in time."

Another silence ensued, and then Dowding said, "They're not completely defenseless, you know. That's a good complement of destroyers we have there and they all have anti-aircraft munitions, including the troop carriers." A heavy silence followed, then he broke it by continuing. "Don't worry, when they come across the Channel, their destroyer screen will be augmented with submarines."

Chagrinned, Crockatt said, "I understand, sir. I promised I'd try."

"And you did. Just one word of advice, my friend. Don't stray too far out of your lane."

Crockatt chuckled as he stroked his brow with one index finger. "Hmph. I gave almost that exact same advice to our young lieutenant last week. In any event, thanks for taking the call. Cheers."

19

Saint-Nazaire, France

Lance clambered up one of the heavy rope ladders draped intermittently over the rail along the ship's length down to the water. To his left and right, soldiers struggled in the rough mesh to keep a handhold and not lose their footholds. Below him, Horton climbed and waited in concert with Lance's progress. Occasionally, a soldier would fall and was quickly fished from the waters, but the troops made steady progress. Soon, both Lance and Horton stood on the ship's wooden deck.

A Royal Navy sailor added their names, ranks, and identification numbers to a list and handed them a card directing them to their sleeping and eating areas. He then pointed them toward an outside set of steel stairs.

"If you go there now," he said, "you might get a hot meal and lemonade. But hurry." He gestured to indicate the multitude of boats still streaming toward the Lancastria. "As you can see, thousands more are on their way."

"Jolly good," Horton enthused. "I'm ready for that." Then he jerked his head skyward as yet another Stuka raced over his head. Seconds later, it banked and descended, lining up on a group of small boats clustered together.

Its machine guns opened up, their terrible noise like rolling thunder accompanying the rain of tracers launched against the boats. Anti-aircraft guns aboard the destroyers and large troop ships engaged the fighters, and all around, soldiers raised their rifles and fired.

They were ineffectual. The Stuka closed the distance, racing only feet above sea level toward its quarry.

In fascination, Lance watched, unable to avert his eyes. Because of the distance, he could make out no details, but none were needed. He heard the sound of the Stuka's machine guns and saw pieces of things fly into the sky, dark figures fall into the water, and a red stain coat the sea's surface.

Meanwhile, the Stuka rolled on, climbed high at a distance, and then circled, its new target obvious. The Lancastria.

The German pilot held his fire until he had leveled out roughly fifty feet above the roiling sea. When he flew within effective range, he unleashed a barrage of lead at the men climbing the ladders and those already hunkered on the decks.

Lance grabbed Horton and pushed into a space below the steel staircase. The protection was inadequate but better than none, and they covered their ears against the roar of gunfire and *thunks* of bullets against the ship's steel walls. The smell of death rose in their nostrils.

Overhead, another Stuka attacked, and then another, following in the path of the leader, taking out small boats and circling to turn its guns on the Lancastria. Then, just as suddenly as they appeared, the sky was clear.

Lance surveyed the deck. "We were lucky," he muttered to Horton. "Those were dive bombers. They must have been at the end of their run and out of heavy ammo."

The cries of the wounded sounded in agonized clamor. Medics and volunteers scurried to provide first aid and drag injured soldiers to greater safety. Lance and Horton joined in. Meanwhile, the flow of soldiers to the ship continued relentlessly.

When, an hour later, the two companions finally stumbled through the crowds filling the decks, lobbies, corridors, and cabins onto an open deck near the stern, they found the space packed with more exhausted soldiers sitting on every available surface. It had been turned into an eating area. Crewmembers dispensed lemonade.

Drinks in hand, Lance and Horton wedged next to each other against an outer wall. Horton looked around, taking in the mass of men crowded together. "Well, Sergeant," he grunted, his head tilted back, his eyes closed, and his legs tucked up tightly to make room for others, "next stop, home."

Lance exhaled. He looked across the faces of anxious men, some in obvious shock, some attempting humor, some already exaggerating war stories. Holding up crossed fingers, he grunted, "Let's hope."

Jacques' little boat plied the waters of Saint-Nazaire, struggling under a load of soldiers that challenged its capacity. Jeremy estimated that the trip would take roughly thirty minutes.

The putter of the engine mixed with the rush of wind, the slapping of water against the hull, and the scattered yells of men giving directions, all punctuated by the cries of seagulls. The smell of the sea combined with lingering gunpowder, the odor of unbathed, sweaty men, and the boat's exhaust.

The Lancastria loomed larger and larger as they approached, and then a speck appeared high in the sky. The whine of a distant aircraft engine descended in tone to a low, throaty growl as the speck enlarged to a dot, morphed into a Stuka, dipped its nose toward the Lancastria, and closed the distance. It flew low over the ship, dropping further until it was barely above the waves and lined up on a group of boats close together.

Jeremy watched in horror as the fighter let loose volleys of lead, erupting its targets in flying chunks of wood and human body parts that splashed into a crimson stain on the frothing sea. When the pilot had finished his run, he turned his aircraft's nose skyward, climbed until the plane was again a bare spot on a blue sky, and then circled, the drone of its engine following it.

From across the water, Jeremy heard cries for help, saw arms and legs thrashing, and witnessed the last moments of men who disappeared under the surface, not to be seen again. In shock, he turned to Jacques.

"We must help the survivors."

Jacques shook his head grimly. "We can't. We're already overloaded.

This boat will founder and sink." He searched Jeremy's despairing face. "I'll circle back after I drop you and the others off and save as many as I can."

Before Jeremy could respond, the pitch of the Stuka's engine caught their attention. The fighter-bomber flew low over the ocean again, somewhat higher than its first run, and lined up on the center of the Lancastria.

As if in a bad dream, the plane cut loose its deadly stream of molten lead at the ship. Bodies spilled over the rails. Men fell from the rope ladders, arms and legs flailing, but soundless from the distance between the Lancastria and Jacques' small boat.

Nausea welled in Jeremy's throat. He fought it off with deep breaths, and his mind slowed to a surreal vision of all that surrounded him. Behind him, the other men in the boat railed against the Stuka, shaking their fists and rifles and hurling empty threats into the sky.

"You bastard!"

"I hope you burn in hell."

"Meet me face-to-face and fight like a man, swine."

Then, before the soldiers had quieted down, the rumble of more fighter-bombers joined the cacophony, and two more planes descended and followed the exact path of their leader. They attacked ships, small boats, and soldiers along the shore or in the water, any targets within the spray of their murderous machine guns.

Jacques whirled and glanced at the shore and then the Lancastria, calculating relative odds of getting to either location. He grasped the throttle and found it already full open. On instinct, he cut the motor and turned the boat, abruptly slowing its forward movement to keep it from running into the machine gun fire.

Seconds later, bullets sprayed the water where the boat would have been but for Jacques' fast action. The plane hurtled past, headed toward the ship, its guns already spilling tracers.

Like a man possessed, Jacques cranked the engine to life and opened the throttle. "Which way?" he called to Jeremy. "Ship or shore? They'll be back."

Jeremy turned to look at the grim faces still turned to the sky, following the Stukas' flight. "We're sitting ducks either way," he called back. "Our best shot of getting back to England is on that ship."

"We were told to watch for you," the young officer listing names and ranks told Jeremy when he finally boarded and showed the strips of ribbon on his wrist. "You are to be escorted to the bridge. Captain Sharp will speak with you there, and then you'll go to the forward dining room for the passage to England." He gestured to a sailor who indicated for Jeremy to follow him.

Startled, Jeremy complied. *I guess Jacques must be tied into British intelligence.* He had hardly had a chance to bid the Frenchman farewell, and now he worried about whether or not Jacques would reach shore and his apartment safely.

Making his way forward, Jeremy observed from the Lancastria's fine lines and quality fixtures that at one time it must have been a passenger cruiser, now pressed into military service. However, seemingly every surface of its tables, chairs, divans, stairs, or the decks themselves were occupied by soldiers; yet as Jeremy glanced over the rail, hundreds more waited to climb aboard.

"How many people are on this ship?" he asked as they struggled through the crowd.

The sailor shook his head. "I don't know. It was designed for seventeen hundred passengers plus three hundred crewmen." He took a deep breath. "We stopped counting at six thousand." After navigating through a series of crowded decks, companionways, stairs, and ladders, they entered through a door marked "Bridge."

The noise and atmosphere changed decidedly when the door closed behind them, with only a few officers working quietly. Captain Sharp stood near the ship's port side, watching as far below yet more men climbed aboard. The bridge crew spoke quietly while poring over charts in front of the ship's wheel and spread along the windshield that spanned the vessel.

Beyond the glass, a gray panorama of troop ships, Royal Navy destroyers, and small boats ranged across the water. The destroyers and many of the smaller vessels ferried soldiers to the larger ones and returned for more. Others that had already filled to capacity lingered farther out, awaiting the naval escort that would provide a defensive shield as the entire fleet convoyed to England. Above them hung a dirty veil of smoke, fed by burning fuel-oil of listing and half-sunken boats destroyed by enemy bombing. Already, a dark film splotched much of the estuary's surface.

The sailor, with Jeremy, approached the captain and made introductions. Sharp was a burly man with dark hair and a jovial countenance weighed down with responsibility. The seaman retreated to a corner of the bridge and waited.

"I'm glad you arrived in one piece," Sharp said, glancing out at the sky. "I received a message telling me to be sure you arrive in England safely. That's almost all I know."

Jeremy did his best to hide his surprise.

"The rest of it is to inform you of a directive coming from high command. When we land in England, you are to report to the director of MI-9. I don't have a location for you, but I presume that's in London. Your unit is informed. Perhaps someone there can help find it. I'm sorry I don't have more details."

"I understand, sir. No problem."

Sharp gestured at the scene below. "I won't be able to spend more time with you. The last ferry just arrived, and we'll be sailing within the hour."

"I'll get out of your way, sir. The ship is a bit crowded."

The captain scoffed. "When we arrived last night, the French pilot who steered us in told me that I had placed a noose around my neck." He closed his eyes momentarily and sighed. "Fleet command signaled that we were free to sail hours ago, but—" He stopped talking a moment and exhaled heavily. "We would have had to go across the Channel on our own. No submarine protection, no air cover. So, I made the decision to wait, and meanwhile, more soldiers climbed aboard." He smiled bleakly. "You know, they say that changing the name of a ship brings it bad luck."

"No, sir, I didn't know that."

Sharp gazed about, taking in the details of the bridge. "This vessel was originally christened the RMS Tyrrhenia, but American passengers had difficulty pronouncing the name. Cunard Line changed it to Lancastria." He closed his eyes again and shook his head while rocking slightly on his heels. "I hope I made the right decision."

Sharp appeared to Jeremy to be a man alone, despite his staff. He was affable, kindly, and professional, but now labored under the pressure of potential life-and-death consequences of decisions already made. The captain started to turn away, but Jeremy stopped him with a question.

"If you don't mind, sir, can you tell me the names of the other ships out there?"

Sharp let his head roll back in thought. "Well let's see, there's this one, the Lancastria; then there's the Havelock, the Duchess of York, the Georgic, the Highlander, the Vanoc." He pointed to a ship about a mile away. "That's the Oronsay. It was hit by aircraft this morning but remains seaworthy."

An officer called to him from across the bridge.

"I must go," he told Jeremy. "I couldn't possibly name all the ships off the top of my head, but between the troop carriers and the destroyers, that's roughly thirty ships. Why do you ask?"

"I want a feel for the effort to rescue our men. Thank you, sir."

"Ah, good point. Farewell. I hope to see you in better times."

Jeremy regarded the captain with compassion, his own senses still numb from the brutal attack on Jacques' boat less than an hour earlier. They shook hands, and Jeremy departed with the sailor, who took him to the forward dining room.

On entering, Jeremy saw that it still contained vestiges of the years it plied the ocean as a luxury liner, displayed in polished wooden tables, artistic murals, and mosaic floors. Now, it too was filled with exhausted men, sitting or standing in whatever small space they had carved out. However, on looking around, Jeremy saw that most men in the room were commissioned officers and senior non-commissioned officers.

No one spoke to him as he entered, and the orderly excused himself and returned to his duties. Looking around, he noticed that a line had formed leading to tubs with bottles of lemonade. He found the back of the line and waited patiently as it moved forward. Not feeling conversational, he stared blankly into nowhere with his hands in his pockets, only moving when the queue did.

Reflecting back, he could hardly grasp all that had happened in the nine days that had passed since he buried himself in the sand. The events of the past few weeks had gone beyond surreal, challenging his sanity.

How did I go from one day building airfields to the next becoming an untrained infantryman in the thick of combat and looking desperately for rescue from Dunkirk? His mind went to Ferrand and his daughters and the risks they had taken to save him and provide him sanctuary. As an image of Amélie flashed through his mind, he inhaled, and his chest seemed to burn.

This time, the memories could not linger, replaced involuntarily with those of the cries of toddlers and mothers separated from each other among hordes of refugees; of families pushing carts holding cherished heirlooms or loved ones too young or old to walk; of packs of dogs and scavengers fighting over carrion, some of it farm animals, some human, some even children; of the mass tramp of a population of millions fleeing south in hopes of finding a safer place; of discarded personal treasures heaped along the roadways for lack of remaining strength to carry them. And then, the brutal attacks by Stukas. The replayed images seared his brain.

The admonition of Nicolas and Jacques echoed again and again, summarized in Jacques' passionate exhortation delivered at the point of a jabbing finger: "You tell them in London that we must win this war. We have no choice, and we free French will fight with or without England."

Looking around at the beleaguered men crowded into this erstwhile elegant dining room, Jeremy lowered his head. "I'll tell them," he whispered. "In London, I'll make bloody sure they hear you."

"Eh? What's that?" a major at Jeremy's elbow inquired. "Did you say something to me?"

"Sorry, sir," Jeremy replied, startled. "I was talking to myself."

"Yes, well, be careful of that." The major cast a doleful look around the room. "A lot of us might be doing the same thing before all of this is over." He smiled with a kindly twinkle in his tired eyes. "Buck up. You'll be all right, and you'll soon be home." He nudged Jeremy's arm and pointed.

Jeremy looked to where the major indicated, through a door leading into a smaller room, and was surprised at what he saw. Inside, men and women in civilian clothes huddled together. Children at their feet clung to them.

"Who are they?" he asked. "What are they doing here?" He fought down sudden anger at the conditions wrought on innocents.

"Embassy staff and their families," the major replied. "I was an attaché there. We brought them down last night."

"God help us," Jeremy murmured as the line proceeded.

Abruptly, from beyond the steel walls and ceiling, the sound of thundering engines grew in intensity. People looked nervously about. Then the ship's sirens wailed.

"Hold tight, old boy," the major said. "We're in for another volley."

No sooner had he spoken than a scorching blast knocked him and Jeremy onto the floor. People screamed, women's and children's frightened cries heard above the din. Smoke and the smell of exploded munitions filled the room. Tables and chairs flew through the air, hitting victims with deadly force.

Stunned, Jeremy struggled to his knees. Below him, lying still on the floor, was the major, his eyes staring vacantly. Panting heavily, Jeremy checked for a pulse on the man's neck. He found none.

The children.

The thought came to Jeremy with blunt intensity and he reeled as he cut through the crowd of confused people toward the room where he had seen the civilians. Black smoke hung against the ceiling and descended to the floor such that he saw only a few feet inside.

A small boy, perhaps two years old, sat near the doorframe, terrified. He rolled to one side and started to crawl back into the room. With waning strength, Jeremy grabbed his shirt. The toddler shrieked and fought as Jeremy pulled him back and lifted him.

"Mummy!" the boy screamed in terror, mouth wide. "Mummy." He struggled as Jeremy wrapped both arms around him and pressed the child against his chest.

"We'll find your mummy," Jeremy said hoarsely. He leaned against the doorframe with the little boy's head near his own while searching the faces of frightened civilians who emerged from the smoke. Men, women, and children pushed out, some together and holding onto each other, some frantically seeking loved ones and joining the crush toward the exit and fresh air.

A woman swept past, calling frantically, "My baby." She stopped and whirled where she stood, her face panic-stricken. "Oh please," she implored to no one in particular. "I can't find my baby." Tears streamed from her eyes. "Timmy," she called.

Hearing his name and his mother's voice, the child pushed against Jeremy. "Mummy!" he cried. "Mummy!"

Just then, the ship began to roll to starboard, the floor sloping as the bow dipped, causing Jeremy to stumble forward. Momentarily unable to stop his momentum, he grabbed the woman's arm. She had stepped backward to regain balance, teetered as she fought for control, and fell into Jeremy.

At first startled, she saw her son in Jeremy's arms. "Oh God, Timmy!" she called. As mother and child struggled for each other, adrenaline coursing through Jeremy's brain cleared his mind.

"We have to get Timmy out of here," he yelled. "Where's your husband."

The mother teared up again and dropped her head. "Dead," she said, her face a mask of grief and fear as she pointed to the room. "In there."

"Then come on," he said. "I'll carry Timmy. Hold on to me."

As they pushed with the crowd to get outside, the ship righted itself and then began listing to port. *She's going down.*

Once on deck, the horrific scene that greeted them belied credulity. Splintered wood coated with a mix of oil and blood caused frightened people desperately seeking escape to slip and slide, a macabre sight. Huge numbers of soldiers had determined that the only route to survival lay in the water and had jumped. Already, hundreds if not thousands of heads bobbed in the water. Some troops flailed, some swam away, and some already floated on the surface, inert. More men leaped without looking for an open spot, many of them landing on top of their comrades, adding to injuries and casualties.

As the ship listed further, Jeremy saw that the deck sloped toward the bow. He paused and looked into the woman's frightened face.

"Listen to me. I don't want to scare you more, but this ship is going to sink."

She nodded, her jaw locked in fright, her eyes open wide. Timmy had stopped struggling, and although quiet in Jeremy's arms, he held onto his mother's thumb.

"We only have minutes," Jeremy yelled above the chaos. "What's your name?"

Her voice shook as she responded, "Eva." The blood had drained from her face.

Jeremy appraised her momentarily. She wore traveling clothes suitable for a diplomat's wife in the summer.

"All right, Eva. Do you swim?"

She nodded and reached forward instinctively to caress Timmy's forehead.

"Good. Listen to me carefully. We're going to jump, but first we'll head forward." He pointed along the increasingly inclined deck. Soldiers pushed past them in the opposite direction, seeking a higher perch. "When I tell you, get out of your clothes. They'll weigh you down. Your shoes too. We'll have to get over the rail and jump together. In the water, we must get as far from the ship as we can, or it will drag us under. Do you understand?"

He saw that color had returned to her face. She gazed at Timmy with a fearful, determined expression. "I'm ready."

They pressed against the wall, Timmy and Eva clinging to Jeremy. The Lancastria's bow continued to sink farther into the water, making the deck steeper, and with blood and oil coating it, footing became even more slippery.

A gap appeared by the rail. Jeremy darted over, pulling Eva with him. "Now," he said.

Without hesitation, Eva drew her dress over her head, shook off her shoes, and climbed over the rail. No one stopped to take notice. Meanwhile, Jeremy had lifted his shirt from over one shoulder and struggled to shift Timmy from one arm to the other in order to remove the rest of the shirt. Eva helped him, and then took the boy so Jeremy could clamber over next to her.

"What about your trousers and boots?" Eva asked.

"No time. Later." He looked down at the swirling water. Fewer heads and bodies bobbed there than closer to midship.

He spotted a clear area below and estimated the drop at roughly twenty-five feet. Pointing it out to Eva, he told her, "That's where we're going. Hold your nose tight but keep both arms close to your body. Don't think of

Timmy now. Give him to me. I'm a strong swimmer. We'll jump together. On three. Ready?"

Eva nodded nervously. "Just take care of Timmy."

"With my life," Jeremy said. He took the boy from Eva and pulled him against his chest. Crossing one arm around the child's tiny back, Jeremy cupped his other hand over the little face and wedged the small head close between his own neck and shoulder. Then he counted off. Together, they leaped.

20

Lance had been sitting with Horton against a wall on the aft deck when the enemy planes struck. Sirens blared before anyone saw the bombers. Soldiers bolted upright, their exhausted eyes raised first to the sky and then to each other. The drone of many engines drowned the wailing sirens, and then a mass of airplanes appeared on the horizon, heading their way.

The soldiers jumped to their feet, their eyes fixed on the fast-approaching Junker Ju-88 bombers. Then they heard the loud reports of the anti-aircraft guns from the top deck, followed by a swift response from the bombers that opened up with sprays of machine gun fire.

The first rounds struck the ship's stern. The next ones pierced steel walls, bodies, wood, and anything else in their path, ricocheting into another deadly flight path and ripping through the deck. Within seconds, the area transformed into a writhing mass of panicked soldiers, sprayed blood, and agonized cries for medics.

The flight of nineteen aircraft closed in over their targets and released their deadly cargoes. The bombs whistled through the air as they plunged. All around the ship, columns of water sprang out of the sea.

At midship, a huge explosion rocked the Lancastria, followed by three more as the projectiles found their targets. The shock sent a shudder through the hull.

Lance and Horton stared. Soldiers sitting on the rails dropped onto the hard deck or tumbled into the water far below. The air filled with the acrid smell of gunpowder and burning oil.

"Direct hits," Lance muttered. "Four of them."

The entire mass of soldiers stood stock-still momentarily as the impact sank in. Then, the clamor started up again at a fever pitch.

Unable to see beyond the heads of those in their immediate vicinity, Lance turned to Horton. "What do you think we should do?" he yelled above the din.

Horton shrugged. "I don't know. Stay here for now, I guess. We don't know how bad the ship's been hit."

No sooner had he uttered those words than the Lancastria began a slow roll to its starboard.

"Bollocks," he said. "It's bad."

Lance agreed. They held their position, standing against the wall while soldiers struggled to move away from the danger, perceived differently by individuals and thus resulting in frantic men pushing against each other in search of safety.

Then, the Lancastria righted itself. The soldiers paused in their struggles, looking skyward and exchanging wondering glances.

Above them, the ship's anti-aircraft guns continued to bellow. The drone of Junkers faded away forward, a view of them blocked by the ship's superstructure.

At first barely perceptibly, and then with increasing rapidity, Lance felt the deck under his feet canting to port. Then, as he and Horton stood with their backs against the wall and facing aft, they sensed that the stern had begun to rise. The bow must be sliding toward the sea.

"Where to?" Horton called.

"Get to the rails," Lance replied. "That way." He pointed to the starboard side.

"Why there?"

"If the ship stays afloat, that side will be high."

"I don't know," Horton said. "If she sinks fast, we'll have a very long jump to have a chance of swimming away from the suction."

"What're the alternatives?"

Horton closed his eyes and shook his head. "No good ones. If we go to the other side and the ship goes down fast, we could still be pulled in by the drag." He exhaled. "I guess we go to starboard."

They headed diagonally across the deck, struggling against men who had decided that their best options were elsewhere. At last, they reached the rail forward of the stern. They felt the deck rise further and saw it sloping toward the bow while the ship continued to list to port at an increasing rate. Already, soldiers leaped into the sea, some with life vests, others without, some wearing full kit, others stripped down. Black oil coated the surface of the water.

"We might have guessed wrong," Horton quipped, forcing a grin. "This doesn't look good."

"Hard to say," Lance replied. Because the ship sank faster on the opposite side, instead of a vertical drop, the hull sloped away. In the water, heads bobbed, bodies floated, and soldiers swam in an expanding arc.

Horton nudged him. "Look." He indicated the hull, which, in the short time they had clung to the handrails, had raised its starboard side to an obvious slant. "We'd better get on the other side of these rails, or we're going to be hanging on to them."

Other men had the same thought. They clambered over to the other side of the rail and pressed against it.

The Lancastria's roll accelerated, and then, unbelievably, the propeller lifted into the air. It hung there, supported by its shaft with its casing clearly visible above the water line.

"The shaft tube forms a shelf," Lance exclaimed. "We can slide to it and have a shorter jump."

"On the way," Horton yelled as the roll continued at a slower pace. Wearing only their field uniforms, they lowered their legs over the side of the hull, turned onto their backs, and let go.

The angle of the hull now was such that gravity had to be assisted. By sitting on their buttocks and pulling with their legs, they descended at a controlled rate, but they felt every bump, nick, and scrape of the Lancastria's rough surface that had seemed so smooth from a distance. To their left and right, other soldiers saw them and followed. When they reached the shaft casing, they rested as other soldiers spread out on either side of them. There, the noise of the chaos had faded, punctuated by faint cries for help from above and below.

Horton peered over the edge. "Clothes on or off?"

"We can swim better without them," Lance replied, "and they would weigh us down, particularly the boots."

A voice behind them cut into their conversation. "I'm keeping mine on," its owner said. "They'll keep me warm."

Lance scoffed, but Horton reached into his shirt pocket and pulled out a small waterproof bag containing a single cigarette and a box of matches. Lance stared at him in disbelief.

"What are you doing? I didn't know you smoked."

Horton sat back against the hull and took his time to light his cigarette. His eyes closed to slits as he inhaled and then sighed in satisfaction.

"Mind if I join you?" the man who had broken in on their conversation asked.

"It's a free country, for the moment," Horton responded. "Be my guest."

Aghast, Lance raised his voice. "What are you doing? We have to go." To his surprise, other soldiers along the casing had also lit up.

Horton turned to Lance with a peaceful smile. "I smoked them until I ran out, except for this one." He waved it in the air, its wispy rings carrying the aroma. "It's my last cigarette, and I've been saving it for the right occasion." He grinned. "This seems to be it, and I'm going to enjoy it."

He shifted his view to the men struggling in the water below and then the small crowd gathered on the casing. "Blokes up there are dead and dying," he continued, "and same for the ones below. For the time it takes to smoke this cigarette, at least I can do it here in peace." He put the cigarette back between his lips and inhaled.

Off to their right, someone started singing "Roll Out the Barrel," and was soon joined by others gathering in greater numbers on the shelf, belting out the jovial lyrics. When they had finished, they became more somber, singing the defiant words to "There'll Always be an England." Then, they fell silent.

Suddenly, a wide-eyed Horton sprang to his feet. "Look," he exclaimed, pointing.

Lance gazed toward the midship. There, a fuel-oil slick had ignited, and soldiers swam desperately to escape the flames, their screams heard clearly across the distance. Some emerged with burned scalps and arms. Some beat the water furiously, attempting to swim out of the flames. Some succumbed and disappeared, not to be seen again.

Lance stepped in front of Horton. "If we're going to get past our own oil slick down there..." He thrust a finger at the area immediately below them.

"I know, I know," Horton snorted, taking one last puff and snuffing out the cigarette on the hull. "We've got to go—" He started ripping off his clothes. "Our boots have to come off now," he grumbled, pulling at them. "It's a lot harder to do in the water, and they are bloody hell for swimming."

Undressed to their skivvies, the two men took only enough time to look over the edge, find an opening among the struggling soldiers, and leap into the oily water below.

21

Streaked with oil, Lance and Horton clung to opposite ends of a thick board floating on the seas. They had survived the jump, swum out of the oil patches, and tried for shore, but found that the current carried them farther and farther out to sea. Each of them wore a Mae West life jacket, taken from corpses whose necks had been broken on impact. The mistake of the unfortunates had been to put on the jackets before leaping. The impact of their chins striking the water had thrown their heads back hard against the device intended for lifesaving, sealing their fates.

Weak swimmers and non-swimmers had thrashed in the water, grabbing for anything or anyone that floated. Before Lance had acquired his Mae West, a big man grabbed for him. Both of their bodies were slick with oil. Nevertheless, the man managed to get an arm around Lance's neck. He held on, and they both sank.

Lance had gulped air just before going down, and the two struggled underwater, the man desperately grasping, and Lance pushing to break contact. Just when Lance thought his lungs would burst, the man's body went limp, his arm relaxed, and he floated away.

On breaking the surface, Lance had heaved for air. Horton, who had not seen the struggle, saw him surface gasping, and swam over to check on him.

"Are you all right?" he called. Lance drew closer and told him what had happened.

Despite the calm sea, wavelets obstructed their ability to see very far. But when they had swum a distance sufficient to be safe from the Lancastria's suction on its final plunge, they turned to watch, fascinated by the spectacle.

The aft section of the ship's keel rolled to the side, high in the air. Soldiers, presumably non-swimmers, still clung at the shaft casing on a slant below the propeller. One by one, they slipped into the brine and struggled in the gathering suction. Then, with an audible rush of air, the vessel slid below the surface and was gone.

—————

Five hours had passed since the sinking, during which time the receding tide and the current from the estuary carried Lance and Horton farther out to sea and dispersed the bobbing heads, bodies, flotsam, and jetsam. At one point, a ship seemed headed their way only to be blown up by a flight of Junkers.

Land was still within sight, but they could no longer make out definitive shapes close to shore. They had seen a fighter plane fly over and drop flares into oil globs, igniting them, and then strafe the ships and men in the water.

For several hours, the two companions floated alone, holding onto a board that might be their final means to salvation. Most of the time, they did not speak, their numb minds dreaming of home, a meal, and clear, cold drinking water.

For Lance, a darker thought pervaded. "I mucked this up," he croaked to himself.

Horton heard the words barely enough to catch their meaning. "What?"

Lance let out a long breath. "I keep thinking about that big man back there. He just wanted to live, like the rest of us. I pushed him away to a horrific death."

"If you hadn't, you'd be dead too."

"I know, but then there are the others."

"What others?"

"Our group from Dunkirk. I lost five of them; I don't know about the two I told to jump onto the coaler at Saint-Nazaire, and then there was François." He paused as his jaw quivered. When he spoke again, his voice caught. "I caused his death."

Horton slid along the board closer to Lance. "I want you to listen to me and listen good." He threw an arm up over the board and rested his chin on it to better see Lance. "If not for you, most of that group would be dead, me included."

"You're a survivor," Lance replied. "You'd have made it."

"Maybe, but you're the one who got us moving, found food and shelter, and led us through all the crap to the coast."

"Thanks." Lance started to speak, but instead laid his head on his hand while clinging to the board. "All the death…"

Horton's reply was immediate and forceful. "Don't you start thinking that way, Sergeant. You reminded the rest of us that we are still soldiers in His Majesty's Army. You rousted us from the shock of what we'd seen and done. You bloody well brought that medic back from the walking dead and revived him into a functioning soldier."

He looked to see if anything he had said registered on Lance. Seeing no change, he went on.

"That German pilot killed François," he said, "just like he massacred all those soldiers and civilians and scattered our mates at the train station. For all we know, all five of them could still be alive. Some might already be back in England, and they would have you to thank."

Lance lifted his head far enough to speak. "I hear you, Corporal. Thanks for the kind words, but that man back there… When I pushed him away, I knew he would drown."

"What choice did you have?" Horton retorted vehemently. "If the situation had been reversed where he was the swimmer and you climbed on him, he'd have done the same thing. I'll bet identical scenarios played out hundreds of times today." He slid next to Lance and grasped the back of his neck. "Listen to me. We're going to get back to England or die trying, but we're not going to give up because we had a moment of self-pity. You're still a soldier with a mission, Sergeant."

Lance remained silent. Horton slid back a little farther on the plank.

Minutes passed. Then Lance lifted his head. "You're right, Corporal. Thank you." He reached his free hand across to Horton, then laughed. "My mother always said that she was brought up without the luxury of feeling sorry for herself. You just reminded me of that."

More time passed, the sun beating down against the cold north-Atlantic water. Horton raised his head. "Sergeant, what are you going to do after the war?"

Lance laughed involuntarily, almost frenzied. "Corporal, I haven't given it much thought. But why are we being so formal, and what are you going to do after the war?"

Horton snickered. "Just pulling a morale check," he croaked. "It's good to see that we're getting less formal. The first name's Derek." He thought a moment. "Let's see. After the war, I think I'll go live in Texas. I've heard it's warm and green and beautiful. I heard that Texans call it, 'Texas, by God,' and people who move there have a saying." He dropped his voice, his head bobbing back and forth as he quoted, "'I wasn't born in Texas, but I got here as fast as I could.' That's the kind of place I want to live in."

"Texas? What will you do there?"

"Oh, I don't know." Horton forced a laugh and wry grin. "I ought to be good for something. Mopping floors or peeling potatoes, maybe."

Without replying, Lance suddenly raised his head as high as he could. "Look over there," he said. "Those blokes look like they could use some help."

Horton turned to where Lance pointed. Two men bobbed in the water, only their heads visible. One of them appeared to be holding onto something just below the surface while supporting the other.

Lance and Horton paddled as best they could and slowly approached them. "Grab the end of this," Lance rasped. "There's room."

The man grasping the submerged object let it go and grabbed the board, pulling his companion with him. "Too weak," he gasped, indicating his friend. "Hurt."

The strain of holding the injured man had sapped his rescuer's strength.

Unclasping his life preserver, Horton said, "Here, give him this." He struggled out of the vest. Together, the three of them managed to get it around the unconscious man. For an indeterminate time, they rotated Lance's Mae West between them and took turns holding onto the injured man, continuing to float, with little conversation.

At some point, Horton's curiosity piqued. "What were you holding onto?"

"Don't know," the man replied in a scratchy voice. "A piece of wreckage that floated and got waterlogged."

"What do we call you?" Lance asked.

"Kenyon."

"What happened to your friend?"

Kenyon put his head down on the board with a forlorn look. "People tossed tables and chairs and anything that would float into the water from the ship. A table smashed into him. It shattered his shoulder, and I think he has internal injuries. Maybe a concussion too."

They lapsed back into silence, and as the sun coursed down to the horizon, the temperature dropped. Cold permeated to their toes. Dusk came, and they knew that their injured comrade would likely not survive the night.

Then, in the twilight, a French fishing boat plowing the waves back to Saint-Nazaire pulled alongside. The fisherman helped them into the vessel and gave them warm coffee and blankets. The injured man lay still but breathed. Kenyon poured life-giving water down his throat and covered him.

"We're from the same village." he said. Tears formed at the corners of his eyes. "We grew up together. We enlisted together."

No one spoke for an extended time as the fishing boat continued its journey to port. Then, Horton stretched out in a corner and pulled his blanket over him.

"No British breakfast in the morning," he grunted. He shot Lance a broken smile and fell asleep.

Nicolas had been at the apartment window when the Junkers commenced their attack, the unmistakable rumble of their engines announcing their intentions. He watched in horror the attack on the ships at least ten miles out, but still identified for what they were by their distinctive shapes. When the assault was finished, he saw billowing smoke rising from a large ship, the black smudge of oil on the ocean's surface, and huge clusters of tiny dots that must be people bobbing in the ocean, spreading away from each other, and drifting farther out to sea while small boats plowed the waves to rescue them. Over the next thirty minutes, the burning ship's bow leaned into the water, its stern raised, and then it slipped below the surface.

Nicolas rushed to the quays still filled with milling soldiers. He searched relentlessly until he saw Jacques' boat limp in, overflowing with bedraggled victims of the Stukas' earlier strafing run. Wading into the water, Nicolas helped the men onto the shore.

"I'm going back out," Jacques called. "Thousands of people are in the water."

Without a word, Nicolas jumped aboard. Grim-faced, Jacques throttled up, and the boat navigated out toward the fleet.

"Did you see which ship went down?" Nicolas asked.

Jacques did not respond at first. Then he closed his eyes and nodded. "It was the Lancastria," he said, sniffing as his eyes moistened. He wiped them with the backs of his fists. "She was the largest ship. That's where I took Jeremy."

22

The little French fishing vessel puttered into the port at Saint-Nazaire. Horton had slept soundly, only stirring when the boat hit a stiff wave. Lance had dozed in and out, keeping an eye on the injured man. Kenyon had tried to stay awake to take care of his friend but had finally collapsed, exhausted. Lance was touched by the man's compassion and that of the fisherman.

As they pulled alongside a dock, Horton opened his eyes, rubbed them, and looked about. Lance reached across and nudged Kenyon, who came to with a start.

"We're back in port," Lance said. "We'll help you with your mate. There must be a hospital where we can take him. Even if the Germans arrive, they're bound by the Geneva Convention to provide him medical care."

Kenyon nodded grimly while fighting back a yawn. Stretching, he bent over his friend. Then he dropped his head, bent further to embrace him, and wept quietly, his chest heaving with constrained sobs. The body was stiff, warmth leaving it.

After tying up the boat, the fisherman set about offloading his catch. When he saw Kenyon's grief, he climbed into the boat and took him by the shoulders.

"I'll take care of the burial," he said in French. "Tell me his name. You must go before the *Boches* arrive." He produced a piece of paper and a pen.

Kenyon looked up, anguished, not comprehending.

"Thank you," Lance cut in. For the first time, he had a chance to really see the fisherman. He was young, probably in his late twenties, with a rugged, windswept look and a lithe build. His complexion, eyes, and hair were dark, and his expression was one of quiet determination.

Lance returned his attention to the dead man and covered the body with a blanket. He took the pen and paper and nudged Kenyon's arm. "What was his name?"

After being prodded a second time, Kenyon muttered a response. Lance wrote it down, coaxed other pertinent information, and handed the note back to the fisherman. Then, streaked with oil and blood, and wearing only their underwear, the three trudged toward the town.

"You know we're not dressed for polite society," Horton quipped, his grim face belying his humor.

"We're short on options," Lance replied. "Maybe someone in town will give us some old garments."

Watching them go, the fisherman looked chagrined. He called to them. "Wait."

They stopped and turned.

"You're tired and hungry. You need clothes and shoes. I'll take you to my house but let me get my fish on ice first."

Gratefully, they reversed course.

"I am Pierre." He saw Kenyon's lingering glance at his friend's body. "Don't worry," he said. "I'll take good care of him." He swept a hand toward the town. "The whole town will take care of him and honor him. We appreciate you."

23

Before dawn, Pierre awakened Lance. "I must go do the fishing. You and your friends stay here and rest. You need your strength."

"We don't want to put you or your family in danger."

Pierre shook his head. "I need time to talk with you. Don't worry about my family. I sent them to Marseille. Later, I might go too. I don't think the *Boches* will go there. The city culture is too independent, and they know it. Everyone knows it. They are still a few days away from here, so you won't be disturbed."

Lance consented.

"Tell Kenyon that his friend's body is at my church. The priest will make sure he has a proper burial." Lance thanked him, and Pierre left for the waterfront.

Although small, the house was comfortable. The three British guests made themselves at home for most of the day. Then, wearing clothes that Pierre had scavenged from friends and neighbors, they wandered into town in mid-afternoon to get a sense of current conditions.

The atmosphere had changed radically from before their transfer to the Lancastria the previous day. Gone were the hordes of soldiers, replaced by groups of twos and threes with markedly different attitudes. Some had apparently accepted as inevitable that they would be captured. They just waited. Of those, some sat staring blankly, and some had drunk themselves into stupors.

Some huddled together discussing their plight in terms of the reality on the ground. A few of them intended to continue along the coast in search of any other ports where a rescue from the sea might occur. The rest planned to strike out overland for Spain. Entirely absent was a vestige of central command or authority. Moreover, a sense pervaded that hostility would meet any attempt to assert authority.

As Lance gazed about, he was struck by another aspect. Saint-Nazaire was beautiful, with quaint, ancient streets and small shops. If the wrecked hulls of ships and small boats were overlooked, the ocean views were breathtaking, and the citizenry was generally friendly despite the ravages resulting from involuntarily hosting an army almost gone rogue. *No one has the state of mind or time to appreciate what's here.*

Horton interrupted his thoughts. "What do you think we should do?"

"Pierre wants to speak with us tonight. I want to hear what he has to say."

Horton agreed. He turned to Kenyon, who was following them much like a puppy attaches to any friendly soul after losing its mother. "What about you?"

Kenyon didn't respond, instead staring around almost trancelike.

Horton repeated his question.

"Oh, sorry," Kenyon said. "Whatever the two of you think."

They gathered in the living room that night. Pierre looked furtive as he opened the conversation. "I told you that Marseille is very independent. All kinds of people are attracted there. It isn't like Paris. If the *Boches* come, the fighting will be hard."

He looked around to ensure he was understood. Horton interpreted quietly for Kenyon. "A resistance organization started there even before the war," Pierre went on. "Its leaders were sure that the Maginot Line would fail, and that Germany would occupy a large part of France. They based their conclusions on the facts that the Maginot was incomplete, and that Germany based its military doctrine on striking hard, fast, and not stopping. The *blitzkrieg*. They didn't think the Maginot or the French air forces would save us or that the French army could defeat them.

"The leaders are in Marseille recruiting fighters. I have friends there who have already joined the resistance. They received a message three days ago from British intelligence asking if groups along the coast could blow up fuel-oil depots to keep them out of German hands. My friends called me yesterday before I went out on the boat."

Lance and Horton stared at him. "Do you mean French soldiers?" Horton asked.

"No." Pierre shook his head. "I mean ordinary citizens who do not accept that Germany will steal our country. We are Free French. We are ready to fight."

Lance cut in. "What do you want from us?"

"We have explosives. We stole them from a construction company. And there are many petrol storage tanks here because this is a significant port. But we don't know how to place or ignite the dynamite without being killed. We need help for that."

While Lance stared transfixed and absorbed Pierre's implied request, his mind flew through the horrifying images of the past two weeks. Meeting Pierre's request for help could put him through similar circumstances yet again.

For several moments he sat in silence, reminding himself of the French people's kindness and generosity toward him and his comrades. Refusing to assist could consign the French to further suffering and would also be shameful.

"I'd love to help," he said quietly, "but I'm an infantryman. My knowledge of explosives is minimal. I could look at what you've got and see what I can do." As he spoke, he saw that Pierre's eyes clouded with disappointment bordering on desperation. Lance turned to Horton. "Any ideas?"

Horton pursed his lips. "I wish I had some." He shook his head and grinned. "I probably know enough to make sure we get killed, but I'll do what I can."

"The three of us ought to be able to figure it out," Lance said. He turned to Pierre. "Let's see what you have."

Kenyon had sat quietly, listening to Horton's translation without saying a word. Now, he placed a tentative hand on the table. "I could help. I'm a demolitions specialist."

Lance and Horton swung around to face him. "You are?" they said in unison.

"Are you up to it?" Lance asked. "You've been through a rough time."

"No rougher than yours."

"But you just lost your friend."

"You've lost mates too." He gestured across at Pierre. "Without him, the three of us we would be dead, and he's been very decent about caring for my chum's body. Pierre is ready to fight for his country. I'm a soldier. I can't turn away."

Lance translated. Pierre's eyes flashed, he leaped up, circled the table, grabbed Kenyon and kissed him on the forehead. Then he bear-hugged Lance and Horton.

"Listen to me," Lance said after a moment of celebration. "We'll need British uniforms. If we're captured in these clothes you gave us, we'll be shot as spies."

Pierre's face turned serious, and he locked eyes with Lance. "I understand," he said. "Do *you* understand that we will probably take them from dead soldiers?"

Lance exhaled slowly and nodded. "We'll need sidearms too, with bullets."

Pierre held his gaze a moment longer. "Then it shall be done."

24

Dardilly, France

For the first two nights after the Boulier sisters had left their father, they traveled on back roads with their Uncle Claude, sometimes with people they did not know, and slept in cellars and barns during the day. Then, having cleared the southern line of the German advance, they moved more openly and rapidly, avoiding the mass of people heading south.

Amélie bore a hollow sensation of having abandoned Ferrand. Chantal sometimes seemed barely conscious, taking little interest in her surroundings or the goings-on of other people, sitting in submissive resignation as they rumbled along in vehicles, lapsing into dazed half-sleep when they were not traveling. Always, she clutched the frame of the family photo. Amélie watched over her worriedly, taking care that she ate and keeping her clean and warm.

After a week, they reached the town of Dardilly, a rural community northwest of Lyon situated among three valleys bounded by towering mountains. In spite of herself, Amélie could not help admiring the natural beauty that surrounded her, the green sweep of hillside fields and the grand vista of distant mountains.

Then, as they drove the final few miles to their destination, she reflected on her conversation with Uncle Claude on the night of their flight from Dunkirk.

"Where are we being taken?" she asked.

At first, Claude had appeared not to have heard her, preoccupied either with driving through the night or the worries of his brother's resistance efforts. Amélie repeated the question.

"Hmm? Oh. Sorry. We're going to our sister's farm near Lyon. Your cousins will be happy to see you. The Germans haven't reached there yet. Ferrand thought you should have time to become established in the community before they arrive."

"What's Father planning with that group he's formed?"

"I don't think he knows yet. He started gathering people together as soon as he saw the British start their evacuation. He knew we were about to be left defenseless." He spat out the last word with angry intensity. "Our leaders betrayed us with their incompetence."

"Have you heard from Nicolas? Did the American get out safely?"

"You mean the British soldier?"

"Ah, yes. He speaks French so well, but he has that *Sercquiais* accent, and once in a while he sounds like an American." As she spoke of Jeremy, her voice caught, and she felt a strange softening in her chest. She turned her head to obscure the flushing in her cheeks. "His father is American. He told me that."

Claude chuckled. "You like him."

Irritated, Amélie snapped, "We're in a war. I don't have time to think about such things. He's dead to me."

"When you went out in the rain, you saved both Jeremy and your father," Claude said, adding softly, "and later you saved Chantal."

"I'm not proud of it. It's something that happened that never should have. Why are we living this way, with the Nazis invading our country, dictating our lives, and all those French and British boys getting killed trying to protect us?" She reached for a handkerchief and sniffed. "Jeremy is beautiful and kind and brave, and he might be on his way to be captured or murdered like all the rest. We *all* risked saving him. I'm worried about Nicolas too. If he gets caught helping…" Her voice trailed away.

"Nicolas knows how to move around and take care of himself," Claude said. "The last time I talked with him, he and Jeremy had made it to the northwest of Paris. The Nazis had not yet cut the lines. The refugee traffic is thick and heavy, though. It helps them hide, but they are in the same boat as everyone else heading south."

Late in the afternoon, they approached the farm in Dardilly. Amélie's mind wandered again to Nicolas, and to Jeremy. Once again, her throat and lungs constricted, and she felt warmth rising in her cheeks. "I can't love you," she whispered to the mental image of Jeremy's strong face. "I don't know you, and I have no time."

When they arrived at her cousins' house, she was surprised to find them in a festive mood. They ran out of the house to greet her, Claude, and Chantal.

"It's so good to see you," Marie, her cousin closest to her age, enthused. "We are excited to have you here, especially at this time." She glanced at Chantal, who seemed barely aware of the activity around her. "Is she all right?"

"She's been very sick," Amélie said, striking a defensive note. "I'll have to look after her."

Andre, another cousin a few years older than Amélie, chimed in. "I'll bring in your things. What an adventure you've had. We're glad it's all over now."

Amélie stared at him without comprehension. "What do you mean?"

"Haven't you heard? Marshal Pétain is negotiating a peace agreement with Germany. He seeks the end of armed hostilities and told French soldiers that the fighting must stop. France will be saved. It was just on the radio."

Claude swore and became silent. No one appeared to have noticed.

Sensing her cousin's enthusiasm, Amélie contained her shock as the five walked a gravel path into the stone farmhouse with a thatched roof. "I-I don't know what to say," she commented. "The news comes as such a surprise."

A few minutes later, as they sat in the living room with refreshments and were joined by Claude's sister and her husband, Andre crossed to a radio on a stand against the wall. He tuned it to the BBC station, and they listened to music while waiting to hear news from Britain.

Then, an announcer stated that General Charles de Gaulle would address the French nation from London. He had escaped from France two days earlier.

Andre snickered. "Doesn't he realize that hardly anyone will hear his speech? *Mon Dieu!* Radios aren't things you can carry around with you or play in your car. Besides, a huge part of the population is out on the roads."

"Some cars have radios," Marie interjected.

"Not many, at least not in France today. Maybe in America," Claude said with a sarcastic edge to his tone. "Either way, I suppose that de Gaulle's audience will be roughly equal to Pétain's, for exactly the same reasons."

They listened to the speech, de Gaulle's voice sounding hoarse and hollow over the electronic crackling of the radio set. "Has the last word been said?" he asked defiantly. "Must hope disappear? Is defeat final? No!

"France is not alone! She is not alone! She has a vast Empire behind her. She can align with the British Empire that holds the sea and continues the fight. She can, like England, use without limit the immense industry of the United States."

He exhorted his countrymen to join him in the fight by all means available. "Whatever happens," he finished, "the flame of the Free French resistance must not be and will not be extinguished. *Vive la France!*"

When he had finished, Andre said in disgust, "That fool wants France to keep fighting. Many of us remember the last war, even if we were too young to fight. Such death and destruction. We don't want that again."

"Pétain is the idiot," Claude snapped back. "He gives aid and comfort to the army that drove us from our homes. He thinks he can negotiate with the madman in Berlin who orders Stukas to fire on a fleeing population." He breathed hard as he struggled to control his rage. "He asks Germany what their terms will be? He sees himself as the great savior of France by surrendering to those monsters who kill our people." He whirled on Andre. "Our hero of the Great War is a Nazi sympathizer. The man now running France seeks to emulate that atrocious Austrian corporal with the silly little mustache."

Nicolas and Jacques had left Saint-Nazaire early that same morning. Although they had intended to get to Marseille as quickly as they could, Nicolas felt compelled to go first to Dardilly.

"My cousins, Amélie and Chantal, are there. They will want to see me and hear about Jeremy; Amélie in particular." He told the story of how she had saved the British soldier at Dunkirk and the obvious attraction between them.

Although sympathetic, Jacques objected. "There is nothing she can do for him now. The Nazi war machine will not pause for sentiment. You're a valued fighter. We need you in Marseille."

"This war won't be won in a day," Nicolas had replied. "At the end, if we've sacrificed our humanity, we will still have lost. My cousins need me for a short while and then I'll meet you in Marseille."

Reluctantly, Jacques agreed. They traveled together to Bourges. Progress was slow. Vehicular and foot traffic congested the roads, and frightened people filled the trains. The two men used each mode of travel intermittently depending on what was available, catching rides when they could, boarding trains when possible, or just joining the mass of trudging refugees.

Late that afternoon, they stopped to rest in a small café in a village south of Bourges. The owner apologized for having nothing to serve aside from water, but he allowed them to rest their legs at one of his tables out of the heat. He refused payment.

Inside, the place was empty, although a radio played from behind the cash register. There, while sipping water and allowing their minds a respite from the atrocities they had seen, the two men listened to General Pétain's address to the nation calling for an end to hostilities.

Their eyes met, fury rising as they understood the implications. They scoffed when, at the end of his speech, Pétain said, "I give the gift of myself to France."

Jacques leaped to his feet, shoving the chair backward and glaring at the radio. "Keep your gift, coward," he yelled at Pétain's imaginary presence. "Your illegal government might surrender, but the people of France never will."

Out on the street, car horns tooted, joined by a jubilant cry from the stream of people going by. Nicolas hurried to look out the door.

Some men and women danced and hugged. The crowd had stopped its forward movement. Apparently, word had spread in the street about Pétain's broadcast. As Nicolas watched more closely, some in the crowd reversed course and headed in the opposite direction with expressions of relief. They engaged each other with animated, happy laughter and conversed with big smiles and bright eyes.

For others, the news did not appear welcome. Their shoulders drooped further, and they continued their journeys with a seemingly heavier tread.

As Nicolas returned to his seat, the restaurant owner entered from the kitchen, worry plastered on his face. He brought with him a tray with a loaf of bread, some cheese and sliced beef, a bottle of wine, and three glass goblets.

"I heard you," he told Jacques, shaking his head. "This is a bad thing. France will pay a heavy price." He set the food and drink on the table. "Please, be my guests. This is from my personal pantry."

While the two men thanked him, he crossed to the radio and fiddled with the dial. "Let's hear what they say on the BBC."

Fifteen minutes later, they listened as de Gaulle called on his countrymen to resist by whatever means. When he finished with "*Vive la France!*" all three men stood and lifted their wine goblets in the air.

"Now there," Jacques exclaimed, "is a leader we can follow." They clinked their glasses together.

25

Later in the afternoon, Amélie went for a walk. Chantal seemed no better or worse, sitting on the front veranda looking across the countryside while clutching her family photograph. Amélie had tried to raise her spirits by gently pointing out various sights, but her sister barely responded.

Her uncle and aunt's farm spanned many acres, with orchards of apricots, peaches, raspberries, and walnuts. They kept a small part of the farm reserved for dairy operations and produced their own branded cheese for market. Situated in the verdant valleys within the Rhône-Alpes, the majestic beauty lifted Amélie's spirits, and she had hoped that it might have a similar effect on Chantal. When she received no indication that such would occur, she struck out on the dirt lanes leading through the orchards.

Deliberately shutting out memories of the past week as she walked, she breathed in the sweet air laden with the scent of blooming wildflowers. A cool breeze sweeping down from the mountains reinvigorated her.

After an hour of hiking, she started her trek back to the house. As she did, her stomach tightened, and the dread that had been her constant companion since hearing the first sounds of war returned. It increased the closer she came to the house.

When she reached the driveway that led out to the main road, she saw another figure advancing toward her in the waning sunlight. She stopped to see who it was, putting the flat of her hand above her eyes to shield them from the sun.

She gasped as she recognized Nicolas' swinging gait. Arms flung wide, she ran to him and embraced him tightly.

"I've been so worried about you," she said as happy tears ran down her cheeks. She stood back to look at him. He appeared gaunt and tired, and she noticed that his signature big smile was gone. "Your father is here, and Chantal. They'll be thrilled to see you." Grasping his hand, she led him up the road to the farmhouse.

Chantal saw them coming. She hurried to Nicolas, buried her face against his chest, and sobbed quietly and uncontrollably.

Surprised, Amélie backed away and let the moments linger.

Claude emerged through the door. Seeing Nicolas, he put his arms around him and Chantal. Very few words were spoken.

At last, the emotional greetings completed, the uncle, aunt, and cousins welcomed Nicolas into their home. Dinner followed, yet Amélie noticed that despite the happiness at seeing Nicolas, an undercurrent of sadness and dread remained. He appeared reluctant to speak about his experiences of the past week, a period that now seemed an epoch.

After dinner, as dusk settled in, Nicolas quietly asked his father to keep Chantal engaged while he spoke privately with Amélie. Seeing the grave expression on his son's face, Claude asked no questions. Chantal had been enlivened a bit by Nicolas' appearance, so Claude cajoled her into walking with him along the farm roads.

When Nicolas and Amélie were finally alone, she asked about Jeremy. "You haven't mentioned him. Did you get him to a port?"

Nicolas nodded, but tightness in his throat prevented him from speaking momentarily. Amélie put her hand on his forearm, her eyes wide with alarm.

"What is it?" she asked. "What's happened?"

Nicolas told her of their hike across France, arrival in Saint-Nazaire, and meeting with Jacques. He spared horrific detail but included his last moments with Jeremy and the sinking of the Lancastria.

"Were there any survivors?" she asked through tears.

"Many. But also, many dead. We stayed out most of last night searching, and we saved as many as we could find, but..." His voice trailed off.

"And other boats were out too?"

Nicolas nodded. "And some managed to get survivors onto other ships."

"So, he could be alive."

"It's possible." Nicolas took a piece of paper from his pocket. "Just before he left, he asked me to give this to you." He laughed quietly, ruefully. "I offered to be his Cyrano de Bergerac. Anyone could see the chemistry between you two."

Amélie dismissed the comment and carefully unfolded the note. It read:

Dear Amélie,

I owe an enormous debt of gratitude to you and your family that is impossible to repay.

You live in my mind. My first waking thought is of you. My last image before going to sleep is of you. I see your hair, your hands, your face, those honey-colored eyes, and I hear your kind voice.

I pray that someday I might see you again, and hope when this war is over, you will welcome me to visit and get to know you better. Until then,

Jeremy

With an almost unbearable mix of emotions convulsing in her mind and heart, Amélie suddenly found breathing difficult. She leaned her head into Nicolas' chest and then patted his shoulder.

"Please, I need some time alone."

Nicolas squeezed her hand and stepped away.

Amélie ran through the half-light of late evening down one of the paths she had visited earlier in the afternoon, head down, shoulders hunched, one hand covering her mouth. She saw her surroundings only in a blur. *How could so many bad things happen in less than two weeks?*

She slowed her pace and walked on, remembering Jeremy's face, strong even when asleep with exhaustion. Darkness overtook the last vestiges of daylight, and the half moon, already high in the sky, shone brightly. She found a secluded place off the path. There, she sat alone on a large stone under the light of the silvery orb, and wept.

"Could I have loved you, Jeremy?" she sobbed. "Were you an infatuation only, because of this war?" She let the tears flow freely until she raised her head to stare up at the moon.

The time with Jeremy had been so short, and yet they had laughed together and learned something of each other's character beyond surface attractions. "I will never forget you," she murmured, "and whether I live through this war or die, with my last breath, I will remember that I was loved, and that I loved."

A thought pressed on her conscious mind. *Nicolas said that some survivors made it to shore, and some were taken to other ships.*

"Could you have made it to England, Jeremy?" she whispered. "How I hope so."

Her thoughts turned to her father. His transformation from sad, retiring widower to a decisive leader in a war against the merciless Nazi machine had shocked her. *And Chantal. She is so young to have gone through what happened.*

Through her grief, Amélie perceived that her father's and sister's emotional states were at opposite ends of a range, and probably tenuous. To survive, the three of them would need each other. Achieving victory in this war depended on fighting to the utmost. Returning to normalcy with a life worth living required being humane.

Jeremy rose again in her mind. "I barely knew you," she breathed, "but I'll hold to the belief that you lived, and that someday, we'll see each other again."

She sat a while longer, her emotions calmed. Then she climbed to her feet, returned down the lane, and found Nicolas waiting for her under a tree.

"You've been my best friend all my life," she said, kissing his cheek.

"We've always been there for each other."

They sat in the grass, lost in thought. Amélie told Nicolas what had happened to Chantal and what she had done to Kallsen.

"That's why we had to flee."

"Will this never end?" Nicolas groaned. He fell back in the grass, seething with anger, and remained silent for a time.

At last, he sat up. "Have you heard from your father?"

Amélie tossed her head. "I'm very worried about him. Uncle Claude calls into that wine cellar under the bombed-out restaurant, but Papa is always out. The lines will be cut sooner or later, I'm sure of that, or the Germans will figure out a way to listen in." She wiped her eyes as tears once again trickled down her face. "What will you do now?"

Nicolas told her about Jacques and the resistance group taking root in Marseille. "He's expecting me. I'll leave tomorrow."

Dismayed, Amélie implored him, "Can't you stay a day or two? I worried about you so much."

Nicolas shook his head. "This war won't slow down or wait, and I've already seen that individuals can make a big difference." He wrapped an arm around her shoulders, and they rocked together. "You and Uncle Ferrand showed the rest of us how to fight. You killed a monster. Your father put a group together very quickly to help people escape. My friend, Jacques, connected with British intelligence on his shortwave radio." He paused as another thought crossed his mind. "You do know that through his network, Uncle Ferrand helped quite a few soldiers escape to southern France."

Amélie looked at him in astonishment. "I didn't know. I'm so proud of him. He's like a man I never knew."

Nicolas nodded in agreement. "He would never talk about his Great War experiences. Something tells me that he draws on them. He set up that network to help British and French soldiers get across the country without being captured. He used it to help get our families away so quickly. Groups like his are forming all over the country. I have to be part of them, to save France."

Early the next morning, Amélie waited for Nicolas on the front porch. Next to her was a small traveling bag. She had looked at a calendar hanging in the kitchen on her way out the door, showing the date of June 20. As she sat, she was once more gripped by all the tragedy that had taken place since Jeremy had appeared on the beach at Dunkirk only twelve short days earlier.

Nicolas emerged a few minutes later carrying two cups of coffee. "I knew I'd find you here." He handed her one of the cups, and they sat next to each other on the steps.

"When do you leave for Marseille?" Amélie inquired.

He sniffed. "As soon as we finish this coffee." He glanced at her. "I'll miss you."

She tilted her head toward him. "You won't have to. I'm coming with you."

Startled, he almost lost his coffee. "No," he retorted. "You can't."

"I can and I will."

"I don't even know what I'm getting into."

"Exactly. No one does. It's a war, and everyone will have to choose sides and fight, one way or another. If I go to help my father, he'll send me away again. I can't sit by and watch while so many people I love risk their lives."

"Men." Nicolas enunciated the word. "Men fight the war."

"Not so," Amélie retorted, her voice rising. "I distracted those soldiers the night we saved Jeremy, and you know what else I did. Kallsen. And when I went into that wine cellar in the bombed-out restaurant, there were men *and* women there, planning for action with the resistance."

Nicolas had no response.

"I'm going, and that's that."

Nicolas remained silent for a few minutes, deep in thought. "What about Chantal?"

"I've thought of that. My cousins will look after her. We might see things differently about this war, but they love her, and she'll be cared for."

"I'm going too," Chantal said from behind them.

Nicolas and Amélie whirled around. "How long have you been listening?" he demanded.

"Long enough," Chantal replied. "My sister is right. We all have to fight. I'm going with you."

"No," Amélie said firmly. "You need to recover. Besides, you're only fourteen."

"That was last week, and I've been feeling sorry for myself." She stepped between them and pivoted to face them. "I can't leave the fighting to everyone else." She leaned over and kissed her sister's forehead. Her voice caught. "Amélie, I'll never forget how you fought for me."

Amélie stood and they embraced.

Chantal pulled away. "Nicolas, your arrival is the first good thing that's happened to us since that awful night. You woke me up." She turned to Amélie. "Papa told us we'd have to grow up fast. I did. I feel like I'm forty-nine years old now, and I'm coming with you. There are things I can do, even if I just make meals for everyone else."

Seeing the hesitance in their eyes, Chantal added, "There's a lot more I can do, I promise you." She took a deep breath. "If I don't go with you, I'll leave on my own and find another group. Either way, I will fight."

Her expression changed to one of curiosity. "I have two questions. Why Marseille? Why not go help Papa?"

"He would never let us," Amélie cut in. "You know that."

Nicolas frowned and sighed. "To answer your questions, Chantal, there are two reasons: resistance in Marseille was organizing even before the war. I can't say more about that now, but believe me, that reason alone is enough.

"The second is that to get back north, we'd have to cross German lines again, and they're much more dangerous now than a few days ago. I talked with my father about that last night. He got you out just in time."

"Isn't he going back?"

Nicolas grunted. "He is, and I wish he wouldn't, but my mother is still there. He says that his wrinkles and gray hair will keep him from being detained, but if not, he'll put on a show of being a most enthusiastic supporter of Pétain and admirer of Hitler.

"I want to fight, but the risk of being found out at home is too high, since we're of military age." He grinned and corrected himself. "Well, Amélie and I are."

"I am too," Chantal muttered stubbornly. "They just don't know it."

26

Marseille, France

The train chugged into the *Gare de Marseille-Saint-Charles* late in the afternoon. The crowds that Nicolas had witnessed bogging them down the previous day had thinned out. All of France seemed to be waiting with bated breath for the outcome of Pétain's overtures to the Third *Reich*. Travel was also much more amiable, the passengers less frantic, more inclined to friendly exchanges, although an undercurrent of unease permeated with furtive glances and instances of suspicious stares.

Nicolas and the Boulier sisters kept to themselves for the most part, only interacting with others when they needed to buy tickets or food. On arrival, they emerged and skirted the front of the station, descended a wide set of marble stairs, turned left onto *Boulevard Marseillaises,* found *Boulevard d'Athenes,* and there caught a bus for the beaches on *Avenue du Prado*.

As they rode through the streets, they took in the relatively relaxed atmosphere, gaping at storefronts burgeoning with merchandise and customers carrying assortments of bags and boxes. Through the bus window, they peered into a grocery store that still flourished with full shelves and mounds of produce, and they passed sidewalk cafés with well-fed patrons enjoying the fair weather.

As they drew near the beachfront, the sweet scent of the Mediterranean Sea greeted them. "Do you know where we're going?" Amélie asked.

"Jacques gave me good instructions," Nicolas replied. "He'll meet us in a café above the beach."

Fifteen minutes later, they sat in Café Gigi, trying not to stare at their surroundings. The contrast between this beach and the ones they had left at Dunkirk and Saint-Nazaire was stark.

"Do they know we're in a war?" Chantal whispered, glancing at customers enjoying a full fare of menu items including café au lait and pastries. The aroma blended with scents of spices and marinated beef wafting on the air.

"They're hoping the war won't reach here," Nicolas replied, "and depending on what Pétain does, it might never get here."

"But our countrymen are dying in the north," Chantal hissed. "Don't they care about France?"

Amélie touched her wrist. "Keep your voice down," she cautioned. "We don't need to make enemies before we even start."

Chantal glowered at her. "But—"

Amélie reminded herself that, despite Chantal having "grown up" in a week, she was still a girl, and an adolescent at that. She interrupted Chantal by squeezing her sister's hand and diverting attention to Nicolas. "Now will you tell us what's so special about Marseille?"

Nicolas did not immediately respond. Instead, he observed Chantal intently. "Listen, my little cousin," he said in a kindly tone that carried a stern note. "I love you, and I hate what happened to you, but if you're going to participate in the resistance, you have a lot to learn, with more growing up to do. A lot of young people your age want to join, but not all of them can handle it. We have to be able to trust that you'll keep secrets and won't say or do something carelessly that could destroy an operation or even a whole network. People's lives will depend on your integrity and competence. Do you understand?"

Taken aback, Chantal stared at him with wide eyes and nodded slowly. Amélie regarded him in a new light. The boy she had known only a week ago had matured into a man.

A waiter brought them water and a menu. They ordered their beverages.

When he had gone, Nicolas spoke again to Chantal. "I'm sorry to say things to you like I just did, but it's better that you learn early." He closed his eyes and sighed. "My father will go back to the hell that is now Dunkirk. On the way, and perhaps even there, he might have to pretend that he welcomes and sympathizes with the German invasion. He'll feel like dying every time, but he'll do it to stay in the fight." He leaned over and kissed Chantal's cheek. "Before this is over, we'll all do repulsive things."

The sun had begun its descent. A cool breeze blew in from the sea, and with it the soft purr of waves breaking along the shore.

Chantal put her arms around her cousin's neck and nodded. "I'm sorry. I'll learn." She sniffed and sat up, wiping her eyes with a napkin.

Amélie broke the tension. "Now, will you tell us about Marseille? And when will this famous Jacques get here?"

Nicolas chuckled. "When he gets here. Soon." He glanced around to check for listeners. "I don't know a lot of specifics, but I can give you a general background. Marseille has always had a culture of independence, from when it first began as a Greek colony a couple of thousand years ago. Even when it was occupied by other armies in times past, its people found ways to rebel.

"It's our largest commercial city and port, and its position on the Mediterranean makes it a major trading hub. The Germans want it, but they're already spread thin." He smiled. "So we have time here to recruit and organize."

Amélie and Chantal regarded him in astonishment. "You were never any good in school," Amélie said. "When did you get so smart?"

"I was a terrible student." Nicolas chuckled, squeezed Chantal's hand, and kissed it. "As my young cousin knows, war makes a person grow up fast." He shrugged. "Jacques and I had a long time to talk. He's the reason I'm *smart*." A sardonic grin crossed his face.

The last fragment of the sun dipped below the horizon, and the waiter brought their meals. As he started back to the kitchen, Jacques appeared at their table, stopped the waiter, and quickly placed an order. Nicolas made introductions.

"Ah, Amélie and Chantal," Jacques said warmly, taking his seat. "I feel as though I know you. Your cousin talked about you both so much."

An uncomfortable silence ensued.

Jacques broke it. "I'm so sorry. I spoke out of turn. Nicolas told me what happened to you."

Amélie teared up. "Thank you for what you did for Jeremy," she said softly.

Jacques acknowledged her sentiment with a nod and a warm smile. After a moment, he said, "May I ask what you're doing here?"

"They want to join the resistance," Nicolas said. "They threatened to look for another group if I didn't bring them along, so..." In a brief aside, he related what had happened to Chantal at the hands of Kallsen and what Amélie had done about it.

Jacques looked back and forth between Amélie and Chantal. "You've both been through a lot, but as bad as it's been, it could get much worse. Some of our people will be captured, tortured, even killed." He turned to Chantal. "Your age won't matter to the Nazi SS or the Gestapo."

She nodded. "They won't be expecting a girl my age to be active. I can move around in bad areas easier than you can."

Jacques scratched the back of his neck and inhaled deeply, obviously uncomfortable with the idea but seeing its merit. He shifted his gaze to Amélie. "And what about you? You've both been through incredible trauma." He started to go on, but Amélie interrupted him.

"Exactly," she said, her voice cold and trembling but controlled. "We both need to fight back. That's how we'll keep our sanity. We were not brought up to be helpless."

Jacques stared into her eyes. The waiter brought his food, breaking the moment.

"All right," Jacques said when the waiter had left. "Let's enjoy this evening. I have a place for you to stay tonight, and we'll talk more tomorrow."

27

Three days earlier, June 17
Saint-Nazaire, France

Jeremy struggled to lift little Timmy into the waiting arms of the rescuers on a small motor launch. For two hours he had held the toddler on a floating piece of wooden wreckage. It was large enough to hold the child, but too small to provide much room for Jeremy to grasp, and so he had treaded water much of the time while working hard to keep Timmy's squirming body perched on the chunk of wreckage. His trousers and boots weighed him down and sapped his strength.

When Timmy was safely aboard, strangers' arms grasped Jeremy under his shoulders and lifted him into the boat. He sprawled on the floor between the other survivors' ankles and feet until two men helped him recline on the wooden bench built into the side of the boat. One of them brought Timmy to him wrapped in a blanket. "His mother?" the man asked.

Jeremy shook his head. He tried to speak but, overcome with emotion, he could not. He held Timmy close.

"There, there," the man said, "let's see to the two of you. Maybe we'll still find her." He pointed across an expanse of ocean. "Do you see that ship? That's the Oronsay. We're taking you there. You'll be in England tomorrow."

Jeremy nodded. *That's what I thought when I boarded the Lancastria.*

The sailor patted Timmy. "Your boy looks healthy enough. I think he'll make it just fine."

The boat's motor revved up, and they started toward the big vessel. Jeremy raised his head and looked around, realizing that the launch was loaded beyond capacity with other rescued soldiers. His mind drifted. Images of his leap off the ship with Eva plagued him. He had held Timmy close, cupping his hand over the child's mouth and pinching his nose on the descent to keep the force of entry from driving water into the boy's lungs. They made a clean plunge into the ocean, and Jeremy had swum back to the surface swiftly with the boy safely in his arms. Timmy had shrieked in terror on breaking into the air, but he had not swallowed much water, if any at all.

Jeremy had looked wildly about for Eva, but she did not appear. Now, their leap replayed again and again in his mind. Eva had leapt at the same time Jeremy did, with her arms held close to her body. *What happened to her? Did she hit someone? Did someone jump in on top of her?*

Her last words haunted him: "Just take care of Timmy."

"With my life," he had replied. Now, as the launch plowed through the waves, Jeremy closed his eyes, dropped his head forward, and squeezed the boy.

They arrived at the Oronsay. Jeremy waited numbly until crewmembers had helped the others board the ship before coming for him and Timmy. When at last they were on the undulating deck, Jeremy stumbled along, carrying the boy. Seeing the toddler in his arms, men in their path moved out of the way and nudged others to make room.

Soon the two were inside, out of the weather. Jeremy nestled on the floor with Timmy in a corner by a bulkhead. Kindhearted soldiers brought him lemonade and sandwiches.

No sooner had he settled in than the ship's sirens blared. Seconds later, the drone of aircraft added to the warning of approaching bombers.

Jeremy's nerves froze. He squirmed around, facing into the bulkhead, and bent over to cover Timmy with his upper body. Other soldiers, seeing what he did, leaned over him against the wall to provide a further protective shield for the little boy.

Timmy cried furiously. Falling bombs whistled. A thunderous explosion rocked the ship.

For an indeterminate span of time, Jeremy held his position, rocking gently to quiet Timmy while visions of his earlier ordeal played non-stop in his head. Then, the men who had sheltered them straightened up.

"All clear," one of them said. "The bridge took a hit and the captain is wounded, but we're not sinking."

Jeremy raised his eyes wearily to meet those of the speaker and held up a hand in thanks. The soldier grasped it and shook it.

"The engine is good," the man said. "The steering was damaged, but the crew is putting together a work-around, so we should be all right for the time being." He reached down and patted Timmy's back. "How's the lad?"

Jeremy nodded without speaking.

"Well, you'll be in England tomorrow."

28

Plymouth, England

The HMT Oronsay tied up at a dock in mid-afternoon after a nerve-wracking voyage from Saint-Nazaire. The room that housed the charts, steering, and wireless had been destroyed, and the captain, Norman Savage, had broken his leg when the bomb hit, but with first aid treatment by good medics, and with his pocket compass, a sextant, and a sketch map, he steered his ship home.

News of the little boy and the soldier who saved him had reached the captain during the night, and he invited them to make the crossing in his quarters so that the child could sleep. Crewmembers brought clothes for Jeremy, some makeshift diapers and a bit of milk and bread for Timmy. The toddler no longer cried, but he clung to Jeremy until finally he fell into deep, exhausted sleep.

Jeremy waited a few minutes, then flipped off the lights and stepped across a narrow corridor into the bridge, closing the door softly behind him. Captain Savage sat in his chair behind the ship's wheel with his injured leg propped up, his compass and sextant on his lap, studying his sketch map. His bridge crew went about their tasks.

Savage appeared to be an unassuming man, exerting quiet authority.

His height was hard to tell in his sitting position, but he appeared to be of medium build and had dark, well-groomed hair over a broad forehead, deep-set eyes, and a narrow chin.

"How's the boy?" he asked when Jeremy approached him.

"Sleeping. Thank you, sir. You were very kind to offer your quarters. How's your leg?"

"It'll hold. I'm chock full of local anesthetics, but I can still steer the boat. I'll be all right long enough to get to port and get this leg seen to."

Jeremy glanced down at the compass. "With that?" he asked, incredulous.

Savage chuckled. "That's all they had not so long ago." His brow furrowed. "Are you that boy's father?"

"No, sir. He was orphaned yesterday. His father was on embassy staff." Jeremy bit his lip as images of Eva's leap flitted through his head. "He was killed in the explosion. His mother jumped with us—" His eyes watered, and his mouth quivered. "She never came up," he said in a raspy whisper. "I don't know what happened to her."

"Steady, lad," Savage said compassionately. He studied Jeremy. "What's your rank?"

"Second lieutenant," Jeremy replied, composing himself. "I'm an engineer."

"How did you come to be on the Lancastria? I'd like to hear your story."

"It's a long one, sir."

"We've got time. We're on course, the weather's good, and I'll be sitting right here."

Jeremy told him of his assignment building airfields in northern France and then finding himself in combat, of his despair at Dunkirk and being rescued by a remarkable French family, and then the tremulous journey across France with Nicolas and meeting up with Jacques.

The captain listened intently. "What are those ribbons on your arm?"

Jeremy looked at his wrist in surprise. He had all but forgotten them. Their colors had faded, but the strips remained tied and intact. He told the captain their purpose.

"Jacques and Nicolas put more faith in me than I warranted," he said.

"British intelligence doesn't know me from Adam, and the message I carry is one they already know—that the French people will fight."

Savage grimaced as sudden pain jabbed his leg. He clamped his jaw, closed his eyes, and rested a moment. His first officer, standing nearby, stepped in closer.

Savage opened his eyes and waved him away. "Perhaps your comrades saw more in you than you think," he told Jeremy. "Be that as it may, all our ships' captains in Saint-Nazaire were told to be on the lookout for you. The loop's been closed, and someone in intelligence knows about you, at least generally. Nothing's lost by your talking with them. You might throw some light on an aspect they hadn't perceived. All of intelligence is a guessing game anyway."

He put his hand to his chin and rubbed it while he thought. "What will you do with the boy? They'll probably take him from you at the port."

A fleeting memory of his last moments with Eva seared through Jeremy's mind again. "And put him in an orphanage? That can't happen. I promised I would protect him with my life." His retort was stronger than he intended. "Sorry, sir."

The captain chuckled and waved away the apology. "Your passion is what your friends saw. Your tenacity. By all rights, you should be dead by now."

He mulled a moment. "The authorities will want to put him with his own family, if they can be located."

"I'd want the same thing. But given wartime circumstances, he's just as likely to wallow in an institution until someone gets around to finding out where he belongs."

"And you'd do what with him?"

"My sister lives in London. She's a kindhearted soul who loves children. I know she'll take Timmy until his family is found. I'd do that myself, but I'm sure I'll be ordered back into the war."

Savage agreed and pursed his lips. "Perhaps I can help."

Startled, Jeremy asked, "How?"

The captain smiled as he put his thoughts together. "Maritime law grants a ship's captain a lot of authority on the high seas." He half-closed his eyes. "Especially in wartime." He called to his first officer, who stepped over sharply.

"Draft a document for my signature. It needs to identify one Jeremy Littlefield and Timothy—" He pivoted his attention to Jeremy. "Do we know his last name?"

"No, sir."

"All right. Put down 'Surname Unknown.' The document should say that the lieutenant is appointed on my authority to be Timmy's legal guardian. Do you understand?"

The first officer jotted the information on a notepad. "Anything else?"

"Throw in a sentence stating that the document is good until the boy's rightful family is found and accepts guardianship. Include a list of legal references long enough to befuddle the smuggest bureaucrat. In particular, quote maritime law in war. If you don't have enough relevant sources, throw some in even if they don't apply."

The officer smiled and departed, notes in hand.

Jeremy watched him go and then turned to the captain in amazement. "Is that legal? Will it hold up after we disembark?"

Savage chuckled and shrugged off another jab of pain. "Who knows? I've never seen a situation like this, and I don't know anyone who has. We can only try." His face took on a conspiratorial quality, one that he obviously enjoyed.

He beckoned Jeremy closer. "Listen, when the ship arrives, you'll wait here and leave with me. I'll push my weight around. They'll think twice about trying to stop me." He grinned. "Especially with this leg."

"Sir, I don't know what to say. Thank you."

"Taking care of that child is thanks enough. Now go and check his diaper or something. I need to get back to running this ship." He reached down to pick up his compass and checked the heading.

When they disembarked at Plymouth, Jeremy was not sure what reception he had expected for the soldiers on the Oronsay, but he thought the one they received was a far cry from what they deserved. Holding Timothy in his arms, he watched from the bridge.

No band played. No crowds of jubilant citizens cheered returning heroes. Instead, customs and immigration officials met the first ones a few yards from the ship.

From his vantage, Jeremy could not hear what took place, but actions plainly revealed a developing hostile situation. The soldiers had surged forward in a mass, their thrill obvious in the jauntiness of their strides. They had stopped short when the officials appeared in a line in front of them. Men pointed, shoving started, and a roar of angry voices arose that could be heard from the bridge. Items flew through the air, hurled at the port officials, and soldiers pushed past them through the gates into the town.

Jeremy's view shifted to the wrought iron fences on either side of the gates. Quiet crowds had gathered there, pressing their faces against the rails, staring into the port.

The first officer came to stand behind Jeremy. "That's a sad lot there," he said, indicating the people at the fence. "Every time we disembark with our soldiers coming home from France, they're there searching every face. They hold pictures up and beg to know if anyone has seen their loved ones." He shook his head sadly. "If you stood here long enough, you'd see some wonderful reunions, but I guarantee that when you leave, your heart will be wrenched out by the grief of those still wondering what happened to the ones still missing."

He took a deep breath. "It's time to go. The captain wants to take advantage of the uproar outside to get you through. He's waiting below in a wheelchair. He figures if you walk close to him, with the mood of the soldiers, you're not likely to be stopped." He handed Jeremy an envelope. "In here is the document you need, all nicely signed and sealed. I hope it does the trick."

They started off, then the first officer paused. "Oh, one thing. Let me have your sister's contact information. We'll call her so she can meet you at the London station."

Jeremy's head lolled back and forth with the clackety-clack of the train headed for London. As Captain Savage had anticipated, they had pushed past port authorities with no difficulty. One customs officer had peered intently at Jeremy and Timmy, but a stern look from the captain had been enough to dissuade him from further action.

They had passed through the gate where family members waited. Jeremy had witnessed the deep anguish of those still searching, and he had seen the joy of hoped-for reunions.

Once through the gate, Savage had bidden Jeremy and Timmy farewell. "My first officer will see to it that you get on the train. He's off getting food and things for Timmy. Best of luck." He had then motioned abruptly for his orderly to proceed pushing the wheelchair, and the two of them reversed course to return to the ship.

Now dozing on the train, a cry from Timmy awakened Jeremy. Exhausted from constant motion despite sleeping soundly on the ship, Jeremy guessed that the little boy must be famished and took out some biscuits the first officer had bought. Sure enough, the toddler grabbed for them and munched blithely.

Other soldiers had packed into the train compartment but left enough room for Jeremy to handle Timmy in relative comfort. Most fell asleep, bunched together, with no space between them. The corridor was just as packed, as was the whole train. Those by open windows sometimes reached out to feel the air and see the countryside. Despite weariness, whether awake or asleep, most wore weary smiles.

If they conversed, they spoke of the horrors they had endured or their disbelief at being on British soil. Jeremy heard snippets:

"That bullet struck so close it left a rip in my shirt."

"My mate went down, right next to me."

"A French family fed us. They let us stay in the barn."

"I thought I'd never make it on that ship."

"I was sure the bombers would get us."

Jeremy's ears perked up at one particular conversation.

"What was with those customs chaps?" one soldier asked. "I was far back in the crowd, so I couldn't hear. I started throwing things when everyone else did."

"I was right up front," another replied. "I saw and heard the whole mess. They wanted us to prove that we had a right to be in England. How're we supposed to do that when we came over to the Oronsay from the Lancastria in our skivvies or worse, not to mention what happened to us in France? And then customs treats us like we don't belong. You'd think our government wanted us to stay there."

Expressions of disgust and resentment followed. Then, the soldier who had made the latter comment turned and stared at Jeremy.

"Hey, you're the bloke who saved that baby from the Lancastria. The story spread all over the Oronsay. Is that him? How did you get to keep him?"

Jeremy smiled. "I'm his legal guardian."

Until then, he had not thought again about the envelope that the first officer had given him. Now he pulled it out of his pocket and opened it. Inside, he saw the folded document and was astonished to see several ten-pound sterling notes attached to it.

Another smaller scrap of paper was folded over them, containing a short message from Captain Savage.

You'll need this to get home and get Timmy settled.
Take good care of him. He represents everything we fight for.

Jeremy dropped his head against the back of his seat. His mouth fell open, and he exhaled in disbelief. His mind still whirling, he extracted the document. It was on Oronsay's ornate letterhead, and as the captain had instructed, it cited multiple legal references authorizing him to confer on Jeremy the legal guardianship of Timmy, signed Captain Norman Savage.

The train moved at a snail's pace with soldiers intermittently sleeping and conversing. Jeremy had to change Timmy's diaper several times. The soldiers smiled benevolently during those events and helped discard the waste out the window. Some cooed at Timmy and played with him. Much to Jeremy's surprise, Timmy played back, raising his hands to them and laughing as only a small child can. He lifted spirits.

Occasionally, he turned around to Jeremy and asked, "Mummy?" When he did, the men in the compartment became quiet, staring distantly, their faces reflecting the horrors they had seen.

After more hours than they could count, the train finally crawled into Paddington Station in London. Jeremy waited until the train was fairly empty before leaving. Then, holding Timmy with one arm, he made his way to a bench near the main street exit and waited.

An hour went by. Jeremy worried that he might have given the first officer the wrong number. Thankful for Captain Savage's kind thoughtfulness in providing him with funds, he found his way to a food vendor and bought a sandwich and other items to make sure that his change included coins. The rest of the money, he put in his pocket.

Timmy had become heavy. The exhausted child slept for the most part, but intermittently woke up, whimpered, and then fell back to sleep. Wearily, carrying the child, Jeremy made his way to a phone booth, dropped in the right coins, dialed the number, and waited. His call went unanswered.

29

Saint-Nazaire, France

Kenyon held back his dismay when Pierre showed him some of the stash of explosives he had stolen. He turned to Lance.

"We're not going to do much damage with that," he said. "Those are blasting caps. The fuel tank walls are thick and strong. With what Pierre has there, we might dent one of them, but we're not even going to create a leak, much less blow up a whole tank."

Lance interpreted.

"We have dynamite," Pierre said. "I need to know if that is the right kind of explosive and how much we need." His voice took on urgency. "The *Boches* will be here soon. We don't have much time."

"You'll need a plunger and wire too."

"Yes, we have it. All of it."

Lance's head swiveled back and forth as he translated between them.

"I can get everything you need," Pierre said. "The security men at the storage place are with us, but the engineer who oversees demolition projects is a Pétain supporter, meaning a Nazi sympathizer. We can't trust him. That's why we need you."

"If I could interject," Horton said. "You don't want that stuff falling into

Hun hands any more than you want them to get the fuel. I know enough to be dangerous, but as I understand dynamite, it's stable. So, why don't you get it all. Take all of it. Divide it up and store it in cellars, barns, and wherever the temperature and humidity conditions are good, and where you can keep it secure."

Pierre listened intently. His eyes glistened. "We are thinking alike, my friend," he responded, "but if we are going to blow any storage tanks, I think we have tonight, and maybe tomorrow night at the latest."

Lance translated the discussion for Kenyon who held up a cautioning hand. "Horton is partially right. Dynamite is nitroglycerine-based with additives and a special clay to make it less sensitive to shock. It becomes unstable with age. Your men can handle it safely as long as they are careful. Is it fairly new?"

Horton relayed the question, and Pierre assured him that the dynamite was new.

"We don't use it in combat operations anymore," Kenyon continued, "because flying bullets will ignite it. If there's a firefight while we're setting it..." He left the sentence unfinished.

Pierre's eyes flashed between Kenyon and Lance as he listened to the translation. "I understand," he said in English with a heavy accent.

"Then get that dynamite with all the other equipment," Kenyon said. "Take me to the staging area with photos and a sketch map of the tanks you want to blow. We'll plan from there." He looked up at the sun's position in the sky. "It's already mid-afternoon. How far are the oil tanks and how soon can you get the dynamite to me?"

Horton relayed Kenyon's thoughts and Pierre's response. "They have five trucks loaded. They'll send four to be stored and bring one to you at the staging area. You can take as much as you need, and they'll stockpile the rest. They can have that done in an hour. Pierre has a question, though. These tanks are filled with oil that is already refined for fuel. So, they will make a bigger bang. Correct?"

Kenyon grinned at Pierre and nodded. "You're exactly right."

Pierre beamed in satisfaction.

The operation could not have gone smoother. Fearful of the imminent invasion by German troops, many residents had already fled. Others stayed in their houses. When Pierre and five other companions along with Lance, Horton, and Kenyon drove to the fuel depot in a car and the small truck, the roads were clear. At the site, the security guards offered only token resistance, and otherwise faded into the night.

Twelve fuel tanks, each a hundred feet in diameter, clustered together in a section of the refinery. Two more larger tanks stood nearby. Kenyon surveyed them, comparing them against the photos and the sketch map Pierre had drawn. He beckoned Pierre. Lance joined them to translate. A bright half-moon hung in the sky.

"Listen carefully," Kenyon told Pierre through Lance. "Nobody's shooting at us tonight, so we're going to take our time and do it right. You won't want to do this under a bright moon when the Germans are here. Your men have their loads and equipment. Tell them to place them just like we practiced this evening, and then run the wires back to the gate. I'll check each one, and when everyone is safely away, I'll show you how to detonate. You'll do the honors."

Pierre nodded eagerly as he listened to Lance, his eyes flashing back to Kenyon. "We're ready," he said.

An hour later, the entire group met back at the vehicles. Kenyon guided Pierre through the steps to connect all the wires. The young resistance fighter pushed the plunger handle down.

The massive explosion rocked the ground and shot flames high in the sky. Frozen in fascination, the men stood watching the inferno until Kenyon grabbed Pierre.

"We must go," he yelled above the roar while gesturing vigorously. "The police! *Les gendarmes!*"

Pierre nodded and called to his comrades. Lance and Horton already waited in the car.

Returning to the staging area, the men were ebullient. They entered a barn on the property amid cheers and yells.

Kenyon quieted them. "Listen to me," he told them. "A triumph feels great, but this is going to be a long war. You can't celebrate out in the open. That could kill you."

Lance translated. The men stared, but nodded acceptance. Then they broke into quiet smiles and exchanged slaps on the back.

"What about tomorrow night?" Pierre asked.

"As my American cousins would say," Lance broke in, "that's a whole new ball game. The Germans will push harder to get here, and local authorities will watch for sabotage activity. Let's spend tonight planning and tomorrow rehearsing your approach and escape routes. Do you have more men?"

"Of course," Pierre responded, "and many more coming."

"Good. Then early in the morning, send some out to reconnoiter the route and set up signals in case the raid needs to be aborted. You don't want to go rolling around a curve and find a new German checkpoint. Do you have the next targets selected?"

"They're on the same compound, but farther down the river. The distance between tomorrow night's targets and the fuel-tanks we hit tonight is about a kilometer, and they are bigger."

"How many?"

"Twenty-eight."

Lance whistled. "You don't think small, do you, Pierre. You should bring more men. You need at least ten." He explained the discussion to Kenyon.

"They'll operate in two-man teams," Kenyon said. "Put each of the ones who were with us tonight with a new one. I won't have time to check all the wiring and placement, so they'll have to do it right the first time."

"We have to assume that we'll be opposed," Lance added, "but tomorrow night will still probably be our best opportunity for a long time."

After Lance had translated for Pierre and the conversation wound down, Kenyon turned to Lance with a thoughtful look. "May I speak to you privately?"

Surprised, Lance regarded him. Gone were the vacant eyes, replaced by intelligence, sharpness. A night of sleep, good food, and a mission had done wonders for him, and he seemed to have momentarily buried his grief for his lost friend.

The two ambled a distance away.

"I'll be blunt," Kenyon began. "I don't know what your plans are, but I'm staying here." His no-nonsense tone indicated that his decision was final.

"I see," was all Lance could think to say immediately. He spread his feet apart and faced Kenyon with folded arms. "Have you thought this through? Horton and I are headed out to Spain right after this next operation."

"I know, and that's why I'm telling you now." Kenyon's brow furrowed. "I came here to fight a war. The last order I received was, 'every man for himself.' That was from my commanding officer."

"Well, I can't order you—"

Kenyon broke into a laugh. "Of course, you can't order me. What's your rank?"

"Sergeant."

"And I made staff sergeant last week."

Taken aback, Lance blinked. "Why didn't you say so earlier?"

"Because I was in a daze, and you were doing such a good job. Look, our country, or at least our government, seems to have abandoned us—"

"I refuse to believe that," Lance interrupted, his voice rising. "Did you see all those ships in the harbor, all those boats going back and forth under fire to rescue us? The same was true at all those ports we bypassed on our way here. We might lack air power, but Churchill gave us what he had."

Kenyon accepted Lance's view reluctantly. "You make a good point, but right now, it's neither here nor there." He squinted through the half-light at the Frenchmen grouped together. "I'm just as likely to get killed trying to get out of the country, and I can do some good here. I can train these men to be effective. With the amount of dynamite they stole, we can wreak havoc on the Germans, and we can find more explosives." His expression fell and he looked away. "Maybe then..." His head dropped and his voice broke. After a moment's silence, he continued in a harder, anguished tone. "Maybe then my chum won't have died in vain."

Planning the operation for the following night proved much more difficult. The French police patrolled in force, inhibiting surveillance. News of the previous night's strike had spread through the countryside, but it had not been the only one. Other clusters of armed opposition had formed and carried out similar raids with varying results at the urging of the fledgling central resistance group in Marseille.

During the course of the day, anxious citizens had called in sightings of German formations moving south, securing supply lines, fuel depots, food storage units, railroads and stations, communications centers, and other key assets.

Pierre's intended target was located along the Loire River on the north side of the estuary. Surveillance had established that no German forces had yet been seen in close proximity, but police presence was heavy, prodded by the Pétain government.

"We can go by boat," Pierre said.

Lance and Horton kept a running translation between Kenyon and Pierre.

"The Loire River current is strong," Kenyon objected. "Going upstream on the return trip could be troublesome. Crossing the river would keep you exposed, and you might find a hostile reception on the other side."

"What if we go in by boat and out by car or truck?" Pierre asked. "We can have our partisans waiting on the far side of the depot to pick us up." He produced a sketch map.

"That looks like a long quay," Horton interjected. "And there's no cover or concealment." He studied the sketch. "What's the distance from the river to the first target? Is that an open field?"

"About half a kilometer," Pierre replied. "And yes, that's an open field."

"How far from the first target to the last one?"

Pierre exhaled. "Another kilometer. Our drivers can meet us on an east-west road past the most northern fuel storage tank." He pulled out a roadmap and spread it on a table, pointing out the features he had mentioned. "That road intersects with a dirt one cutting north across a farm. Several villages are near the other end." He pointed them out. "We can hide in the towns until things quiet down; or once past them, the country is wide open with farms."

Kenyon scrutinized both maps. He pointed to three storage tanks in a row near the bottom of the sketch. "We'll wire these." He gathered his thoughts and then pointed to a group of four tanks to the east. "We won't touch these."

As Pierre started to protest after Lance translated, Kenyon held up a hand. "Hear me out. They're too far from the rest and away from our direction of travel." He indicated a group of fourteen tanks in two lines running to the northeast. "As soon as we have these wired, we'll blow the first three. That will bring security to that location and keep them busy. Then we'll wire these last eight to the north and blow the group of fourteen. Once we're safely in our getaway cars, we'll blow the last ones. Does that make sense?"

Pierre looked dismayed as Lance translated and hovered his hand over the group of four fuel tanks that would be left untouched.

Kenyon read his thoughts. "Don't be greedy," he said with humor. "Blowing those is a needless risk." He straightened up. "This fight just became real for you. You're in it now. Some of your men could die tonight." He locked eyes with Pierre. "You could die. We've got to mitigate risk, get in, blow what we can, and get out. That's how you're going to be around for the next operation and the one after that..." He waved his hand in a circular motion to indicate a continuing string of missions.

"I understand," Pierre responded after Lance had translated. "We should go very early in the morning when the fishing boats head out to sea. We'll be among them, and then divert to the quay by the depot."

Kenyon considered that. "We need at least two hours of darkness."

"I'll get some of my fisherman friends to start their day early."

"You might need to overpower some guards and cut some phone lines."

"We can do that."

30

Two hours before dawn just over twenty-four hours later, a fishing boat belonging to a friend of Pierre's navigated into the current upstream of the fuel depot and held steady. Lance, Horton, Kenyon, Pierre, and the five partisan fighters of the first night's mission crouched behind the wheel-house with three additional men and two women. The vessel was soon joined by a fleet of fishing boats that took up positions around the first one, all of them with their running lights on. They started downstream.

Lance had observed the partisan group of men and women as they had rehearsed during the day, and he was pleased with what he saw. Several men, like Pierre, made their livelihoods by navigating the waves daily as fishermen. The others were farmers who regularly worked the fields. All were lean and physically fit; the women too. He didn't know how the latter related to the men, and he chose not to inquire. All wore looks of zeal tempered by a realization that the war had come to them.

Having women present and participating in combat operations made Lance uneasy. Doing so had never before occurred to him, and he did not like the idea. Pierre explained their role, and the women were eager to do their part, so Lance accepted the decision to include them without further objection. His uneasiness persisted, but he was gratified that one of them spoke broken English.

Her name was Elena. She was small and curvaceous, having been chosen partly for those attributes. Her blue eyes over a ready smile would brighten any room, but she was also strong and athletic, her blonde hair currently held in place against the wind by a tight scarf. The other woman enjoyed similar characteristics but did not speak English.

The moon had begun its ascent and cast its reflection on the dark water, further illuminating the boats. The fuel depot came into view, and for the first time, Lance saw that the huge tanks were set well back from the water's edge. A seawall of sorts, built from stacked stones, ran for several hundred feet along the bank. The field behind lay wide open with no cover or concealment all the way to the dimly lit storage tanks. Two guardhouses stood close to each end of the quay.

Lance's heart pounded harder.

When they had navigated a quarter of the bulkhead's length abreast of it, the boat's owner choked the engine. It sputtered. He pointed the vessel toward the quay and manipulated the choke enough to power it there. Then he doused the motor.

The men crouched on the dark deck below the sides of the boat. Elena jumped out. The fisherman tossed her a rope. She tied it off and started up the bank to a gravel utility road that paralleled the river.

A door slammed on one of the guardhouses. Peering out of the darkness, Lance watched as Elena spoke with a sentry. They headed for the guardhouse. The other woman jumped from the boat, climbed the bank, and started toward the opposite end.

Two of Pierre's men slid over the side of the boat onto the bank. Crouching low and staying close to the water, they moved swiftly in opposite directions.

Meanwhile, the women had entered the guardhouses at their respective ends of the service road. Pierre's two men reached positions just below them. After the women disappeared inside, the men crept up the short, shallow grade. Arriving in front of their separate doors simultaneously, they jerked them open. Inside, they were met with the same scene: the women bent over the unconscious guards who had succumbed to the effects of chloroform applied by charming women ostensibly seeking help.

Working together quickly, the men and women cut the phone wires and headed back to the fishing vessel. Even before they arrived, the rest of the men piled out and dispersed, carrying their equipment, which included an aggregate of fifty-six sticks of dynamite. As soon as they were offloaded, the fisherman headed out to sea.

Using maneuver tactics practiced the previous day, the group of thirteen, including the two women, moved swiftly across the field. Ten minutes later, they arrived at the bases of the first set of three tanks. While six fighters moved into the shadows on the opposite side to set their charges, the remainder continued north to the field of fourteen tanks.

They worked rapidly and methodically. When the first charges were finished, those teams uncoiled thin wires from spools as they headed toward the larger set of tanks. Arriving there, they ran the wires to the northwesternmost corner, carefully joined them together, and set them down. Then they moved out to affix dynamite sticks to the remaining tanks in the larger set.

When all wires had been run to the designated corner of the field and the teams were accounted for, Pierre, under Kenyon's watchful eye, attached the wires to the plunger.

"Make sure you give us ten minutes," Lance said.

Pierre nodded. Sweat poured down his face and he breathed heavily. While he and Kenyon prepared, Lance, Horton, and the other nine men continued on to the third field, unspooling wire as they went.

Next to Pierre, Kenyon watched the minutes tick away. When the time was reached, he signaled.

Kenyon checked the connections and gave a thumbs-up.

Pierre took a deep breath, turned the handle, and pushed. Without waiting to see the result, the two men took off at a full run to rejoin their comrades.

The explosion ripped the night. The ground shook. Flames leaped into the sky.

In the distance, sirens blared. Cars raced with bright headlights along a curved road that skirted diagonally along the depot's eastern edge, to the site of the three tanks now jetting flames high into the night sky.

Kenyon and Pierre arrived at the third field and sprinted to their designated targets. Now the full, undivided team worked on the eight remaining tanks, setting the charges and stringing wires to the northern boundary. Seven minutes later, they converged.

Once again, Pierre leaned over a plunger, twisted it, and thrust it down. Another explosion rocked the ground and lit up the sky. The full blast dwarfed the one of the night before, the roar of flames casting infernal heat in all directions and generating its own wind. The smell of burning fuel seared the nostrils and filled the lungs, leaving an acrid taste on the tongue.

Still running wire from the third field, the group continued north to a road crossing from east to west. They approached a stand of trees on a curve.

While Pierre connected the last wires to the plunger, three Citroens emerged from the trees, flashing dimmed parking lights. They pulled alongside the group.

Three men and Elena piled through the back door of the first car while the other woman took the front seat. The car took off, crunching gravel.

Two men entered the second vehicle, one of them taking the front, while Lance and Horton waited by the rear doors on either side of it. Two others crawled into the back of the third car.

One more time, with Kenyon standing next to him, Pierre pushed the handle down. One more time, the earth shook, and a cauldron turned night into day.

Lance and Horton dived into the waiting Citroen. Its tires spun as it raced away.

Kenyon and Pierre ran for the third automobile. No sooner had they closed the doors than it took off, taking a different route than either of the first two.

Lance turned in his seat, straining to see that the third car had escaped. The small rear window prevented him from seeing it. He faced forward again, leaned his head against the back of the seat, and exhaled.

Next to him, the partisan fighter stirred. Lance looked at him. The man smiled broadly and nodded. "*Merci,*" he said. "We could not have done this without you and your friends."

In the left rear seat, Horton grinned. "I'd say that went well."

The eastern horizon showed the first signs of dawn with a fine glimmering line of red stretching across the horizon. Then, golden fingers shot into the sky and spread as the little car turned toward a village. By the time they passed through it and headed west toward the staging area, full daylight revealed the early morning beauty of the countryside. The grass along the roadside gleamed with dew.

Whether because of fatigue or spent emotional energy, no one spoke, the driver content to wend his way through the curves in the road in silence. They came to a place where trees on both sides created a canopy, almost like a tunnel.

For a second, Lance's eyes closed, and in that flash of time, he saw his beloved Sark Island, with its wide, flat fields perched on steep cliffs rising three hundred and fifty feet above the sea. Images of his parents appeared so real, joined by those of Paul and Jeremy, and his sister, Claire. A lump formed in his throat with the realization that he missed them more than he had ever thought possible.

He felt the car rounding a curve and then slowing. He opened his eyes. The driver brought the vehicle to a full stop.

There, where the canopy broke not two hundred feet away, a German panzer blocked their path, its long, thin main gun pointing to one side. Immediately, dark uniformed soldiers emerged from behind it, rifles held waist high. They broke into a trot toward the Citroen.

The driver panicked. He ground the gears trying to get into reverse, but then he popped the clutch. The engine stalled.

The turret on the tank rotated. Its barrel dropped, lining up on the car. Its engine roared, and it rolled toward them.

On his side of the car, Lance threw the door open and dived into the road. The French partisan followed, as did the passenger in the front seat.

The tank fired a warning shot over the roof. The German foot soldiers stopped, lifted their rifles to their shoulders, and took aim.

Lying flat on his stomach in the road, Lance raised his hands in the air. The two partisans followed suit, and then all three struggled to their feet.

The Citroen driver, seeing their surrender, put both hands out the window. Then carefully, he opened the door and stepped out, leaving it wide open in front of him.

In the back seat, Horton watched. Seeing that the driver's side of the car was very near the edge of the road and a ditch, he ducked his head below the seat.

Counting on the German soldiers' attention being locked on Lance and the partisans, and their view being obstructed by the front door and the driver standing behind it, Horton opened his own door just enough to squeeze through to the ground. Then he rolled into the ditch and lay still.

The Germans motioned at the driver to join his comrades. One captor moved in front of Lance and took the service pistol from his belt. Then he stepped back and uttered those words no soldier wants to hear at the point of a gun. "For you, the war is over."

———————

Kenyon fidgeted. Three hours had gone by since they had blown the fuel-oil tanks, and he had heard nothing from Lance, Horton, or any of the men who had been with them. Elena did her best to translate reports coming in of sightings of German units entering the area, including several accounts relating instances of British soldiers having been captured and partisans executed.

Kenyon beckoned to Pierre. "We have to assume that our chaps were taken," he said through Elena. "They might be tortured. We have to relocate, now, and those other truckloads of dynamite have to be moved."

31

Dunkirk, France

Resplendent in his new gray uniform with silver epaulets, black collar with an SS symbol, and a diamond-shaped patch on the sleeve with the letters SD embroidered on it, *Hauptman* Bergmann strode into *Oberstleutnant* Meier's office unannounced, stood to attention, and clicked his heels. Immediately below his chin, he wore a black Iron Cross, signifying combat service, and under his arm, he carried his cap with a black band over its brim and a silver skull emblem.

Meier looked up from his desk with contained annoyance. "You've been gone nearly a week. I trust your trip to Berlin was productive."

"Very." Always haughty, Bergmann's demeanor had taken on an air of suppressed patronization. "You'll be happy to know that I'll add greater capability to your command." Unbidden, he sat in a chair in front of Meier's desk.

Meier returned to various documents he had been reading prior to Bergmann's entry. A pall hung over the room.

After several moments, Meier looked up again. "By all means, *Hauptman*, fill me in."

"I met with my direct-line commander. Obviously, I'm attached to your command, and will continue to take my immediate orders from you."

Meier scoffed lightly. "I am aware that you have an avenue to circumvent my authority. My admonition on how to handle our civilian population stands. Your way will get my men killed. What added capability do you bring?"

Bergmann locked cold eyes on Meier for a moment. Then he reached into his tunic, removed a document, and handed it to Meier. "My orders, sir."

Meier opened and scanned it. "I see," he said without emotion. "So, you are now an officer of the *Sicherheitsdienst*, the SD branch of the SS. Congratulations." His tone carried less enthusiasm than the word implied. "What does that mean?"

"Thank you. It means that I am attached to your staff in a special intelligence capacity. My mission is to find and weed out threats to the *führer* and our Nazi regime, both from internal and external sources."

An unctuous smile crossed his lips. Meier was unable to discern whether or not the expression suppressed malicious intent.

"I was fortunate that *Reichsführer* Himmler personally attended my induction ceremony and gave me those orders. He had been advised of the situation here with the rebels. He approved of my actions and toasted them at a reception. His last words to me were, 'Nip this in the bud. Do not fail me.' I assured him that I would not."

Meier's expression remained impassive, almost bored.

"Further down the page," Bergmann said, "you'll see mention of a mission to seek out and destroy rebel activity here, subject to your orders, of course."

"Of course," Meier said, peering through slitted eyes.

"When the occasion warrants, I can bring in SS units to support your command at almost a moment's notice. That will alleviate pressure on your soldiers to perform tasks outside of their normal duties."

Meier observed Bergmann as though seeing a new species of insect for the first time. "So then, please tell me, how do you intend to proceed?"

Bergmann smiled thinly. "I'm not satisfied that our military police are equipped to pursue criminal elements like the Boulier family. They're too busy with directing traffic and conducting regular police work to apply the needed priority and resources. The Kallsen situation is a case in point, and it is still an open investigation. I'll start there and take it where it leads." He stood. "If that's all, *Herr Oberstleutnant,* I will take my leave and get to work."

Meier's expression did not change. He leaned over his desk. "Stand at attention when you speak to me," he commanded in a low, firm voice.

"Sir?" Bergmann queried, surprised.

"I said, stand at attention," Meier ordered again, coming to his feet.

His face flushing crimson, Bergmann clicked his heels and stood straight, his arms locked at his sides.

"Now you listen to me, *Herr Hauptman,*" Meier growled. "You came late to this party, receiving your previous command when your predecessor fell on the last day of combat operations in this area. You haven't seen a single day of fighting; despite that you wear the Iron Cross.

"You have your authorities and I have mine, and until I receive orders through *Wehrmacht* channels that say otherwise, you will take my direction. That will start with proper military decorum. You don't breeze into my office unannounced, and you don't release yourself from the position of attention until I give you leave to do so. Finally, don't insinuate to me that you and your 'greater capability' have a free hand within my command. You will take orders from me and clear with me in advance any action you wish to initiate. Do I make myself clear?"

"Very clear, sir."

Meier fell silent, eyeing Bergmann. "Here are my initial orders. Draw up a plan on how you intend to proceed on your *special mission* and submit it to me within three days. Do you understand?"

"Yes, sir."

"Good. Now go see my executive officer to coordinate support for your operation. Dismissed."

Bergmann's cheeks and the back of his neck were aflame as he left Meier's office. He could not recall ever having received such a scathing rebuke. He had been so taken aback that he had forgotten to give the extended arm salute with the crisp Nazi farewell.

Like a man on a mission, he went straight to the adjutant's office. The major who filled the role was much more intimidated by his uniform than Meier had been and was only too pleased to allow the duty driver to take Bergmann to the *maison d'arrêt*.

There, Bergmann stalked into the administrator's office. Without offering a greeting, he presented himself in front of the official's desk and clicked his heels. On seeing him, the man rose nervously.

"Please update me on the status of the investigation into Kallsen's murder."

The administrator trembled slightly. "Nothing has changed," he said. "We have not established that the death was a homicide."

"What about the autopsy."

"Sir, your last instruction was that we should store the body and wait for your own medical examiner to perform that operation. We followed your orders, but no German coroner has appeared."

Bergmann grimaced, remembering that he had, indeed, given such an instruction. "Has anyone from our *feldgendarmerie* coordinated with you?"

The administrator shook his head.

Angrily, Bergmann returned to the battalion headquarters and strode into the adjutant's office. "If you will be so kind," he said perfunctorily, "I need to use your secure telephone line."

Two minutes later, he recognized the voice of his new higher SS commander's second-in-command. "Things are progressing well," he said. "If possible, I need a squad here in two days fully prepared to act." For justification, he cited his intent to seek out Kallsen's killer.

"I'll also need a medical examiner. The unit here is dragging its feet on establishing the cause of death for the Kallsen case." As an apparent afterthought, he added, "And could I possibly receive the full background dossier on *Oberstleutnant* Meier? I'd like to learn more about my local commander."

He listened to a read-back of his requests and hung up. Satisfied, he went to seek out the battalion executive officer. Passing by Meier's office once more, he sneered, nearly tripping over a woman on her knees mopping the floor.

"Get out of the way," he berated her, and then glanced at the door to Meier's office. "Weakling," he muttered. "You have less authority than you think."

In the wine cellar under the destroyed restaurant, Ferrand Boulier gathered his group. It had grown since the night he had sent his daughters south with Nicolas. The numbers alone presented a security risk as members entered and exited the building. Sooner or later, an enemy soldier would notice. Worse yet, Nazi sympathizers could already have infiltrated. Beyond that were common-sense safety concerns: too many people in too small a space with a single exit. *One hand grenade would cause a massacre.*

"It's been too quiet," he told his partisans. "We can't operate the way we have been. The security risk is too high. That said, we evacuated a lot of threatened people into the south of France, including family and friends, and British and French soldiers." He paused to let that sink in.

"We have to disperse into small teams where only the members of each group will know what their teammates are doing. I'm sure the phone lines will be cut soon, so we'll set up a system of couriers.

"The German army will not let Kallsen's death go easily. We just received word that Bergmann is back in Dunkirk, and now he wears the uniform of the SS. His first stop after checking in at his battalion headquarters was at the *maison d'arrêt*. He wanted to know about the progress on the investigation into Kallsen's death."

A murmur floated through the cellar.

Ferrand held up his hand. "We don't have much time. When you leave this cellar tonight, you won't come back. Right now, we need to form into three-person teams. Each team will designate a courier. Choose that role carefully. It is a dangerous one. He or she needs to blend in, not draw attention. Tell no other teams who that is, where you're going, or where you'll operate. I'll untangle any conflicts. We'll establish identity codes so that when you receive a message by courier, you'll know it's genuine."

"We'll have a lot of teams," someone called out. "Can you handle them all?"

"Good point," Ferrand replied. "We'll establish a communications structure. Everyone should remember the founding principles of our French Revolution: *'Liberty, Equality, Fraternity.'* We're all equals, and we don't have time for petty jealousies. Any hierarchies will result from operational needs whether that be a skill, experience, proximity, or some other mission imperative."

Men and women had already begun discussing among themselves. Ferrand held up his hand and called for quiet.

"We have two more things to resolve," he said. The murmuring died down. "Bergmann will take retribution in my neighborhood again," Ferrand continued. "I'm sure of it. We have to get those people out."

Total silence descended on the room. "That neighborhood is guarded," someone called out. "No one is allowed in or out."

"And that is exactly the type of situation we are coming together to handle," Ferrand replied. "We won't leave our friends and families to the horror of the Nazis without a fight."

"What if the residents won't come out?"

"Then whatever happens to them rests on their shoulders. We'll do our best, and that's all we can do." He let the moment linger as people exchanged comments.

"I'm looking for volunteers," he said, and the room quieted down again. He raised his hand. "And if you volunteer, I will be there with you."

A clamor broke out in the room as people celebrated his gesture, but Ferrand quickly hushed them. "We'll establish a secure means of choosing and notifying the men and women who will participate. Right now, we have one more matter to discuss."

The group trained expectant eyes on him. "Monsters like Bergmann will use every means possible to get information. We already saw that. Our brothers and sisters, mothers and fathers, sons and daughters will be put in compromising positions, and then coerced to collaborate with the enemy. When that happens, we have to exert equal pressure to counter it."

"What should we do?" a voice called from the back of the room.

Ferrand looked around sadly at the faces before him. He rubbed the back of his neck, his reluctance to speak on the subject evident.

"We are at war, and our actions must acknowledge that always. When we find collaborators, we'll show no mercy. We will make public examples of them by slicing their throats, men or women, and leaving their bloody bodies where they can be seen. We'll hang signs around their necks written in their own blood that say, *'Collaborateur!'*"

In the early hours of the next morning, Ferrand was alone in a dark room well within the burned-out wreckage of an apartment complex deep within the ruins of the city. The area had been struck by many bombs but nevertheless contained livable dwellings with beds, left-behind food, and in some instances, running water. He stood in front of a mirror. Pulling a lighter from his pocket, he flicked it, then held it close to his face and peered at his reflection in a mirror.

A gaunt face stared back at him, with deepened lines, eyes sunk in dark sockets, hair and beard uncut and scraggly. "What have I become?" he whispered.

The internal struggle that had brought him to the point of advocating for the summary execution of his own countrymen in the event of collaboration was one that had waged over the past week. He understood that the policy might one day require him to slice the throat of someone close to him, but he saw no other way to counterbalance the retribution that the German SS already meted out at the *maison d'arrêt*. His decision had been precipitated by the reappearance of *Hauptman* Bergmann. The lady who mopped the floors in the headquarters had given warning.

He stepped back from the mirror where he could see the shadow of his full self, his old body bent with age. His thoughts went to Amélie and Chantal, to Claude, and Nicolas. *Are they safe?* His heart fairly burst at the thought of his daughters, so far from home.

Ferrand regarded his dark reflection in the mirror once more. "What I am," he muttered, answering his own question of moments before, "is a man who knows the ravages of war and will fight the devil with no holds barred to save my daughters, my family, and my country."

32

One day earlier, June 19
London, England

Major Crockatt arrived at work early, as was his habit. His secretary, Vivian Brown, sprang up to meet him and intercepted him before he could enter his office.

"There's a man sleeping in your office. I put him on your cot—"

"Why is he here?" He started to shove past Vivian, but she blocked his way.

"He came in early this morning, a soldier, and he looks wretched; like he'd been through hell's trenches before coming here. I found him at the entrance. He asked anyone passing by how to get to MI-9. And sir." She hesitated. "He has a little boy—a toddler."

"A what? How did he get in here? Who let him pass through security?"

Vivian handed him an envelope. "This might explain things. After I read the document inside and the attached note, I vouched for him and brought him up."

Slightly annoyed, Crockatt took the document and scanned it, his eyes pausing over "Littlefield" and "Captain Norman Savage." He looked up. "Littlefield. Is that—"

"I think so, sir. He has three ribbons on one wrist. They're faded, but aside from looking like death, he's a dead ringer for MI-6's Lieutenant Paul Littlefield. I took the liberty of calling down to Plymouth and managed to get Captain Savage on the line."

She told him Jeremy's story as related to her by the ship's captain. "This Lieutenant Littlefield arrived at Paddington late last night, and he couldn't find his sister. I take it he went by her house in a taxi, but it was empty, and he didn't know how to reach his brother, so he asked the driver to take him to the MI-9 headquarters."

"So much for secrecy," Crockatt muttered. Then he rubbed his chin. "Poor sap," he mused. "Amazing what he's been through and that our thrown-together identity scheme actually worked. Call his brother. Get him over here, but don't tell him why." A perplexed expression crossed his face. "I didn't know about the sister. Do we know her name?"

"Claire."

"See if you can track her down as well."

He stepped around the secretary. "Don't worry. I'm just going to have a peek. I won't wake him." He cracked the door open and peered inside.

Jeremy slept soundly on the cot, curled up and facing the wall. Sleeping next to him and held against his chest was the little boy, as Vivian had said.

Crockatt gently pushed the door closed.

Paul Littlefield hurried to Crockatt's office. He had taken Vivian's call and tried to get her to divulge the subject, but she insisted that the major had instructed her otherwise and that the matter was urgent.

Making his way through the corridors, he hoped against hope to learn something about the status of his brothers but knew that the likelihood was slim. *He probably wants to press me about the transfer again.*

When he entered, he was surprised to find the major stretched uncomfortably on a wooden chair in front of the secretary's desk with his arms crossed. Vivian's eyes shone with excitement. As Paul looked from one to the other, he noticed that even the major seemed to struggle to contain a smile.

"You wished to see me, sir?"

Crockatt stood and placed his hands on his hips sternly. "Have you given any more thought to my offer?"

Bewildered, Paul just stood there. "Sir, I—"

Vivian giggled and the major chuckled. "I can't do this," he told her. Then he faced Paul seriously. "We have news for you, Lieutenant, of the mixed variety. You must prepare yourself."

"Is it one of my brothers?" Paul breathed. "Which one?"

"Jeremy," Vivian burst out while Crockatt frowned at her. She pointed at the office door. "He's in there."

At first speechless, Paul whirled around to look at where Vivian pointed. "In there?"

"He's asleep," Crockatt said. "You can look in on him, if you like, but I'd let him be a while longer. He's been through several ordeals."

Together they crept to the door and opened it slightly. Paul peered inside. He studied the figure lying on the cot in the half-light, then drew back and closed the door.

"Is that a baby with him?"

Crockatt nodded and gestured toward a chair. "A little boy. Have a seat. Vivian will tell you his story as she heard it."

Paul listened in awe.

When Vivian had finished, Crockatt showed him the document Captain Savage had signed.

Paul inhaled and let his breath out slowly. "Unbelievable." He leaned his head back. "Unbelievable," he repeated.

"We tried to find your sister, Claire, so we could let her know as well."

Paul swung around, startled, and checked to see if anyone else was listening. "She's at Bletchley Park, sir."

Crockatt stared a moment and then tossed his head back. "I should have guessed."

"She wanted to do something more active in the war effort, but I convinced her that having two sons already in the combat areas, her going into danger might be enough to push our parents over the edge. She agreed but wasn't happy about it. I'm hoping this job she has out there will be enough of a challenge for her."

"Well," Crockatt said. "Let's see if we can get the three of you together."

"Thank you for bringing me in, sir," Paul said. "At risk of sounding ungrateful or opportunistic—"

"I know what you're going to ask." Crockatt stood and paced. "We have no news of your other brother."

33

Jeremy had been in a half-sleep, dozing in and out of consciousness while his aching body protested against every toss and turn. He came to with a start and whirled around on the bed. "Timmy," he called.

From across the room, a female voice replied reassuringly, "I have him."

Jeremy looked in that direction through bleary eyes. Recognizing his sister, he dropped back into the sheets and instantly dozed off again. When he reawakened a few minutes later, she stood over him, smiling. She held little Timmy asleep in her arms.

His mind still numb, Jeremy sat up and pivoted awkwardly to sit on the edge of the bed. Claire sat down next to him. He took Timmy and held him close, recalling as though through a fog that he had woken up in a strange office with Paul and his sister there. He remembered nothing past that.

"I thought I had dreamed you," he murmured to Claire.

"No, I'm real," she said, wrapping an arm over his shoulder and brushing a shock of hair from his face.

"Where are we?" His voice sounded distant as he looked about the room, the furnishings a blur.

"You're at a place called Bletchley Park. We moved you here by gurney and ambulance, and a staff doctor checked you out." She dropped her hand to his shoulder and squeezed him. "You've lost a lot of weight, and I gather you've been through one ordeal after another. You'll need some time to recover."

Timmy stirred.

"He'll be hungry," Claire said. "I have a bottle ready for him. He's a little old for it, but in his condition, he might just take it." She handed it to Jeremy, who slipped the nipple between Timmy's lips just as the tiny boy began to cry. Timmy quieted, and his eyes fluttered and closed as he drank.

Jeremy circled his free arm around his sister's waist and leaned into her. "Was Paul there too, or did I imagine that?" His voice sounded low and hoarse.

"You didn't dream it. He's just outside. I'll fetch him." She left and returned with Paul, who crossed the room and stood in front of Jeremy. Wordlessly, the two men regarded each other, and then Paul hugged Jeremy around the shoulders.

"I'm so glad you're alive," he whispered. "We worried that we had lost you."

After an extended moment, Jeremy pulled away. "Any news of Lance?"

Paul shook his head.

"How are Mum and Dad?"

"The last we heard, they were doing well," Claire interjected, "but we haven't been able to reach them in several days."

"What is this place?" Jeremy asked around mid-afternoon as the three siblings took Timmy for a stroll about the stately gardens and ponds of the Bletchley Park estate.

The front of the mansion looked like a row of six two-story town homes, each with its own roofline and colorful façade. Wide lawns and meticulous gardens surrounded the building.

"The historical version is that this estate was built in 1883 for a prominent financier and politician of the time, Sir Herbert Leon," Claire said.

"And what are those?" Jeremy pointed to a row of similar squat, single-story buildings on both sides of the manor. Most were built of brick halfway up their exteriors, with horizontal wooden siding interrupted by windows in the upper parts of their structures, and steepled roofs. Others looked like they had been thrown in as an afterthought. Despite being clean and orderly, their presence struck a discordant note on the otherwise elegant estate.

"We call those buildings 'huts,' but I'm not allowed to say much about them or what we do here," Claire said apologetically. "That's a standard rule, which my boss emphasized before agreeing to let us bring you and Timmy to stay out here."

"Claire's work is very hush-hush," Paul interjected. "I'm not allowed to know anything about it either."

"My job is not any more hush-hush than yours," Claire responded, bumping against Paul playfully.

"Why were we brought here, in particular?" Jeremy asked.

"That was Major Crockatt's idea," Claire replied. "I work here. Anyone can see that you need time to recuperate, and Timmy needs constant care, like any child that age. At my flat in town, that would be impossible. London's a good hour from here by train.

"The apartment we're staying in was not being used, and since it opens onto the gardens, there's plenty of room for Timmy to play outdoors. I hired a nanny this morning to take care of him while I'm working, and I'll be close by." She laughed. "My co-workers are mainly women, and they're all excited to help out. Timmy won't lack for attention. Your job now is to get back your strength."

Jeremy smiled, his eyes and body feeling heavy. "We have to find Timmy's family. He belongs with them."

"Don't you worry about that," Paul said. "Major Crockatt's secretary, Vivian, is checking with the Foreign Office. They'll have the list of embassy staff. Like all the other departments, they're still trying to figure out who made it back to shore in France, who got on the ships, and who..." He caught himself, leaving the remainder of the thought unsaid.

Jeremy nodded without replying.

They wended their way back to the apartment. While Claire put Timmy down for a nap in a back bedroom and Paul made tea, Jeremy sat on a divan looking across the landscape through the massive window. Eventually, he dozed, and the cycle of memories that had plagued him while evading across France started up again, now in dreams.

He woke up in a sweat and saw Amélie, her soft smile, her musical voice, just beyond his reach. He stretched his fingers out to touch her, and then realized dimly that he was still asleep, still dreaming.

He came fully awake, breathing hard, perspiration streaming down his face.

Paul stood in front of him, bearing a tray. He stared down at Jeremy. "Are you all right? You were having a nightmare."

Jeremy closed his eyes, his face pained. "I'm tired." He sat up, blinking to clear his vision. "I'll have some of that good English tea," he said with forced enthusiasm.

Claire joined them. "Timmy should sleep for a while."

After a time, Jeremy asked, "Who is Major Crockatt?"

Paul set his cup down. "He's the head of MI-9. That was his office you went to in the middle of the night and his cot you slept on. How did you know to go there?"

In broken sentences expressing disorganized thoughts, Jeremy told them, and spoke of Jacques and Nicolas, and the trek from Dunkirk; of Amélie and her sister and father. "She plays the piano, you know," he told Claire. "She plays Chopin like you do."

His siblings listened quietly, sometimes with moist eyes, sometimes aghast at the atrocities he described, and then angered at the abandonment of the soldiers in France. At one point, Claire crossed to the divan and sat close to him, holding onto his arm as the story unfolded.

"It's not over," Jeremy rasped when he had finished, his eyes sunken. "I have to go back."

Claire leaped up from her seat. "What? You can't possibly go back." Her eyes blazed. "You've done your part. You've done more than your share." She spun around to Paul. "Tell him. Tell him he's not going anywhere."

Paul stared at Jeremy, stunned. "After everything you went through to get here, you want to go back?"

Jeremy sat still, his eyes closed, breathing deeply. "Strangers risked their lives for me," he whispered at last, his lips trembling. "I saw horrors that should never have happened. Hitler's war machine is ruthless. It's wanton. It enjoys killing and kills anything."

Claire sat back down and leaned into him with one arm around his back. Paul remained quiet, speechless.

"They need our help. The French government surrendered. The people didn't. And if we don't fight, France and all the countries the Nazis occupy will be raped and ravaged, and then that monstrosity will come here."

He leaned against the divan and rested his head on its back, his eyes closed. Suddenly, he sat forward. "What happens to the Channel Islands when Germany occupies France?"

Neither Paul nor Claire uttered a word.

"What will happen to them?" Jeremy demanded. As realization dawned, he stood abruptly, red-faced with anger. "We're not going to defend them, are we?"

From the back of the house, Timmy wailed. Claire rushed to quiet him.

Jeremy sat back down and leaned toward Paul. "Tell me. What is being done for the islands? Mum and Dad are there."

"The Channel Islands were declared an open territory a week ago." Paul spoke slowly, reluctantly.

"Left unprotected?"

Paul nodded. "They've been de-militarized, all our forces moved out. Somehow, the Foreign Office failed to inform Berlin. The Germans bombed Jersey and Guernsey two days after the decision was made. There's a big row about that at the highest levels."

Jeremy's lips curled with disgust.

Paul continued. "Our government sent ships there to evacuate anyone who wanted to be taken off the islands."

"And have they come?"

Paul shook his head. "If by 'they,' you mean the good citizens of the Channel Islands, seventeen thousand were evacuated from Guernsey in a single week. If you mean our parents, I haven't spoken to them in nearly a fortnight. I couldn't get through on the phone, and by now, those lines have probably been cut. Mum's and Dad's names have not been listed among the arrivals. I check daily."

Jeremy took a deep breath and exhaled. "And we know nothing of Lance."

"I've tried tracking his unit. It was supposed to deploy to the north of France to reinforce there, but that was before the German blitz through Belgium.

"We've had no news of his unit. I'm sure he was not evacuated at Dunkirk, or we would have heard. Reports are coming in from partisan groups about British soldiers making their way across France to other ports, like you did, but so far, he's not among those listed as arriving here. The reports also say that some of our men are making their way overland to Spain in hopes of getting home from there, but so far none have arrived, at least none that we know of."

While he spoke, Jeremy toyed with the three faded ribbons still tied around his wrist. Paul noticed.

"Do you mind if I ask what those are?" Paul asked. "We started to cut them off last night when we cleaned you up, but you wouldn't let us."

Jeremy stopped toying with the ribbons and stared at them as if just discovering them. "These," he said at last, "might have made the difference between whether I lived or died. They were the recognition signal that put me near the bow of the Lancastria, where I had a greater chance of survival. They got me through to Major Crockatt's office." He stood and walked to the window, peering out at waning rays of sunlight as dusk approached.

"Jacques tied them there," he said. "I owe him my life, as I do Nicolas, Claude, Ferrand, Chantal, and Amélie. So many. They are my family now too, as close to me as you and Claire and—" His voice trembled. "And Lance."

He remained silent a moment, and then continued. "I wasn't the only one. You'll hear stories of French families helping our soldiers by the thousands." He breathed deeply and turned toward Claire, who had just re-entered the room. "Don't you see?" He spoke in a hoarse whisper. "We must help them."

"And we will," Paul said. Rising from his seat, he crossed to Jeremy and grasped his shoulder. "Until you have proper clearances, I can't tell you more, but I will tell you that England is not defeated, and we will not desert our French brothers and sisters."

Claire also crossed the room and embraced him. "I'm so glad you've come safely back to us."

"When can I speak again with this Major Crockatt?" Jeremy asked. "I have a message to deliver."

"He wants to debrief you," Paul replied. "He's already notified your unit of your whereabouts, and you've been transferred to his organization..."

Jeremy's eyes flashed in surprise.

"...at least temporarily," Paul continued. "It was part of an arrangement he made with your headquarters so you could be with Timmy. He wants you to rest up for a day or two, and to be interviewed by a psychologist."

Again, Jeremy reacted.

"Sorry," Paul said, hands extended in a placating gesture. "Standard procedure, to make sure you don't have underlying anger or some other disorder that could endanger yourself or others."

"I'm solid."

"I'm sure you are. It's routine."

"And what of Mum and Dad?"

"I put in calls to them. I'll keep attempting to call and checking the arrivals from the islands. The Red Cross is putting the mechanism in place to send messages back and forth. Hopefully, that'll be up soon."

34

Jeremy studied Major Crockatt, who in return, studied him. They sat in the front room of the apartment at Bletchley Park, awaiting the arrival of one Lord Hankey. Paul and Claire were both at their jobs, and the nanny played with Timmy on the front lawn.

Jeremy felt his physical strength and mental acuity returning, but his muscles still ached, and he found putting coherent thoughts together difficult. A tray with a pot of fresh tea was on a low table in front of the divan, and the two men held cups of the steaming brew and sipped it.

"Sir, if you don't mind," Jeremy ventured, "I'm not accustomed to such high-level attention. I really know nothing about your organization other than I was directed to seek out MI-9, and I've never heard of this Lord Hankey, although with that title, he must be something exalted. What's his interest? For that matter, what is yours? You both came out a distance from London to see me on this grand estate I'm allowed to know nothing about, and I know less about the purpose of your visits." He smiled. "That said, I'm grateful that you took in Timmy and me. Thank you."

Crockatt smiled. "You can thank the resourcefulness of your French friend in Saint-Nazaire. He stayed on his shortwave radio until he convinced a loyal citizen to seek out a contact inside British intelligence. Fortunately, my group is new and small enough that we could give the matter some attention. Working out and communicating the identification signal with the ribbons was a little dicey, but, well, here you are." A look of curiosity crossed his face. "I'm a little puzzled, though. With all the thousands of troops to be rescued, why did *you* receive such special attention?"

"Luck of the draw, I suppose." Jeremy sighed. "Nothing more than that. This wonderful French family in Dunkirk helped me. A nephew of the father took me across France, and Jacques, the shortwave operator, was his contact. They had already set up a network, and I was fortunate enough to be their first customer."

"I get that," Crockatt said, "but I sense there is more to it. This man, Jacques, has been in touch since the Lancastria went down. He wants news of your safe arrival, and he insists that you have a message for me. Your brother told me the same thing.

"By the way, Jacques moved on from Saint-Nazaire to join a group in Marseille that had already been in contact with MI-6. We haven't told them your status."

Jeremy rose and went to stand by the window looking out to where Timmy played. "I'll tell you honestly. I'm a poor emissary. The message is simply that the Free French are ready to fight. You already know that from de Gaulle's speech. My brother told me about the radio address."

Crockatt poured more tea into his cup and offered to refresh Jeremy's, who declined with a shake of his head. "If you don't mind," the major said, "when Lord Hankey arrives, I'd like you to go over your story again from beginning to end, starting with your escape at Dunkirk. Maybe we can figure things out from there."

"I can do that," Jeremy agreed, "but who is this lord? I know nothing about him."

Crockatt's brow furrowed while a bemused smile crossed his face. "We're competitors, of sorts," he said. "My group is organizing to build networks across Europe to help downed pilots, separated soldiers, and escaped POWs evade and escape like you've just done, and get them home to safety.

"Lord Hankey has quite a bio. His full name is Maurice Pascal Alers Hankey, and he's also known as 1st Baron Hankey. He's an old acquaintance of Churchill's, who convinced him to take this new post. You must have heard of him. He's been the Secretary to the Imperial Defense Committee for the past twenty-three years and was simultaneously Secretary of the War Council. In fact, he's the man who sold the idea of a tracked armored vehicle to Churchill back in 1914.

"His new unit is still in the incubator. It hasn't been launched yet, but it's a Churchill brainchild, at least partially. It's being formed by combining the functions of three existing agencies, so it will gain a lot of high-level support, but it already has detractors. I don't think MI-6 likes it much because, like MI-9, they'll be trying to recruit and use the same assets.

"I expect it'll go active next month. It's to be called the Special Operations Executive, or SOE, and its purpose is to set up networks across Europe like ours, but for the express purpose of carrying out acts of sabotage. Essentially, it aims to open up a new front behind enemy lines by training and supporting local partisans."

Jeremy had listened intently without interruption. Now he interjected, "That's a great idea. The partisans will welcome it. And what an incredible career Hankey has had. But how did he learn about me, and what does he want?"

Crockatt chuckled. "You stood at the door of intelligence headquarters with a crying toddler in your arms in the middle of the night asking anyone who went by how to get to MI-9. That drew attention, and I'm positive that the Oronsay's Captain Savage told your story at high levels. Word got around. Both of us want to interview anyone who escaped France after Dunkirk. We want to know how it was done, what contacts were made, and if they can be renewed." He hesitated. "I'm sure, like me, he might want to recruit you. We'll be going after as many chaps as we can who show promise."

"Sir, I appreciate that, but I have to tell you that I'm not a trained combatant or intelligence operator. I'm a civil engineer. I want to go back, certainly, to help the people who helped me, but for your purposes, I probably know only enough to get in the way."

As he spoke, they watched a man walk across the gardens from one of the huts.

"That's Lord Hankey now," Crockatt said. "Before he gets here, let me say two things very quickly. Your tenacity at Dunkirk, your experiences in crossing France, and your courage and perseverance in rescuing that child are remarkable, well above the norm. Coupled with your language ability in French, well, you're just what MI-9 is looking for, and we'll train you for whatever else you need to know."

Lord Hankey drew closer on the front sidewalk. He stopped to watch Timmy a moment and patted the child on the head. Timmy looked up at him with a big smile.

"He's not a bad sort," Crockatt said, watching Hankey. "The other thing I want to say, and you should know, is that your brother, Paul, was a fiend for seeking out information about you and Lance. He pestered me almost daily, and I'm sure he did the same thing with other sections. I've been trying, unsuccessfully so far, to recruit him. You carry the same characteristic of perseverance. Must be a family thing. But you can be very proud of his dedication to you and Lance, and your family."

Jeremy coughed to relieve his constricting throat. "Thank you, sir, for telling me." In spite of himself, his voice cracked.

Lord Hankey arrived at the door. Jeremy met him there and welcomed him inside. He was a thin man, slightly below medium height, in his sixties with a high forehead and a heavy mustache.

After niceties, the three men sat down in the front room. The questions inevitably led to a request for Jeremy to recount his experiences, beginning with how he found himself in combat north of Dunkirk to how he ended up in Crockatt's office. Occasionally, they interrupted to ask for more detail or seek clarification.

Halfway through, the nanny brought Timmy inside. When the little boy came through the front door and spotted Jeremy, his eyes lit up, and he ran over with uplifted arms. Then, he stopped and looked around.

"Mummy?" he said, eyes wide and questioning, his palms turned outward. "Mummy?"

Jeremy picked him up and held him close, hiding his own misted eyes. Then the nanny took the child for his bath before supper. For a time, the room remained uncomfortably quiet. Hankey stifled a cough and looked away, while Crockatt stared straight ahead.

After Timmy and the nanny had disappeared into the back rooms, Jeremy finished telling his story and responded to questions. Then,

Hankey said, "I suppose the major told you his interest, which is the same as mine."

"He did," Jeremy responded, "and I'm a little overwhelmed by it all. I don't see myself as anything special; I'm a common chap trying to survive in an unexpected situation. That said..." His eyes alternated between Hankey and Crockatt. "I will tell you plainly that I've fought tremendous anger in the last two days. Paul and I discussed and even argued this morning about what happened. That was before and after the psychologist was here. I suppose I passed the assessment, or neither of you would be here now. Is that right?"

They stared at him blankly and nodded in unison.

"I've come to grips with why we were abandoned at Dunkirk," he said, and watched the two men closely. They sat stone-faced. "We were deserted, and the whys didn't make the ordeals any easier." He looked away. "Maybe if we had been allowed the opportunity to volunteer, that would have made a difference. I imagine that to a man, we thought we'd be rescued the same way those who got out at Dunkirk were evacuated. Instead, we found ourselves alone, every man for himself. Our reception back on English sovereign soil wasn't very pleasant either."

The silence in the room was thick, the air suddenly stifling. Hankey started to speak.

Jeremy held up a hand. "Bear with me, sir. I'm not bitter, but I need to get this off my chest to someone representing high authority, and you, Lord Hankey, are about as high as I'm likely to get."

"Go on," Hankey said, without expression.

"I understand why our prime minister made the decisions he did." Jeremy tossed his head with a tinge of disgust. "God knows if our parliament had heeded his warnings years ago, we might not be in this mess." He exhaled. "But they didn't."

"I must interrupt," Lord Hankey said. He stood, placed his hands on his hips, and turned to face Jeremy. "I cannot let your last statement go unchallenged." He took a deep breath while Jeremy drew back, startled.

"I agree that Mr. Churchill made the right call at Dunkirk, and that more should have been done to improve our bomber forces, but what you do not know is the extent to which his predecessor built up our defensive capability. Mr. Chamberlain needed time, and he bought it at Munich. When the war comes to our shores, which will happen within days, Hitler will find more fight than he bargained for, thanks to preparations the public knows little about. It could not have been done without active cooperation between Sir Neville and the parliament. Without them, we would not have had our radar screen, our fighter squadrons, or--" He interrupted himself. "I'll leave it at that."

While Hankey spoke, images of Neville Chamberlain flashed through Jeremy's mind. Most prominent was a filmed news clip of the previous prime minister arriving home after a meeting with Hitler in Munich, waving a piece of paper in the air and proclaiming that he had secured "peace in our time."

"I don't know how to respond to that, sir," was all that Jeremy could think to say.

"No matter now." Hankey waved a hand and took his seat. "Always keep in mind that things are not always the way they seem. Carry on."

Jeremy cleared his throat and shifted forward on the sofa. "I know our air forces are spread thin. On that awful day at Saint-Nazaire, I saw the large numbers of ships that were mustered, and I appreciate that we convoyed home under the protection of Royal Navy destroyers and submarines. That tells me that Mr. Churchill gave us what he had, and there's no argument that getting the army back to protect our homeland was an imperative." He shook his head with a look of awe. "I don't even like to think of the moral dilemmas the prime minister faces every waking hour of every day."

He sat quietly to the extent that his two listeners thought he might have finished, but then he continued speaking low, his voice cracking with emotion. "I'll tell you frankly that I'm incensed that my home, the English Channel Islands, where my parents still live, was also abandoned, but I even understand that we just don't have the resources now to defend there. We're in a long war.

"So, I'm fine with the decisions the PM made. But we left tens of thousands of our mates in France, including my brother. Those of us lucky enough to get home were helped by thousands of strangers who risked their lives for us. We owe them a debt we can never repay, and I'm not sympathetic to the notion that France let itself down. Its government surrendered. The people didn't. They are ready to fight, and I'm ready to fight shoulder-to-shoulder with them."

Crockatt's staid expression broke slightly into his ethereal, distant smile. He started to speak. Once again, Jeremy raised a hand.

"Hear me out, please. I'm almost done. I want to be where I can do the most good, and I'm partial to the family that saved me at Dunkirk. I don't want to be an analyst sitting behind a desk. If I must be in this fight, I want to be in the fight."

The two men sat up straight. "Your friends in Saint-Nazaire sent the right messenger," Crockatt said.

"Now comes determining where to place you," Hankey joined in. "I'll explain your options simply. MI-5 does domestic counterintelligence. Probably not your cup of tea."

Jeremy agreed.

"MI-6 is the big deal in British intelligence. They run foreign agents. That's your classic spy scenario. You'd recruit and manage spies in other countries. I'm sure that section would love to have you."

He gestured toward Crockatt. "The major here is standing up a new crew—" He interrupted himself with another wave of his hand. "He's probably explained to you what his unit does, running escape lines, etcetera.

"My new section, SOE, is all about blowing up things behind enemy lines. The way that MI-9 and SOE operate will be roughly the same with a different emphasis. As you've probably already gathered, the tension between us is that we're likely to be trying to use the same assets more often than we'd like to. The same goes for MI-6."

He looked at his watch, stood abruptly, and handed Jeremy a business card. "I've taken up enough of your time. Think it over and let me hear from you. My number is on that card." Major Crockatt also excused himself, and the two men left together.

Late that night, Jeremy lay in his bed, feeling a modicum of peace for the first time in weeks, resulting from a sense of having some control over his future. Then he dozed off, and the cycle of recollections began. This time, he took his mind deliberately to memories of Amélie. He lingered over visions of her face, her eyes, her lips. He listened to the echo of her voice in the recesses of his mind, and her laughter. He imagined taking her in his arms and kissing those wondrous lips.

Uneasiness suddenly gripped him as he remembered that Nicolas had said Amélie's family had fled their home. *Where is she? Is she safe? Her family?*

He sat up in the dark. *They're still in danger. I have to get there.*

Almost immediately, a sense of guilt pervaded, of deserting his own mother and father, and Lance. He struggled with the notion that he should be doing something to help them. *Help those you can when you can,* he admonished himself.

35

Marseille, France

"You're going to be treated like an adult," Amélie told Chantal earlier that morning. "Are you up to it?"

"I don't know," Chantal had replied. For a split second, she looked like the vulnerable young girl she had been the night Amélie had spotted Jeremy on the beach, afraid of what might happen if they helped him. The expression disappeared, replaced by a fury that evoked its own concern in Amélie.

"I will try my best," Chantal continued. Her voice hardened, and her eyes flashed anger. "I won't be a victim of these Nazi animals. Whatever our resistance needs for me to do, I will do it. That includes..." She drew her hand across her throat in a slicing motion. "Just name the target."

Amélie studied her sister. Chantal's tone concerned her. She recalled that Chantal had used that same slicing motion the night they had rescued Jeremy. She had been fearful and used the gesture to show what the Nazis would do to their family if they were caught aiding a fugitive. The new context worried Amélie, but she tucked the sense away in her mind.

"Jacques and Nicolas will be here soon," she said. "If you'd like to come along, we're going for a walk on the beach where we can talk without being overheard."

Fifteen minutes later, the four of them meandered through the sand by the water's edge, keeping their distance from other beachgoers.

"There's a woman here in Marseille," Jacques began. "I know her only by her codename, Hérisson, and I've never met her. She leads a resistance network. It's the one British intelligence put me in contact with before I closed down my shortwave radio."

"Why did you close it?" Chantal asked.

"The governments in a lot of countries in the war are closing down licensed operators. Without codes, the radios are insecure, and with them, they're too easy for spies to use. Pétain already outlawed their use, and British intelligence won't respond to my transmissions now."

"Who is this Hérisson?" Amélie said.

"A very smart woman, from all I can learn about her. She lives in Marseille and is good friends with a man who was high up in the French government before the German attack. He went to join the Pétain government and expects to be appointed in an intelligence role. The rumor is that, a long time ago, he anticipated exactly what the Germans did in attacking through Belgium and decided that the best way to fight them was to be close to the intelligence center. He'll do that while running a resistance organization through Hérisson. He'll feed useful information to her for action. That's as much as I've heard about them, and more than I'm supposed to know."

"That sounds almost impossible," Amélie interrupted.

"I have a hard time believing it too, but so far, the story checks out. What I can tell you is that all three of you have been referred to Hérisson. There's a vegetable vendor here in Marseille. He sells to all the big hotels and restaurants. Hérisson set the man up in business as a great way for him to circulate in places where people gather and talk, so he can learn what's going on. It's a very profitable business and helps fund the resistance locally. You'll meet him later today."

"He already knows about us?" Nicolas cut in.

"I told him about you before yesterday," Jacques replied. "I went to see him early this morning to let him know about your cousins. Under the circumstances, surprises are not a good thing."

Nicolas grimaced. "Sorry—"

"That was my fault," Amélie cut in. "I gave him no choice."

Chantal also started to speak, but Jacques held up his hands.

"It's all right," he interrupted. "Nicolas had no way to reach me, and anyway, I told him the whole story when I learned it. The man wants to meet you to make his own assessment. Their organization already has defined roles. The question is, how can you best participate?"

The vegetable vendor, Maurice, was huge, a man suited in appearance to be a butcher. His cover lacked any subtlety whatsoever, which is how he was able to maneuver around so freely: surely a man with such a friendly, in-your-face manner could not be engaged in resistance activities. His eyes bulged below a wide forehead, and his demeanor appeared guileless. Despite his size, his overpowering, engaging personality compelled people to open up to him, and talk.

His real value, however, lay in his ability to recruit and manage scores of patriots wishing to join and be active in the resistance. Within days of the German advance around the Maginot Line, still less than a month ago, people across France joined in small groups to oppose the German war machine as best they could.

Jacques made introductions at a warehouse as Maurice loaded his truck with vegetables. "Keep moving," he told the sisters. "You need to look like workers while we talk. Help me carry the vegetables out."

Jacques and Nicolas left for another safehouse.

"Your story for the moment is that you're my nieces, refugees from the north of France, and need the work to survive. Your parents were killed." He laughed a full, jocular belly laugh. "I'm helping you from the goodness of my heart."

The Boulier sisters liked him immediately. The two of them bunched together on the small passenger seat as Maurice made his rounds, and they helped him make deliveries. Chantal could not help wondering who among the people she met were active members of the resistance.

That evening at Maurice's sprawling farmhouse on the edge of the city, they met his wife, Suzanne, and their three young children, two boys and a girl. The children warmed up to the Boulier sisters, thrilled to learn of cousins that were new to them.

Suzanne was as bulky and gregarious as Maurice. Whether or not she knew anything of their backgrounds she did not indicate or ask, and they did not volunteer. She showed them to a comfortable room, and then brought them down to dinner.

Late that night, after the children had gone to bed and Suzanne had retired for the evening, Maurice sat across from the Bouliers at the kitchen table. Aside from their earlier conversation establishing their initial cover stories, nothing had been said about how to proceed. Now, for the first time all day, Maurice's expression turned serious. The girls watched him anxiously.

"You're good girls," he said, "good people." His big eyes turned to Chantal with kind intensity. "I'm so sorry about what happened to you." He shifted his view to Amélie. "And what you had to do about it. No one should have to suffer such brutality. No one should have to remember killing another person. If you wish to talk about it, we can. Suzanne is happy to help too. Otherwise, we won't mention it again.

"Now, as to what you can do to help." Once again, he shifted his eyes to Chantal. "I'm thinking that you can go with me on my deliveries. Suzanne could probably use help as well."

Chantal listened with a noncommittal expression.

"As for you." Maurice turned his attention to Amélie. "We have positions that will be difficult to fill and are almost always open, but they are very dangerous. In fact, it is the most dangerous position inside the resistance. You'll have to receive specialized training that will take you away for several months."

Amélie and Chantal exchanged horrified glances. "We've never been away from each other," Amélie said. "I need to be where I can look after my sister."

Chantal objected immediately. "You don't need to worry about me. If we're going to win this war, we can't hold back." She turned to Maurice. "I didn't come here to be a nanny or somebody's assistant. I want a real function inside the resistance, or I'll go somewhere else."

Surprised at her obstinacy, Maurice gazed at Chantal. "All right," he said, "I'll give it some more thought. Maybe you could be a courier. That's also very dangerous, and most people won't suspect a child; I mean a young woman."

"I know the risks. I came to fight," Chantal said.

Across the table, Amélie sniffed. Maurice and Chantal watched as she rubbed her eyes. "The truth is, I don't know if I can be away from Chantal." She gave a small, mirthless laugh, directing a concerned look at her younger sister. "I said you'd be the bravest among us," she murmured. Reaching across and taking Chantal's hand, she whispered, "I killed that German so you could live. Please don't get reckless."

Maurice cleared his throat with a cough. "I'll get you both in to see Hérisson," he said. "She'll make the final decisions."

36

Dunkirk, France

Hauptman Bergmann looked up slowly from a document he had been reading, his mind distant. "Approach with care," he murmured aloud, despite being alone in his office. "This man could do me some damage."

The document bore the title *Oberstleutnant* Meier, and markings on it indicated that it was confidential. Bergmann had read it through three times, and now ruminated on how best to handle the commander.

Meier, the dossier revealed, belonged to a centuries-old Prussian aristocratic family with an equally long history of military service. A favorite of General Rommel, he had been at the point of the *blitzkrieg* into France, executing the battle plan in his sector flawlessly, halting his advance only when having received an inexplicable order to do so ahead of closing in on Dunkirk. For his skill and tenacity, he had gained favorable attention not only from Rommel but also from the *führer* himself. As a result, Bergmann concluded, Meier enjoyed a degree of immunity.

As the captain saw the larger picture, the dilemma for Hitler in dealing with the German army, the *Wehrmacht,* had been that its officer corps largely consisted of the sons of aristocracy, raised with the notion of loyalty and duty to the fatherland. That commitment had often set them at odds with the dictator's own vision of where he wanted to take the country, resulting in mutual distrust and suspicion, but he had no choice but to rely on his officers to meet his military aims. Bergmann understood that alienating the military that possessed the weapons of war and the experience of ground combat ran the risk of inviting a coup.

He hated the aristocracy, seeing its members as privileged without merit and an impediment to his own ambitions. In the *Wehrmacht*, he could probably never hope to be promoted into senior ranks. That factor had been what led him to seek transfer to the SS, where he saw his opportunities for promotion to be more plentiful.

Under the hands of Hermann Göring and later Heinrich Himmler, the SS had been created initially as an eight-man bodyguard for the *führer*. Over time, Himmler grew and developed the organization into a multi-armed colossus that rivaled the Wehrmacht. Its power was limited only by Hitler's will, such authority already confirmed by a German court. The SS exercised its terrifying authority through its investigative arm, the SD, and through its executive arm, the *Gestapo*. Together, the sister organizations used their clout without reservation to hold in check anyone posing a threat to the regime, including private citizens, public officials, and the highest-ranking military officers, never hesitating to arrest, torture, and execute.

Bergmann recalled well the bloody purge of the so-called "night of the long knives" that had eliminated many officials of a competing element, the *Sturmabteilung*, or SA, a predecessor organization raised by the Nazi party early in its existence. It had gained power and influence such that it and its leader, Ernst Röhm, had been seen as threats to the authority of the *führer* himself. Brutal action eliminated the threat.

Bergmann envied those of the SS with low membership numbers signifying that they had joined the organization early. They had participated in its growth to become a paramilitary force to match the size and capability of the *Wehrmacht* itself, loyal only to Adolf Hitler. But he contented himself with the notion that his opportunities now appeared boundless. *At some point, I might want to transfer into the Gestapo.*

He realized a difficulty in dealing with *Oberstleutnant* Meier. As long as the smell of victory with lust for more permeated Berlin, the combat leaders were untouchable. Their triumph resulted in the signing of a Franco-German armistice, planned for the next day at the very site of Germany's previous humiliation, in a train car near Compiègne. In Meier's case, the commander operated under an umbrella of protection that started with his rank and battlefield successes and ran through his family name and General Rommel to the *führer.*

Bergmann's own background did not lack for achievement. His father had fought in the last war, and his family had suffered the privations resulting from the onerous conditions imposed by the Treaty of Versailles.

The elder Bergmann had also been among the first to recognize the economic benefits accruing to Germany by the firebrand Hitler's positions. He had not only read Hitler's biographical manifesto, *Mein Kamf,* as soon as it was published, but he had also pressed his son to read it. Then, when Hitler rose to power and formed the Hitler Youth, the son had joined early and enthusiastically.

When Hitler began clandestinely building his armed forces, Bergmann's father landed a contract that eventually led to his founding an armaments factory specializing in munitions. When the younger Bergmann reached military age, he applied for and received acceptance into the *Kriegsschule* at Potsdam, one of several military academies across Germany for training combat officers. His father had glowed with pride when he graduated and accepted a commission.

From there, Bergmann had gone on to learn armor tactics at the *Panzertruppenschule* I in Munson. However, on finally emerging into active duty with the *Wehrmacht*, he had been frustrated to see that the plum assignments went to officers with long family connections to the military. He became consigned to staff roles, only achieving command, as Meier had reminded him, when a company commander had been killed in action. With Germany's military at war in far-flung places, replacement officers were already scarce, and thus Bergmann got the call.

Shortly after entering active duty, he had observed the differences in opportunity and treatment between the *Wehrmacht* and the SS. Perceiving greener pastures, he had submitted his application.

He had reveled in the recollection of the shift in perceived authority when Meier had been required to inform him of his new commission. Then, he had burned at Meier's remonstrance regarding military decorum. To him, it was deliberate humiliation at the hand of a member of the undeserving aristocracy.

A knock on the door interrupted Bergmann's ruminations. When he called out to allow entry, the door opened, and an SD sergeant appeared. He advanced to halt in front of the desk and presented himself with the obligatory click of his heels.

"Sergeant Fleischer reports for duty."

"Good, Sergeant. Welcome. Have you read the plan I forwarded to you?"

"Yes, sir, and I understand it completely. My squad is to reinforce the guard on a neighborhood at the eastern edge of Dunkirk just above the shore. No one is to be allowed to enter or leave."

"Exactly. We will start interrogating the residents tomorrow or the next day at the *maison d'arrêt*. Someone in that group knows something about where Ferrand Boulier went. He is the head of a family of terrorists who murdered a German soldier. They cannot be allowed to escape. This is my first case to resolve as an SS officer, and I won't let it go. Have you done your reconnaissance?"

"We have, sir. The mission is straightforward. Thirteen houses. Roughly fifty people, including the children. That should not be difficult. Any special instructions?"

Bergmann thought a moment. "Feel free to shoot if need be but try not to kill anyone. I need the information. I can't get it from a corpse."

"What if we have to kill to prevent an escape?"

"If you must, you must."

The sergeant looked thoughtful. "Sir, may I ask a question, one of curiosity?"

Bergmann assented.

"I've read the case, but I'm not clear on why you are so determined to get this particular individual. The *feldgendarmerie* is already investigating."

Bergmann pursed his lips and nodded. "A fair question. I'm convinced that this case is more than just a murder. It took place too quickly, too cleanly, with very little evidence left behind. Then, not only did Ferrand

Boulier and his daughters vanish, but so did his extended family and close friends, all within hours of Kallsen's disappearance. I believe this is the beginning of a resistance network, and it cannot be allowed to grow. That's what I told *Herr* Himmler, and why I have his personal support for this mission."

37

Dunkirk, France

Ferrand Boulier looked over the thirty young men assembled in front of him. All were in their late twenties or early thirties and physically fit. They were gathered in an empty warehouse.

"Training and practice are over," he said grimly. "Tonight, we go out to save our friends and neighbors. In the process, we might kill some Germans."

A murmur of approval arose.

Ferrand lifted his hand for quiet. "We don't want to become them," he said. "We take no joy in this fight, and we don't kill wantonly. Your mission is to save French families, not kill Germans. If you *do* kill, your friends and families can expect retaliation. Try first to render the guards unconscious. Failing that, do not hesitate.

"Remember, they will shoot. We only have knives and clubs. Surprise is our equalizer. If you find you must kill, then like we practiced, slice their throats or stab them. Regardless, take their guns and ammunition."

Ferrand looked around at the faces of his group, some eager, some afraid. *So young.* A lump formed in his throat. "All right. We've been over all this before. Final reminders: I'll be at the site in the designated place. Each two-man team will come to me. You have the schedule. At the site, I'll give final clearance to go rescue the family at your target house. Use the shadows on your approach. The moon will be high, shining on the front of the houses. We'll make our approach from the rear, among the shadows. Make best use of them.

"If anyone in the house chooses not to go, leave immediately. Don't linger, don't try to convince anyone. Just go.

"Those families that come with you should bring only the clothes they're wearing. Take them to your designated safehouse. Someone else will take charge of them from there. You don't need to know where they're going or who takes over. You'll leave immediately. Is that clear?"

He waited for the murmurings to subside, indicating that his instructions were understood. "Surveillance teams are watching the neighborhood now, and we should hear from them soon. Any last questions?"

"Ferrand," a man called. "Shouldn't we wait for a night that will be darker?"

Ferrand nodded with an air of resignation. "Good question," he replied. "I'd like to wait, but time is not on our side. *Hauptman* Bergmann is back, and he wears an SS uniform. We know he's going to press this neighborhood for that soldier's death. He won't wait. Any other questions?"

"Wouldn't it be better," another man called out, "for all of us to go at the same time? We could be in and out more quickly."

Ferrand blew out a breath of air, the weight of his decisions lining his face and bearing on his voice. "I honestly don't know. If everything goes smoothly, your suggestion would be best. But if shooting starts, we could have a lot of defenseless people caught in the open with bullets flying at mothers and children. It could be a bloodbath." He paused. "Our way keeps our casualties to a minimum in case something goes wrong." He closed his eyes momentarily in quiet reflection. "I hope I don't regret my decision."

Grim silence descended as his words settled in. "Any more questions?"

He received none.

"Everyone knows what to do in case we abort?"

The group's members nodded and murmured assent.

A man suddenly stumbled into the warehouse through a side door. Sweat streamed down his red face, and he was out of breath.

"Bad news!" he called out. He leaned over panting, cupping his hands over his knees and supporting his torso with bent arms. "The Germans just added nine more soldiers to guard the neighborhood. There are now thirteen. The new ones are SS shock troops. There's a guard on each house."

Ferrand's face became resolute. He held up a hand. "We need to modify our plan," he said, "but we still go tonight."

Ferrand sat cross-legged in deep shadows among the ruins of Dunkirk on the opposite side of the alley running behind the row of houses that included his own. Two men hunched at his shoulder. A third hovered behind them. He turned to the third man.

"You are from the last team?" he asked in a low voice barely above a whisper.

"Yes."

"Brief me on what you are supposed to do under the new plan."

"I'll go with the two members of the first team. I'll help subdue the guard and will be their lookout while they go inside to get the family. The team leader will take the rescued family to the safehouse. I'll return here with the other team member. He'll stay here with you to do the same for the next group, and I'll return to my team and await our turn."

"Exactly," Ferrand said. He turned to the team leader. "Go, and good luck."

He watched as the three men hunched over, moved out, and scurried through the moonlit rubble to the alley. One by one, they crossed the narrow passageway and disappeared into the shadows.

Less than five minutes later, the second team arrived at Ferrand's side. Two minutes later, two of the men who had gone out with the first team returned.

"Success," one of them said. "The guard will not regain consciousness tonight. The family is on its way to its safehouse." He joined the second team while the other man returned to his own, the last one in the queue.

Three more times, teams went out with the same result. Then on the fourth, all three team members returned.

"The family wouldn't leave. The SS guard stood right at their back door. The wife panicked when she saw him lying there after we clubbed him. She ran to a bedroom where she has two young children and wouldn't come out. She's terrified. Her husband tried to convince her, but she wouldn't listen."

Ferrand let out a slow breath. "I was afraid of exactly that," he said. "Well, it can't be helped. You did your jobs."

"We can try again," the team leader said. "The guard is already subdued. Two of us can go back, and the third man can stay here to help the next team."

"Too risky," Ferrand said. "There must be a roving guard checking on the others."

"We haven't seen one and earlier surveillance didn't mention it," the team leader replied. "I think this is a thrown-together mission that the SS takes more seriously than the *Wehrmacht* does. If we had waited, security would have tightened. I think we can do this."

"All right. If the family agrees to go, both of you stay with them until you reach the safehouse."

With that, the two disappeared once more into the night, followed shortly by the next group.

Waiting alone in the dark, Ferrand looked up at the sky and breathed in deeply, exhaling slowly. His nerves on the raw end, he expected the night to erupt into gunfire at any moment.

"We won't get away clean," he muttered. "Bergmann is vengeful. He'll get even." *Still, we must resist. They cannot take our country without a fight.*

Four more teams went through. Ferrand breathed a little easier. With only two more families to rescue—

His thoughts were interrupted by the sound of machine gun fire. Tracers lit up the night sky. He leaped to his feet. The next to the last group arrived, but no third man returned from the previous set.

"Go!" he told the team members. "Abort the mission. Tell the ones behind you. Follow your escape plans."

38

Oberstleutnant Meier paced, his face red with anger while *Hauptman* Bergmann stood at attention. Both men had received early morning calls about the skirmish that had taken place last night in the neighborhood on the northeastern edge of town.

"I specifically instructed you to clear your plans with me before taking action," the commander bellowed.

"Increasing security where it already exists is not 'taking action,'" Bergmann replied tersely without breaking his stance. "Obviously, the partisans had a plan already underway when my men took their posts in that neighborhood, and my report will say—"

Meier swung around in fury. "Are you threatening me?" he interrupted. "Your narrative might be obvious to you, but it is not obvious to me. What is blatantly clear is that you had a soldier out of control: Kallsen. Without provocation, you entered a peaceful neighborhood to interrogate its inhabitants, you executed a man without the slightest investigation, and then inflamed the population by your continued harassment. From the time you left for Berlin until your return, they had given no problem.

"You haven't been back even a day, and now I have four men being treated for concussion, and you have seven in the same state. Three of those received bullet wounds, probably from their own rifles, and the weapons and ammunition belonging to the wounded are gone, taken by the partisans. That's what my report will say."

Bergmann started to say something.

"I'll tell you when you can speak," Meier stormed. He whirled and shook his finger in the captain's face. "We don't wage war on women and children."

"My job is to seek out and eliminate threats to our *führer* and the Third *Reich*," Bergmann blurted.

Meier's tone mocked. "You're going to make the argument that a tiny neighborhood with mainly old people and families with young children represents such a threat?" He barely contained his exasperation. Taking a deep breath, he lowered his voice. "Your job is to do as you are told. You are not alone in defending the *reich*. We all share that job. During and after the end of this war, Germany will have to govern these people. We should avoid starting a new front behind our own lines by inciting the population to violence against us. Their actions will be aimed primarily at our soldiers whom we need alive and well to fight our wars. Tell me you understand that."

Bergmann said nothing, standing stone-faced, eyes looking straight ahead.

"Dismissed," Meier said.

Bergmann did not move.

"Did you hear me, *Hauptman*. You are dismissed."

"Sir, may I speak?"

Meier hesitated, holding back his disgust. Then, he gave permission with a nod.

"You might be right," Bergmann said, "and I have no wish to be at cross-purposes with you."

Meier shot him a searching glance. "At ease. Speak."

Mindful of the Meier dossier he had read, Bergman spread his feet apart and relaxed a bit. "If I brought this trouble on us, then I apologize. Regardless, we now have a situation in which our soldiers were attacked, their weapons taken, and probably used against them. Someone organized and led that raid. My considered opinion is that we cannot let that pass."

"Agreed," Meier said, only slightly mollified. "What do you suggest?"

"What if we were to announce that we seek the criminal individuals who mounted the attack, in particular their leader? We can offer a reward and state that a reprisal will occur after so many days if we are unable to make arrests."

Meier continued to pace, rubbing his chin. "I'll tell you plainly that I'm not a fan of reprisals, and I won't go after the remaining families in that neighborhood. The last thing we need is to make martyrs out of them and turn their names into battle cries.

"What would you offer as a reward and how would you carry out the reprisal? Keep in mind that a threat is most effective prior to its execution."

"The answer to the first part of your question is simple," Bergmann replied. "Money. We need to pick an amount." He took a moment to put additional thoughts together. "We could structure the reprisals over a number of days. For instance, when we make the announcement, we could say that if we do not have the information we seek by the following day, we will arrest a single person. We'll double the number each day for the next four days. On the sixth day, if we have nothing satisfactory, we will shoot one of those arrested, double again the next day, and so on. If we reach day eleven without information, we will have arrested and shot thirty-one people."

"And achieved nothing."

"I don't believe it will come to that. When fathers are torn from their homes and jailed, people will talk. I am sure that if we hear nothing by the time of the first execution, we will have something before the order to fire is given. Sir, if you want to spare our soldiers' lives, this is the way to do it."

Meier remained pensive for several minutes. "I want to think this through, but a condition I will impose if I agree to your plan..." He looked directly into Bergmann's eyes. "And that is a big 'if.'" He stared across the room at nothing in particular. "If I were to issue such an order, it would stipulate that no execution is to be carried out without my written order, and you would be required to sign a statement attesting to your under-standing. Is that clear?"

"Yes, sir."

"Then go prepare your plan. Run it by the executive officer before bringing it back to me."

39

Ferrand lay on his bunk within the bombed-out ruins, falling in and out of sleep, held in that nether state by sheer physical exhaustion, and rousted awake by the emotional calamities that confronted him. He ached to see his daughters but forced thoughts of them out of his mind.

"There will be repercussions," he murmured during a lucid moment. The eruption of gunfire between partisans and the German SS had assured swift, violent retribution.

His sole consolation was that of the thirteen families; all but two of them had escaped, including the family of the reluctant mother. The rescue party had also evaded capture, only one of them having taken a bullet that grazed an arm. By now, the families had scattered to homes across northern France. Partisans there would move them steadily south, past the German front. Fortunately, the Nazis were still engaged in consolidating and pressing south on the Atlantic coast.

Ferrand's eyes popped open, and he sat up. A sound had awakened him. He strained to hear it again, but when he did not, he allowed his body to fall backward onto the mattress and closed his eyes once more.

He heard the sound again and recognized it as a voice projected through an electronic loudspeaker, but he could not make out the words. "It can't be good."

As the minutes ticked by, he realized that the broadcast message repeated. It stopped for a time, he fell asleep, and then he was awakened by another iteration of the message.

Pulling a pillow over his head muffled the noise, but when he awoke again an hour later, he heard the electronic voice once more bellowing in the distance. After a couple of hours, he decided he had better find out what was being said.

He waited until the shadows had grown long and then made his way carefully through the ruins, using the shadows and debris for concealment. Reaching a safe place where he could make out the words, he sat amidst the wreckage and listened.

"To the good people of Dunkirk, you have terrorists and traitors among you, led by Ferrand Boulier, and including his daughters, Amélie and Chantal. They murdered a German soldier, escaped, and then led an attack on a squad of German troops. Three of our brave soldiers were shot, and several others are in critical condition with severe head injuries.

Such criminal acts should not go unpunished, and you, the good citizens of Dunkirk, should not be exposed to the dangers they bring. Therefore, be advised of the following:

- A reward of one thousand francs is offered for anyone bringing information leading to the arrest of Ferrand Boulier.
- The daughters are controlled by their father. When he is arrested, they will be allowed to go free.
- If by tomorrow at noon, we have received no information, we will arrest a resident of Dunkirk. That will double the next day, and so on through five days.
- If by the sixth day, we have received no information, other measures will be considered.
- Anyone with information may communicate that such is the case through any German soldier or officer, who will escort you to the appropriate office.
- This announcement will be repeated periodically until no longer necessary."

Ferrand dropped his head into his hands. He felt nothing other than profound fatigue. His mind descended into an empty space in which no thought registered. Darkness gathered around him, the electronic voice scratched the night, yet still he did not move.

For two more hours, Ferrand sat alone, immobile. His breathing slowed, his eyes closed, and he fell over in the rubble.

Above him, a waning moon moved across the vestiges of a once proud city. The stars glimmered against a dark sky, and the chill of night set in.

At dawn, the hateful blare of the electronically broadcast voice awakened Ferrand again. Strangely, he felt refreshed. Checking around his immediate vicinity to be sure he was not observed, he once more made use of the shadows to retrace his steps to his room among the ruins.

When he arrived, a woman waited for him. She was bent like he was and a few years younger. She had waited for him inside the wreckage of the building's first-floor corridor, out of sight.

"You are a treasure, Anna," he said on seeing her.

She put a sorrowful hand to her mouth. "Oh Ferrand, you look so awful. This war is killing you slowly." She looked around at the crooked walls that lacked ceilings and a roof. "It's killing us all."

"You're making so many sacrifices and taking such chances," he told her. "I don't know how you do what you do, mopping the floors of those beasts."

"That was my job there before the Germans arrived. They let me stay. I need to eat. I hope the information I bring you is helpful."

"Most helpful, Anna. I can never thank you enough." He put his arms around her shoulders and held her.

"We've been friends for so many years," she said, pulling away. "Who would have said that our beautiful city could have been destroyed the way it was?" Looking around again as if seeing things the way they had been, she shook her head, and her eyes filled with tears. "We had happy memories here while we were children, and then when we had children."

Ferrand put his arm around her shoulder and nudged her toward his room. "And now we fight so that all of them can create more good memories. Come. I think I can make some coffee."

She held her hands in front of her face. "No, I would be late for work."

"Did you have news for me?" Ferrand asked.

She nodded. "You heard the message over the loudspeakers?"

Ferrand acknowledged that he had.

"That was the work of that *Hauptman* Bergmann. He's not very popular with *Oberstleutnant* Meier. They've had several big fights. Meier doesn't like the way that the captain came into your neighborhood. He had forbidden Bergmann from taking more action without approval. Then that shooting happened. I think Meier doesn't like the Nazis, and I'm sure he despises the SS. The two men hate each other."

She started to walk back toward what had been the main entrance. "I don't know what they plan if they don't find you, but I do know that Bergmann cannot execute anyone without Meier's written order. The captain is arrogant, and is throwing his SS weight around, but he's afraid of Meier. I don't know why."

Ferrand had listened carefully. "So, I have at least five days?"

"I think that's right, but I can't say for sure."

"That information you brought about the animosity between Meier and Bergmann could be useful someday, and about the commander being hostile to Nazis. Thank you, Anna." With his arm around her shoulders, he squeezed her. "You shouldn't be doing this. You should be somewhere safe and warm, with family looking after you."

Anna looked around and laughed quietly. "And you? We do what we must."

"When you're ready, we'll get you to a safer place."

Anna started toward the exit again, and then paused. Turning, she shook her head and wiped her eyes. "It's too late for me, but I will do everything I can to help my family." She reached up and stroked the side of Ferrand's face. "You are a good man. Be careful. I hate to think of what Bergmann will do to you if he finds you." She started to leave, and then turned with a parting comment. "My sister was very lucky to be married to you."

40

Marseille, France

Amélie sat at breakfast with Chantal, Maurice, and Suzanne. A knock on the outside kitchen door interrupted them. Maurice saw through the window that Jacques and Nicolas stood on the landing. He waved them in.

Nicolas looked worried. "I just spoke with my father," he blurted. "He had to travel far south to find a working phone. The Germans are cutting the lines in the north."

He related that some partisans had rescued several families out of the Bouliers' old neighborhood in Dunkirk, and a firefight had resulted. "Our groups got away, but several German soldiers were wounded. Some of them were SS."

He alternated his eyes between Amélie and Chantal. "*Hauptman* Bergmann is in the SS now. Yesterday, he announced that a man would be arrested today, and they'd double the number of arrests for five days. Bergmann said that if they still did not have the leader in custody by then, they would consider other measures. You know what that means. They'll start executing until the leader surrenders to them. That's your father."

Her eyes wide, her hands shaking in a frenzy, Amélie said, "I have to go to him."

"I'm going too," Chantal echoed.

"You can't," Nicolas insisted. "Neither of you. Look, Amélie, he sent you away so he could make good decisions without worrying about your safety."

"He didn't make good decisions. He got himself caught."

"He's not caught yet, and he made excellent decisions. He not only saved you and his own relatives and friends but also several families who escaped because of him, and lots of soldiers. His risk was shared by others who accepted his leadership. You can be proud of him."

"Of course, I'm proud of him," Amélie retorted. Her voice descended into a hoarse whisper. "I'm scared for him."

As she listened, tears began to run down Chantal's face. Her lips quivered. "This is my fault," she said, barely above a murmur.

Amélie leaned over and embraced her, while Nicolas grasped her shoulders. "This is not your fault," Amélie said. She turned her eyes to Maurice. "Do you see why we must be in the fight?"

The big man nodded, studying the girls compassionately. He excused himself and went to another room. There, quietly, he called Hérisson. "We need to meet," he said. "We must get an urgent message to London."

Late in the afternoon, Maurice returned from his rounds. He had gone alone and now he called for Amélie and Chantal to join him at the kitchen table. From another room, Suzanne could be heard taking care of the children.

"I met with Hérisson today," he said. "She'll meet with you. She knows about your father and she understands the situation. She sent a high priority message to London and received a reply a short while ago. They're going to send a team here within a few days."

Chantal's eyes sparkled and she jumped in the air with excitement. "That's wonderful," she cried. "They're coming to save Papa."

Almost immediately, she noticed that Maurice did not smile, and his brow furrowed. She glanced at Amélie and saw that her sister's eyes were fixed on his face.

"What's wrong?" Chantal asked.

"Nothing's wrong," Maurice replied, "and this is a good thing. The British are implementing a program they had already planned, and they're doing it ahead of schedule."

"Then why aren't you smiling?"

"Because, my young friend," Maurice said, tousling her hair, "it is important that you understand the realities of war."

Chantal started to protest, but Maurice held up a hand. "Please listen to me, and I will tell you all.

"The team that's coming will be here to save the network your father established. If they save him too, so much the better, but that isn't their chief objective. They'll bring with them weapons, ammunition, and money, and Nicolas will guide them back north to rendezvous with Claude, but their mission is to safeguard the network. Do you understand that?"

Wide-eyed, Chantal watched Maurice's face. She nodded vigorously. "I do," she said, almost breathless with excitement. "I'll go with them. We can rescue Papa, and the British team can do whatever they want, as long as we have the weapons."

Maurice pursed his lips and shook his head. "It's not going to be like that."

Dismay spread over Chantal's face. "What do you mean?"

"I know what he means," Amélie said quietly. She faced her sister. "Papa sent us away so that he could carry on the fight without worrying about us."

Chantal's anger flared. "So, are we going to sit by and watch while he is tortured and killed?"

"Not at all," Amélie replied. "We have to fight here while we trust our family and friends to rescue Papa; well, his network, and hopefully him as well."

Chantal crossed her arms, her chin jutting forward with obstinacy. "I'm going."

"Listen to me carefully," Maurice replied. "If you insist on going, the British mission is off. Hérisson's London contact made that very clear. Neither you nor you sister can be involved. They're pulling the resources together months ahead of schedule and before the team is fully trained.

These people are putting their lives on the line just by parachuting in. We need to live by their conditions."

"But why?" Tears ran down Chantal's face.

"Like Amélie said, if they can rescue your father, they will, but personal emotions come second to making good decisions. Only three are coming, and they have specific jobs. Your friends and neighbors in Dunkirk will carry out most of the action."

"Then what are the British bringing?"

"Resources and organization. They demonstrate clearly that London is in this war with us."

Chantal's face knotted into adolescent bitterness. "Like at Dunkirk?" She slumped into a chair, buried her face in her hands, and choked back sobs.

Amélie rose and hugged her.

Maurice stood against the opposite wall, at a loss for words. He made an attempt to console. "I understand how you feel—"

"No, you don't!" Chantal screamed, leaping to her feet. "How could you? Our city was bombed, we were driven from our home. We saw all those soldiers getting massacred. I was nearly raped, and Amélie killed—"

Her sobs made further speech impossible. "And now," she managed after a few moments while wiping her eyes, "our father, who did nothing but help people, is being hunted down. Maybe they've already arrested him."

She continued trying to control her weeping, her lungs heaving with the effort. After several minutes, she calmed down and took her seat.

"I'm sorry," she said to Maurice, regarding him through eyes still brimming with tears. "You've been kind to us."

"No worries, my little friend," he replied with a gentle smile. "I have broad shoulders."

"And this," Amélie said quietly while stroking Chantal's hair, "is exactly why we can't get in the way." She turned to Maurice. "Give us something meaningful to do, something that lets us strike back."

"I'll see what I can do," Maurice said. "I'm sure there's a way."

41

Somewhere east of Saint-Nazaire, France

Tramp, tramp, tramp. The incessant shuffling of footwear by the thousands along the roadway bore down on Lance's exhausted mind, otherwise occupied with only one conscious thought: food. Days had passed since his last full meal, and all his waking hours were now spent walking, pushed along by unsympathetic guards in a miles-long throng for twenty-three out of each twenty-four hours toward the east, always east.

His original captors had treated him decently. Being the only British soldier among the group taken prisoner on that fateful morning after blowing up the fuel-oil tanks, he had been separated from the French Resistance fighters captured with him. He had no idea what had happened to them, nor, for that matter, what had happened to Horton. *I hope he got away.* For an hour, he had been held at gunpoint, seated on the ground with his back against the wall of a barn while curious German soldiers filed by, staring at him as they would an animal in a zoo, as if trying to discern how such a creature had come into being.

Aside from being held captive, they treated him well, some bringing food, water, coffee, and even offering cigarettes, and some posing for pictures next to him. For his part, Lance attempted a look of neutrality, fighting down an overwhelming sense of dejection. He had not anticipated spending the war as a POW.

Regardless of his effort to appear stable, his captors seemed to sense his personal turmoil, for they treated him as though both respecting and feeling sorry for him, a step above pity.

After an hour, a lorry had pulled up to the barn that the Germans had used as a quick, makeshift headquarters. Using prods and gestures, the senior non-com had indicated for Lance to load onto the canvas-covered truck-bed. By then, the extremes of actions and events of the past few days wore into his body such that every motion weighed like lead on his muscles and further dampened the cognizant operation of his brain. Painfully, he did as instructed.

Aside from two armed soldiers perched at the back end of the truck, Lance was the only passenger. He sat on the wooden bench at the front by the cab. The truck jolted into motion, and he was alone, his only company the cruel memories of the past few days and a dismal sense that he had failed his comrades, whose whereabouts remained unknown.

Deliberately, he shoved his thoughts toward home, but doing so brought no solace. Even as he pictured his mother's stoic face with her subtly smiling eyes, his stepdad climbing among the cliffs of Sark, his sister pounding out the strong chords of Chopin on the piano, and his two brothers wrestling in the grass, his sense of isolation and failure deepened.

The lorry made several stops, and each time, captured British soldiers loaded into the back. They barely acknowledged each other, only enough to claim a narrow portion of the bench, which became even smaller as more and more prisoners clambered aboard, sat, and stared into empty space.

After what seemed like interminable hours, the truck pulled to a stop. From outside the canvas, gruff voices yelling in German barked out orders, and at the back of the truck, the prisoners began to dismount. As Lance climbed down, a hand from below grabbed his shoulder and shoved him. He stumbled in the direction of his new comrades while managing a glance at this latest set of guards.

They were older than the soldiers who had captured him, most appearing advanced in years sufficient to have fought in the last war, and they bore a common expression of anger, as though resenting having been brought back to active service. Regardless, the curious admiration and respect of his original captors had disappeared, replaced by harsh commands, abrupt jostling, and outright hostility.

They disembarked in front of a vast, muddy field with strands of barbed wire reinforced intermittently by armed German soldiers keeping careful watch.

In the field, thousands upon thousands of men in British military uniforms languished, each a testament of dejection. Some sat cross-legged, some back-to-back with a buddy, others in various contortions seeking comfort on the wet ground. If they spoke at all, they did so in low murmurs, most of them with downcast eyes, looking up only to see the latest newcomers before returning to their own internal struggles.

Almost in a trance, Lance staggered into the field with the group from the truck until an unconscious consensus had been reached that a spot had been found, and he sank to the ground with the others. He had no idea how many hours had passed, only that a rain shower blew in, the sun came back out before sinking on the horizon, and he shivered in darkness. Then, immediately after dawn, the guards began shouting, barking orders, and moving among the mass of prisoners, prodding them with their rifles, and pushing them to the road. There, surrounded by German troops, they formed into a line, four to six abreast stretching back as far as required to absorb a procession of thousands. The first captives on the road were immediately led off toward the rising sun, and the rest followed as they trudged onto the road.

Mile after endless mile passed under their ragged feet, the tramp, tramp, tramp almost the only sound they heard on the open road. Occasionally, they had to pause to allow other such processions to cross their paths at intersections. As they passed through villages, the French citizenry lined up on either side of the streets, calling to them and trying to hand them food and water.

On seeing this, the guards shoved the offending French men and women aside, stomping on the gifts of sustenance and threatening the offenders with weapons pointed their way. Lance slogged along just inside the long phalanx. Witnessing the cruelty provided enough of a shock to revive his senses a tad, and he took more note of what transpired around him.

He moved to the outside of the procession, and as it entered and left more villages, he made a mental note of them: Savenay, Nantes, Ancenis, Angers... The trek seemed endless, each mile, each step becoming more painful. On the third day, he found a small notebook in the jacket pocket of the uniform Pierre had scavenged for him, and as they passed from village to village, he scribbled the names down.

That same night, he scrawled a message to his parents. The next day and in succeeding days, he held the note tightly in his hand, marching stubbornly on the outside of the formation, searching for an opportunity.

They trudged through the days and into the night, stopping again in wide-open fields, allowed to sleep for an hour, and then put on the march again. On arrival at each successive resting area, their guards dispensed a few dry crackers, their only food for the day. The farther east they walked, the more their plight worsened. Gone were the well-maintained war machines of the front and the crisp combat soldiers sympathetic to their predicaments. Each new day brought a new crew of guards, each angrier and more brutal than the last and having older and older machinery, some of it horse-drawn.

On this morning, the seventh since his capture, Lance's struggle to his feet was more pronounced as the guards shouted their commands to start the day's trek. He shuffled to the roadway with the mass of prisoners, pushing in an almost catatonic trance to the edge of the formation. Hours passed before the eastern horizon began to lighten, signaling the approach of dawn. He had continued his record of towns and villages passed through, noting that their captors reveled in exhibiting their captives to the French populace in Orléans, Sens, Troyes... And still, he clutched the note.

The procession of pitiful soldiers continued through Saint-Dizier. The citizenry lined the road on both sides, pressing close to the prisoners, throwing bread, cheese, fruit, and other food into the passing throng. The German guards shoved them back.

Ahead of Lance, a prisoner stumbled. The hapless man fell to his knees outside the line of POWs. A woman reached in with a bottle of water to offer him a drink. A German soldier pushed her to the ground. Turning on the prisoner, he kicked the man and beat him with his rifle butt.

The procession continued on, but the prisoners had bunched as they attempted to step around the disturbance. A British officer-prisoner stepped between the guard and the victim. Then, a German officer appeared, angrily demanding an explanation for the commotion.

"I must protest the treatment of this prisoner," the British officer said.

While he spoke, the German officer looked questioningly at his subordinate, and then glared at the offending prisoner.

"He is protected by the Geneva Convention," the British officer continued.

Without uttering a word, the German officer pulled his pistol from its holster and pumped three bullets into the British officer's chest. The man fell to the ground as women screamed and the crowd of onlookers scattered. The line of lurching prisoners staggered around him.

Shocked, Lance stumbled past. Nausea overcame him, but he had no food in his stomach to heave. Ahead of him, people who had not seen or heard what had transpired crowded more closely for a better view, sensing that something had occurred that they could not see. The German guards too had momentarily diverted their attention, and in that moment, the crowd had moved closer to the prisoners, some offering food or just gestures of encouragement.

Lance spotted an empty outstretched hand. He could not even see the person to whom it belonged. He grasped it with both hands, pressed his note into it, and pushed the fingers closed around it.

Then he moved on without missing a step. He raised his eyes to the heavens, let his head fall backward a bit, and breathed in deeply, a momentary sense of relief. Then he continued putting one foot in front of the other, enduring his sojourn toward Germany.

42

Bletchley Park, England

Claire Littlefield called Paul's office at mid-morning. Failing to reach him there, she tried his apartment.

"Sorry," he said. "It's Saturday. I was trying to get some domestic chores—"

"It's urgent," she said. "I need to speak with you at once."

"Shall I come out to Bletchley?"

"Yes, but not the apartment. Knock on the door of Hut 6. Show them your credentials and wait for me. I'll tell reception to expect you, and they'll page me."

Almost two hours later, Paul presented himself as Claire had instructed. When she appeared, she shot him a quick smile and set out walking without a word.

"What is it?" he asked, as she led him over the mansion's broad lawn and through the gardens to a pond. He tried to ease her stress with levity. "You're being rather cloak-and-dagger here, of all places."

"I'm breaking protocol a bit," she said at last, breathless from the brisk pace she had set, and slowed down. Finally, she stopped and faced him. "I can't tell you all that I do in there," she said. "I'd be canned, or worse. Maybe jailed."

"What is it? Don't tell me anything you're not supposed to."

"There are always gray lines. Does the name Boulier mean anything to you?"

"Boulier," Paul repeated. "Is that the surname of the family who helped Jeremy?"

"I'm quite certain it is. Let's just say that I came across that name. Ferrand Boulier. And the context was not benign. In fact, it was quite threatening. He and his daughters are the subject of a manhunt in northern France. An SD chap by the name of Bergmann is after them."

"Are you sure? Maybe the names are similar."

Claire shook her head. "I double-checked. I have the correct names, and I'm sure they are the ones who helped Jeremy. What can we do? We have to help them."

Paul stared at her. "How? I'm not even supposed to know about whatever you learned or how you got it."

Claire bristled. "So, turn me in. Jeremy would be furious if he thought that we knew of a danger to the people who saved his life and did nothing to help them. Besides, he's in love with the older daughter, Amélie."

"He what? How could you know that? He seldom talks about her."

"Call it intuition. You should see his eyes light up when her name is mentioned."

"But they barely know each other. He couldn't have seen her more than a day or two."

"It might be nothing if they get a chance to know each other, but he met her under extreme conditions. Regardless, he cares for her and her family. We owe them." Paul took a hard look at his sister. She stood facing him, eyes burning, arms folded, and jaw set.

"I'm taking this to the top of my organization," she said. "That man, Boulier, started a network in northern France that's been effective across the country, even in its infancy. He's the type of ally we need to help our soldiers who were left over there. From what I gathered from Crockatt, he's doing exactly what that new MI-9 section was created to support."

"But you're not even supposed to be telling me as much as you have.

How are we going to bring this up in any context that doesn't get us arrested, maybe even hanged? Then what will we have accomplished? I'm not exaggerating."

"What about that man Jeremy met with yesterday? Lord Hankey, I believe. Isn't he supposed to be setting up a commando capability of some sort?"

"It's not even operational yet, and I'm sure Hankey won't be directing it. They'll bring in someone else of lesser rank to do that."

"Well Churchill must have thought Hankey could do something to put him in that position." Claire's eyes flashed as she spoke, and her fingers poked the air in exasperation. "This is war. Our classifications are meant to protect information, not keep us from acting when we know there's something to do."

Paul peered at his sister and laughed.

Taken aback, Claire asked, "What's so funny?"

"You're doing to me what I've been doing to Major Crockatt," he said. "All right, how do you get along with your boss?"

"Fine. It's a fairly small organization at the moment with a flat management structure, so I interact with him regularly. It's expected to bring on many more people, so it won't stay small for long. We see a lot of activity, and Bletchley belongs to MI-6."

"Then here's the approach. Explain to your boss the situation, tell him that the information could be critical to Lord Hankey, and ask to run the situation up the staff.

"Meanwhile, I'll go to Crockatt and tell him I've learned of a newly formed network in northern France that's in danger of being broken up. His interests and Hankey's coincide. I'll even agree to transfer over to his unit if he'll help follow up. Let's see how far we get, and then we can figure out next steps."

Suddenly exuberant, Claire swooped on her brother, throwing both arms around him. "I knew I could count on you to come up with something."

Paul laughed. "By the way, security is not airtight around those secrets inside that mansion and those huts, even though they're an enigma."

Startled, Claire stared at him, her cheeks flushing. "What do you mean?"

Paul ducked his head and waved his hands in the air. "That's all I'll say. Now go."

"What do we tell Jeremy?"

"Nothing, for the time being."

Major Crockatt held a steady gaze while he listened to Paul relate his conversation with Claire. "You do realize," he said sternly, "that you and your sister have probably already broken through thin ice."

"Yes, sir. We both know that. If we had done it for a self-serving purpose, then I would expect disciplinary action. In this case, neither of us stands to gain anything other than, perhaps, satisfaction from helping good people who saved our brother. If that's an offense worthy of incarceration, then put me away. Meanwhile, if we manage to save the Boulier network, then we've served the purposes of both MI-9 and SOE."

Crockatt drew back. "Got it all figured out, have you? Why come to me? Why not your own boss?"

"MI-6 is set up to run spies, not execute rescue operations. But besides that, Claire is already trying to run it up through the Bletchley Park hierarchy, so it has a good chance of winding up there anyway. If it also comes to the higher-ups through another channel, it has a greater probability of gaining some attention and being acted upon."

"MI-9 isn't being set up for rescue operations either."

"But Lord Hankey's organization and yours are organizing networks inside the country to be run by the partisans themselves. You'll arm them, equip them, fund them, and train them, and in many instances, the same people will accomplish missions for both organizations, probably for MI-6 too. With no outside assistance, the man we're talking about already built a network like the ones you intend, and he saved the lives of his own people and our soldiers. We must help him save his organization."

Crockatt sat silently for an extended time, pressing a pen across his upper lip while he thought, never taking his eyes off Paul's face.

"And you'll come over here if I help you?"

"If that's what it takes."

Crockatt smiled and tossed the pen on the desktop. "I would never make such a bargain, Lieutenant. I'll help because, as you say, it's the right thing to do. I can't promise success. The last time you asked for help with the air support in Saint-Nazaire, we got nowhere. But I'll try."

"Thank you so much, Major." Paul started for the door, then paused midway across the office and turned. "Sir, if you'll still have me, I'd be honored to work in MI-9."

Crockatt broke a slight smile. "I'm pleased to hear that, Lieutenant. We can talk more about it when we get through this business. I'll place a call to his lordship now."

43

Sark Island, English Channel Islands

From the front window of the stone *Seigneurie* mansion, Dame Marian watched a man striding along *Rue de la Seigneurie*. Rarely given to emotion, she nevertheless felt her stomach tighten as if alerting her to a premonition. She recognized him as the mail carrier coming from the post office a few hundred meters away, but he was off schedule. Today was Saturday, and he should not be delivering mail. *He brings no glad tidings.*

She ruminated as she watched his approach. The news circulating about the war had not been good, and events occurred so fast she could barely keep up, and then only from what came over the BBC. She knew that General Rommel, one of Hitler's favorite generals, had burst out of the Ardennes Forest through Belgium and breached the Maginot Line. She scoffed. *That expensive and "impenetrable" hunk of junk that was supposed to stop the German army along the French border.*

A rumor floating around told of Rommel ordering his tank commanders to point their guns to their own rear and charge across in front of the line waving black and white flags and yelling at the tops of their lungs. By the time the hapless French understood that the charging tanks were not those of the fleeing Belgian army, so the story went, the Germans were past their fortifications and poised with guns pointing at France's unprotected rear.

Whether true or not, Marian had no way to know, but regardless, the German army had flanked the Maginot in the northwest where it was weak and incomplete. Then they had penetrated into France and trapped the British Expeditionary Force at Dunkirk with thousands of fighters from the French 10th Army. Rommel had given his forces a six-day leave and traveled to Berlin for a planning conference with the *führer*. By the time he returned, the evacuation at Dunkirk had been completed.

Another rumor was that Hitler had let the British and French armies escape so that their countries would be demoralized by the scenes of defeated fighters returning home and leaving their war material to him. A more sober explanation was that the fast-moving *Panzer* divisions had outrun their infantry and logistical support. The terrain around Dunkirk was not ideal for armored vehicles, and the pause allowed time for the trailing elements to catch up. Rommel's men needed to rest and conduct critical repairs to and maintenance on their war machines before continuing the offensive.

Marian sighed. *Who knows why the maniac in Berlin does what he does?* The news was that the Luftwaffe had been unmerciful in the air over Dunkirk, dropping bombs and mowing down troops on the beach. *Maybe Hermann Göring convinced Hitler than he could destroy the fleeing army from the air.* "That's as good a theory as any," she muttered.

Dunkirk was only three hundred miles away, and now Continental Europe lay bare for Hitler's army to overrun at will. Only Switzerland, Spain, and Portugal, protected by the Alps and the Pyrenees mountain ranges respectively, were poised to withstand him. Those countries had declared neutrality, but if push came to shove, Spain's dictator, Franco, was decidedly pro-Nazi.

To make matters worse, five days ago, the French government had determined that fighting Germany no longer made sense and moved out of Paris to Tours, where Marshal Pétain, the "Lion of Verdun," promptly sought surrender terms.

The next day, Marian had listened to de Gaulle address the citizenry on

BBC. When he announced that the flame of French resistance would not be extinguished, she had muttered, "I hope you're right."

Only four days ago, she had listened as Prime Minister Winston Churchill announced to the nation, "...the Battle of France is over. I expect that the Battle of Britain is about to begin... Let us therefore brace ourselves to our duties, and so bear ourselves that if the British Empire and its Commonwealth last for a thousand years, men will still say, "'This was their finest hour.'"

Does Britain's finest hour mean abandoning her loyal subjects?

Today, this very day, Hitler was in a train car at a park near Compiègne in France to seal a Franco-German armistice. *And our tiny Sark Island is only a short boat ride from Normandy.*

With her reflections in mind and still observing the postman making his way toward the *seigneurie,* Marian put her hands along the sides of her temples and massaged them. "God help us," she breathed.

As the postman approached the main door of the house below Marian's window, he moved out of her sight. Moments later, his errand completed, he reappeared and began his return journey.

Marian waited. Minutes passed, more than anticipated. She heard footfalls on the stairs and turned, expecting to see the maid. Instead, her husband, Stephen, mounted the staircase. Even before he cleared the top, she saw that he bore an uncharacteristic expression, one that was at once grim, horror-filled, and sorrowful.

Stephen was a tall, thin man with thick gray hair. He was tanned from constant exposure to sun, sea, and wind, and known to laugh often and long. Loved by his fellow islanders for his humor and humility, he lived the irony that he was their legal ruler despite having been born in America.

Sark Island, although a British possession, governed itself under ancient Norman law. Being an only child, Marian had inherited her title upon her father's death and had ruled Sark. Then she married Stephen.

Under the legal concept of *jure uxoris seigneur*, meaning "by right of wife," Stephen had gained the title of *Seigneur of Sark Island* and became its senior co-ruler. Although he carried out his ceremonial responsibilities dutifully, he was content to leave the real governing to Marian and otherwise enjoy his idyllic life.

Now, alarmed by Stephen's demeanor, Marian braced herself. Respected and admired by the populace, she was nevertheless known to be stoic. Her father had raised her to be independent, teaching her to shoot, climb the cliffs that encircled Sark Island, and think for herself; but he allowed for little emotional expression. She had once told Stephen, "I am fortunate to be unbound by the useless sense of self-sympathy."

Stephen entered the grand landing of the second floor holding a yellow paper between shaking hands, and he kept looking down at it with tormented eyes as he advanced. When he drew near Marian, he tried to speak but could not, and then she saw that tears ran down his face.

"What is it, Stephen?"

He stood in front of her holding out the yellow piece of paper. "A telegraph from the War Office..." was all he could manage.

Marian steeled herself. Already, the war had raged long enough that such missives throughout the British Empire were things to be feared, for with increasing frequency, they brought news of a war death within the family.

"Was one of our sons killed?" she asked softly. "Which one?"

Stephen shook his head numbly. "It's Jeremy and Lance. I don't know if they're dead." His voice broke. "Jeremy was at Dunkirk. I don't know where Lance was. They're both missing in action."

Marian and Stephen sat together in a small salon off the landing on the second floor of the mansion. She had taken a seat in a richly upholstered chair before a mahogany desk by the window, and he sat on a divan near the center of the room. She remained poised, unmoving. He lowered his elbows to rest on his knees and held his head in his hands.

After several minutes, Marian broke the silence. "What was Jeremy doing at Dunkirk?" she asked, a rhetorical question. "He was an engineer, not a foot soldier. He's not like Lance, who was eager to be in the war. The army sent Jeremy to France to construct airfields. He knows nothing of combat."

Stephen raised his head to hear his wife, and then returned his face to his hands. "As I understand things," he said after a time, "Jeremy's unit was thrown in with others to provide rearguard protection so that the units on the beach at Dunkirk could evacuate. That was a tiny force compared to the German divisions, so our army took every spare non-combatant soldier, including the engineers, and put them at the front."

Marian closed her eyes and breathed in. "So, our sweet Jeremy was fed to the wolves."

"Along with many other fine young boys."

Marian nodded almost imperceptibly. "Do we know how many of them survived, how many were captured, or how many died?"

Stephen shook his head. "News is scant. The BBC hasn't had much detail to report. The Germans claim they took tens of thousands of men as prisoners. I think Paul is still safe in London, and of course Claire is there, but I haven't been able to reach either of them."

Marian stood, smoothed her skirt with a sweep of her hands, and crossed to her husband, laying a hand on his shoulder. "Our people will want to know about Lance and Jeremy," she said. "They love them."

Stephen stood, and they embraced.

"The times ahead will seem impossible," Marian said, stepping back. "But I don't have to tell you that." She closed her eyes and rubbed her temples again. "The Germans will come. We have to prepare our islanders to meet them."

44

Word went out that the Dame of Sark had called a meeting for that evening. She did not stress a priority but did not need to. All the islanders had seen the smoke rising over the ocean in the direction of Normandy two weeks ago and understood its significance; and among a populace of roughly four hundred and thirty people, few secrets survived. They murmured, horrified at the news that Lance and Jeremy were missing in action.

Being the sole population in western civilization still ruled under the ancient Norman feudal system, albeit with greater benevolence than that recorded in other places at other times, the lives of the *Sercquiais*, as the citizens of Sark called themselves, were at once well-ordered and interference-free.

Although Marian Littlefield held the fief by inheritance, she had gained her surname by marriage. During the last war, Stephen, the son of investment bankers in New Jersey, had taken up residence in Canada with several college friends so that he could fly fighters for the British Royal Flying Corps. Afterward, he remained in London as a banker and became a British citizen. It was there that he met Marian, a widow with four lively children: three sons and a daughter.

On moving to Sark, he had been much surprised when he learned that he was legally the senior co-ruler of the island. His only objection to living there was that the island, at just over two square miles, was not large enough for a golf course. He contented himself with exploring the jagged cliffs of the forty-two-mile coastline with his stepchildren, sailing with them in the rough waters of the Channel, or engaging them in sport on the flatlands.

When in 1565, Queen Elizabeth I conferred the fiefdom in perpetuity on Helier de Carteret and his heirs, she required that he keep the island free of pirates and that forty men live there who were British subjects. Helier met his obligation by subletting the island in forty parcels to tenants who agreed as a condition of their leases to build a house on their acreage and keep a man on each parcel armed with a musket.

That arrangement had continued through the centuries even with the sale of the fiefdom. Marian, descended from the last purchaser of the lease, exercised the rights of lordship; and the families of the tenants descended from the most recent owners of their respective subleases retained their respective rights.

Laws governing Sark were promulgated in the Chief Pleas, a parliamentary body with the tenants also inheriting voting membership. Pressure had built to convert to a more democratically elected representative system, but on this night, Germany subsumed all other concerns. Residents crowded into the ancient stone Chief Pleas Assembly building to hear what the Dame had to say.

As Marian and Stephen entered and made their way to the front of the hall, the crowd parted to make way. The citizens' sympathetic expressions signified that many had heard the news, conversation ceasing as Marian reached the front and turned to look across the concerned faces. Stephen, always supporting his wife, moved to a chair to one side at the front of the assemblage where he would remain unobtrusive.

Marian took a breath. "My friends," she began, "I don't have to tell you that we face precipitous times." She lowered her eyes to the floor momentarily, and when she raised them again, emotional pain creased her face. "You might have heard that our sons, Lance and Jeremy, are missing in action." Tears welled in her eyes. She sniffed and wiped them away.

She acknowledged audible gasps and sounds of empathy about the room with a bow of her head. "Thank you. The good news is that, as far as we know, Paul and Claire are still safe in London." Her strained smile expressed that the optimistic tidbit did not overcome the worry.

"I didn't ask you here to sympathize with my personal concerns. We face a shared danger coming from the continent, and it is lethal."

She caught Stephen's eye and took another breath. "As you know, I went to Guernsey three days ago. I wanted to see how our local higher government and neighbors prepared to meet the menace. What I saw disturbed me greatly. I am sad to say that our friends there reacted in panic. I saw lines at stores, at banks, and at wharves where desperate people jostled for passage to England. Our neighbors on Guernsey buried family treasures and heirlooms in their gardens, and they crowded veterinary clinics to put pets to sleep rather than leave them to the mercy of the Nazis."

The emotion of having to speak of her personal considerations passed, and her voice became stern. "You know from the news that, a week ago, our national government decided that these Channel Islands are to be demilitarized, meaning that the Crown will not defend us. The Germans will come, and no pretense of trying to stop them or put up a military defense will be attempted. On Guernsey Isle, the panic over that decision caused over seventeen thousand people to evacuate in one week."

She looked across her audience, her glance settling on many friends she held near and dear. "My visit affected me deeply. I watched the Guernsey we knew fade into history. Regardless of the outcome of this war, it will never be the same. Returning home afterward, I took some time to think before speaking with you about how we could best preserve our unique oasis of quiet and rest."

Waiting for her words to settle in, Marian continued. "We are the last feudal system in existence, at least in the west, and while such governance has a dismal history in general, it works for us. We write our own laws, empanel our own courts, have our own culture, even enjoy our own language. Those ethereal elements that define the character of a people will be gone from Guernsey and will not come back. We cannot let that happen here, on Sark Island."

Approving murmurs arose from various quarters. "Dame Marian," a voice called, "do you believe the Germans will come here?"

"I do," Marian replied somberly, "if only for the propaganda value of seizing British territory."

"Let them come," someone else piped in. "I still have my musket."

A ripple of laughter circulated in the crowd. Marian smiled with genuine humor.

"Yes, under our obligations to the Crown, we still defend our island with at least forty muskets, and we know they are all rusty." Then she became serious again. "With London's demilitarization announcement last week, as you know, came an offer to evacuate any of us who wishes for that. We will help anyone who chooses to go."

She paused to let the gravity of her pronouncement sink in. "Before you decide, think carefully about what your departure could mean. I believe that if we leave, the island we come back to will not be the one we know and love. Everything that makes us unique in this world will have been wrenched from us."

She took a deep breath as her eyes swept the room. "Therefore, Stephen and I have decided that we will not leave, and I appeal to you personally to stay with us."

No one stirred, no one spoke. Individual faces showed the weight of decision pressed on them.

Laden with concern, a single voice broke the silence. "How will we meet them?"

With a glance at Stephen and then at the floor, Marian lifted her head and steepled her fingers against her chin. "I have a few ideas. Hear me out. When the Germans come, the principle they must grasp is that while they occupy our beloved Sark Island, they will never dominate us. We are and always will be proud British subjects, and *Sercquiais*."

45

London, England

The head of MI-6, Brigadier John Menzies, stared coldly around the room. Present with him were Lord Hankey, Major Crockatt, Paul, Jeremy, Claire, and Commander Alastair Denniston, deputy head of the Government Communications Headquarters at Bletchley Park. All looked serious, but Jeremy was also bewildered.

Menzies first glared at him. "You, Lieutenant," he said, his voice high-pitched and cracking. "I understand you're at the center of this discussion. Please explain."

Startled, Jeremy uncrossed his ankles and stood up. He wore a new uniform supplied by Crockatt. "Sir, I don't know what the subject matter is, who you are, or why I'm here. Forty-five minutes ago, I received an order from Major Crockatt to be present for this meeting. Aside from that, I'm in the dark."

Menzies studied him. "You're that officer who was rescued by the Oronsay, aren't you? The one who saved the little boy?"

Jeremy nodded. "I suppose I am, sir, but I hardly—"

"Save your modesty," Menzies interrupted irritably. "Please wait outside in the next office."

Feeling his ears turn hot with humiliation and the eyes of everyone in the room following him, Jeremy rose and exited, closing the door behind him.

When he had gone, Menzies looked around at the others. "Is there anyone else who claims to be unaware of what we're here to talk about?" When no one spoke up, he continued. "I brought you here by request of and in deference to Lord Hankey." He scowled. "Understand that I could have frog-marched each of you in here in handcuffs and leg chains. Bletchley Park's security has been breached. That risks one of our most closely guarded secrets, which so far is our greatest hope for victory. How and why did the breach take place, and how do we contain the damage?"

He looked around at each face, his anger evident, and then spoke directly to Denniston. "I would like you to remind the people in Hut 6 at Bletchley Park that it is their job to intercept German communications and decode them. It is not to translate and analyze them or recommend action based on them. Is that understood?"

Denniston coughed and threw a look at Claire. "I'll deal with it, sir."

Menzies fixed his cold gaze on her. "I understand that you are the source of the breach."

"She is not, sir." Paul stood. "I knew about the purpose at Bletchley independent of her."

His discovery of Bletchley's major role in the war effort had been accidental, although given his job at MI-6, he surely would have learned about its secrets sooner or later. That special section belonging to MI-6 was home to the band of cryptologists and codebreakers, and to Enigma, the cypher machine used by the German army to generate code that was supposed to be unbreakable. Using an Enigma given to British intelligence by Poland just before their own German invasion, not only had the staff at Bletchley Park broken the code, but they also did it at such speeds that they read virtually every message emanating from German high command and its field units. Indeed, it was such messaging that had alerted Churchill to the need and opportunity to evacuate at Dunkirk.

Menzies leaned back in his chair, clearly angered by the interruption. "Please explain, Lieutenant, concisely."

"I work in your organization, sir. I read and analyze lots of intelligence.

While I was not specifically authorized to know about the goings-on at Bletchley, if I did not know about it, that would mean I am not doing my job thoroughly, because I would have missed the documents that *are* associated with my work."

Without changing expression, Menzies broke in. "Hmmm. We'll have to talk about that later. I take it that you are an analyst?"

"Yes, sir."

"Did you have any other aspirations for the duration of this war?"

With a glance at Crockatt and mindful of the major's pending offer, Paul replied, "I had thought I might transfer to one of the fighter squadrons. I hear they are in desperate need of pilots, and flight school is not very long these days. I'm already a licensed pilot."

Menzies scoffed. "Well you can get that idea right out of your head. You know too much about Bletchley. You won't be allowed out of the country for the duration of the war. We can't risk your being shot down and captured. Too much is at stake. You'll be lucky if I don't have you prosecuted and ask for the death penalty."

Paul listened with dismay and a sinking heart. He glanced again at Crockatt, whose expression remained blank.

Hankey stood, looking impatient. "Lighten up, John. You're not going to hang anyone in this group."

Menzies shifted his eyes, shielding his surprise with a deadpan expression.

"We're all loyal subjects here," Hankey continued. "I agree, though, that this young lieutenant cannot be put in a position in which he could be captured, tortured, and thus jeopardize exposure of Bletchley."

"That's policy," Menzies interrupted. "No exceptions."

"Yes, well, let's get to the heart of the matter, shall we? What is pertinent is the information that Miss Claire retrieved, not how she got it. It's germane to all of our missions. The secrets of Bletchley need not be endangered."

Menzies sniffed. "Go on."

With occasional input from Crockatt and Paul, Hankey told the pertinent parts of Jeremy's story, dwelling on the particulars of how Ferrand

Boulier had saved his life and those of many other British soldiers and French citizens.

At his conclusion, he said, "The only breach of Bletchley in this instance is that Miss Claire highlighted significant information, which, to my mind, she should have done. She went through channels. In doing so, she shed light on something none of us had yet realized, that the very type of network we wish to establish is growing up of its own accord in northern France. We should capitalize on that."

Claire held her breath, feeling the hard scrutiny of Menzies' stare.

"You broke the code for those particular messages?"

Claire squirmed uncomfortably. "Yes, sir."

"The decoded messages are in German," Menzies snapped. "How did you know what they contained?"

"I studied German in school, sir. We all did. Me"—she glanced nervously at Paul—"and my brothers. We're all fluent in it. My mother saw to that. She lived in Germany for a while, picked up the language, and wanted us to know it."

Appearing somewhat flummoxed, Menzies turned to Denniston. "Did you know that?"

Denniston shook his head. "I knew she speaks French. She grew up on Sark Island, but I didn't know she also knew German."

Menzies directed his next question to Claire again. "Didn't you ever tell anyone?"

"No one ever asked," she replied. "I was recruited because I play the piano. Musicians make good decoders—something about the discipline involved."

For a moment, Menzies just stared at her. Then he grunted and waved his hand. "Sark, eh? Sorry we couldn't do more down there."

Without waiting for a response, he turned his attention back to Denniston. "She went outside of channels."

"To a member of your own staff."

"Then how did it get to MI-9?"

"I did that, sir," Paul broke in. "From my view—"

"The view of a lieutenant," Menzies growled.

"Yes, sir," Paul replied. "May I continue?"

Menzies assented with an impatient nod.

"I regard Major Crockatt as a mentor. I wanted advice on getting the matter in front of you as quickly as possible. Lives hang in the balance, particularly those of Mr. Boulier and his daughters. If we are to believe the communications, Bergmann is after not only the family, but also the network that Boulier established."

"I'm sure you feel very self-righteous in your assessment," Menzies fired back, "but let me clue you in on an aspect of Bletchley so that you rein in your propensity to take independent action." He poked a finger in Paul's direction. "We've let convoys of ships be attacked when we could have sent messages that would have saved them. We've let attacks go forward against our forces when family members of our staff and close friends were in jeopardy. Some were killed. Do you have any clue about why we would do that?"

Aghast and confused, Paul shook his head.

"The Germans think their code is unbreakable. They change the setting each morning, but they use it every day. What do you think they would conclude if suddenly, every convoy they assaulted or every objective they attacked was abruptly and miraculously met and defeated by our forces?"

"I'm not sure, sir." Paul still reeled from what he had just heard. "I suppose they'd guess we had their code."

"Exactly, and what would they do?" Without waiting for a response, Menzies continued. "They would change it. We expect the activity at Bletchley to shorten the war by two years. It's taken us a long time to get to where we can decipher volumes of encrypted messages and do it rapidly.

"Have we played God and sacrificed lives? Yes. I freely admit that. But we've saved many more thousands than we've lost, and ultimately, the lives saved could be in the millions." He glanced at Claire, his eyes piercing. Ferocity tinged his voice. "And we only allow our brightest and most trusted codebreakers inside the huts at Bletchley."

Claire squirmed but remained silent. Paul broke the discomfort. "Sir, I don't know what to say."

Menzies was not finished. "Her job is to decode, not translate and analyze what's received. We have other departments for that."

"Which missed it altogether," Hankey broke in sternly. "We have an opportunity to support an established network, and a high price possibly to be paid if we don't take it."

Menzies peered at Claire in silence. She held his stare a moment, and then dropped her eyes.

He shifted his view and scrutinized Paul. Finally, he addressed Lord Hankey again. "You feel strongly that this network in northern France is one that should be preserved, if possible?"

"My sense is that it probably is, but none of us is informed well enough to give a reliable response. We can say that it is one of the first to form, and to date, it is one of the most effective. Failure to preserve it could discourage others from becoming active."

"I see," Menzies said. "Major Crockatt?"

"I concur."

Menzies sat quietly, his anger dissipated, alone with his thoughts. "What do you think should be done about it?" He alternated his view between Hankey and Crockatt. "Neither of your sections is even up and running yet."

The lord and the major started to speak at the same time. Crockatt deferred to Hankey. "Your calling this meeting preempted discussion before we could fully analyze the situation," Hankey said, "but we're talking about saving the Boulier network. Doing so would advance our combined missions by preserving a proven asset. If in the process we rescue the family, so much the better. If anyone deserves to be rescued, they do."

"And what about my point that neither MI-9 nor SOE is operational yet?"

"That's only a matter of filling positions in both organizations," Hankey said. "Our missions are defined, the hierarchy established, and we are now in recruitment and training phase. Besides, this is a war. The enemy didn't wait on our convenience or when we were fully prepared to launch their attack.

"We have the assets. I know that you, that is MI-6, are in touch with new groups forming in the south of France, the very ones who alerted us that young Jeremy Littlefield was on his way here. He sits just outside the door because of them, and he's left wondering what the bloody hell is going on. They already know him and trust him."

Hankey stopped talking, a look of realization dawning on his face. Glancing across at Claire, he saw an expression of horror in her eyes. She held her hand in front of her mouth to throttle a gasp. Standing next to him, Paul sucked in his breath.

"Are you suggesting that we send that lieutenant back in there?" Menzies asked. He too seemed taken aback at the implied suggestion.

"I suppose I am," Hankey replied, "although I hadn't had that notion before I said it. He'd have to volunteer, of course."

A pall descended over the room. Menzies was the first to speak.

"Essentially what you are proposing," he told Hankey, "is to send a battered evader from Dunkirk who has not yet recovered back into the combat zone to conduct a potential suicide mission. He's untrained, and he's emotionally attached to an objective that's different than the one you propose. That's what this boils down to. He's after saving that family, and you want to save the network. Succeeding in one *might* preserve the other, and his support would come from two sections of British intelligence that are not yet operational. Is that accurate?"

Hankey did not immediately speak, but then he bobbed his head. "You've sized it up, John, although with the assets at your disposal, I expect that you'll provide whatever additional support we need. *Is that accurate?*"

Menzies' eyes narrowed, but he nodded slightly.

"This mission can serve as a signal to the Free French that we fully intend to support them throughout this war," Hankey added.

Claire fidgeted while the discussion took place. She suddenly blurted, "No."

All eyes shifted to her. "You can't ask him to go back in. You saw him. He still looks wretched from what he's been through."

Silence.

"He'll go," Paul said quietly.

Attention switched to him. He looked across at Claire. "You know he'll go. We won't be able to keep him away. He already knows something's up, and he'll put two and two together. Lord Hankey is right. He's the key to overcoming the trust factor, and for that reason alone, he's the best man to go. If we wait longer, the Bouliers could be dead, and their network demolished."

The room remained quiet for a few moments, broken again by Menzies. "The prime minister will want to know about this mission. It won't go forward without his approval. We'll have to mount a simultaneous disinformation campaign to protect Bletchley as a source." He looked across to Claire, and his expression softened. Then he spoke to Paul. "Bring him in, and let's hear what he says."

A knock on the door interrupted the discussion. When it opened, a clerk hurried in and handed a note to Menzies. He read it quickly and dismissed the messenger.

"Gentlemen, Miss Littlefield," he said, "if we are going to do anything, we'd better move. We just received word from Marseille. Bergmann just made his first arrest."

Twiddling with a pencil, Menzies looked directly at Claire. "I have one more stipulation for securing my cooperation."

46

Jeremy's reappearance before the group assembled in John Menzies' office was short and concise. Paul had gone to the door and summoned him. As he entered, Claire made her departure. She turned her face as she passed by him. Neither brother sat down.

"Lieutenant Littlefield," Menzies said, directing his gaze at Jeremy, "I understand all the particulars. Your brother can fill you in. I have one question for you: would you volunteer to go back into France to save the Boulier network?"

Without hesitation, Jeremy replied, "I would do anything for the Bouliers. When can I leave?"

Menzies broke a rare smile. "I appreciate your zeal, but you need to understand a subtlety. The objective is not to save the Bouliers, although if you succeed, that is a likely outcome. Your mission would be to keep the network intact that Mr. Boulier put in place and that helped you and others escape and evade across France. Is that something you'd agree to do?"

"Without hesitation, sir. How soon can we get underway?"

Menzies remained silent for several moments and then turned to Crockatt. "Major, this mission falls in your purview. I won't speak for Lord Hankey, but I suspect that if any ancillary blowing-up needs doing, his section will be happy to oblige.

"I'll get to the PM, brief him, and request priority across the services. The mission must leave no British fingerprints. To save the viability of Bletchley, it should look like a purely French partisan operation. And, you'll need other backing. For starters, you'll need air support of some kind to get our man over there." He indicated Jeremy with a jut of his jaw. "Any questions?"

There were none.

"Well, then," Menzies said, finality tinging his voice as he redirected his attention to Crockatt. "Keep me apprised, Major. I'll second young Jeremy's brother, Lieutenant Paul Littlefield, to you for the duration of the mission; I'm sure it would be a distraction to him anyway. All of this assumes that Mr. Churchill approves. I don't see why he wouldn't, except that this mission jumps ahead of established plans. You should have your answer before the day is out. I suggest you start work."

<hr />

"I'm not sure I understand the mission," Jeremy said when he was alone with Paul and Crockatt. "Are we to rescue Ferrand Boulier or not? Has he been arrested?"

The major responded, "We don't know, but he might get captured, or even turn himself in to save his friends. Regardless, the network needs to continue to function. You'd normally be considered too close to the issues to be part of the task, except that the participants in France already know and trust you. We don't have time to formulate a better alternative."

"So, what am I supposed to do?"

"I've barely had time to think things through," Crockatt said. "The first hurdle is getting you over there. Teams are to be structured with a leader, a radio operator, and a courier. The other members joining you are mostly trained, but you're not, at least not for this specific leadership role. Again, we don't have time. You'll have to rely on what you picked up in combat and while evading across France. We need you on the ground there tomorrow night, but even the way we get you in and out of the country has to be worked out." He smiled sardonically. "You caught us in our infancy. Everything is experimental."

A puzzled look crossed Jeremy's face. "What happened to Claire? She seemed upset when she left."

"She doesn't want you going on this mission," Paul cut in. "Menzies sent her back to Bletchley to care for Timmy. They'll stay in the apartment while you're gone."

"You won't be going back there at least until after your return," Crockatt added.

"But why?" Jeremy asked, startled. "I should say goodbye to Timmy. He'll be confused when he doesn't see me, and he's lost enough people that were important to him."

"There's no time," Crockatt said brusquely. "If we're to get you into France tomorrow night, we need every minute to plan and prepare."

Something about his tone caused Jeremy to scrutinize the major's face, which remained impassive. Jeremy swung around to search Paul's expression. His brother only shook his head.

Jeremy's concern rose. "What happens to Timmy if something happens to me?"

"The Foreign Office is still searching for his relations, and until they're found, you are still his guardian. Claire and the nanny will take care of him on your behalf."

"Timmy will always have a home with the Littlefields for as long as he needs one," Paul interjected. "Rest assured of that. I'll be looking in on him regularly."

Not quite mollified, Jeremy asked, "Can't I at least see him before I leave?"

Crockatt shook his head. "You can't go back to Bletchley, unless you want to cancel the mission."

Jeremy shot the major a piercing look but said nothing. An image formed in his mind of the first time he had seen the little boy crawling back into the smoke and flames on the Lancastria. The memories flooded in again.

He turned on the major fiercely. "Promise me," he rasped, his voice suddenly hoarse. Then he whirled on his brother. "Swear to me that you will let nothing bad happen to Timmy. I promised his mother."

A knock on the door interrupted the conversation. Vivian opened it. "The operations and logistics people are ready for Jeremy," she said.

Jeremy glanced at her without seeing her. When his eyes focused, he was startled at her presence. He peered at Paul again with a probing expression.

Paul nodded with a set jaw and furrowed brow. "I swear."

Jeremy shifted his gaze to Crockatt.

"Count on it," the major said. "Now," he continued, changing the subject, "while you meet your team, draw your gear, and get up to snuff on procedures, Paul and I will put a mission concept together. We'll be ready with it this evening."

After Jeremy had left with Vivian, Paul turned to Crockatt. "Do you think he knows why he can't go back to Bletchley?"

"He's not dumb," Crockatt replied. "He knows he's going to France in civilian attire, and if he's captured, he could be shot as a spy. Or he could be tortured, in which case he would want to know nothing about Bletchley. Thankfully, he knows nothing of Enigma.

"From his view, all factors that precipitated this mission emanated from radio transmissions coming out of Marseille to Lord Hankey's fledgling organization. For him, Bletchley Park was just a place to stay. We must keep it that way."

Paul agreed, but refrained from mentioning his other concern. *If Claire is right, and Jeremy is smitten with Amélie, they could endanger each other and the entire Boulier network.*

47

"You'll have to jump, ol' boy," Major Crockatt said. They were in an old farmhouse north of London. Its pastures had been converted into an airfield, its barns into supply huts and training facilities. "You'll fly across the Channel in a Lockheed B14L Hudson bomber." He was almost apologetic. "We're contemplating having Lysander aircraft land in France for future missions, but we don't have time to make the necessary preparations for this round. We'd have to find fields, establish air and ground signals, train reception teams. All of that is infinitely more difficult for landing a plane than flying over and dropping people off."

While the major spoke, a senior sergeant held up assorted items, called them out, and put them in various pockets of Jeremy's kit. Further down the room, other non-coms checked out Jeremy's courier, Théo, and the radio operator, Brigitte, a very small woman. Jeremy had met them earlier in the day.

Watching them while being briefed, Jeremy struggled to surmount misgivings over the woman. Then he remembered Amélie facing two German soldiers on a rain-soaked night on the road above the beaches at Dunkirk while he and Ferrand hid in the gully. *Courage can show up anywhere.*

Now, as they ran through final inspection, her eyes met his. She gave a slight nod. She seemed poised, yet behind the dark eyes, he saw or imagined a hint of fear.

"Here's your map," the sergeant said to Jeremy.

"It's a night jump," Crockatt continued.

"Sir, it's really all right," Jeremy said. "I practiced a few landings in the mockups in a dark barn. I know what to do. Keep my eyes on the horizon, roll as soon as my feet touch the ground."

"Here's your compass," the sergeant went on, despite the interruptions.

"They've selected a fairly narrow field for the drop zone," Crockatt interjected, "but it's long and the prevailing winds blow along its length. You'll come out of the plane on a static line, so your chute will open automatically. Get your bearings as quickly as possible, then steer to the center of the field. Did they teach you how to do that?"

Jeremy nodded. He treated the attention with bemusement. "And they taught me how to use the toggles to crab back and forth so I don't overshoot the field."

Watching from the side, Paul was both somber and amused. He found Crockatt's mother-hen-like care for his brother and his teammates heartwarming and reassuring.

"Your torch," the sergeant said. "I'll put it in this coat pocket. Don't forget it. You'll need it as soon as you're on the ground. Now, would you please empty your pockets?"

Jeremy complied, finding a one shilling coin as he did so.

"I'll take that," the sergeant said. He handed Jeremy a wad of banknotes. "And here are your French francs. That's carrying money. We'll drop three equipment cylinders with your team. They contain rifles, ammunition, foodstuffs, and more money. Now we need to check the tags on your clothing. Mustn't have any British ones."

Jeremy waited patiently while the sergeant checked. "You're good, sir. All French tags."

"I say," Paul remarked to Crockatt, "these chaps are very thorough."

"We want our people back in one piece," the major said. To Jeremy's relief, he went to check on the other team members.

"Here are your French identity papers and your Webley MI907 6.35-mm pocket pistol," the sergeant went on. "Mind you, it's loaded. Let me have your British ID."

Jeremy looked at the man dumbly, and then smirked. "Mine was lost on the Lancastria," he said. "I haven't been in England long enough to get a new one."

The sergeant gave him a searching look but continued to go through the various items, including emergency rations, extra rations, and first aid bandages. As he did, he quizzed Jeremy on his cover story. At one point, he lifted his head in concern. "Sir, you seem to be unsure of crucial details."

Jeremy chuckled. "I am, Sergeant. I just learned them today. But no worries, if worse comes to worst, I'm versed at playing the fool."

The non-com shot him a look that was both perplexed and skeptical, but he let the matter ride. Next, he held up a worn wine cork, complete with a purplish-red end. "Inside this are your lethal pills."

He slid back a small cover on one side to reveal a hollowed-out interior. When he turned it over, two small tablets rolled into his hand. "You've been briefed on these?" He arched his eyebrows. Jeremy nodded.

Aircraft engines spinning up to power sounded through the small farmhouse. Jeremy looked around anxiously for Paul.

His brother had the expression of a deer caught in a bright light, frozen. He broke his trance and hurried over to Jeremy, throwing his arms around him. "Come back to us, brother," he muttered. "You've been gone far too long."

"I'll be back," Jeremy said. "Take care of Timmy and give my love to Claire. Keep trying to get to Mum and Dad and keep an eye out for Lance."

Paul hesitated, but then blurted in a whisper, "Claire thinks you're head over heels for the French girl. Don't let personal feelings get either of you killed."

Jeremy chuckled and squeezed his brother's neck. "I must be more transparent than I thought. I'll keep your advice in mind. I probably won't even see her."

Paul stepped back and eyed him skeptically. "Don't try to pretend that she's not a big reason you're so keen on going back."

Jeremy stood still, his eyes in a faraway place. "I hadn't thought of it like that," he admitted, "but if I'm honest with myself, she's in the mix. The last I heard, though, she's safely away from Dunkirk. It's her father that's in the soup, and I owe him."

"But you're keeping the preservation of the Boulier network uppermost in your mind, right?"

"Of course."

Paul looked skeptical, but he made no further comment. The two of them joined the team heading toward the back door with the sending-off party.

Behind the farmhouse, the pastures had been turned into aircraft parking areas and rutted runways. The group piled into a car with their parachutes and equipment packs and drove through the myriad aircraft parked in long lines.

On a nearby taxiway, silhouetted against a twilight horizon, a big plane squatted, its rear turret prominent on its back, its gun barrels still visible against the sky, and its propellers spinning while its engines roared. Two additional gun barrels protruded from the glass nose that gleamed dully in the fading twilight.

The car stopped parallel to the airplane. Behind the wing, a round hatch just large enough for a person to fit through opened within the tri-colored roundel of the Royal Air Force logo painted on the bomber's side.

The crew emerged through the opening and dropped to the ground. Crockatt introduced them. Then he drew Jeremy and his comrades around him while Paul stood close by. "Try to get some sleep on the way over," he said. "You'll need it." He shook hands with each of them and helped them climb aboard.

Five minutes later, Crockatt and Paul stood side by side as the big bomber taxied down the runway, turned into the wind, and revved its engines. The major cast Paul a sidelong look. "Fighter squadron, eh?"

"Sorry, sir. It was a thought." Paul sighed. "It's not in the cards now."

"No worries. I'm sure your contributions in the war will be far more valuable on the ground."

As he spoke, the bomber began a slow roll down the runway, gained speed, thundered past them, and lumbered into the night sky. After it had disappeared, they rode back to headquarters. Paul sat silently, the lump in his throat making breathing difficult.

Crockatt watched him closely. "Are you all right?"

Paul murmured, "I hope I didn't just take part in sending my brother to his death."

48

Marseille, France

"Do we know who they're sending?" Maurice asked.

Madame Fourcade, codenamed "Hérisson," shook her head. "I only know that he is codenamed 'The Fool.' Not very inspiring." She let out a small, sardonic laugh. "But it's good to see that someone still has a sense of humor. I'm told he already has experience in France and speaks the language fluently."

Fourcade was a petite woman from the upper crust of French aristocracy who became disgusted with the Nazis long before they made known their broader intentions beyond the return of historically Aryan lands. The turning point for her had occurred before the war began, while on a touring visit to Vienna shortly after the *Anschluss*. There, she had witnessed Jewish shopkeepers and professionals, with their families, rousted from their homes and places of business, humiliated in the streets, and forced to wear big, yellow Star of David emblems on their outside clothing. From that single episode, she had concluded that nothing good could come from a regime that not only refused to protect the rights of individuals but also participated in their persecutions.

Returning to Paris, she had sought out those people among her socialite friends who seemed less enamored with the uniquely mustachioed dictator to the northeast. At one particular cocktail party, she had listened intently as two guests argued heatedly about the danger to France coming from Germany, and what measures should be taken to stymie it.

One of them was Charles de Gaulle, then an ambitious lieutenant-colonel on the staff of the French war hero, Marshal Philippe Pétain. The other was Major Georges Loustaunau-Lacau, an intelligence officer also on Pétain's staff. They were fellow graduates of Saint-Cyr, France's foremost military academy, and both were vocally and unabashedly critical of Hitler.

Fourcade quickly ascertained that the two officers, in addition to being contemporaries, were fierce rivals. Entering into conversation with Loustaunau-Lacau, later codenamed "Navarre," she found she shared opinions with him.

A few days later, Navarre called Fourcade and asked if they could meet for dinner. She agreed, and they spoke for many hours. Together, they had sought out like-minded individuals and begun building an organization to resist in the event that the Nazis attacked.

When Germany invaded France, Fourcade had driven south from Paris among the six million refugees clogging the roadways. *Was that only one month ago?* Fortunately, she had friends along the way who were happy to house her, but she had been shocked to find so many of them applauding when Marshal Pétain set about to save France by capitulating.

After several stressful days on the road, she had arrived in Marseille to find that early preparations she and Navarre had made had paid off. She rendezvoused with him there, and they discussed plans.

They differed in their approach. She wished to stay in Marseille and operate from there. He believed they could do better by his continuing in high position inside the intelligence apparatus where he had access to closely guarded secrets. Those of operational value, he could feed to Fourcade.

They had set Maurice up in business several months earlier and his vegetable vending enterprise had flourished, as had his recruiting efforts. He had already built a sizeable group of patriots willing to carry the fight.

Communications methods set up by Navarre with British intelligence were operational, despite that coding and decoding required further development; radio transmission then employed more euphemisms than codes or ciphers. Nevertheless, they had yielded effective results as word spread among Frenchmen who refused to accept their country as a vassal of Germany and were thrilled that an active resistance movement was building in Marseille. Among recruits were patriots from along the Atlantic coast who had blown up fuel-oil tanks.

Within days of Pétain being named head of government in Tours, Navarre had traveled there. Since Pétain knew him personally as a competent and dedicated intelligence officer, he had appointed Navarre as his head of intelligence.

As a result of Fourcade's and Navarre's combined efforts, within a week of Hitler entering Paris, their organization was up and running.

"To give you a more complete answer to your question, Maurice, we don't know anything about The Fool," Fourcade said. "This is the first mission like this. We can't even call it a proof-of-concept since it was thrown together so quickly. The larger idea is to send teams all across France to coordinate plans among resistance groups with British intelligence. The British teams include a leader, a courier, and a radio operator. They'll also bring arms, ammunition, equipment, and money.

"In this case, we have a patriot in the north who set up a network almost as quickly as we did, but he's being threatened with exposure, capture, torture, and the destruction of his network. The imperative is saving his network. The nice result would be to save him too."

Maurice sighed as he regarded Fourcade with doleful eyes. "You know you're talking about the father of the two girls I brought here yesterday, Amélie and Chantal."

"I know," Fourcade said. "I'm struggling with that." She lit a cigarette and stared across the cityscape below her. The Mediterranean sparkled in the distance. "Whatever we do," she said, her voice filling with passion, "we cannot become like those beasts who invaded our country. But we have to be careful not to mix personal considerations with mission requirements. From what I learned about Ferrand Boulier from his daughters, he understands and accepts that. Our aim has to be preserving the network. If we save him too, so much the better."

"What about the girls themselves? They want to be involved."

"And they could be effective, both of them, but not on this mission. They told me their stories. Such a tragedy, but they're strong, intelligent, and resilient."

She took a puff on her cigarette. "Take Chantal with you on your rounds," she mused aloud. "Let her collect and drop off a few messages, give her a sense of doing something important, but don't expose her to real danger. The threat here is limited for the moment anyway, but if Pétain keeps acting like a Hitler copycat, the French police will be a force we'll have to contend with. We have time to let her grow up a bit. Maybe her father will agree to move down here."

"I'm relieved to hear you say that," Maurice responded. "She's still a girl. She should not be fighting in a war. What about Amélie?"

"Until we're finished with the Boulier mission, we need to limit her involvement. She could be an excellent radio operator, but that will become such a dangerous position. The Germans will bring in signal detection technology and spread it south. Count on it. Operators will live in isolation, and their only direct contact with us will be through the couriers. Psychologically, it could be devastating, and I have to wonder about what their life expectancy will be. Probably not long. The radios are their lifelines, but they will also bring death to many of their operators."

She took a last puff on her cigarette and stuffed it out in an ashtray. "There's one other person we need to talk about," she said. "Jacques."

Maurice arched his eyebrows in surprise. "Is there a problem with him?"

Fourcade shook her head. "Only potentially. He's completely trustworthy, but he's Jewish. If he's found out, what the Nazis will do to him is unspeakable. We need to make sure that we always have his back."

"Of course," Maurice replied. "He's a good man."

Fourcade sighed and leaned back. "What a world we live in." She closed her eyes as if to blot out despairing thoughts. "All right, to finish up today's business, the team coming in tonight is only the first of many. We'll need to train more people on how to prepare for arrivals, how to signal from the ground so that the pilots see them at night, and how to wave them off if we need to abort. That's a good place for Amélie to start. If you like, she can be part of the reception committee for our friends coming in from England tonight."

49

A field north of Marseille

The big Lockheed Hudson bomber lumbered south. Its flight path remained high and well west until it was just north of the Pyrenees, avoiding German anti-aircraft guns already taking up positions along the coast of France. Then it turned east, flying along the valleys that skirted the great mountain range. When it reached the Mediterranean, it continued out over the sea until the lights of Marseille twinkled beyond its left wing. Then it banked north and began its descent.

In the back of the plane, Jeremy's three-person team prepared to jump. They were incongruously outfitted with their parachute and equipment over jumpsuits, and beneath that they wore the street clothes intended to allow them to blend with the French public immediately.

The crew performed last-minute checks under a red light.

The bomb bay door opened.

Jeremy approached it gingerly, his breath coming in short gasps as the reality sank in of jumping from an aircraft flying swiftly through the night at hundreds of feet in the air. A crew member guided him to sit on the rim of the bay, his legs dangling below. He clung to its sides, sweat stinging his eyes inside his goggles. Wind blew through the aircraft, but it was surprisingly quieter and less violent than he had expected.

The red light turned to green.

Jeremy pushed himself off and dropped, his nerves strung tight. The wind tossed him around a bit, and at first, all he saw was darkness. Then he was past the turbulence of the aircraft's propwash. He looked up, saw his parachute inflate, and felt the tranquility and thrill that comes from feeling safe under an open canopy before factoring in that someone below might shoot, or that trees or jutting rocks might cause a tragic end. The illumination of a half-moon added to the ambient light over Marseille, allowing him to see his surroundings better than he had expected.

Far below, he recognized the shape of the field, seeing in the same instant a flash of signal lights. He searched around in the sky, spotted his teammates and the three equipment cylinders under open parachutes, and prepared to land.

On the ground, Maurice was the first to hear the aircraft's low rumble. Some of his team had spread out on one end of the field where the chutes were expected to land. Others positioned themselves at the opposite end to signal the pilots.

The bomber appeared as a dark shadow with a deep, throaty roar as it reached its nearest end of the field. Six dark objects fell in sequence from its underbelly, and then the canopies opened, and the three team members and their equipment containers floated to the ground.

"The first jumper will be the leader," Maurice had told Amélie. "I'll take care of him and find out what orders he carries. The radio operator is a woman. Help her. She'll probably be glad to see a female welcoming her."

Amélie had watched in awe as the parachutes drifted down, barely visible blots against the night sky. The remark Maurice had made earlier rang true about these people endangering their lives just by making the jumps, and that did not even consider the risk of being shot down on the way to France.

"Be careful as you approach them," Maurice instructed. "They'll be armed and ready to shoot, so be sure to whistle the tune I taught you earlier and wait to hear the right tune in response."

Her heart beat furiously as the dark figures touched the ground and rolled. Maurice trotted out to the leader as Amélie started toward the other two jumpers. She watched as Maurice slowed his approach and proceeded cautiously. He whistled a faint tune and she heard the musical response. Then she saw the man in deep shadows. In the darkness, she could make out none of his features. As she passed by, he ran to unclasp and deflate his parachute while Maurice moved in to assist.

She went on to the second person, another man, and continued to the third, the female radio operator. She stopped in the darkness, her heart still pounding, whistled as instructed, and heard the correct response.

Another of Maurice's men arrived at the same time. Together, they helped the woman out of her parachute harness and jumpsuit and gathered her equipment.

"We have a safe place for you to stay tonight," the man told her. "You can transmit from there to let London know everyone arrived safely."

"And did we?" the woman asked in French with a perfect Parisian accent. Her voice was calm but held an inflection of anxiety.

They looked around in the ambient light. All three parachutists were busily engaged, securing their equipment and preparing to move out.

"You did," Amélie said, and held out her hand. "Thank you for coming."

The woman exhaled audibly. "Thank you. This was more nerve-wracking than I had thought it would be." She grasped Amélie's outstretched hand.

"You're safe now," Amélie told her. "The Germans haven't yet come to this part of France. Hopefully they won't."

"I'm Brigitte," the woman said.

"I'm—" Amélie hesitated. Maurice had briefed her that the woman would not use her real name, and he had assigned Amélie a code name. "I am Colibri."

"Hummingbird. Nice," Brigitte said in English. She tried to study Amélie's face, even in the dark. Then, reverting to French, she asked, "Will I be staying with you tonight?"

"No. This reception ends my participation in your mission. You'll meet the team to take you north tomorrow. I won't see you again, but you are in good hands."

———

"I've been impressed so far," Jeremy said. The group conversed in French. "How was your treatment?" They were together in a farmhouse on the northern edge of Marseille. Maurice had taken them there, seen to it that they were comfortably settled in with the host family, and set out a guard. He had left with a parting comment that their escorts would arrive in the morning.

"Nicely done," Brigitte said. "I met a young woman in the dark who goes by Colibri. She was very sweet and happy to see us. I'm almost sorry she's not coming along. And the family downstairs is so nice."

"I have to say, Brigitte," Jeremy said, "I was surprised to see a woman on the team."

She nodded. "Wartime exigencies. I was the most qualified and available on short notice. Officially, women are still not authorized to be in combat areas, so officially, I'm not here. There's a lot of discussion taking place at high levels on the subject and the policy might change soon." She laughed sardonically. "It's amazing what can be done when there's a need."

Jeremy scrutinized her a moment. "Well, thank you for coming." He changed the subject. "The leader uses the codename 'Renard.' He said that a team will meet us tomorrow to guide us north. There'll be four members, one to help each of us move through enemy lines, and one to watch out ahead of the whole group when we travel. We'll head north as far as we can on the east side of the country, and then turn west and travel behind the lines."

The third member of the team, Théo, the courier, had so far not said a word. Now he spoke up. "We didn't get much chance to talk before leaving England," he told Jeremy, "but I overheard the sergeant who checked you out say that you're weak in knowing details of your cover story. If you trip up, we could be exposed. Your codename, 'The Fool,' doesn't exactly build confidence."

Jeremy shot him a glance. Théo was a wiry man, in his late twenties, of medium height and build, and with a florid complexion and dark hair. His eyes showed no malice, but they bore a pugnacious expression that warned against nonsense.

"I think we'll be all right," Jeremy replied. "I left France less than a week ago. I was one of those left at Dunkirk. I think I'm good for another go. I'm on this mission because I already know the people there who are resisting the Germans. They got me out, and they'll get us through. I'm 'The Fool' because I played the fool. That was my cover story."

Théo stared at him. "*Vive la Résistance*," he said at last. "I understand the mission is to protect a network," he said, "give it some backup. Can you give us more detail?"

Jeremy nodded. "Sorry we didn't have time to do that before departure." He explained who the Bouliers were, that Ferrand had set up a network, and the success they had realized in aiding British and French soldiers as well as his own family members evade capture. "Their ability to communicate is going to be constrained as Germany destroys telephone hubs and lines, and they currently have no direct contact with Britain or any other networks.

"That's where we come in. I'll assess the needs. Théo, you'll courier my messages to Brigitte"—he turned to face her—"and you'll code and transmit the messages to London. One thing to know is that I won't be with you long. As soon as we're settled in, London will pull me back there for training."

"You seem to be doing a fair job so far," Brigitte cut in. "Why send someone else whom we don't know?"

"You're making London's point," Jeremy replied. "So much of the resistance effort will rely on trust. My replacement will be someone you've already trained with. Whoever it is will bring the benefit of having been fully up to speed and will be more familiar with the country than I am. I'm the stopgap intended to establish initial trust. You'll have to fill in the new leader." Neither Brigitte nor Théo seemed fully mollified, but they did not press the matter further.

50

The farmhouse north of Marseille

"Jeremy! I can't believe it's you," Nicolas enthused when they saw each other. He wrapped his arms around Jeremy in a bear hug. "No one told us you were the one coming. You've been gone barely a week. And you survived the ship that sank."

Jeremy was equally surprised and thrilled to see Nicolas and Jacques. "I made it thanks to you two. I didn't know you'd be our guides. This is great." He introduced them around. "These are the men who got me out of France. Nicolas brought me out of Dunkirk down to Saint-Nazaire. He knows the country. Jacques got me out to the ship."

"Seeing you is like seeing a ghost," Jacques chimed in. "I didn't know if you had survived."

Théo regarded Jeremy with new respect. The farmer and his wife called everyone to breakfast. While they ate, Jeremy noticed an undercurrent of anger coming from Jacques and Nicolas despite the pleasant surprise of seeing each other, and they both appeared distracted.

Then the farmer asked, "Have you heard anything about what agreement Marshal Pétain is making with the Germans?"

Jacques scowled. "The swine," he muttered, and looked across at the farmer's children. Seeing that as a cue, the farmer's wife shooed them into another room.

"What's happened?" the farmer asked.

"That damnable traitor gave away more than two-thirds of the country. It was in the news this morning."

Nicolas looked equally disgusted but let Jacques do the talking. He just shook his head and said, "It's true," while seething with fury.

Jacques uttered a string of epithets. "That cowardly 'hero.'" He said the word with animated contempt. "He gave the Germans the industrial north of France all the way south of Bourges and a wide swath of land along the entire French Atlantic coast. Most of our army is to be disbanded down to one hundred thousand men. Citizens will be disarmed, and the French police have to assist in putting down anti-Nazi unrest."

"So that part of France belongs to Germany now," Jeremy asked, appalled.

"In theory, no. The French government supposedly has administrative control over all of France with the capital still in Paris, but Pétain's government is moving from Tours to Clermont-Ferrand. The Germans will occupy most of the country, and you know they'll never give it back. Not willingly."

"What about our navy?" the farmer asked.

"Oh, we get to keep it," Jacques said, his voice thick with sarcasm. "But what good is it? It's parked on the coast of North Africa." He laughed, a loud, angry guffaw. "We call our new country New France."

His face had flushed a deep red. It contorted with rage. He dropped his voice, striking a threatening note. "I promise you, that traitor, that *collaborateur*, will learn what it means to betray France. Death to him, and death to all *collaborateurs*."

The small group sat in stunned silence.

Jacques started up again. "He ordered a change to our national motto. According to this great defender of France and our culture, it is no longer, 'Liberté, Égalité, Fraternité.'" He jerked from his seat in fury. "Now, according to him, it is, 'Work, Family, Country.' He thinks he can take freedom away from us with the stroke of his pen. Who does this scum think he is? God? And he gives away our country."

He jabbed a finger in the air. "I'll tell you who he is. He's not just a Nazi sympathizer." He spat out his next words. "He is a *fils de pute* Nazi!"

While Jacques ranted, Jeremy kept a close eye on Brigitte and Théo. If their discomfiture rose, they did not show it. They sat in their chairs, stoic and listening.

When Jacques had run down, Jeremy said softly, "Should we be going soon?"

Jacques seemed to come out of a reverie. "I'm sorry," he said. He stood, stepped around the table, and offered his hand to Brigitte. When she lifted hers, he took it in both of his cupped palms. "I apologize. I was rude." He did the same with Théo.

"Perfectly understandable," Théo said. "If Mr. Churchill had given away most of our country, I'd be upset too. But that's why we're here, to help get it back, isn't it?"

Jacques bowed his head graciously and made apologies to the farmer and his wife. They waved it off, sharing his sentiment and rage.

Only much later in the afternoon did Jeremy and Nicolas find themselves alone with a chance to talk. The group had already divided up into their traveling mode. Jeremy resumed his persona as "The Fool," led by Nicholas. The others traveled singly under the watchful eyes of their escorts, and Jacques maneuvered out front. Before leaving the farm, they checked and double-checked each other's forged papers, and ran through reviews of their cover stories. Théo was much more comfortable and even amused when Jeremy morphed into his brain-damaged alter ego.

"How's your family," Jeremy asked when he and Nicolas had placed distance between themselves and anyone else. He noticed that his friend had lost much weight, that his skin was tanned, and he looked much more serious than when the two first met in the barn of his family's dairy farm in Dunkirk. He quickly found out that Nicolas had not shed his humor.

Nicolas grinned. "Why don't you ask the question you want to ask?"

Jeremy's cheeks flushed. "All right, how is Amélie?"

"She's fine and thinking of you all the time. She's in love." He laughed. "I told you, the two of you are right for each other."

Jeremy shoved Nicolas' shoulder. "Where is she?"

The humor dropped from Nicolas' face. "Think, brother. I cannot tell you that. What if you get captured? Under the circumstances, do you really want to know?"

Jeremy closed his eyes and breathed in and out slowly. He shook his head. "Is she safe and well? What about Chantal?"

"Yes, they are both well. Chantal is having to grow up too fast."

"Aren't we all."

Nicolas' face grew serious. "I couldn't tell you where they are anyway. By now, they've moved. I won't know to where." He grimaced. "I need to tell you some things."

He recounted what had happened at the Boulier house after Jeremy had left. "That's the reason the family had to flee. We have no time to waste."

As Nicolas spoke, Jeremy felt a boiling rage welling up such as he had never faced, recalling that he had first arrived in France to build airfields, a young, recently graduated and commissioned engineer wanting to do good. Finding himself in combat with almost no training, his primal instinct had been survival. Then in the Boulier house he had experienced emotions with Amélie that he had never before known.

After surviving the haunting trip across France with Nicolas and out to the Lancastria with Jacques, another drive, that of caring unselfishly for a child, had guided him through his actions on the ship, and then in the waters with Timmy.

Timmy! He realized that he had barely thought of the child since accepting the mission to return to France. *Oh my God, how is he?* His heart wrenched on remembering how the toddler had clung to him, and he realized that he did not want Timmy's relations to find the child. *But he needs them. I might not be around.*

Now he felt intense internal conflict, rage pitted against caring, and he thought of what Nicolas told him had happened to Chantal and what Amélie had done about it. His mind went to Amélie again, and he imagined her in the beauty of their short time together.

Then he pictured Chantal, small, frightened, exuberant; a teenage girl, full of life, having to contend with evil monsters. He saw Ferrand in his mind's eye, the gentle, bent old man who had gone out into a storm to save him from the Nazis.

The Bouliers are family now. This just became personal.

51

Coudekerque-Village, France

"This is one of those out-of-the-way villages that was passed by as the Germans attacked Dunkirk," Nicolas told Jeremy. "There's not much here, no one had the means to resist anyway, and neither the French nor British armies bothered with it, so the Germans didn't either. I guess the villagers should count their blessings; it's only about six kilometers to Dunkirk, which is almost completely destroyed."

They had arrived during the night after nerve-wracking journeys in tiny farm trucks, buses, cars, and whatever modes of transportation that friends of the Bouliers had or could arrange that took them in the right direction, including horse-drawn farm-carts. Jacques had steered them around German checkpoints so that they were able to arrive at this small village without being challenged.

Exhausted, they fell into beds in another farm, this one owned by a longtime family friend. Claude arrived to greet them the next morning, overjoyed to see Jeremy alive and well. "We didn't expect to see you so soon," he said. He gave a sidelong grin to Nicolas and jutted his chin at him. "I hope my no-good son didn't steer you in the wrong direction," he teased.

"Come to think of it, I haven't seen him either since before you left." He gave Nicolas a jocular bear hug and tousled his hair.

"He did well by me," Jeremy replied, smiling, and introduced his team and Jacques.

"Thank you all for coming," Claude said. "I won't say I'm glad you're here. I hope we can gather again in better times."

A somber silence followed. Jeremy asked him, "Do you understand our mission?"

"I'm not sure," Claude replied. "I secured housing for Brigitte and Théo separate from you and each other, and well away from here. I got them employment that fit their cover stories. I received word that Brigitte is a trained nurse, so I put her in for a job at a clinic. The area is short of medical help, but the need is great, as you can guess. She'll be able to travel around to visit 'patients,' and she can camouflage her radio case as a medical bag, so she should be able to make her transmissions from various places to avoid detection."

Jeremy nodded. "Good. And the people in the area where she'll live and do her rounds, they don't know where she comes from?"

"Correct. As far as they know, she was assigned there by the Pétain regime." He spat out the name derisively. "We forged papers that say so."

"Good, and what about Théo?"

"He's a mechanic, *oui*?"

Jeremy and Théo both nodded.

Claude laughed. "That's good. I have some vehicles needing repair." His brow furrowed, and he directed his comments to Théo. "Seriously, a lot of vehicles in the area need work. There's a garage in a nearby village that's looking for a mechanic. They want to talk to you. You'll be able to move around to meet people's needs too."

"How about transportation?"

"Everyone travels around on bicycles these days. With all the destruc-tion..." Claude bowed his head, wiped his eyes, and coughed. "So many dead," he mused. He looked toward the horizon. "We just had another cousin die, fortunately of old age, but we couldn't even give him a decent burial." He caught himself. "Getting on with business, we had no problem finding spare bicycles."

He looked at Jeremy questioningly. "What do we need to do for you?"

Jeremy grasped Claude's shoulder. "I won't be around long," he said. "This team came here months ahead of schedule. I will be replaced. My headquarters sent me because I already knew the people here."

"And we trust you," Claude added. "Are you here to rescue my brother?"

Jeremy did not answer directly. "Let's you and me take a walk." He glanced at Brigitte and Théo to indicate that he needed to speak to Claude alone. They nodded.

Secluded as the farm was, the countryside gave only a few hints that a savage war raged. But for knowledge of the real situation, the sterling weather beneath a blue sky among rolling fields would have given reason for a sense of well-being. Only a few of the crops had been trampled by passing engines of war and infantrymen, although smoke still rose on the southwestern horizon in the direction of Dunkirk. Occasionally, the tranquility was broken by the low rumble of explosions in the far distance.

"It's hard to believe that not even three weeks have gone by since you were here," Claude said after they had walked a ways into the fields. Then he sighed. "You didn't come to rescue Ferrand?"

"Officially, I'm not here for Ferrand. Where is your brother? Bring me up to date."

"He stays in an apartment he found in the ruins of Dunkirk," Claude said. "His sister-in-law, Anna, knows where it is. She's like a courier to him, but it's very dangerous for her. She works at the battalion headquarters where this Nazi SS vermin, Bergmann, has his office." He leaned back and furrowed his brow. "I worry about Anna. She's old and should not be working so hard, but she gets valuable information. If we manage to rescue Ferrand, I think she'll be in even greater danger, so we need to think of pulling her out."

He provided further detail, and Jeremy absorbed it. When Claude had finished, Jeremy explained that the MI-9's concern was to preserve the network that Ferrand had established, assist in training for more effective resistance, and pass intelligence back to headquarters; but mainly, to be ready to help the large number of British and allied airmen and soldiers expected to pass through when the war was brought back to the Germans.

"We will be bombing targets in Germany and France," he said. "Planes will be shot down. Crews will be on the ground evading capture. Others will get caught and then escape. Soldiers will be separated from their units. We need the network in place to help them, and that's what Ferrand did so fast and so well. We need to ensure that those people stay active as much as possible."

Claude listened with anxious eyes. "And what about my brother?"

Jeremy smiled kindly. "I told you the official reason why I'm here. Your brother saved my life. So did his daughters, and you and Nicolas, and all those others who helped get me back to England. I could never forget you, and I could never leave any of you in the lurch, especially Ferrand."

Claude wiped tears from his eyes. "You're a gift from God," he said in a broken voice.

"No," Jeremy replied, "your family is a gift to me."

"Why can't you stay? If your bosses are going to keep someone here anyway, why not you?"

"Two reasons, the first being that I haven't been trained."

"Neither have any of us." Claude chuckled. "We're getting on-the-job training."

"And that's exactly the point. I was good for bringing in the team and settling in, but there's a lot I don't know to be most effective. My replacement will be someone who is fluent in French, knows the area, and is fully trained for the mission. I know only enough to be dangerous."

Claude dropped his head and nodded reluctantly. Then he cast Jeremy a sidelong glance. "And what of Amélie? She's in love with you."

Jeremy swallowed hard as his throat constricted. "Nicolas tells me she's safe." He coughed. "I can't think of her right now."

"Ah, my boy," Claude said, watching Jeremy's face and placing a hand gently on his shoulders. "We fight for better days ahead." He took in Jeremy's gaunt appearance. "You look like you haven't eaten or slept in days."

Jeremy grunted. "I haven't had much time or opportunity for luxuries."

Claude chuckled. "Whoever could believe that in France, eating would be a luxury. Still, we have food at the house. We'll fatten you up."

"If there's time," Jeremy replied sardonically. Then he brightened. "We brought rifles and ammunition with us."

"They were good to see," Claude replied. "Our fighters thank you." His face scrunched with a question. "You mentioned two reasons you could not stay. What's the second one?"

Jeremy told Claude about Timmy and how the little boy had fallen under Jeremy's care. "He's so small, and as far as we know, he was left alone in this world." He bit back emotion. "I love him like a son. I have to make sure he's cared for until he's united with his own family. He's already lost so much."

The two men continued walking across the fields. When they reached the end, they turned and walked back, still talking.

"You said that this Bergmann threatened retaliation?" Jeremy asked.

"He hasn't said he'd execute anyone, but I think that's what he means by 'other measures.' If you add up the numbers, he's talking about killing thirty-one people if Ferrand is not arrested. We can only pray that he will not take women and children too, but that man has no soul."

"I'd like to see him face-to-face," Jeremy said, gritting his teeth. "The challenge is to get Ferrand away from here without inciting retaliation."

"How do we do that?"

Jeremy outlined a plan formulating in his mind. When he had finished, he said, "I only have one question. Is my French accent good enough?"

Claude grunted. "You sound like you come from the south of France. The Germans won't know the difference."

52

Dunkirk, France

Bergmann worked at his desk sorting through papers, reading documents, signing others. Several days had gone by since he issued his ultimatum concerning Ferrand Boulier, and he had filled the time by delving into his other areas of responsibility. Certain that prior to the first execution someone would reveal their whereabouts, he felt no frustration as each day passed with no information. As a result, he had delegated responsibility for making arrests to the SS sergeant, and otherwise he had maintained a hands-off stance. That seemed to have eased tension between him and Meier.

Today marked the sixth day since the pronouncements had been made in the streets over the public address system, and still no one had come forward. That meant that as of today, thirty-one people had been arrested, and by midnight tonight, barring something unforeseen, they would conduct their first execution. He smiled. *Someone will come forward.*

Late in the afternoon, a soldier knocked on his door, presented himself in front of the desk, and clicked his heels at attention.

"Sir, I have a man waiting outside with news about Ferrand Boulier. His name is Villere."

Bergmann grinned with self-satisfaction. "Bring him in."

Villere had a haggard appearance, as though events of the past weeks had taken their toll. He wore a long, wrinkled overcoat despite the warm weather, and he hunched over and presented a nervous demeanor, holding his hands in front of his chest and wringing them. His hair had not been cut in weeks, and his eyes had sunk in their sockets.

"Papers," the captain demanded.

Villere nodded wordlessly, his hands shaking as he reached into his coat pocket and pulled out his documents.

"Why are you wearing that coat in this weather?" Bergmann asked.

"I don't want it stolen," Villere replied. "All that I have is what you see." He handed his papers across the desk.

Bergmann examined them. "It says here that you are a schoolteacher. What did you teach?"

"Basic elementary topics. My pupils were very small. I'm not much good at technical subjects, so I stayed with the younger children."

"I see," Bergmann said with no effort to hide his disdain. "Why are you helping in the search for your fellow countryman?"

"He's endangering us all, sir. I need to eat."

Bergmann eyed the man dispassionately. "You look hungry, not starved."

"I've been able to scrounge some food, but it's gone," he pleaded. "I don't have another source."

The captain continued to scrutinize the man. "Tell me where Boulier is and how you know he's there."

Villere hesitated. "Sir, the reward—"

"You'll get your reward," Bergmann snapped. "Now answer my questions."

Villere's body shook, but he nodded. "I stay in the ruins. There are a few places that have only a little damage, but they're hard to find and get to. My apartment was damaged, but it's livable. When my neighbors fled, they left food behind, so I found things to eat, but as I said, it's gone. I need to buy more." He took a step forward, his face anxious. "You know it's dangerous for me to be here. If I'm labeled as a collaborator—"

Bergmann pushed his chair back impatiently and rose to his feet.

"You've told me your personal problems," he sneered. "I want to know about Boulier and how you know where he lives."

Villere's mouth went slack, and he peered sideways at Bergmann while his head bobbed up and down. "Yes, yes," he said. "I'm coming to that. He's staying in one of the deserted apartments that's still habitable. It's not far from mine, and he has to pass by to get out to the main street. I've seen him several times."

"Do you know him?"

Villere shook his head. "Only by sight and reputation. He's an artist and fairly well known in the area. You surely know how to verify his identity."

"And how would we do that?" Bergmann growled.

Villere looked at him with a startled expression. "His sister-in-law works in this building. You must know that."

Disbelief crossed Bergmann's face. "She works here? What does she do?"

"Unless her job has changed, she's a cleaning lady, a janitor. She tidies the offices, mops the floors... Anyone could have told you that. Her name is Anna."

Stunned, Bergmann's eyes bulged. He yelled for his sergeant.

When the SS non-com appeared, he ordered, "Get me that cleaning lady."

Before dusk, Villere led Bergmann and his SS squad deep into the ruins of Dunkirk. With them, terrified and trembling, was Anna. Her head bent, a handkerchief to her nose and mouth, she struggled to keep up. An SS man pushed her along when she faltered.

Gloom had settled into the bombed-out shell of Dunkirk as the group proceeded through the rubble-strewn, abandoned streets. Shards of glass from storefronts crunched beneath their boots on the cobblestones. Above, intact outer walls leaned precipitously, weighted down by half-roofs and partial floors. Surreal sights met them, of bedrooms half destroyed, with fully made beds teetering at the edges of the floors, and beyond them, views into untouched kitchens and dining rooms. They maneuvered around ruined cars and trucks with heavy crusts of dust and tossed about at impossible angles; and everywhere, the smell of stale explosives mixed with decomposing bodies and other stenches that accompany unbridled warfare. Stray dogs and cats, their bones poking under stretched skin, watched them go by, some desperate, some hopeful, some snarling, all filthy and starving.

Villere turned into an alley blocked by piles of toppled bricks. He climbed over them along a faint pathway and entered a passage that forced proceeding in single file.

The SS men nudged each other for increased alertness as they followed behind Bergmann, with the last two dragging Anna along.

Fifteen minutes later, they came to an area that had been surrounded by the rain of fire and brimstone, but by comparison to its immediate environs, it had survived in fairly good shape. Several of the apartments looked intact.

Villere pointed. "He stays in there."

Bergmann nodded to his sergeant, who, with a slight motion of his hand, caused his men to line up abreast of each other, their weapons locked and loaded and pointing at the hollowed-out entrance.

"Get him," Bergmann ordered Villere.

The schoolteacher peered at him in resignation, walked forward, and disappeared into the shadows. Moments later, he reappeared.

He bore a shocked face. "He's dead," he said. "Do I still get my reward?"

Anna shrieked her anguish. "No," she cried, and started toward the door.

Disconcerted, Bergmann swung around to his sergeant. "Come with me."

The two of them followed the old woman into the deep shadows of the apartment. Above them, the hall opened beyond successive collapsed ceilings to the wreckage of the roof. At the far end, the old lady entered an intact doorway.

When the two men arrived in the room behind her, she had already bent over a man lying on a bed. He stared up, sightless. Lifeless.

Anna turned grief-filled eyes on Bergmann. "You did this." She dropped her head onto the corpse's chest and sobbed. "Ferrand, what have they done to you? To us?"

Suddenly, she stood and hobbled over to Bergmann, fists raised. "You did this. You. What do you want with us? Why do you destroy people's lives and their homes?"

Bergman grabbed Anna's wrists and tossed her into a corner. She landed in a heap, weeping, her hands covering her face.

Bergmann walked over to the bed and stared at the still figure, observing that the man had been deceased for at least a day, maybe more. The body was bloated, the skin mottled, but behind the scruffy beard and balding head, Bergmann thought he recognized Ferrand Boulier.

He instructed the sergeant to move the body to the morgue and set out to return to headquarters.

Villere stood at the entrance to the narrow passageway. "My reward?"

"He wasn't arrested," Bergmann snarled. "He's dead. Show me the way out."

Shaking, Villere complied, and Bergmann followed.

53

Bergmann shoved Villere into the dark passage, ignoring his faint surprise that the man he pushed was solidly built. "You were useless," he barked impatiently.

Villere did not respond. They advanced into the alley illuminated only by the half-moon, which nevertheless gleamed off the brick walls on either side.

Behind them, a firefight erupted, darts of light from tracers piercing the night. Bergmann turned, alarmed. Suddenly, a strong hand jerked him backward by his shoulder. Spinning around, he saw that Villere had dropped his overcoat to the ground and straightened up, revealing a potent, shadowy figure advancing rapidly on him.

Villere grabbed Bergmann's left shoulder with one hand and delivered two powerful right punches to his gut. Bergmann doubled over, air driven from his lungs, pain shooting through his upper torso and down into his groin.

"You kill defenseless people. Coward," Villere hissed. "You beat up old women." He let go of Bergman's shoulder and pummeled the SS officer's face with both hard fists. "Let's see how you do against a fighter."

Bergmann sprawled backward onto the ground. He rolled and scrambled to his feet, gasping for air, his mind grappling with this turn of events.

He tasted blood trickling into his mouth and spat it out, his eyes fixed on this formidable, unknown opponent.

From the direction of the apartments, gunfire exploded. Bergmann turned his head slightly to listen. The guns fell silent.

A surge of adrenalin spawned from rage cleared the captain's mind. He felt a return of strength. Crouching, he faced Villere and reached for his Walther P38. He fumbled a moment too long with the strap that held the pistol inside the holster.

Head low, Villere charged into Bergmann's waist just as the weapon cleared the top of the leather. It fired wildly. The bullet buried in a wall with a loud smack. The pistol flew through the air, and then slid along the ground into a mound of debris.

Bergmann dropped his chest over Villere's shoulders and brought his knee up into his attacker's face.

Villere hung on, his arms around Bergmann's waist, his legs and weight driving Bergmann back against a wall.

The German captain raised both fists over his head and brought them down hard into his foe's back, above the kidneys.

Villere let go and fell to the ground, writhing.

Bergmann waded in, kicking the prone body.

Beneath him, Villere ignored the pain and, rolling over, caught the toe and heel of Bergmann's boot in his hands and shoved.

Bergmann lost balance and fell backward. He rolled and lurched to his knees.

Slowed down by the pain in his back, Villere climbed upright, with one knee still on the ground, the other bent to push to his full height.

Bergmann rushed in to deliver a hard blow to the side of his adversary's head.

Villere saw it coming and ducked. Bergmann fell on him, and the two grappled and bashed each other.

From the end of the alley nearest the apartments, voices called out in French. Adrenaline once more surged through Bergmann, who scrambled to escape. He fought and kicked his way, distancing himself enough from Villere to get to his feet, and he fled down the dark alley into the night.

Breathing hard, Villere struggled to his feet, peering through the darkness after Bergmann. Hearing running footsteps behind him, he turned painfully and dropped his hands to his knees to regain his breath and support his upper body. His head drooped.

Feeling a hand on his shoulder, he looked up at Ferrand Boulier. Claude stood next to him. "Are you all right, Jeremy?"

Jeremy nodded without straightening up. "I'll live. I think. Good to see you, *Monsieur* Boulier." Slowly, he raised to full height and turned to hug Ferrand, taking in the old man's scruffy appearance. "How's Anna? She did an incredible job."

"She's scared, but she's safe. She won't be going back to work. Our family will take care of her."

"What about your cousin?"

Ferrand took a kerchief from his pocket and wiped his brow. "We were close," he said mournfully. "We grew up together. People always said we looked like twins. I'll miss him." He sighed. "We'll bury him with my name. He would be proud to make this contribution to the resistance. If questions come up, the medical examiner knows to have him identified as me."

"And the SS men?"

"Some are dead. Some wounded. All incapacitated," Ferrand said. "I'm sure their comrades will be along to pick them up." He grunted. "We're a fighting force now."

"Not for long if we stay here," Jeremy said. "Let's go."

54

The battalion executive officer waited inside *Oberstleutnant* Meier's office when the commander arrived the next morning. He looked grim.

"We have a situation," he said.

"I caught some rumblings on the way in," Meier replied. "We had some shooting inside the ruins?"

The major nodded. "*Hauptman* Bergmann—"

At mention of the name, anger crossed Meier's face. "What were the casualties?"

"Three dead. Six wounded."

"Do we know who the attackers were?"

The executive officer shook his head. "The SS men were ambushed." He related the facts as he knew them. "Here is Bergmann's report," he said, handing over a document.

Meier scanned it, his eyes narrowing further with fury. "The fool carried out the first execution too," he snapped. "Get that captain in here."

Three minutes later, Bergmann came to attention in front of Meier's desk. He started to speak.

"Shut up, *Herr Hauptman*," Meier said in a low, threatening voice. "You're here to listen."

He turned to his executive officer standing just inside the door. "Release all the prisoners taken under *Hauptman* Bergmann's reprisal order and cease further arrests based on it. At once. His order is null and void."

While Bergmann's cheeks flamed red and his eyes bulged with fury, the executive officer left the room to carry out Meier's command.

"You've made a big mistake," Bergmann said. "My report will say—"

"You'll be able to provide your report in person," Meier stormed. "I'll be returning you to Berlin. You are relieved of your duties."

Bergmann started to speak again.

"I said shut up," Meier cut him off. "You wear a military uniform, but even with all your academy training, you seem to have missed out on the most fundamental parts of it. Either that or your arrogance grew exponentially with putting on your SS uniform."

He took a deep breath. "When you took command of your former company, you neglected to handle a disciplinary problem. You let Kallsen get out of hand. You went into a neighborhood unprovoked and got several of your men laid up in the hospital with serious head injuries.

"You disobeyed my orders. You neglected to seek guidance or coordinate beyond your own whims, and as a result, you've gotten several of your men killed. That's what my report will say.

"We're in a war against an army, not a population, and you'd better learn that. We destroyed the houses and the livelihoods of Dunkirk's people, but until your silly forays, they saw their dead and wounded as collateral damage, and as painful as that must be, they accepted it. But when you attack the population directly, they fight back directly, as you just found out. Now, you have the questionable distinction of having taken casualties in the first skirmish with civilians, which *you* provoked. Were any of them killed or wounded?"

"I don't know, sir."

"I suspect not since you don't mention any in your report."

Unable to contain his anger, Bergmann blurted, "The people just learned that they can kill German soldiers without repercussion. You taught them that."

Meier's eyes bulged and he swallowed hard, fighting to control his rage. "You infantile fool," he bellowed. "What they learned is that they can capture German weapons, and when they shoot our soldiers, they bleed and die. You destroyed the image of an invincible German army, and you've generated a fighting force behind our own lines."

He jammed his face close to Bergmann's. "And now they have more of our weapons. And you have what? A man who died of old age lying in the morgue. He was your fierce terrorist."

Meier took a deep breath, circled his desk, and sat in his chair. "Report back to your SS superior in Berlin," he said without looking up. "Dismissed."

Bergmann clicked his heels and threw his arm out in the Nazi salute. "*Heil* Hitler!" he roared, and stormed out of the room.

A few minutes later, the executive officer returned. "Do you think there'll be repercussions?"

Meier discarded the thought with a wave of his hand and a toss of his chin. "Not as long as General Rommel commands the 7th Panzer Division and the war progresses favorably. They need me."

55

Six days later, July 3
Sark Island, English Channel Islands

On the tenth day after Marian Littlefield's entreaty to the citizens of Sark, she received word that the old lifeboat that regularly ferried between Guernsey and Sark had been spotted with German officers aboard.

That morning, Stephen had joked that, with the next day being when Americans celebrate their independence from British rule, "...if I had stayed in New Jersey after college instead of heading out to Canada, we would be spending tomorrow barbecuing hamburgers and watching parades and fireworks rather than playing host to Huns."

"And they're almost here," Marian had replied. Then, in a rare emotional display, she hugged Stephen. "I'm scared. I convinced our people to stay on with us, and now I worry that I might have sealed their fates."

"You're the bravest person I've ever known," Stephen said, lifting her hand and kissing it. "Now give them hell, just as we planned."

"Is everyone prepared?"

"Informed, rehearsed, and ready," Stephen replied. "These Germans have no idea who they're dealing with."

William Carré received an official note from Marian at mid-morning. As *Seneschal* of Sark Island, he performed the dual role of head of the Chief Pleas and judge of the island. The former role was the one that Marian's directive addressed.

Carré had expected it and knew his responsibility. Already having heard that a boat with German officials had arrived at the port, he was dressed formally. At his door, the messenger handed him a sealed envelope, which he slid inside an inner pocket of his jacket. A tractor pulling a passenger wagon awaited him. He boarded and took his seat for the short ride to the top of the steep road leading down to the harbor.

People stood in their doors along the way, grim-faced, with mothers holding lively children behind them. Farmers and workers along his route paused in their labor to watch him go by, some waving and calling good wishes to him as he passed.

Within minutes, Carré stopped at the top of the harbor road. There, he alighted, looked around at a small crowd, dismissed his ride, and began walking down the steep road and through a tunnel to the harbor. Soon, he saw the boat bobbing in the water, and in front of it on the shore, two men in German uniforms. He strode up to the one who seemed to be in charge.

"Good day," he greeted in *Sercquiais*. "I speak no German." With both hands, he proffered the envelope delivered by the messenger from Marian.

Startled at the lack of obeisance, the officer snatched the envelope from Carré and tore it open. His expression changed to one of surprise. There, in perfect German with flourishing handwriting, was a note signed by Marian Littlefield, Dame of Sark.

I am informed that you arrived on Sark Island and wish to speak with me. I will be most pleased to receive you in the Seigneurie at your earliest convenience after receipt of this message. I designated our most honorable Seneschal William Carré, president of our parliament, to welcome you and guide you to the official seat of Sark Island's government at my residence and office. I look forward to your visit.

Flustered, the officer looked around and spoke with his companion in German.

"Do you at least speak English?" the second officer asked Carré in perfectly enunciated English. "My colleague speaks none."

Carré nodded. "Of course. We are British subjects."

"That is a matter to be taken up with your *Seigneure*," the officer replied haughtily. "Where is your car?"

"No cars are allowed on Sark," Carré replied. "We will have to walk."

The officer stared past Carré at the tunnel leading away from the port. Then he tilted his head to scan the high cliffs overlooking the harbor. After a brief consultation with his senior colleague, he said, "Very well. Lead on."

Out of breath and perspiring in the warm summer weather and from the steepness of Harbour Hill Road after they had climbed through the tunnel to the flat ground eighty-one meters above sea level, they turned onto *Chasse Marais*, their clothes drenched with sweat. "Don't you have any vehicles at all?" the English-speaking officer asked, his face red. "Surely you must have something we could ride in."

"Only wagons pulled by tractors," Carré responded amiably, "but none were available on short notice."

As they turned onto *Rue de la Seigneurie* and proceeded, people barely took note of them, continuing about their business as though nothing unusual were taking place and greeting them pleasantly when passing by. Field workers seemed oblivious to their presence, and mothers only glanced out of windows at them while their children played in their yards, seemingly unmindful of their passage.

"Do your people not realize that a new order is taking hold in this world," the English-speaking officer said to Carré.

"So we've heard," the *Seneschal* replied, "but we don't know the details. We're a small island of little interest to anyone else. We mind our business and keep on living our lives."

"Well as of today, you are of interest to Adolf Hitler and will fall under the rule of the Third *Reich*."

With no change in his pleasant demeanor, Carré replied, "I'm sure you are right, and you can take that up with Dame Marian."

At last, after walking nearly two miles, the group arrived at the main entrance to the *Seigneurie*. One of the officers stepped to the door and was about to knock when Carré stepped ahead of him.

"Allow me," he said with an ingratiating smile. "A matter of protocol."

He lifted the knocker and banged it a few times.

The officers fidgeted, their annoyance clearly expressed in their eyes and the glances they exchanged. While they waited, they dusted off their boots.

Moments passed, and then a servant girl opened the door. "Ah, *Monsieur Seneschal,* I'm so pleased to see you," she said. "What business do you have today?"

Carré bowed with a flourish. "I came to present these two officers to *la Seigneure.* I believe she is expecting us."

The girl pursed her lips under amused wide eyes. "I hadn't heard. I will have to announce you. Please wait here." She closed the door.

The senior officer turned angrily to Carré. "I demand to see the *Seigneure* at once. Please open the door." The other officer translated.

"Patience," Carré said matter-of-factly with a gesture of his open palms. "I'm not sure she expected you this early. We probably interrupted her morning tea, and she will not want to make a bad impression. We won't have to wait much longer."

Ten minutes later, when the Germans seemed near the peak of frustration, the door opened again. "Dame Marian will see you now," the servant announced. She led them through a foyer, down a long hall, turned into another corridor, and finally knocked at an imposing door with intricate carvings. Another servant opened it and ushered the group inside.

Marian and Stephen sat together at adjacent desks at the far end of a large reception hall. She wrote busily while Stephen seemed preoccupied in reading what appeared to be correspondence. Neither looked up for a few moments.

The servant indicated for the group to wait and walked softly across the room. "Sir, Madame," she said in a proper voice, and stood until she had been recognized. At last, Stephen looked up and nodded.

"Sir, the *Seneschal* is here to present the German delegation. Madame sent out the invitation this morning on receiving word of their arrival."

Stephen looked past the servant at the officers. "Ah yes. I had forgotten."

He stood and nudged his wife. "Dear, the delegation you mentioned is here. Do you wish to see them now?"

Marion looked up with a neutral expression. "Give me a minute." She looked down at her papers again, signed a document, and then stood.

"Gentlemen," she called in perfect German. "We've been expecting you."

As Carré and the officers approached, she held her hand out for them to kiss. Taken aback, the German officers exchanged bewildered glances.

Carré stepped forward and kissed Marian's hand. She lowered it to her side. "Madame *la Seigneure*," he announced, "I am pleased to present the delegation of the *Wehrmacht* of the Third *Reich*."

Marian shifted her eyes to the senior officer. "I am pleased to receive you," she said, and as he stepped forward, she held her hand out again. On reflex, he reached for it and kissed it.

"And you are?" she asked.

"Major Lanz," he replied. "I am the commandant on this island."

Marian remained silent, studying him. He was a tall man, with a dark complexion and dark hair. His alert eyes showed intelligence, and his demeanor was that of a fair-minded person.

The other officer stepped forward. "I am Dr. Maass," he said in English. "I will serve as medical officer."

Marian appraised him, and she did not care for what she saw, although noting that his English accent was flawless. He seemed a man too pleased with himself, too smooth, and she wondered how much time he must have spent in England to gain mastery over the language and what information he might have gathered and passed on while there.

She held her hand out with the unspoken message.

After an uncomfortable silence, Maass reached for it and kissed it without a word.

"Now," Marian asked in German, "what can I do for you?"

Many hours later, a physically and emotionally spent Marian collapsed on the sofa in the upstairs lounge.

"You were brilliant," Stephen said, "and you were absolutely right about their observance of protocol. They can't help themselves."

"We can thank Benito Mussolini for the idea," she replied. "He forced German visitors to be announced and walk past the grandeur of his surroundings, to approach him across a long, huge office.

"I knew we were winning when I heard them dusting off their boots at the front door. That showed they intended to treat us with respect.

"Besides, Germany wouldn't send their combat-seasoned leaders to oversee our tiny island. Lanz is an aristocrat. He's here burnishing his reputation without putting himself in real danger. He'll never be at the front. We'll play on that, at least for as long as it works. Now that I know whom I'm dealing with, I'll research his background. I'm sure we have acquaintances in common. We might even share ancestry."

The servant girl appeared at the top of the stairs and interrupted the conversation. "Sorry to bother you, ma'am," she said. "The operator of the boat from Guernsey came by while you spoke with the Germans. He had a piece of mail for you."

She hesitated before handing the envelope to Marian. "He wanted to slip this to Mr. Carré to bring to you, but the German officers were a bit agitated and in a hurry. The letter arrived yesterday in Guernsey. He said to tell you that there won't be any more mail coming from or through the British mainland."

Marian took the letter, and the servant departed. It had been postmarked in France. When she opened the envelope, she saw that the message inside was scrawled on dirty, wrinkled paper. Scanning to the signature line, she brought her hand to her mouth and gasped. "It's from Lance."

Stephen bolted across the room and hovered at her shoulder as she read aloud.

"Dearest Family, I'm alive. I hope Jeremy got out all right. I'm a POW, on a forced march with thousands of British and French soldiers—no, tens of thousands—to Germany. The French people have been good to us. They line the roads and slip or

throw us food and give us water when they can, but the guards are a sadistic lot and push them away when they see that happening.

This note has our address on it, so maybe it'll get sent on. If you are reading it, we owe a debt of kindness to a stranger on a street in a town somewhere in France east of Saint-Nazaire.

I think of you always. Mum, I know I was a handful. I wish I could have done better. Dad, I think of all the cliff-climbing and ball-kicking we did. I miss my brothers and sister so much. Thinking of my family sustains me.

I'll try to get a Red Cross message to you when I reach a destination.

I love you all dearly, Lance"

Marian Littlefield, Dame of Sark, clutched the letter to her breast and sobbed.

56

Marseille, France

Madame Fourcade welcomed Jeremy, Nicolas, Ferrand, and Anna to her rented villa to the northeast of Marseille. Jacques had stayed in the north to fill in until Jeremy's replacement arrived.

"We can't do this often," Fourcade said, "but getting together to see the faces of friends who go in harm's way warms my heart." They sat around a table on a large covered veranda. The city sprawled below them, and the blue Mediterranean glimmered in the warm air.

Fourcade put her arm around Anna. "You were so brave," she told the old lady, who still peered about with apprehension.

"It was nothing," Anna replied in a high-pitched voice barely above a whisper. "I didn't have to do much acting." She pointed at her brother-in-law sitting across from her. "Ferrand's cousin looks so much like him that at first I thought it *was* him, and my anger with the Germans is real."

"Well, we lost a valuable asset when you left that battalion head-quarters."

"Not so valuable," Anna replied, waving a hand. "Bergmann's gone. He was the only one who learned about me. The Germans don't check much on the invisible people who do their cleaning. Someone will take my place and get even better information."

"Well, you did an incredible thing," Fourcade said. "That information about Meier's hostility to the Nazis might have long-term value. I'll get word up the channels."

"I must go back," Ferrand cut in. "I only came to bring Anna."

"I have to go too," Nicolas interrupted. "I have to be with my father in this fight."

"Ferrand, you need to rest," Fourcade said firmly. "I just met you, so I won't take too many liberties, but you should lie low, take a breather, eat"— she shoved a plate of meat and potatoes his way— "and get your strength back. You've been under killer pressure for a long time. *If* you go back, we need you in top condition. Nicolas and his father can stand in for you until the team leader from London arrives in a few days.

"As for you." She turned her attention to Nicolas. "You'll have our full support. You did a marvelous job getting Jeremy across France and then back up to Dunkirk with the team. Jacques too. You both proved your worth. Let us know how we can help."

Nicolas beamed, bowing his head in appreciation.

"Would it be possible to see my daughters?" Ferrand cut in again. "I understand they are somewhere in this area."

Fourcade's expression melted to one of compassion. She smiled. "We'll see what we can do."

Jeremy had been sitting facing into a breeze, enjoying the chatter and the ambience. His heart skipped a beat at Ferrand's request and again at Fourcade's response.

A French door behind them suddenly flew open. Amélie and Chantal burst onto the veranda, arms outstretched. They ran to their father, who had half-risen from his seat when he saw them. They buried him in hugs and kisses. Chantal jumped up and down in excitement like the young girl she still was.

Amélie had her arms around her father, her face on his shoulder, swaying with him. She glanced up, saw Jeremy, and their eyes met. She sucked in her breath and her cheeks flushed scarlet.

"Jeremy!" She pulled away from her father, rushed to him, and threw her arms around his neck. "We thought you were dead."

Hearing her sister, Chantal jerked her head around to see Jeremy, and then she too ran to embrace him.

"Was that you who parachuted in the other night? I was there. I helped the woman."

"Brigitte?"

"Yes, Brigitte. I looked right at you when I went to help her, but in the dark, I couldn't see that was you."

Fourcade watched the reunion with amused interest. Maurice walked out onto the patio and took a seat next to her. "Sorry I was late," he said. "We ran into trouble on the way over."

Fourcade shot him a look of alarm.

"Don't worry," he said, grinning. "This was of the mundane type. A vegetable truck spilled its load all over the road."

She looked dubious.

"Not mine." Maurice laughed. "But we had to wait until the road cleared." He looked across the gathering, locking in on the girls still hovering over Jeremy. "Their father is not the only one they're happy to see."

"I noticed."

While they observed, Chantal broke away to welcome Nicolas, her Aunt Anna, and then her father again. Amélie and Jeremy remained where they were, standing, talking, their hands touching. Ferrand watched with a contented smile.

"Is it my imagination, or do I see some chemistry there?" Fourcade asked.

Maurice laughed quietly. "They're in love. I'll tell you the whole story."

Two more men walked onto the patio with another woman. They had dark complexions, but one man spoke only English, and the other only French. The woman spoke both languages. They did a double take on seeing Jeremy, but he did not notice them. Fourcade introduced them quietly to Maurice.

"This is Kenyon, Pierre, and Elena," she said in French. "They blew up the tanks in Saint-Nazaire."

"Impressive," Maurice said. "Welcome. We're glad to have your expertise."

Elena translated for Kenyon's benefit, and Fourcade noted with amusement the way she flashed her eyes at him. *We might be sensing more magic in the air.*

Kenyon gestured toward Jeremy. "Who is that man?"

"His name is Jeremy Littlefield," Fourcade replied. "He was brought over a few days ago from England to put a team in place. He's leaving tonight, by submarine. We have a boat taking him out to the rendezvous. Do you know him?"

"No, but we had a chap with us at Saint-Nazaire with that surname. He saved my life when the Lancastria went down. That man looks enough like him to be his brother. Unfortunately, we lost him." He peered more closely at Jeremy. "The mission went off all right, but everyone in his getaway car disappeared. We don't know if they were captured or killed."

"Oh, that's depressing," Fourcade said. "I wouldn't tell him. Not now. Whether he is or isn't your friend's brother, Jeremy deserves to enjoy this evening."

Late in the afternoon, Jeremy and Amélie finally had a chance to be alone among the villa's gardens. They walked hand in hand through the lanes, admiring the flowers and the beauty of the scenery.

"This is so much better than the last time we saw each other," Amélie said. "I thought we would never again see something resembling normalcy."

"Your family risked so much to save me," Jeremy said. "Your father is an amazing man. I haven't stopped thinking of any of you since Dunkirk." A shadow crossed his face. "Unfortunately, this is going to be a long war."

"Shh." Amélie turned in front of him and raised one delicate finger across his lips. "We must enjoy the good moments." Then she kissed him lightly. "Everyone says we're in love."

"Are we?" Jeremy asked.

They resumed walking along the path. "I don't know. I honestly don't,"

Amélie replied. "We met under such intense moments. You're a good man. A wonderful man. And brave. I know what you did to save my father. Whatever debt you might feel you owe us is paid. We're even. I think about you every waking moment, but is that love, or is that worry? Would I feel differently if we had met under other circumstances? What about you, are you in love?"

Jeremy stopped in the middle of the path. He locked his fingers behind his head, stretched, and breathed in deeply. Finally, he chuckled, and took Amélie's hand again.

"I've had the same thoughts," he said. "Do I love you, or am I infatuated with a beautiful girl who faced such danger to save me? Would I feel differently if I had met you at a party, or at a library, or in a store. I don't know." They resumed ambling through the flower garden, enjoying the fragrance.

"Do you really have to go tonight?"

"I'm afraid I must. That's the bargain I made for British intelligence to support this mission. I have to go back for training."

"To do what?"

"I'm not sure, but if I were to guess, I'd say it is to do what I just did, except to learn to do it better."

"Then you'll be back?"

"Maybe. But one thing I can tell you for sure. I'll come to find you when this war is over, no matter how long it takes."

Amélie circled in front of him again, threw her arms around his neck, and kissed him, gently at first, and then with passionate energy. "I believe you," she murmured. "Are we being too logical about our feelings?" She kissed him again.

Jeremy's whole being seemed about to burst. He held Amélie tightly, returning her kisses until he felt almost incapable of catching his breath.

She leaned back slightly, her eyes looking into his. "I love you," she said.

Jeremy reached back, unclasped both of her hands from around his neck, and held them in front of him, cupping them with his own. Then he put his right palm flat over his chest, cupped it again, and pressed it between hers. "I'll leave my heart right here," he murmured, "where it belongs."

EPILOGUE

Around nine o'clock in the morning, Jeremy heard the phone ring in the apartment he shared with Claire and Timmy. His sister had already left for work.

His return trip from Marseille via the sea had taken several days. On arriving back in London, he found that Claire had moved to a guest house on an estate near Stony Stratford, a village nine miles from Bletchley, arranged by Crockatt. The MI-6 head, Menzies, had been uncomfortable with the former living arrangement. An alternative had been sought.

The new place allowed Claire to be close to work at Bletchley as well as near Timmy whenever Jeremy had to be away. The nanny had a private room too, and the house had a nursery with plenty of space for Timmy to play indoors and outdoors.

The middle-aged couple who owned the estate were only too happy to help out. The request coming from a military intelligence officer made them feel like they were doing something important for the war effort, and they loved having Timmy around.

The reunion with the child had been joyous. On first seeing Jeremy, the toddler had looked confused. Then he let out an excited shriek, clapped his hands, and burst into happy cries. He ran and locked his arms around his guardian's neck. Jeremy lifted him into the air and pressed the boy's cheek against his own. "Ah, I've missed you."

The little boy gazed into his eyes, then looked around questioningly. "Mummy?"

Jeremy buried his head between Timmy's cheek and shoulder, smothering a grief-filled gasp. Claire and Paul stood watching nearby, holding in check their desire to hear as many details as he was allowed to share.

"Did you see Amélie?" Claire had teased when they finally settled down to talk. She poked his ribs.

"I did," Jeremy replied, fighting her off. A smile had broken across his face in spite of his best effort. "All right," he said, "I'll admit it. We're fond of each other."

"Just fond?"

"I won't go any further on that subject now." He laughed, then his expression had become serious. "She and her sister and father are together in Marseille for the time being, and that is still a relatively safe place."

"You'll see her again, little brother, in better times," Claire said. She circled behind him and snuggled her head against his back. "I believe that."

Jeremy had diverted his attention to Paul. "Any news on Lance?"

When Paul shook his head, Jeremy asked, "Do we know how Mum and Dad are doing?"

"Red Cross messages are finally getting through," Paul replied. "I let them know you're safe. They'll be thrilled to hear that." A note had arrived from them indicating that they were doing well under the circumstances. Given that the communiqués were confined to twenty-eight words and subject to censorship, the siblings could not expect to learn much about conditions on the island. One phrase was cryptic and concerning though: "Pray for Lance, that he can persevere."

Paul had informed Jeremy sadly that the Germans now occupied all of the English Channel Islands. "We sent reconnaissance patrols to both Guernsey and Sark, but the operations got muffed up. Some of our soldiers were killed. We got nothing."

Jeremy sighed heavily. "What about Timmy? Any news of his relatives?"

"The Foreign Office thinks they might have found some grandparents living in India," Paul said. "Apparently, the father was an only child who was educated and joined the foreign service from the Far East. They haven't learned anything of Eva yet."

Jeremy was not displeased, but immediately felt guilty for being selfish. "Surely, they must have a record of whom to contact for emergencies."

"If the father was injured or killed, they were to contact Eva."

"Oh. I see the difficulty," Jeremy replied gravely. "Well," he went on with a subdued smile, "until his relations are found, he'll just stay with us." He had plopped on the floor next to Timmy and wrestled with him until the child squealed with laughter.

That had been a week ago. Jeremy had spent the following week resting up, playing with Timmy, and thinking of Amélie. Now that she and her family were safe in Marseilles with Fourcade and Maurice, he finally felt free to let his feelings about her roam without dread. *But it's going to be a long war.*

The phone rang again. Jeremy was not expecting any calls this morning.

Paul was on the other end of the line. "Could you come in to Major Crockatt's office." His voice sounded urgent. "Can you make it by eleven o'clock?"

When Jeremy pressed for a reason, Paul's voice broke, and he insisted, "Just please get here, quickly."

Getting dressed and taking the train into London took two hours, and that was without taking time to see Timmy. When Jeremy arrived at the headquarters, he was startled to bump into Claire at the entrance. She was as surprised as he was, and her face was equally serious. "You were called too?" he asked.

Claire nodded. "Any idea what this is about?"

"None."

They made their way through the various security checkpoints and arrived at Vivian's desk. She greeted them warmly but with an air of reserve, and instead of taking them into the major's office, she ushered them down a hall to a conference room.

When they entered, Crockatt and Paul were already seated. Paul looked grave. With them was a soldier, a boy really, one who looked like he had aged rapidly and recently. His skin was darkened, more unwashed than tanned, but he looked fit, if undernourished. He sucked in his breath when his eyes landed on Jeremy.

Crockatt rose and showed Jeremy and Claire to their seats, and then took his own. "You know, of course, that a number of our stranded chaps made their way overland through southern France and Spain to try to get on boats coming to England."

Jeremy and Claire nodded.

"Is this about Lance?" Claire broke in, her eyes wide with anxiety. "Is he dead?"

"Maybe not," Crockatt replied. He introduced the third man. "This is Corporal Derek Horton. He is among the first of those who arrived on our shores via that route. They arrived yesterday. We put out word that we wanted to interview any who made their way home, to get the details of how they did it. It's pertinent to rescuing more."

"I want to know about our brother," Claire interrupted again.

"He's the best man I've ever known," Horton broke in, his voice rough. Speaking obviously took effort. "He's a real leader, he is."

He leaned back with a faint smile. "Would you believe that when we got to Saint-Nazaire, a bunch of soldiers were raiding a train full of liquor. He set it on fire so they wouldn't get too drunk to get themselves to the docks to be rescued."

Jeremy stared at him, stunned. "I was there. I saw that fire." He put his hand to his face. "We were so close. I didn't know he'd done that."

Horton sighed. "That was him." He paused and shook his head. Then he alternated his eyes between the siblings. "I wish I had some good news for you."

"Is he dead then?" Jeremy asked.

"I wish I knew." He told Lance's story from the time the two had met northeast of Dunkirk to their rescue after the Lancastria went down.

"You were on the Lancastria?" Jeremy jumped from his chair in disbelief. He sank back down, numb with the realization of how narrowly they had missed each other, twice.

"Yeah, we were there." Horton resumed his story, telling how he and

Lance had found a staff sergeant by the name of Kenyon and his friend struggling in the water.

"Kenyon? Are you serious? Is he a demolitions specialist?"

"He is."

"I met him in Marseille last week. He was with a Frenchman called Pierre and a woman—Elena. He must have recognized me."

"I'm sure he did." He glanced at Paul. "The three of you are dead ringers for each other." He smiled at Claire. "You too, Mum, if you were a bloke."

He chuckled at his own joke and went on, "I'm glad to know Kenyon and Pierre got away. Elena, too. She's a nice lady." He told of François leading them across France and of his death from a Stuka attack, and he explained the mission they had undertaken with the French resistance. "We succeeded. We blew up those fuel tanks, but then while we made our getaway, we got stopped by a German panzer sitting in the middle of the road with a squad of infantry soldiers. The last time I saw Lance, I was lying in a ditch, and he was being marched away by the Germans."

He closed his eyes. "I love your brother. I wouldn't be here but for him, and others might have made it home because of him." He opened his eyes again and gazed at each of the siblings. "I hate to be the one to tell you, and I hate to put it this way, but if Lance is alive, he's a prisoner of war on his way to Germany." Then he grinned. "If I know your brother, he's giving 'em hell and trying to escape right now, as we speak." He glanced up and made eye contact with each of the siblings. "One thing I can say." His eyes probed each of their faces. "He loved you dearly. Each of you. And your parents. He was very devoted to your family and your Sark Island."

On the other side of the conference table, Claire broke down sobbing, letting tears run freely. Paul and Jeremy sat quietly, their heads bowed, shoulders drooping. Crockatt looked away as though to avoid intruding on private moments. For a few minutes, no one spoke. Horton dropped his hands into his lap and hunched forward in his chair, looking helpless. "I'm sorry," he said glumly. "I was never any good at manners."

"Oh, no!" Claire said. She wiped her eyes on a handkerchief, stood, and hurried around the table to hug him. "You've suffered a great deal," she whispered between barely controlled sobs, "and you cared for our brother.

How can we do anything but love you? You're welcome with our family anytime."

———————

Crockatt excused himself, stating that he would interview Horton further later, and Vivian brought in sandwiches. The group lingered in the conference room, eager for any detail about Lance, and Horton obliged. Then, after bidding farewell, Jeremy and Claire rode the train back to Stony Stratford together. They took a first-class compartment so they could be alone in their grief, riding in silence for most of the trip, tending to their separate thoughts. Paul had work still to do at his office and promised he would be there later and bring Horton along.

When the train was well out of London and into the countryside, Claire said, "I'm so glad we came. That Corporal Horton is a wonderful person. We must stay in touch with him. He is family now."

"Agreed," Jeremy replied. "He gave all the credit to Lance, but I get the feeling that he deserves a lot of it too. I hope someday we can hear the full story with the two of them together."

Claire nodded and wiped her eyes. She smiled, and then teared up again as her thoughts returned to their missing brother. "We kept talking about him in the past tense, but he might be alive. We must cling to that hope and pray that he comes home safely."

Jeremy nodded distantly while staring out the window at the passing villages and rolling fields. The train's rhythmic purr brought a hypnotic effect. More minutes passed, and then, to relieve the distress, Claire asked, "Did you see in the news that the Germans dropped their first bombs on England two days ago, against our shipping?"

Jeremy nodded. "It's as Mr. Churchill said, the Battle for France is ended, and the Battle of Britain has just begun." He sighed. "We know we are in strange times when we use a bit of news like that to lighten the mood." Then he leaned toward Claire and touched her face. "I want to say thank you."

Claire regarded him, once again on the brink of tears. "For what?"

"I know you can't acknowledge what I am going to say, and I don't want you to." He paused, searching for the right words, and felt the return of composure as he spoke. "I know you had something to do with generating my mission to France. I don't know what you did, but whatever it was, without you, Ferrand Boulier would likely be dead, and his network destroyed. Now it's a valuable asset, and I got to see Amélie again. That wouldn't have happened for a long, long time."

Claire gazed at him through teary eyes. "Oh, little brother," she cried, hugging his neck and kissing his cheek. "I love you." She clung to him for a time. "Things will work out for you and Amélie, you'll see."

Jeremy adjusted himself in her arms so that his shoulders lay flat against the back of the seat. He stared up at the ceiling. *There must be a way to use that network to find Lance and bring him home.*

EAGLES OVER BRITAIN
Book #2 in the After Dunkirk series

As WWII intensifies, the German Luftwaffe attacks Britain from the skies in a major air campaign. With no allies at hand, she stands alone.

Individual American pilots, ignoring US neutrality laws, rush to aid England and join her fighter squadrons.

As the Battle of Britain rages on, British pilots are joined by these, "The Few", as well as refugee pilots from Poland, Czechoslovakia, and other embattled nations.

The story of the Littlefield family continues in the next installment of the After Dunkirk series.

Get your copy today at
severnriverbooks.com/series/after-dunkirk

AUTHOR'S NOTE

The tapestry that is the history of World War II boggles the mind in contemplating what is generally known about it. Common knowledge of it is a tiny fraction of the full scope of accomplishment by courageous men and women who sacrificed their fortunes and their lives to bring in the cause of freedom. I learned that in researching for this series of books of which AFTER DUNKIRK is the first. For example, little is known about the sinking of the *HMT Lancastria*, and I have taken particular pains to describe that tragic event and pay respect to the memories of those lost, those who suffered through it and survived, and their affected families.

When my publisher suggested that I write about the war, and despite that the genre always appealed to me, I was sure that all that could be written probably had already been published. When I dug in, I found myself awed by the contributions of people at critical turning points in the war—there were so many of them, but their names are seldom known or mentioned.

One such person was Yvette Lundy, a Resistance fighter who died in late 2019. An article about her appeared in the news in late 2019. I found her story intriguing: as a schoolteacher in Épernay, France, she had been a forger, producing false documents for refugees from the Nazis, and she worked with the Possum Escape Line to help downed pilots, separated soldiers, and escaped POWs evade capture. Eventually she was arrested and held in the notorious Ravensbruck prison camp, being released at the end of the war.

In researching the Possum line, I learned of myriad other networks across Europe. Some were set up to help refugees and escapees; others to engage in sabotage. Many were developed with outside help from the Allies. Others sprang up independently. One book I acquired for research covered a single network. That book was 800 pages long, and each page listed entries: names, dates, and places; no narrative details.

Isolated stories abound. The English Channel Isles' lie very close to France, one of which is Sark Island. Only recently has it changed its government from a feudal to a democratic form. And yet, through most of its history, the people of Sark have loved their way of life and their governing system. During the war, the real Dame of Sark, Sibyl Hathaway and her husband anticipated that Germany would occupy the Isles, and they planned to meet that challenge. A sad note about their story is that they lost a son during the Blitz.

A point of confusion sometimes surrounds the timeframe of Dunkirk, the Battle of Britain, and the Blitz. The evacuation occurred over eight days, but in the immediate weeks following, additional evacuations took place along the French Atlantic coast. That led into the Battle of Britain which lasted for roughly three months and which British historians account for as separate and distinct from the Blitz. During the Battle, the *Luftwaffe* bombed RAF airfields (with an accidental bombing of London leading to an RAF reprisal bombing of Berlin). When Churchill showed no sign of relenting and seeking a negotiated peace with Hitler, he changed tactics and began bombing cities, which continued for eight months. That action was the Blitz.

This book, AFTER DUNKIRK, limits its scope to the timeframe immediately following the evacuation until a few days into the Battle of Britain. The next book, EAGLES OVER BRITAIN delves further into the Battle; and the one following will center on the Blitz.

Over the course of the year that incorporated the Evacuation, the Battle of Britain, and the Blitz, both Great Britain and Germany changed elements of strategy, tactics, and equipment. Those elements appear in each book to the best of my understanding, characterized by how they were seen in each successive period, which might differ from a view looking back.

On the British side, in the early days, there were more Hurricanes than Spitfires because the former had been in the inventory longer, and the latter were far more difficult to manufacture and thus took more time to deliver. On the German side, the Messerschmitt was the most capable aircraft, however, the Germans also relied on the Stuka dive bomber/fighter, Ju 88s, Heinkels, Dornier DO17's, and other aircraft. As a result, in any given battle, an unexpected combination of aircraft might have appeared.

During the Battle of Britain, the limitations of the Stuka as a fighter became manifest, and from thence was used almost strictly as a dive bomber requiring ME109 escort. That was not the case across the entire length of Germany's many fronts, and Stukas strafed and bombed ships, trains, convoys, tanks... Interestingly, the most decorated of all German pilots was Hans Ulrich Rudel, a Stuka pilot.

There is no doubt of what Churchill said of those who fought during the Battle of Britain, that so much was owed to so few. Nothing can take that away. What is little known is the radar screen and the command and control system designed and established by Air Chief Marshal Sir Hugh Dowding. His determination and force of personality built the system of men, women, machines, and technology that allowed Great Britain to see well in advance where Germany was sending its bombers and fighter escorts and dispatch "The Few" to engage them in mortal combat at the places and times that would bring down an otherwise overwhelming, implacable foe. Of equal value was the decoding and analytical facility established at Bletchley Park that developed the ability to read any and all coded radio messages transmitted across German networks. The combined effort of all these men and women who sacrificed themselves helped win the war.

This book is a work of fiction, but it is based on real people and events. Where I have used actual names, their actions herein are fictitious, and a figment of my imagination. I hope I have done the real participants justice

ACKNOWLEDGMENTS

The people who helped me with AFTER DUNKIRK, are numerous. I put out a call for anecdotes about WWII escapes and evasions and received piles of them. I am humbled by the heroism of so many mothers, fathers, grandparents, uncles and aunts, and other relatives of that time without which, we would be living in a much darker world.

Friends and family contributed technical knowledge. Others read and re-read either sections of the draft, or the entire manuscript, several times. Others proofread. Still more provided encouragement.

I have expressed my gratitude to each person who helped me with this project, so rather than risk missing someone here, please accept my thanks again, here.

I will extend my gratitude to my publisher, Andrew Watts at Severn River Publishing. He pushed me to write about World War II. I had read many books about the war and had studied it at West Point, but I had never researched it in depth, digging into the corners and crevices to find the little-known details of that history. They must number in the billions. I have probably not both read and written so much in as short a time, and a major element I learned is that if I study that epoch daily for a thousand years, I am sure that each day I will learn something new and astounding that reinforces the awe in which I hold all who participated to keep the western world free. We call them the greatest generation. They were giants.

ABOUT THE AUTHOR

Lee Jackson is the Wall Street Journal bestselling author of The Reluctant Assassin series and the After Dunkirk series. He graduated from West Point and is a former Infantry Officer of the US Army. Lee deployed to Iraq and Afghanistan, splitting 38 months between them as a senior intelligence supervisor for the Department of the Army. Lee lives and works with his wife in Texas, and his novels are enjoyed by readers around the world.

Sign up for Lee Jackson's newsletter at
severnriverbooks.com/authors/lee-jackson

LeeJackson@SevernRiverBooks.com